DANCE

As the soft strains of music rose above the din, the duke slipped his hand through Valentina's arm. Amazed by the transformation from disapproving lord of the manor to debonair gentleman, she managed a polite smile and tried to ignore the envious glares from the debutantes clawing her with jealous eyes.

As he whisked her effortlessly onto the dance floor and drew her near, the heady scent of scandalwood invaded her nostrils. She liked his clean, fresh scent, she realized with a rush of heat. She had never noticed how utterly gorgeous his dark brown eyes were. His sheer height alone exuded an imposing strength. Of course, she'd never been this close to him before, she thought with a tingle of excitement.

"I scarcely recognized you," he remarked softly against her ear, "fully clothed."

—From _"Be Mine,"_ by Stacy Brown

CUPID CALLING

Stacy Brown

Karen L. King

Patricia Waddell

ZEBRA BOOKS
Kensington Publishing Corp.
http://www.kensingtonbooks.com

ZEBRA BOOKS are published by

Kensington Publishing Corp.
850 Third Avenue
New York, NY 10022

All Kensington titles, imprints and distributed lines are available at special quantity discounts for bulk purchases for sales
promotion, premiums, fund-raising, educational or institu-
tional use.

Special book excerpts or customized printings can also be created to fit specific needs. For details, write or phone the office
of the Kensington Special Sales Manager: Kensington Publishing Corp., 850 Third Avenue, New York, NY 10022. Attn.
Special Sales Department. Phone: 1-800-221-2647.

Zebra and the Z logo Reg. U.S. Pat. & TM Off.

First Printing: January 2003
10 9 8 7 6 5 4 3 2 1

Printed in the United States of America

CONTENTS

Be Mine

Stacy Brown

Prologue

England, 1814

"Come on, boy," Valentina Rutledge shouted to the black mastiff that barked and leaped at the prize she held in her outstretched hand.

She tossed the grubby, drool-covered stick. "Go on. Fetch it, boy!"

Scrambling about, he bounded on all fours across the expansive green. Lifting her hand to the rim of her straw hat, she smiled as she watched her furry companion romp happily across the lawn. Just beyond the place where the dog lay enjoying his mangy stick stood a large, stately brick mansion. Set in the distance on the hill, Compton Hall loomed large against the lush English countryside. The enormous estate was fashioned in a semicircle with four large white pillars in front. The main house was red brick flanked by side north and south wings that enclosed the gardens.

The majestic estate was famous throughout Essex. Of course, the fact that the Duke of Westmoreland took up residence in Chelmsford from time to time helped secure the steady stream of avid tourists. But of late, the Harwicke family was seldom at home. The duke was fighting on the Peninsula and had not returned home in quite some time. His mother preferred to remain in town, salving her worried heart with the help of close friends.

The enormous mastiff dropped the stick at Tina's feet. He whimpered and pawed her skirt.

"What a spoiled playmate you are." She crouched down and scratched the dog playfully behind his ears.

The summer sun beat down mercilessly. She was nearly melting. Brushing her forearm across her cheek, she glanced over her shoulder at the cool lake. It glistened beneath the hot sun. She all but envied the weeping willows bowing down to take a dip.

"Oh, why not take a refreshing swim? Eh, boy?"

The dog let out an excited yelp and trotted toward the inviting water. Removing her straw bonnet, she laid it in the grass and unpinned her ebony hair. Long curly tresses cascaded down her back. She untied her white muslin bandeau and removed her peach muslin gown. Unlacing her hot vamp boots, she tossed them aside and peeled away her stockings. Her bare feet padded through the plush grass. It was deliciously soft, like silk beneath her feet. Her companion was already in the water, his dark, wet head bobbing up and down.

"Wait for me. Silly dog!"

Splashing into the water, she dove headlong into the cool abyss. When she came up for air, the dog was curiously absent.

"Here, boy!" she called to him. But he made no appearance. Frowning, she swam toward the bank. Placing her palms on the grassy ledge she hoisted her midriff out of the water. She was about to get a leg up when a pair of black Hessians planted themselves squarely on the bank in front of her.

Her head jerked up.

To her complete dismay, the mirror-polished boots contained buff-colored britches that fit snugly over two large, muscular thighs. She gulped. Her horrified gaze climbed higher to discover two impossibly broad shoulders encased in a fine white cambric shirt. Her eyes slowly crept higher. Two piercing dark brown eyes fringed with thick black lashes stared down at her.

Good Lord! She slunk into the water. "*Who* are *you?*"

"I might inquire the same of you," his deep, commanding voice imparted coldly.

A gentle breeze tousled the man's hair. One solitary raven lock fell haphazardly across his forehead. It did precious little to soften the harsh, forbidding lines around his mouth however. With his hands slung low on his narrow hips, he looked rather large and forbidding, whoever he was. Jet-black hair, sharp chiseled features, endless legs and broad, muscular shoulders blocked out any hint of the blistering sun that had driven her into the cool water. She shivered and glanced about her and wondered how on earth she was going to extricate herself from this dreadful situation, when his large, masterful hands reached down and hoisted her none too gently onto dry land.

The breeze picked up once more, plastering her white sheer cotton shift to her glistening wet skin. His dark, hooded gaze swept over her firm breasts straining against the sheer wet fabric. Hot color scalded her cheeks. She shivered and hastily folded her arms across her bosom.

The large black mastiff bounded toward them. Wagging his tail, he shook his wet fur. He danced eagerly around the two, jumping and barking.

"Down!" the man's booming voice commanded. The dog uttered a defeated whimper and immediately sank onto his belly.

Talons of dread closed around Valentina's heart. She knew in an instant the identity of the man standing before her. This paragon of masculinity, this intimidating, hulking man, was none other than the celebrated master of Compton Hall, the Duke of Westmoreland. Her desire to disappear into thin air increased tenfold.

"Precisely who are you?" he demanded gruffly. "And what the devil are you doing on my land?"

"I—" she began, casting a desperate glance about for her clothes. "Swimming," she offered lamely and scurried across the grass to where her abandoned dress and bandeau lay.

He angrily stomped across the grass after her.

Lord, what a disaster, she thought as she tried unsuccessfully to wriggle into her muslin dress. What would her mother say? Swimming in the duke's lake half-naked. Zounds! There would be hell to pay. Her shift was soaking wet. It would take some doing to squeeze her wet body into her dry clothes. She could not imagine how the situation could get any worse. The duke tramped after her, and she knew.

Ignoring the tug-of-war her uncooperative garment was waging, he snapped at her. "That much is patently obvious. At present, however, what evades me is your name. I should very much like to know your name."

Mortified, she gave up the struggle and clutched her garments to her chest. She bobbed a quick curtsy. "Er . . . My name is Tina, Your Grace."

His scowl darkened. *"Tina?"* he echoed sharply. "What the deuce sort of name is Tina?" He stared at her, the crease in his forehead deepening. "Are you a servant girl from the village or something?" he muttered with impatient rancor.

She stiffened. "No, I am not a servant girl from the village or something. My proper name is Valentina Rutledge." She stuck her hand out. "Pleased to make your acquaintance, Your Grace."

He dismissed her outstretched hand by ignoring it. *"Valentina?"* he clarified. "You cannot be serious?" he scoffed.

Her lips pursed. "I assure you, I am in earnest. I was born on February fourteenth."

"One would hope so," he drawled with icy mockery.

"Saint Valentine was a fourth-century virgin martyr," she imparted with pride. Her knowledge of antiquities was quite extensive, indeed, especially when it came to all people and events relating to Valentine's Day.

He looked at her aghast. "I beg your pardon," he burst out in disbelief. *"What* did you say?"

"I said—"

"No," he cut her off, raising his hand to silence any further shocking elucidations she intended to make. "Cease. I have heard quite enough."

"I have made an extensive inquiry into my patron saint, you see."

His lips turned down. "Observably."

"You would be astonished to learn as I myself was that the day in question dates back to pre-Christian times."

He blinked at her as if she were barking mad. "Fascinating, to be sure," he muttered dismissively, "but I think it is fair to say, should you continue on your present course, you are scarcely likely to follow in the footsteps of a virgin or a martyr." She turned crimson. "A martyr is the last thing I wish to be," she countered swiftly.

Her chin jutted out. "I merely happen to enjoy nature. Is that a crime?"

A hard smirk edged his mouth. "No. But you still have not answered. Why are you taking your leisure in *my* lake?"

"It is the only lake I could find."

He gave her an exacerbated look. "Who gave you leave to swim here?" he fired at her.

"No one, Your Grace. I came on my own since I was allowed to walk about."

He looked at her askance. "Alone? Here, on my land? To swim in the nude?" he burst out, incredulous that any gentle-bred young lady would dare such a thing.

Her cheeks burned hotter. "On the contrary, I am fully clothed."

His heated gaze swept over her. *"Clothed?"* he spat. "In a thin shift that barely conceals your modesty? Have you no manners, no breeding at all? No concern for convention? Good God, anyone might have seen you."

"Someone did," she pointed out before she could stop herself.

He offered her a blistering look of contempt. "Explain yourself," he barked, outraged that any young lady would conduct herself in such a shocking manner. "How is it that you came to be on my land in a complete state of undress?" he grumbled, motioning to her immodest condition.

"I walked."

His brows snapped together. *"Walked?* From where?"

She pointed across the green to the thick hedgerow. "Morely House."

A glimmer of recognition dawned in his dark eyes. He seemed to see her in a new light. He folded his arms over his chest. "Ah, yes, Henry Rutledge, lately of India, I do believe."

She braced herself for the insupportable assessment of her stepfather's character that was sure to follow. It was generally understood that the late earl had sent his only son to India in total disgrace. Only upon his father's death did her stepfather dare return to England. But the duke did not berate her on that score. Oh, no, he was far too preoccupied with her lack of clothing.

"I presume you are his wayward daughter fresh from your inexpert governess's care?"

She bristled. "Hardly wayward and I am not his daughter," she corrected tersely. *Inexpert governess's care, indeed,* she scoffed inwardly. He might be a peer of the realm second only to the Archbishop of Canterbury, but she was an earl's stepdaughter and deserved some measure of respect. Why, he treated her like a lowly servant girl or worse. "My natural father is dead. My mother and I have been in residence for quite some time now, Your Grace," she explained, a decided edge to her voice. "I am loath to discover you were not aware of our society."

One end of his mouth quirked slightly. "Forgive me, I have been engaged elsewhere and have not frequented Compton Hall for quite some time, nor have I been inclined to enjoy much *country* society, Miss Rutledge. Perhaps that explains it."

His social slight hit its mark. He was a duke, and she was plain old Miss Rutledge, lately of India. Never the twain shall meet.

"Indeed," she ventured to say, flying deliberately in the face of his interrogation. "You are returned from Spain, I do believe."

His dark eyes narrowed speculatively. "How is it that you come to know of me, and I have never before laid eyes on you?"

One dainty bare shoulder lifted petulantly. "It is common practice for me to walk about the countryside. The steward said I might enjoy the estate in your family's absence," she said with bold impudence. "I am sorry to learn you know nothing of it."

Truth be told, she was not a bit sorry; she never paid much heed where one property began and the other ended. Nor, for that matter, where her furry companion's master was. Before today it had been wholly insignificant. For months now, she and the playful dog cowering at his master's feet had been the solitary occupants of the sprawling landscape. She loved the impeccably manicured grounds. Compton Hall had fast become her favorite place to escape Mama's shrewish ranting and infernal gossiping. At Compton Hall, Tina could walk for hours on end. She could read beneath the elms and daydream by the lake. But she would rather die a thousand deaths than admit all that to the pompous duke who was standing before her.

"You seem rather well informed," he remarked, clearly annoyed that his personal affairs were common knowledge. "Regardless of who is currently in residence, young ladies should not trespass on private property. You would do well to remember that in future."

Her temper flared. His haughty condescension nettled her sorely. The man was perfectly dreadful. A more charitable duke would be sympathetic to her plight, perhaps even mildly diverted by her innocent mishap. *He* continued to regard her as if she were a strange aberration of some kind sprung to life from the bottom of his lake. What was more, the rag-mannered man sought to humiliate her at every turn. His unceasingly correct attitude was insufferable. "I scarcely think a walk through the woods qualifies as trespassing. And as I've said, I had permission."

His critical gaze examined her wet ebony tresses, sun-kissed cheeks and up-turned nose dotted with far too many freckles to be fashionable. His lips turned down.

Apparently, her appearance was as disarming to the opposite sex as her mother claimed. The duke's expression left a great deal to be desired. It was not that she was unaccustomed to disparaging remarks and disapproving glances; she knew her looks were unconventional. Dark violet eyes, wild raven curls, were hardly all the crack at the moment. It was the blond, blue-eyed gel that was fashionable in London. But for some inexplicable reason, she found his frank, open appraisal rather unnerving, intensely so. She squirmed.

"Am I to assume," he clarified, his exacting gaze examining every inch of bare tawny skin, "that you were *born* in India?"

He intoned the word *India* as if it were a highly contagious disease. "My father died when I was eight; my mother remarried shortly after his death. Lord Rutledge brought us to England."

"I see," the duke muttered in a colorless tone, dragging his gaze away from the soft, round swell of her breasts straining against the low-cut cotton shift. "Tell me, Miss Rutledge, I am but curious. In India do all the young ladies swim naked for all the world to see?"

Hateful, wretched man! Her hands balled into angry fists. "Oh yes," she countered, tossing her long raven tresses over her shoulder. "Only, in India the gentlemen enjoy a nice refreshing swim, too."

A mantle of furious color streaked across his face. "You impudent, little hussy," he growled, taking a menacing step toward her.

Good Lord! Her eyes rounded owlishly. Another inch and she would be pressed against his hard, muscular chest.

"Allow me to assure you that an *English* gentleman conducts himself with the utmost propriety, which is more than I can say for you, gallivanting around the countryside half-naked."

Instantly indignant, she glared up at the giant of a man towering over her. "I was *not* gallivanting," she corrected tersely. "I was swimming!"

"In *my* lake," came his thunderous retort.

"I have never been more displeased to suffer a gentleman's acquaintance in all my days," she fumed, at the end of her tether. "You have the dubious distinction of being the most insufferable man I have ever met!"

"If you wish to be treated like a lady, I suggest you comport yourself like one. You would be well advised to cover yourself," he snarled, his smoldering gaze riveted to her full, round breasts practically spilling over the top of her thin cotton shift. "And stop parading around the countryside in your skivvies like a common trollop, baring your body to every man you meet. Else this gentleman might forget himself and give you what you deserve."

Her mouth dropped open. She uttered a choked squeal that was something between shock and outrage. Presenting him with her back, she tramped, with as much dignity as she could muster, across the soft green carpet toward home.

"Aggravating, ill-tempered, horrid man!" she fumed. "Common trollop, indeed! Hah. Swimming naked! As if I were. I have never been more put out in all my days. And Valentine *was* a virgin martyr," she muttered aloud.

Nonetheless, the sting of his rebuke lingered. As she tramped angrily across the countryside, she found herself morbidly curious. Did he actually know any *real* trollops? And for that matter, did she truly resemble one?

She stopped in her tracks. Her brow wrinkled slightly. What precisely did he mean by giving her what she deserved? It sounded rather wicked and decidedly unpleasant. But not half as disagreeable, she decided, climbing over the thick bracken, as the fact that her knees felt like lemon pudding when he looked at her. What was more, she decided, as she rounded the drive and approached Morely House—whose sturdy brick walls covered with thick ivy looked to be a mere cottage compared to the illustrious Hall rising up in the distance—despite his obvious faults that were far too numerous for her to count, he was a damnably attractive man. Well beyond handsome, he was quite deliciously debonair. And a duke. Living right next door. Were it not for the look of disdain permanently etched on his darkly handsome features, he would be the most pleasing gentleman of her acquaintance. As it was, however, she wished never to suffer his loathsome company again. At least, she amended with a rush of tingles, not without the benefit of proper attire.

One

Six months later . . .

Lady Octavia Rutledge sat in the rose room at Morely House. Perched like a hairpin on the edge of the white-and-pink-striped settee in the small sitting room, she drummed her fingers on her knees. The floral porcelain clock on the mantel ticked. "Oh, why has it not arrived?" she snapped, her brittle voice shattering the peaceful silence.

"Calm yourself, dearest," her stout, balding husband remarked from across the room where he sat in the matching rose velvet wingback. His short, sausagelike legs were propped on the delicately embroidered stool. His red, bulbous nose was firmly entrenched in latest edition of the *Times*.

"It simply *must* come," she cried, her thin red lips working with displeasure. "How could the vile duke overlook us? It is too much to be borne! He cannot throw a Valentine's Day ball and exclude us."

"Pray do not fret, dearest. It will not be the first time or the last that we have been overlooked."

Heaving an irritated sigh, Octavia glared at her dense husband. "Indeed, it is not." Her tone was heavy with bitter accusation. "I do not know how you can bear to see me set so low."

Henry lowered his paper to his lap and offered her a miserable look.

A knock sounded at the door. The servant girl, Mary, bobbed a quick curtsy. "Beggin' yer pardon, my lady, this just come," she said timidly.

"Oh, my stars!" Octavia exclaimed and jumped to her feet. Snatching the missive, she tore it open. "It is an invitation to the *Valentine's Day ball!*" Her long bony fingers caressed the pristine invitation with reverence.

Mary bobbed another quick curtsy and took her leave.

Sighing, Octavia pressed the ivory parchment that bore the Westmoreland red wax seal to her breast. The thought that they may not have been included on the exalted guest list for the Valentine's Day ball had her nerves in shreds. The duke's exalted social status was never far from her mind.

A relieved smile blossomed on Henry's portly face. "What a delightful house party that promises to be," came his nebulous reply. "There will be partridge shooting, to be sure."

"Valentina will, of course, be delighted. It is well known the duke is searching for a wife. Ever since that dreadful woman, Lady Winston, broke his heart, he has been positively desolate. And now, we are invited! I can scarcely contain my excitement. He has seen fit to entertain our society."

"Mmm," Henry readily concurred and resumed his reading. "It would be a much needed diversion, to be sure."

"If the servants' gossip is to be believed, and I very much suspect it is," she chattered excitedly, "the duchess was heartbroken by the duke's firm resistance to enter the marriage mart. And she greatly feared when he left for the Peninsula that his gallantry might well cost the family an heir. Now he is returned safe and sound. That horrid woman Gwen Winston betrayed him in a perfectly heinous manner. He has no choice but to procure a bride at the Valentine's Day ball. I can see no reason that our daughter may not well be chosen his bride."

That piqued Henry's ear. His head perked up. "Have you lost your wits entirely? He is a duke."

Octavia took immediate umbrage. "Any man would be proud to take our daughter as a wife. And she will make a fine duchess," she averred, her cunning mind at work.

He looked dumbfounded.

Leaning forward, she intoned in a conspiratorial whisper, "Our little Tina may well find comfort among their society." Her tone was pregnant with possibilities. "We have only to prepare her."

"But," Henry sputtered in dismay. "I daresay the duke has other more eligible girls at his disposal?"

Octavia pulled a face. "Nonsense." She waved away his objection. "Do you think that we would have received an invitation if our little angel was unsuitable? And who can be more in need than we are at this very moment? Do you not see the hand of providence? Only consider, dearest, now may be the proper time to encourage such an advantageous union." As her sharp features narrowed with intrigue, she prattled avidly in his ear. the earl paled considerably and sank into his chair.

"We have only to play our hand, dear husband, and prepare our child for the most excellent ball of the year. The rest should fall into place rather nicely, I should think. After all, cupid requires a helping hand now and again," she murmured, her long fingers stroking his arm.

Henry offered her a wan smile. "I cannot think why the duke would not welcome our little Valentina."

"But of course, he shall," Octavia purred, "and for our part, we shall be only too happy with the alliance. What with your horrid gaming debts, we are fortunate not to be in debtor's prison this very minute. But thanks to my ingenuous scheme, if we conduct ourselves accordingly, our names may never appear in the *Gazette.*"

Paling at the mention of his losses, Henry cowered. "You know how I try. Upon my honor, I never meant to lose so much." Wringing his pudgy hands in despair, he pleaded with her, "Don't be cross with me, Octavia. I try to control myself—"

"Oh, do be silent! I loathe your caterwauling even more than your preponderance for gaming hells." Drawing a deep, calming breath, she smoothed the lines of her regal muslin and silk gown and regained her composure. "All must be made ready. And, Henry, we must succeed. I will not suffer the bailiff. And I will not auction my possessions." She pinioned him with a mordant stare. "We must triumph."

"I will do whatever you wish," Henry mumbled in defeat.

Three weeks later, despite strenuous protests to the contrary, Valentina Rutledge entered the majestic ballroom at Compton Hall. Gazing about her, she stood in awe of the gilded mirrors, marble polished floors and opulent chandeliers aglow with candles. She had never experienced such grandeur. From the liveried footman to the finely etched crystal flutes, every extravagance imaginable was on display. It was quite magnificent. She allowed herself a momentary tingle of excitement. Slinking about the duke's lavish ballroom hoping against hope that one's esteemed host did not recognize her was not at all what she imagined her coming of age would entail. Still, she had to allow it was quite thrilling.

Her gaze surveyed the ballroom. Verily, from the crush it would appear every young eligible maiden in the county was here, all hoping to be noticed by the duke and perchance to persuade him that she should be his duchess.

Valentina wrinkled up her nose. Try as she might, she could not imagine fretting over such trifles. Titles and family bloodlines were an absolute bore. It was perhaps a good thing. She could certainly never aspire to anything as lofty. Life among such wealth and privilege was out of her meager reach. Not that she longed to attain any such wealth and position; that was strictly her mother's domain. She cast a speculative glance at her mother garbed in the finest silk lavender and black lace gown. Her hair boasted an enormous purple feather that protruded in a ridiculous fashion from the back of her head.

"What a lavish household the duke possesses," she murmured in Tina's ear as she eyed the gold silk brocade drapes on the large casement windows with greedy appreciation. "Must have cost a king's ransom."

"Mother," Tina admonished under her breath, "I hardly think you should discuss such things. Anyone might overhear."

"Fustian." She waved away her daughter's objection. "One can ill afford a lack of appreciation for such grandeur. No matter how humble our circumstance may be," she instructed Tina in strident tones. "One must consider these things."

"I beg to differ, Mama," Tina countered sharply under her breath.

Ignoring her daughter's discomfort, she turned to address her husband. "The wealth and influence the duke possesses . . . boggles the mind, does it not?"

"Indeed, it does," Henry chortled, rocking on his heels as he gazed about him, ogling the luxurious surroundings.

"The rules of the house insist all gaming bets be no larger than one hundred pounds," she chastised, wag-

ging her gloved finger at him. "I suspect even you cannot get into mischief this night, Henry."

"You've no reason to fret over me, dear wife."

Valentina turned away. Her mother's grasping nature
was vile. No help for it, the woman was frightfully super-
ficial. Tina was convinced that her mother had taken a
second husband strictly for the position and the wealth
such a scrupulous move might offer. It must be true, for
poor old Henry Rutledge was not much of a catch. His
balding head and rotund belly made him frightfully un-
appealing. Poor man was utterly impotent in character.
His main preoccupation seemed to be whining most of
the time.

"The Valentine's Day ball is the most sought after social event in Chelmsford," her mother advised in a low
tone. "Look lively, girl, *he* may arrive at any moment!"

Tina heaved a sigh. *Lord, I hope not.* Unlike all the
other eager girls awaiting an introduction to the duke,
the very last thing she wanted was another encounter
with the dour duke.

"We should consider ourselves extremely fortunate to
have received an invitation," her mother advised, her
gaze avidly searching the room.

On that point, her mother was entirely correct. As it
was, however, Tina fervently wished the duke would *not*
take notice of her. She cringed at the mere thought of
seeing the unfailingly handsome, impossibly correct
duke. It simply would not do for him to make mention
of their previous meeting. Her mother would have her
guts for garters.

"Faith, what an absolute throng there is tonight! Let
them all hope for success, but you, my dear," her mother
declared, her critical gaze assessing Valentina's white
gauze gown, "shall suit very well, indeed."

Tina scoffed inwardly. After watching her mother ma-
neuver every gentleman of her acquaintance, with an

almost Machiavellian skill, Tina had decided to avoid arranged matrimony at all costs.

"White is the perfect choice. I daresay His Grace shall not be able to tear his eyes away. And your curls and braids are very becoming," she demurred, patting Valentina's wild black hair reined under control for once.

"Oh, yes, indeed," Henry chirped, looking exceedingly pleased with himself. "You are a picture of loveliness in that gown, my dear."

Frowning slightly, Tina managed to stumble out, "Thank you." Her nerves were rapidly in decline. She was beginning to suspect her mother was up to something. The very last person on earth she wished to impress anything upon was Roland Harwicke. And yet, here she was perched on the precipice of social disaster with her mother at the helm. "I sincerely doubt the duke will take a second look at the likes of me. You mustn't build up false hopes."

Octavia merely smiled and hummed a cheerful tune. Tina looked at her as though she were a candidate for Bedlam. She darted a desperate glance at Henry for support. But he merely smiled at her. Sighing, Tina looked away and prayed the evening would draw to a quick end.

Roland Harwicke entered the ballroom. His gaze surveyed the crowded hall. A grim frown edged his lips. Damn his meddling mother and her foolhardy Valentine's Day ball. The entire notion was absurd. Infuriating. And downright insulting. His lips twisted. He glanced about him. Bloody hell. The confounded room was teeming with grasping, vacant women all clamoring for his attention.

Catching sight of Lady Ashcroft and her plump, hopelessly unattractive daughter waving from across the room, he forced a faint smile to his lips. The mere thought of conversing with the hideous creature nauseated him. Turning away from their obvious attempt to attract his attention, he made his way toward the ridiculous throne of sorts that his mother had arranged for this evening. From her perch atop her red velvet chair, she might scour the crowd for a desirable candidate for matrimony. He felt like the sacrificial lamb being led to the slaughter. After the infamous scandal he had suffered, he heartily resented having to show his face in polite society. But Gwen Winston had left him no choice. Less than a fortnight ago, his beloved fiancée had issued her stunning blow to his fine, upstanding name. News of her jilting him and her marked preference for another man spread like wildfire through the *ton*. Her hateful deception was bitter gall to swallow.

He could still see the gloating look on her face as she rebuffed him. She had actually found pleasure in seeing him set so low. To think that she had willfully deceived him was untenable. For years, while he was off fighting in Spain for king and country, she had lied to him, plying him with letters of love and eternal devotion. And all the time, she had been entertaining another man behind his back. It was beyond the pale. What a daft fool he was to fancy himself in love with her, or any woman for that matter. They were all alike.

Her malicious plot to set him low was enough to make a lesser man pull up sharp. The news would have been hard to bear under any circumstances. But the public forum that she chose had been no less than paralyzing.

Were it not for his mother's insistence that he marry before his thirtieth birthday and set up his nursery, he would have feigned a ferocious stomach illness or temporary insanity—anything to avoid the probing stares of the *ton's* watchful eye and the soft murmurings of his grand faux pas.

Despite his deep resentment, he knew honor must be upheld at all costs. That was the code by which he lived and from which he never strayed. The enormity of the family title weighed heavily on his broad shoulders. He had no choice but to accept his mother's advice and make an appearance tonight in the vain hope of finding some inoffensive chit to wed and bed and get with child by year's end. He despised the notion of being fodder for young debutantes eager to ease his broken heart and to dip into his very deep pockets with their fat, sticky fingers. But that was the way it was.

"Ah, there you are," his mother remarked. Sitting in her ridiculous crimson velvet chair, the gray-haired matron peered up at him through her quizzing glass, her dark, piercing gaze as exacting as his own. "It is high time you made an appearance."

Planting his fisted hands firmly on his hips beneath his immaculate black velvet superfine cutaway, he scowled at her. "I am here," he growled under his breath. "That is enough."

"Temper, temper," she muttered. "Do try to be agreeable. Tell me if you see anyone worthy of your esteem," she murmured, her eager gaze surveying the crowd.

He sniggered. "Do you honestly expect I will judge any of them worthy? Aside from wreaking havoc on men's well-ordered lives, the sole preoccupation of the fairer sex," he intoned with venom, "is to connive their way into a judicial alliance with a sufficiently wealthy gentleman."

She waved away his objections. "You are in a mood tonight."

"May I remind you that we are in the country? Can there be an eligible miss for miles?"

"I daresay a gently bred country miss is less likely to run amok. And the courting may be achieved in infinitely less time. The fact remains you must produce an heir. You are not getting any younger, Roland. You must set up your nursery. Your initial choice for a bride turned out to be less than desirable. Now it is down to this, we are left with my approach."

His bored gaze appraised the endless sea of ball gowns. "Not one in twenty of them, for all their finery, strike my fancy. I wish them all to the devil. Satisfied?"

"You become tiresome. For heaven's sake, Roland, it hardly signifies whether you find love or not."

"I am not being tiresome, merely honest. On the surface, it is possible for a woman to appear a quintessential lady. Perfect in every way. That is, until such time as she decides to reveal her true character. Then the man in question has only to be glad he has not been so blind as to exchange vows with the little witch."

"Yes, all right. We are agreed; the things of which the fairer sex is capable are quite vexing, indeed. But the fact remains you must contemplate a wife and make a wiser choice on this occasion. Just," she sputtered with frustration, "find someone, anyone."

His lips thinned. Find someone, hah, as if that were a real possibility. If he was lucky, he might escape this waking nightmare and slip upstairs before the dawn to savor the only worthwhile moment of this horrific exhibition with a very large brandy in one hand and Robert Owen's *A New View of Society* in the other. He was eager to read Owen's discourse. During the war, Roland's rigorous reading habits had fallen off. He must adhere to his strict schedule else relinquish the all-important discipline entirely, and that would never do. He prided himself on being well informed.

"Do not let that horrid woman, Gwen, get the best of you."

His jaw clenched hard enough to crush enamel. "Never mention her name to me again," he spat through his teeth.

The duchess winced. "Do not fly up in the boughs. I

merely meant that the best way to forget one chit is to find another."

A dark shadow of anger swept across his face. "This is the last of your matchmaking I intend to suffer," he gritted in a fierce under breath. "Do I make myself patently clear?"

"I wouldn't dream of inconveniencing you again," his mother derided. "You're an absolute prince. If either of us lives through tonight," she added in a terse under breath, "it will be a miracle."

"There he is!" Octavia exclaimed, pointing from across the room at the duke in a vulgar fashion. "At last!"

Catching sight of him, Tina gulped and willed her knees to stop buckling. Fresh from the fashionable grouse moor in Scotland, he looked quite breathtakingly handsome. He was exactly as she recalled, tall, broad shouldered and flawlessly male. And perfectly handsome . . . unbelievably handsome. Impeccably elegant, he was dressed in a black velvet cutaway and silk striped waistcoat and a soft, snowy white cravat. His gray britches clung to his strong, powerful thighs like a second skin. His ebony hair was slicked back from his face, accentuating his dark, chiseled features. She sighed. He was entirely too good looking, she decided, too perfectly proportioned to be real.

"Who?" Henry mumbled stupidly, slurping down his ratafia in a sloppy gulp.

"The duke," Octavia snapped with irritation. "He has arrived. Come, Valentina," she said, her tone determined. "We must present you."

Tina opened her mouth to object. But the hard yank on her wrist effectively quelled her resistance. Her overbearing mother practically dragged her through the swarm of eager bodies. "No. Mother, please, I have no wish to—" she began. It was no use. Her domineering mother was not listening. She had other ideas.

As the crowd parted like Moses at the Red Sea, the duke's head turned to see what the commotion was all about. His disapproving gaze swept over the scene with mild distaste. His gaze jerked back. His ebony eyes narrowed on her face. A glimmer of recognition lit his dark eyes.

Well, well, well, he thought, mildly diverted, *if it is not the rather dishonorable Miss Rutledge.*

Letting his gaze drift over her, he allowed himself to indulge in a frank, bold appraisal. He could not quite believe she was the same unruly chit he had happened upon swimming in his lake. No hint of the wild hoyden who once brazenly argued the merits of swimming in the nude remained. Where the devil had all her freckles gone? Her buttery soft skin that had once glistened in the summer sun had faded to a respectable shade of ivory. And her long, riotous curls were reined into stylish coiled braids. The vivid recollection of how she had looked that day, all wild and wanton, took hold in his mind. With shocking clarity, he recalled her wet cotton shift that had clung to every inch of her firm, ripe breasts and her rosy nipples straining against the gossamer-thin fabric. Bloody hell. Frowning at his bizarre train of thought, he forced himself to push the image from his mind.

"Your Grace," Lady Rutledge said, practically thrusting Tina at him, "may I introduce my daughter, Valentina Rutledge?"

"No, Lady Rutledge, you may not."

A shocked gasp pervaded the room. Tina felt her stomach drop to her knees. He would not dare reveal the nature of their first meeting . . . or would he?

"Roland, really, you are beneath contempt," his mother interjected beneath her breath. "Remember yourself."

"Your Grace," Lady Rutledge was quick to say, "do not

be hasty. As you can see, she is a diamond of the first water."

"Mmm, yes," he murmured, his lazy, hooded gaze assessing her obvious attributes nicely revealed by her tight, daring neckline. "But we have already met."

That took the wind out of Octavia's sails. *"Already met,"* she repeated dully. "There must be some mistake, Your Grace."

He shook his head, his gaze never leaving Tina's flushed face. "I make no mistake."

The blood raced to Tina's ears with a deafening roar. Now he would decimate her, reveal her scandalous conduct in the most devastating venue imaginable and watch with relish as she suffered the consequences. Oh, he was hateful. She despised him. But she could not understand why her heart was hammering in her chest.

She darted him a helpless look, beseeching him to remain silent. He met her gaze with a glint of amusement. His full, sensuous mouth curved slightly. Oh, he was enjoying the upper hand! Her lips thinned. Vile man! If he planned to expose her for a wild hoyden, why did he hesitate?

"I beg of you," her mother went on to say, "pray do not dismiss her out of hand. She has many admirable qualities, Your Grace."

"Has she, indeed?" he queried, cocking an ebony brow. Folding his arms over his formidable chest, he regarded her for a long moment, his gaze roaming over her white, gauzy gown.

Tina bristled. The way he looked at her! Good gracious. It was as if she were a pound of horseflesh at Tattersalls. Scurrilous knave.

"I will allow she has a certain beauty, madam," he imparted at his most arrogant, "that cannot be denied, but I am persuaded her disposition is entirely lacking."

"Lacking?" Lady Rutledge echoed. "In what way, Your Grace?" she queried, floundering on a sea of dismay.

"If memory serves, she is something of a bluestocking." He bared his teeth in a humorless smile. "I seek a meek, mild-mannered bride with more grace and dignity."

"One who doubtless knows her place and heels at his feet like a well-trained dog," Tina grumbled under her breath and earned a kick in the shin from her mother for her trouble.

"On the contrary, Miss Rutledge," the duke replied, loosing his wrathful gaze on her, "I already have a dog, as you well know."

Tina's cheeks burned. She lowered her gaze to the floor. Drat the man. She had not intended the words reach his ears.

The duchess glanced from Tina's red face to her son. His reaction puzzled her.

"I must say I admire your taste in jewels, my dear. Wherever did you get such an unusual stone?" she asked, pointing to the enormous amethyst that lay just above Tina's daring cleavage.

"The stone was a gift from my late father," she said, fingering the pear-sized pendant with affection. "It is the last thing he gave to me before he died. I have always treasured it."

The duchess offered her a pleasant smile. "Gifts from loved ones often are irreplaceable. Such an unusual piece," she ventured to remark, eyeing the jewel with appreciation.

"In India, it is said that amethyst protects all who wear it against thievery and drunkenness."

"Oh, my!" the duchess murmured. "Do they, indeed? How . . . very . . . intriguing," she added, her voice trailing off.

Realizing her blunder, Tina was quick to explain, "It is only a superstition, Your Grace."

"Is that so?" the duke coaxed, his faintly amused gaze fixed on her. "What else do they say in India?"

She lifted her dark lavender gaze to his. Her chin rose with impudence. "It is claimed to be a love charm, Your Grace."

"Ah," he said sagely amid the shocked murmurings from the crowd. His gaze lingered on the gleaming purple stone shimmering against her alabaster skin. "That explains why you chose to wear it tonight."

Wishing the awkward interview were at an end, the duchess drew an audible breath. "Well, Roland, I suppose you should ask this lovely creature to dance," she prompted him.

"Oh, no!" Tina rushed out. "On the contrary, that is not at all necessary. Pray do not put yourself out on my account. I do not dance overly well. Not at all. I don't. Truly."

"Nonsense, child," Octavia contradicted. "She is elegance itself, Your Grace," she advised, shoving Tina at him.

The duchess glanced up at Roland sharply. "Will you not ask her to dance?" she pressed under her breath.

"My mother is quite correct," he said, stepping forward. "It was remiss of me not to ask you sooner. Will you do me the very great honor of dancing the quadrille, Miss Rutledge?" he asked, etching a polite bow before her.

"I—" Tina hesitated, searching for a polite way to refuse. But the sharp thrust of her mother's elbow in her ribs silenced her protest. She took a hard swallow and politely inclined her head in acceptance. "I would be delighted, Your Grace."

As the soft strains of music rose above the din, the duke slipped his hand through her arm. Amazed by the transformation from disapproving lord of the manor to debonair gentleman, she managed a polite smile and tried to ignore the envious glares from the debutantes clawing her with jealous eyes.

As he whisked her effortlessly onto the dance floor

and drew her near, the heady scent of sandalwood invaded her nostrils. She liked his clean, fresh scent, she realized with a rush of heat. She had never noticed how utterly gorgeous his dark brown eyes were. His sheer height alone exuded an imposing strength. Of course, she had never been this close to him before, she realized with a tingle of excitement.

"I scarcely recognized you," he remarked softly against her ear, "fully clothed."

His breath was warm and soft and a ripple of unwanted pleasure coursed through her. "Your particular brand of charm always renders me bereft of speech, Your Grace," she replied, holding his hand to circle him.

His dark, hooded gaze settled on her tight, low-cut bodice. "I was given to understand," he bantered in a low whisper, "wild harridans with a penchant for scandal were strictly forbidden from attending Valentine's Day festivities."

Her blue-violet eyes flashed temper. "I was coerced into making an appearance here tonight. Nothing grieved me more than the thought of our next encounter," she uttered coolly.

"I cannot help but wonder at your continual impropriety. It speaks very ill of your temperament."

She lifted her chin a notch. "Your opinion of me does not signify in the least."

"Ah, then, why suffer the unnecessary introduction?" he murmured in a suggestive undertone that made her quiver.

Unwilling to lay the blame at her overbearing mother's feet, she fell silent and effortlessly moved through the quadrille dance steps with lithe grace. Her mother's lack of tact and decorum was a constant source of humiliation. It was not that her mother intended to be gauche and uncouth; she simply could not help it. The hateful man would doubtless use the truth to lay further insults at Tina's feet. That was an advantage she simply refused to grant.

"Allow me to assure you, Your Grace," she murmured as she passed him, "that I am not in need of a husband, nor am I desirous of finding one among your society. So you are quite safe."

"That comes as a relief to both of us, I'm sure," he countered with a sardonic smirk.

She heaved an irritated sigh. "Your Grace." His title sounded like a rank insult on her lips. "Pray believe me when I tell you, no one could be more astonished by your invitation than I myself was."

His head came up sharp. "I sent no such invitation," he told her bluntly.

"Of that, I can have no doubt," she replied, an acerbic edge to her voice. "Your mother doubtless is responsible for the unfortunate circumstance that precipitated my presence here this weekend."

"*Weekend?*" he growled on a fierce whisper. Good God. "You have plans to stay the night?" he asked, surprise mingling with displeasure.

"Yes. Mother says Henry wants an early rise for the shooting in the morning."

Roland's entire body stiffened. He looked beyond her and wished the interminable dance would come to an end. He had a sneaking suspicion his mother was playing cupid. Damn her. Undoubtedly she had a part in Lord Rutledge's invitation. They had never been invited to Compton Hall. And they certainly resided close enough to come and go easily enough.

"I am persuaded we shall do admirably well avoiding one another." His tone was as discourteous as it was patronizing.

"Indeed." She glanced over her shoulder at the scores of young ladies impatiently watching from the sidelines.

"With so many eligible, eager young ladies to chose from this evening, Your Grace, I am flattered by your attention."

"It is not my intention to flatter you, Miss Rutledge," he imparted brusquely.

She pulled a mock frown. "Verily, Your Grace, I am all astonishment. Such a remark does not do your fine, dignified and proper character justice."

His features hardened like granite.

The brazen chit had the audacity to laugh. At him. The Duke of Westmoreland. How dare she be amused at his expense? The little baggage had gone too far. He despised being ridiculed. And would not suffer her insults lightly.

"I daresay, with that scowl upon your face," she teased, "Eros will need to be your ally if you hope to find a proper young miss tonight."

He stared down at her, his face a glowering mask of rage.

Another gurgle of laughter escaped her throat. "Faith, you could frighten a girl half to death without half trying. But I suspect you are trying very hard, indeed, to make me think ill of you, are you not? Never fear, you are the very last person with whom I should ever wish to dally."

He uttered a furious, choking sound. "You silver-tongued little witch—" he spat under his breath.

"Uh, uh, Your Grace," she tsked. "A bad temper is never in good regulation."

The look he gave her was purely contemptuous.

The little tart was baiting him. How dare she taunt him? "You outrageous little scamp," he gritted furiously under his breath. "I am sorely tempted to give you the spanking you richly deserve."

She glanced up at him from beneath dark, sultry lashes. "Oh la! What a bounder you are, to make such idle threats," she said cheekily. "Another girl might be tempted to put your forbearance to the test."

His nostrils flared. Anger roiled in the pit of his stomach. The shameless hussy was flirting with him! By God, she was a hoyden to her very core. Once more, the image of that shocking summer day took shape in his mind. Her soft, sun-kissed shoulders bare to his touch, her round, full, ripe breasts peaking against the sheer cotton fabric of her shift, the dark circles of her areolas tempting him to touch her, to taste her, and to kiss her swollen, wet lips and have his way with her in the grass. By God, he should have done. Not that he ever had. It was improper, most improper. He prided himself on excellent morals and an undying sense of decorum. Such base instincts did not become a man of his station.

Still, he could not deny he felt suddenly overwarm. His pantaloons grew tight against the swell of his manhood. Disgusted, he chided himself for noticing her soft, feminine curves revealed by her shockingly low neckline. Her obvious display of sensuality in her dampened gown was wicked. *And devilish tempting,* an unbidden voice reminded him.

Bloody hell. He was a duke, for God's sake. He should not give in to the animal side of nature that all men possess. And yet he was fighting the nearly overwhelming impulse to smother those pert, full lips and to taste her. Hear her breathless sighs against his lips. And see her beg him for more. He could only guess at what untold pleasures lay beneath her soft, shimmering gown. Right about now his imagination was working wonders. Dash it all. Heaven help him, he wanted to discover every inch of her soft, luscious little body.

The music came to an end. The dancers all quit the floor in search of libation. Standing alone in the middle of the empty dance floor, he came immediately to his senses.

His face burned with shame.

Stepping back, he etched a curt bow, turned on his heel and left her where she stood. Dazed and a bit confused, she watched him stalk off the dance floor. Frowning, she gathered her skirts and went in search of her mother. She was at least relieved to be able to herald the unhappy news of the duke's firm and resolute rejection.

Despising the tug of attraction he felt for the little siren, Roland vowed to take his mind off her. He must focus his intellect on higher ideals where it belonged and retrieve his mind from the gutter. He would engage in a lively political debate. Yes, that would do the trick. The discord at the Congress at Vienna and the unrest in France were fascinating topics. He could and would keep his baser urges at bay. But Lady Diana Newell approached him before he had the chance to escape.

"Good evening, Your Grace," she purred, cozying up to him like a sleek kitten.

"Lady Newell," he replied with a polite nod inwardly hoping their dialogue would be brief so that he might impart his views on Bourbon government in France over a much-needed glass of brandy.

"I was hoping to find you," she murmured, waving her ivory fan languidly to and fro.

Clasping his hands behind his back, he uttered a nebulous, "Indeed." Sensing the buxom blonde's obvious attempt to ingratiate her self, he inquired blandly, "And why is that, Lady Newell?"

"I should very much like to offer my services in your hour of need," she stated with a bold, sensual smile.

Pretending to misunderstand her meaning, he frowned slightly. "In what capacity, pray, madam?"

She leaned closer to whisper, "I am told I have a way with broken hearts. Just ask my first two husbands."

His lips twitched. "They are dead, Lady Newell, else I would."

"All the more reason you and I should get better acquainted," she murmured, practically rubbing up against him. "They both died happily, Your Grace."

He was about to issue a curt rejection when, out of the corner of his eye, he caught sight of Valentina once more. She was standing on the sidelines. That perfectly horrid woman she called Mother, Lady Rutledge, looked very cross, indeed. Verily, she was reading her bedraggled daughter the Riot Act. For once, he felt sorry for the little imp. Although why he should think of her at all was beyond his reckoning. He watched her raise the glass of lemonade to her full, sensual mouth. As her soft, supple lips caressed the rim, he found himself wondering what it would be like to taste her, to feel that pert rosebud mouth open beneath his, to caress her tongue with his. Rousing himself from his wicked reverie, he tore his gaze away. A dark frown marred his forehead. What the devil was the matter with him? His thoughts were oddly preoccupied with the Rutledge chit.

What he needed to rid himself of this pent-up frustration was pleasure, fresh, sweet pleasure. And from all reports, Lady Newell's unrestrained performance in bed was a carnal experience not to be missed.

He turned back to the widow who danced attendance eagerly at his elbow. "You've convinced me your idea has merit," he acquiesced with a smooth smile.

"How utterly delightful," she crooned. "I look forward to furthering our acquaintance, Your Grace. You may rely on me to seek you out. I am on excellent terms with the servants," she whispered softly against his ear.

"Until tonight," he replied, kissing her outstretched hand.

Two

Hours later, the dreaded Valentine's Day ball finally drew to a close. All the guests who planned to spend the weekend were happily ensconced in their rooms, and the servants were dismissed for the night. Roland glanced at the large clock in the marble foyer. A crooked smile touched his lips. It was nearly three o'clock, ample time for Diana to have slipped unnoticed into his private quarters. Taper in hand, he made his way through the sleepy house to his bedchamber.

Eager as a schoolboy, he mounted the red-carpeted stairs two at a time. As his feet padded noisily across the carpeted landing, impatient fingers tugged at his suffocating silk cravat and pulled the intricate knot loose. Tonight, he would get that silly raven-haired chit out of his blood once and for all.

A pale yellow hue gleamed beneath the heavy paneled door. He smirked and quietly eased the door open.

The bed hangings were partially drawn. Smiling to himself at her forethought, he shut the door behind him and undid the pearl studs of his silk embroidered waistcoat.

"You found my rooms with no difficulty, I see," he said, shrugging out of his black claw-hammer tails velvet coat and hastily discarding his waistcoat on the chair.

She moaned slightly. Her legs rustled beneath the sheets.

His smile broadened.

He made short work of his remaining attire and walked to the bed. Leaning down, he snuffed out the taper. Pulling back the heavy green-velvet and gold-brocade counterpane, he slipped into the large tester bed. Despite his inexperience, he planned to enjoy every moment of tonight.

"*It is I,*" he murmured, drawing her near.

Sighing, she eased into the curve of his body and rested her head on his shoulder. To his surprise, she was in her night rail. Mildly diverted by her bizarre sense of discretion, he chuckled softly in the darkness. Who would have thought her modest?

Cupping her face with his hand, he tilted her mouth to receive his kiss and covered her lips with his own.

"Mmm," she mumbled sleepily and wrapped her arms around his neck. He pressed her back against the soft feather mattress.

Showering kisses over her face, he let his hands drift lower to caress her soft, round breasts and round, full hips. Pleased by her breathless sighs, he slipped the tiny buttons open at her neck and eased her night rail off. He kissed her bare shoulders. His eager hands caressed her hips, the flat of her stomach, and reached up to cup her full breasts.

"What . . . are you doing?" she murmured groggily, her voice slurred from sleep.

He laughed softly in the darkness. "What do you think?" he whispered, trailing kisses along her neck and nibbling at her collarbone with his teeth.

"*Ummm,*" she moaned sleepily.

Frowning slightly, he wished he had come to bed a bit earlier. The woman sounded half asleep. But as his mouth covered her naked breast, she seemed to rally.

Mewing with pleasure, she feathered her fingers through his hair and clutched him to her, eager for more.

Leaving her breast to savor the rest of her luscious body,

he smiled to himself. He had to admit her timid approach strangely heightened his desire. Coming over her, once more he murmured against her lips, "You are lovely."

"Am I?" she whispered hazily, kissing him.

Laughter rumbled in his chest; her performance was quite titillating. He covered her mouth with his. His tongue caressed the seam of her lips, urging them apart. When at last she opened and his tongue slipped inside, she was well worth the wait. His mouth slanted hungrily over hers. She sighed against his mouth and smoothed her hands over his shoulders. Her soft, supple lips eagerly met his passionate onslaught. Her tongue joined his teasing love play, fueling his desire. Her ardent sighs and tentative yet wildly uninhibited response nearly drove him to the brink of control.

His hand caressed her satiny thighs and slipped in between. Finding her soft, slick petals, he probed her honeyed depths, exploring her dewy apex until she trembled and tilted her hips, opening herself fully to his agonizingly sweet touch. Relishing the slow, deep, tantalizing strokes with baited breath and wildly undulating hips, she moaned. Her fingernails dug into his shoulders. She shuddered against him. Her spontaneous reaction was nearly his undoing. Uttering a guttural groan of need, he rolled on top of her. His mouth covered hers in a deep, ardent kiss. Pushing her legs wide with his thighs, he settled against her. His hard shaft probed her soft, slick, surprisingly tight channel. At the feel of his hard, probing invasion stretching her wide, she gasped against his mouth. Her palms pushed against his shoulders.

The bedchamber door banged open.

"Confound it!" he growled, shaking his head as if to clear it. He withdrew from her and rolled onto his back. The bed hangings tore open.

"What the devil?"

Henry Rutledge towered over him, blazing taper in

hand. Shackles of dread closed over Roland's heart. It dawned on him that Diana had not sounded at all like herself. In fact, he realized with a surge of panic, she had been behaving completely unlike an experienced widow of two husbands. She sounded very much like another woman, a much younger woman, a completely inexperienced woman. His head jerked around. Lying naked in the middle of his enormous tester bed was Valentina Rutledge, her soft ruby lips swollen and wet from his passionate kisses. Her wild midnight tresses curled wickedly about her bare ivory shoulders. She looked every inch a wanton enchantress. She blinked at her parents, turning from one to the other. And then she looked at him. Her startled violet eyes widened. Her hand flew to her mouth to stifle a horrified cry.

Henry glared down at Roland. "A fine, upstanding gentleman like you taking advantage of my innocent stepdaughter," he railed loudly. "There'll be hell to pay, Your Grace!" he bellowed, fisted hand raised in the air. "You'll not get away with this."

The outraged Octavia sank down on the bed beside Tina. "What have you done to my poor darling?" she demanded, brushing Valentina's tousled hair.

Pushing her hand aside, Tina grimaced and rubbed her temples in a vain attempt to clear her head.

Roland's blazing gaze burned into her. "Perhaps you would be good enough to explain how *you* happened to be in *my* bed?" he spat with venom.

Her brow ruffled. She looked about her in confusion. The hunter green velvet bed hangings and paneled walls were completely alien to her. The distinctly masculine dark mahogany surroundings did not remotely resemble the accommodations she had been given for the night. Her eyes darted back to his. Her cheeks colored fiercely. She took a hard swallow. "I . . . have not the slightest idea," she admitted in a horribly small voice.

Leaning over her, he planted his palms on either side of her hips. "No?" he blazed angrily.

Eyes wide and misty, she shrank back against the headboard. She looked dazed, like a frightened doe.

"Allow me to elucidate. You snuck in here hoping to lure me into scandal."

She stared at him in blank disbelief.

"She most certainly would not do such a scandalous thing!" Henry bellowed. "How dare you suggest that our innocent little girl planned this?"

"Really, Your Grace, the very last place our chaste daughter would contrive to be in the middle of the night is *your* bed," Octavia added for good measure.

Roland's head came up sharply. He fixed Octavia with a murderous glare. "Then, perhaps you would be good enough to explain what the hell you are doing here?" he gritted angrily.

She looked taken aback. "I went to check on Tina before I turned in for the night. She was gone. Her bed untouched. Naturally, I roused the house and went in search of you, Your Grace. As our esteemed host and master of Compton Hall, I thought you the best person to aid in our search. We never dreamed," she exclaimed in horror, "of finding you *together.*"

"How could you possibly?" he sneered at her. "Allow me to commend you on a well-laid scheme."

"See here," Henry blustered, "we are entirely innocent of any wrongdoing. 'Tis *our* daughter *you've* compromised. You're in no position to cast the blame."

Terribly groggy, Tina clutched her head in her hands. It ached with a thundering beat.

Glowering at Henry, Roland angrily kicked off the sheets and vaulted off the bed.

Tina's head came up. A strangled squeal of shock escaped her throat. A little dazed and a lot fascinated, her spellbound gaze drifted over his well-toned, powerful physique. She had never seen a man in the nude. At seeing the hard evidence of his desire, she flushed and quickly lowered her lashes. Vivid recollections of her body stretching to accommodate his large manhood assailed her. A mantle of red crossed her cheeks. Glaring at her, he snatched his black-velvet dressing robe from the end of the bed and threw it on.

Uttering a string of oaths, he drove his fisted hands into the pockets. As his bare feet tramped a path in the hunter green Aubusson carpet, he tried unsuccessfully to rein in his temper.

His emotions were always under admirable control except where *she* was concerned. The cursed woman bedeviled him. Ever since their initial encounter, the chit had gotten under his skin. And now this! Good Lord, what a dreadful situation! One thing was for certain: it had all been carefully orchestrated, of that he had no doubt. That Valentina virgin, voluptuous vixen, had tricked him.

His icy glare swept over her with blistering contempt. She leaned over the edge of the bed, inadvertently baring her lovely backside to his eager gaze. He took a hard swallow. His brow grew moist. Her current position afforded him an excellent view of her curvaceous back and round, full bottom. The same backside he had clutched only moments ago while he drove into her impossibly tight, unbearably slick feminine channel. The renewed throb of desire rushed to his groin. Damn and blast. Dragging his gaze from the fetching sight, he snatched her night rail from the floor and shoved it at her.

One bare arm appeared from behind the wall of sheets. "Thank you," she said and snatched it from him.

Giving her a disgusted look, he resumed his agitated prowl. He had to focus on the situation at hand. Good Lord, he could not believe how close he had come to claiming her virginity. Bloody hell. His mouth went dry. He had compromised her completely. Think, he must think of what to do. But all he could see was her, lying naked beneath him, hungrily kissing his mouth, clutching at his shoulders, urging him to join his body to hers and how it felt to breach her enticing, soft, impossibly tight feminine core.

Confound it. He could still taste her. She was as fresh and sweet as ripe strawberries. And the way her silken thighs had quivered beneath his touch was almost too much for him to endure. Even now, he was heavy with the need to possess her. Devil take it. He could not truly harbor smoldering passion for Valentina Rutledge, could he? No. He could not. He did not. It was unconscionable. Impropriety seemed to follow the infernal chit wherever she went. While he possessed a fine, upstanding character and embraced all that was good and decent.

He did not want her. She had deliberately duped him. Otherwise, he would never have responded to her soft sighs and hungry kisses and silken caresses. He cast a furtive glance in her direction. Oh, hell. He did want her. He could not deny it was she who dominated his thoughts and drove him toward his nearly desperate need for passionate release. It was she who filled him with mindless desire, and she made him ache for exquisite release. Blast. Blast. Blast. Her very existence had driven him to accept Lady Newell's invitation. All the while he had kissed her, fondled her, wanted her, he had envisioned a raven-haired temptress, lush and ripe and eager, lying in his arms. Bloody hell! This was sheer madness. It must be.

Try as he might, he could not seem to reconcile the fact that he, a dignified and proper duke, had gone beyond the bounds of self-control with *her*, a wild, impetuous scamp barely out of the schoolroom. Sitting in the middle of his bed, she was fumbling with the buttons to her night rail. His lips turned down. She was all thumbs from the look of it. The soft linen sheets tangled about her legs, baring naked thighs to his hungry gaze.

He quit breathing. Dragging air into his lungs, he pulled his gaze away from the fetching sight. And tried to no avail to produce a plausible, nonincrimenating explanation for what she was doing sitting half naked in the middle of his bed.

By now, the hallway was practically swarming with guests, sinking the nails in his coffin. Pushing through the crowd, the duchess entered the room. Roused from her bed in the middle of the night, she was, as always, the picture of regal propriety. Her startled gaze swept over Valentina's disheveled appearance; her eyes widened slightly. She glanced at Roland in disbelief.

Through the din of the galloping horses in her head, Valentina heard her mother decry the shocking state of affairs. "Just look at my poor innocent. Ravished by the duke!" she wailed, burying her face in her hands. "Oh, what is to be done?"

"It was not like that," Valentina cried, but her plea fell on deaf ears. She tried, with an appalling lack of success, to clear her cotton-filled head and to make sense out of what was happening. She herself was not entirely certain how she came to be in the duke's bedchamber. But she was just as stunned by her parents' inopportune appearance.

She dearly wished her recollection were not so hazy. Try as she might, she could not seem to remember anything save for the wickedly delicious dream she was having. No, not a dream. It had been real. All of it. The shocking way he had touched her. The incomparable way he had made her *feel*. She could not quite believe it had been the duke who had set her aflame. It had been his hands that caressed her and his hungry mouth that kissed her.

To her murky brain, it had all seemed a delightful fantasy, featuring a handsome prince who bore a striking resemblance to the duke. His passion quite took her breath away. Perhaps it was the Valentine's Day ball that had set her imagination aflame and allowed her to indulge in such a scrumptious fantasy. Whatever the reason, she could not resist his fiery touch. It occurred to her now that she had never been kissed before, and she could not possibly have imagined all the wonderful things he was doing to her. But in her delirious dream state that had scarcely seemed relevant. Her handsome prince had been kissing her and touching her in her most secret, delicious places. She had been helpless to resist. Try as she might, she could not clear her mind long enough to fully register the circumstances. The pleasure had been so intense, so utterly irresistible, that she had willed it to go on and on. And heaven help her, it had. Now, of course, it was patently clear why the erotic, scandalous dream had seemed so real. It had been real. All too real.

She still couldn't quite believe he was capable of such passion, or that she could respond to his touch with such wild abandon. The shameful truth was, she wanted him. The dour Duke of Westmoreland was her dream lover.

To her enormous relief, he took immediate control of the harrowing situation. With admirable calm, he addressed the gathering pack of onlookers.

"Go back to your beds," he advised. "Nothing more to see here tonight." Ushering them into the hall, he closed the door on their shocked faces and blotted out their scandalous murmurings. He leaned back against the door and folded his arms over his chest. His hard, piercing gaze locked with hers. The look he gave her was lethal. A shiver crept up her spine. He looked as though he hated her. It did not take her long to understand why.

"What the devil do you have to say for yourself?" Henry's booming voice demanded to know. "You've sullied my stepdaughter's reputation and taken her virtue for a night's pleasure."

"No," Valentina cried, frantic to put a halt to the waking nightmare. "It was not like that!"

Henry arched a bushy brow. "No? Did he seduce you, then, girl? Claimed to love you, did he? Is that how you ended up in his bed?" he accused.

"N-no," she stammered, feeling all topsy-turvy, the meager contents of her stomach threatening to make an unwanted appearance. "I'm not . . . precisely sure. But the duke is not to blame. Truly, he is not."

The duchess cocked a dubious brow. "Is this true, Roland?" she asked her son. "Dare we hope *you* have a satisfactory explanation of tonight's events?"

"I am sorry to disappoint you," he uttered stiffly, "but I have nothing satisfactory to report."

"Tell us nothing untoward occurred," she prodded him in desperation. "You must give us assurances," she urged, her voice climbing an octave.

Shoving his hands in the pockets of his black-velvet dressing robe, he replied stiffly, "I cannot offer the innocuous explanation you seek. Although the young *innocent,*" he derided, glaring at Valentina with blistering contempt, "appeared in my bed uninvited, I am ultimately not entirely without blame in the matter."

The duchess's eyes drifted shut. She clutched her forehead between her thumb and her forefinger.

Henry swore out loud.

A satisfied smile spread across Octavia's lips. "We have at last arrived at the truth," she purred like a cat cornering a helpless mouse. "He entrapped our daughter in his bed and now seeks to escape his honor-bound duty."

A ripple of alarm swept over Valentina. She suddenly saw quite clearly the alarming direction this catastrophe might take. "This is all a simple misunderstanding," she insisted, on the verge of hysteria. "You see," she began, searching for a reasonable explanation for the totally unreasonable circumstance, "I must have gotten confused.

Somehow, I ended up in the duke's bedchamber. It was an accident. I—I made a silly mistake, but it is all cleared up now. We can forget about this mix-up and go back to our beds and forget this unfortunate mishap."

"On the contrary," Roland countered icily, "I do not believe your stepfather will allow it."

Henry seized his cue. "Indeed, I will not. What the devil are you going to do about this?" he charged the duke angrily.

"Do?" Roland replied, his scathing gaze never leaving Valentina's pea green countenance. "What would you have me do? It was your stepdaughter crawled into my bed. If her virtue has been compromised, she has no one to blame but herself."

Valentina's eyes widened. A horrified gasp escaped her lips. "I did no such thing!"

His jaw turned to granite. "The hell you didn't," he ground out, taking a menacing step toward her.

"Why would I?" she demanded, indignant.

His lips curled in a vicious sneer. "As if you don't know."

Her enormous violet eyes rounded slightly. She had the nerve to look baffled.

Sensing her son's simmering wrath, the duchess wisely interjected, "I suggest we discuss matters in the morning when cooler heads prevail."

"Yes," Lady Rutledge concurred, "after breakfast when the shooting party has departed, we shall discuss what is to be done."

Panic took root in Tina's heart. "On the contrary. Nothing is to be done," she stated with bold conviction. "I have no wish to pursue the matter. And I am persuaded the duke shares my desire to put the unfortunate incident behind us." She was rewarded with a painful bite of her mother's nails in her arm.

"Nonsense," Octavia insisted with a chilling smile. "You are naturally overwrought by what this brute has done to you. Retribution must and will be made. The sooner, the better."

Before Valentina had the chance to object, her mother propelled her from the bed and ushered her none too gently toward the door.

She paused at the threshold to cast a disdainful look at the despicable duke. "We shall see what the morning's light brings," she huffed haughtily.

"Indeed, Lady Rutledge," came his steel-edged retort. "The truth shall be known. One way or the other."

Piqued by his insolence, she ushered her bewildered daughter from the room.

Closing the door in their wake, the duchess let out a miserable sigh. "Is there no end to the calumny you intend to bring upon this family? First that horrid Winston woman and now this!"

Roland cast her a withering look. Crossing the room, he lifted the decanter and poured himself a much-needed brandy.

"What *do* you plan?" she pressed him.

He shrugged and downed the contents of his glass in one gulp. "Not a great deal I can do," he replied and slammed the glass down on the table.

She looked scandalized. "You cannot seriously intend to offer for that—that common trollop?"

Roland gave his mother an irritated look. "Under the circumstances, what else can I do?" The truth of his unseemly conduct grated on him excessively. And yet, honor dictated he marry the wily chit. Hell, he thought with a blaze of renewed fury, her maidenhead was a mere technicality. He had kissed her, fondled her and almost joined his body to hers in the manner that only her husband had the right. Now all that was left was for him to make restitution. Regardless of how unthinkable such an act on his part might be.

"Well," his mother sputtered. "I must say I raised a

prized fool idiot. How could you be so infernally stupid as to let her dupe you? Simple misunderstanding, indeed," she scoffed. "Anyone can see the little tart planned it. I expect she hopes to be duchess by week's end. It is too much to be borne, first that ghastly Gwen person and now the gypsy girl. I am glad your father is not alive to see this."

Roland's jaw clenched. He knew he had conducted himself badly. His late father doubtless would not be proud. "Gypsy or not, I cannot ignore her stepfather's threats. He means to make good on them, of that you can have no doubt."

"Honorable young ladies do not skulk into men's beds in the middle of the night. Surely, there must be a way out of this. If you have not taken her virtue, then it is simply a matter of honor, and a marriage need not take place. Tell me that her virtue has not been compromised completely. At least leave me some shred of hope."

The feel of her soft, unbearably tight entrance sheathing him like a second skin as he entered her assailed Roland without mercy. A flush of heat suffused his prominent cheekbones. He cleared his throat and pushed the memory from his mind. He forced himself to recall that she had duped him. He must concentrate on hating the girl. And never again think of the unbearable pleasure that fleeting moment of passion in her silken arms had afforded him. "I am afraid I cannot give you the assurances you seek," he admitted with a good deal of regret.

His mother paled considerably. She sank down on the edge of the large tester bed. "The conniving little witch and her odious parents have got the upper hand," she bemoaned, her spirit gravely dampened.

"It would seem so, yes," he conceded begrudgingly.

"No," his mother countered with energy, shaking her head in violent reaction to the mere thought of that ill-bred charlatan as her daughter-in-law, "it is unconscionable. Find a way to thwart them. Pay Rutledge off. Anything. You cannot mean to stoop to marriage? Not with such a girl?"

"I will never be free of him. He plans to milk me dry for years. That much was obvious. Or do you imagine the hoards of guests arrived at my door last evening on their own?" he asked her archly. "What assurances do we have that the vulgar Lady Rutledge will not take the blunt *and* tarnish my fine, upstanding name? If I offer payment, I will be entirely at their mercy. And I refuse to put my head in their noose. That I will not do," he imparted with icy resolve.

"Clever, I must say. They've orchestrated the perfect scandal."

Roland's jaw clenched. Smarting from their little ruse, he reflected on the wicked siren they had employed to do the deed. She had performed well beyond anyone's expectations, especially his. "Once I am wed, no matter how distasteful a prospect that may be, I am free of the odious man and his unctuous wife for good."

"Yes," his mother was quick to point out, "but married to their little harlot, what then? Such a match . . . is unthinkable. Only consider your position, your title. You must not do this, Roland. Regardless of what transpired here tonight, you must cry off. Get rid of her."

"How can I?" he snapped angrily. "Honor dictates—"

"*Honor?*" she echoed in dismay. "How can you speak of honor at a time like this? Your entire life hangs in the balance. It is a folly, my boy, as ill-conceived as your engagement to that grasping witch, Gwen."

"I am not in a position to suffer another scandal. Given the nature of my conduct, I must offer her the protection of my name. The burden of decency rests on my shoulders. I am to blame. I can not and will not evade my obligation."

His mother heaved a miserable sigh of defeat. "I suspect Henry Rutledge presumed that much already. He has assessed your unfailing sense of decency and employed it to his advantage. You are to be congratulated, my boy." Reproach filled her voice. "You have earned the dubious distinction of being the only Duke of Westmoreland to be duped twice by two cunning females. And this time you've no one to blame but yourself. If you wanted to enjoy her wares for the night, you should have made it clear that you had absolutely no intentions of marrying the little Cyprian for it."

"Yes. Thank you, Mother, for that edifying piece of advice," he gritted through his teeth. "In future, I'll be sure to follow your judicious advice, should the unfortunate circumstance of utter disgrace ever arise again, but at present, I am still reeling from my most recent unpardonable folly, I've a smashing headache, it is four o'clock in the morning and I am more than a little tired!" he bellowed loudly.

Astounded by his uncharacteristic display of temper, she got to her feet. "Pray, Roland, do not shout," she replied and hastily quit the room in search of her bed.

Anger roiled inside of him. He paced the confines of his room like one of the caged animals at Menagerie at the Tower of London. His mother was entirely correct and that was the rub.

Valentina had deliberately hoodwinked him. What was more, Lady Newell must have been her ally from the start. No wonder she had cozened up to him and practically begged him to take her to bed. It was all a carefully orchestrated scheme to trick him. His lips curled into an angry snarl. Befuddled, indeed. The hell she was. Her attempts to smooth things over would have been humorous were her duplicity not so bloody obvious. It was entrapment, pure and simple. And he was the damned fool who had gotten snared by her clinging kisses and breathless sighs. She was a talented actress who had been primed for the role by her grasping mother. The muscle in his jaw pulsed. She might be able to garner a wealthy husband by this gambit. But she would pay dearly for her machinations. He would see to it personally.

Three

The next morning, after most of the guests had departed or joined the shooting party, the Rutledge family lagged behind.

If Valentina had thought herself ill last night, this morning her condition was nothing short of acute affliction. If she did not know better, she would have sworn she had been poisoned. She could not think why, but something was wreaking havoc with her stomach. And an aggravating little man was hammering inside her head. Having spent the balance of the dawn retching, she was thoroughly exhausted and hot and clammy.

She entered the library, trailing submissively behind her mother. The large marble fireplace blazed with a warm, crackling fire, taking the chill off the morning. Her gaze swept over the bookshelves that curved in a semicircle behind the enormous desk. Roland was present, of course. Garbed in a hunter green superfine coat that accentuated his broad, muscular shoulders, a crisp white linen shirt, olive silk cravat and buff-colored pantaloons, he looked every inch a cool, remote duke. His freshly washed black hair was combed back from his razor-smooth face, accentuating his masculine features.

Taking her seat before the large maple desk, Tina found herself uncomfortably sandwiched between her overbearing parents. Situated in a large Queen Anne chair beside the desk, the duchess cast her a venomous glare. Her piercing black gaze raked over Tina's plain lavender muslin. A frown edged her aged lips. Drawing a disgusted sigh, she looked away.

Dropping into the large dark brown leather chair behind the desk, Roland swept his gaze over Tina's pale, drawn countenance. Frowning at her ashen complexion, he directed his attention toward Henry.

"I'll come directly to the point." His manner was cold and impersonal. "I am willing to make the necessary retribution. To avert scandal and retrieve your stepdaughter's tattered reputation from the jaws of ignominy, I offer marriage."

A look of shock crossed Valentina's ashen face. Sitting bolt upright, she cried, *"Marriage?* No. Oh, no! That is not necessary. Truly, it is not."

Henry piped up. "No one is trying to force your hand, Your Grace. We all understand our little girl's ruin was not intentionally done."

"Yes," Octavia chirped with an ingratiating smile, "I am certain we can settle on an appropriate sum that would salvage our daughter's reputation without the necessity of nuptials."

Startled, Tina shot her mother a perplexed look, but Octavia merely smiled in the face of her daughter's dismay.

Roland sat back in the leather chair, his hands steepled in thought. "Indeed?" he murmured, cocking a dubious brow. "You've decided to be lenient, then? Under the circumstances, that is excessively magnanimous of you. I rather thought you might try to elicit a hefty settlement in return for your silence."

"Why," she gushed, "we are only thinking of what would be best for our little Tina, Your Grace. She is quite determined to marry for love."

His dark, penetrating gaze swerved toward Valentina. As his bold, impudent gaze roamed over her, she had the

scandalous impression he was recalling every moment of
last night's torrid encounter. Her lashes fluttered down.
Her head was still reeling from their passionate interlude.
She shifted beneath his searing regard. The man seemed
to have the uncanny ability to look right through her. It
was decidedly unnerving to have his piercing gaze fixed
on her. He was not at all pleased with her most of the time
and certainly never less so than at the moment of their
forced betrothal. Seeing him now, looking terribly dark
and unfailingly handsome, she was reminded that he was
a duke, in a long succession of dukes, and she was plain
old Miss Rutledge lately of India. His imposing stature cut
an intimidating figure. His stern, forbidding features and
his impossibly correct attitude could make a saint falter.
And heaven knew, after last night, she was as far a cry from
sainthood as any girl could be.

"Do you reckon my money will ease your plight, Miss
Rutledge?" he asked her with biting sarcasm.

Her chin came up. She opened her mouth to assure
him she cared for neither the protection of his name nor
his money, but her mother squeezed her wrist hard
enough to crush bones. She flinched and fell silent.

Henry cleared his throat. "I shouldn't like to put it
that way. Come now, let us be civilized about this. Name
your sum."

Dragging his dark, accusing glare from Valentina's
miserable face, the duke loosed his lethal stare on her
stepfather. "I intend to make no offer of money."

"No money?" Octavia echoed sharply. "But you must!"
she cried, vaulting to her feet.

"On the contrary, I have made an offer of marriage
which your daughter has seen fit to reject. The matter
would appear to be closed. I bid you good day, madam."
Planting his hands firmly on the desktop, he pushed
back his chair and got to his feet. "You will, of course, understand if I do not show you out?"

"Not so fast," Lady Rutledge snarled. "Tina is a child, naturally tentative and frightened of marriage. She can have no idea what humiliation she will suffer now that you've had your way with her. But I do. If you do not settle with us and put the matter to rest, I can make your life very difficult, Your Grace. And don't think I won't."

Valentina took in her breath. *"Mother,"* she gasped.

"Hush," Octavia hissed at her.

Roland regarded the crass woman with blatant dislike and reclined once more behind the desk. "I have little doubt you would be willing to do anything to achieve your ends."

Baffled, Valentina's forehead creased. "What ends?" Turning to her mother, she pressed, "To what ends does he refer?"

"The man has wronged you, and now he refuses to make retribution," Octavia barked irritably. "It is beyond the pale."

"Understand me, madam," Roland warned in a deadly tone. "I will not suffer blackmail."

"Blackmail?" Tina erupted in horror.

"I scarcely think retribution is blackmail," Henry muttered.

Roland's ferocious glare threatened to skewer him where he sat. "I do."

"Oh, very well then, have it your way," Octavia snapped testily. "Marriage it shall be."

"Nothing will ever induce me to accept your offer," Tina stated, resolute. "I am sorry, Your Grace, I confess I do not fully comprehend the nature of this discussion, but I do know that I must refuse the protection of your name."

He met her adamant refusal with cool disdain.

"The devil!" Henry exploded hotly, blundering to his feet. "If you think for one moment I'll have you under my roof after the duke's had his way with you, you are sadly mistaken, girl. It is marriage to the duke or naught!"

Valentina drew a deep, steadying breath. "Very well," she said, squaring her shoulders. "It is nothing."

A flicker of surprise crossed Roland's dark eyes.

"You must be mad!" Octavia sputtered in disbelief, gawking at her. "I will not hear of it. Think of your reputation. You must marry."

"I have a small stipend from father," Tina ventured bravely. "I shall make out well enough on my own."

Octavia waved away her suggestion. "Gracious, child, that was spent ages ago."

A look of stunned disbelief crossed Tina's pale, delicate features. "What are you saying?" she breathed. "What have you done?"

"I did nothing untoward," her mother remarked brusquely. "I am your mother. It is my duty to look after your welfare. You know nothing of these things."

"You spent my inheritance?" Tina murmured, greatly distressed. "Behind my back . . . without so much as a word?"

Heaving an impatient sigh, her mother said sharply, "The simple fact remains you are homeless. The duke does not see fit to offer a monetary settlement. And unless you agree to his offer of marriage, you will be out on the streets. Penniless."

Dazed, Valentina blinked at her mother. "You cannot mean turn me out?"

Octavia's lips thinned. "Your reputation is in shreds. We must consider our situation and protect our interests. Why, we would never be able to show our faces in polite society again."

The color drained from Tina's face. A deafening ring sounded in her ears. Her head began to spin. The room blurred. To her horror, her fate now rested in the duke's hands, the one man in the world least likely to be merciful. She raised her eyes to his. His cold, unwavering stare held her captive. A shiver of dread crept up her spine. He sensed his power over her and doubtless planned to use it to his advantage. "As usual, Mother, you leave me no choice," she said, her tone desolate. She bowed her head in defeat. "I will marry you, Your Grace."

"Well then, the matter is settled," Octavia said, triumphant. "It seems there is to be a wedding, after all. The best and most expensive wedding of the year. You'll be the envy of all, my dear," she crooned, completely indifferent to her downcast daughter.

"No," Roland countered sharply. "The marriage ceremony will be private, here at Compton Hall. No pomp and circumstance. You may attend or not; the choice is yours."

Valentina's head came up. "So soon?" she cried in alarm. She needed more time. Time to prepare herself. Time to become accustomed to the idea. Time to get to know him.

He offered her a hard, cruel smirk. "But of course. We do not want to risk the threat of scandal to besmirch your fine, upstanding name. As it happens, I am on excellent terms with the archbishop. All can be arranged in very little time."

Lady Rutledge sighed her disappointment. "Very well, if you insist," she conceded begrudgingly. "But I do think my little angel deserves better."

Sickened, Tina turned her face. Her mother's main thought was the duke's exalted station and that her daughter would be his duchess. Happiness did not enter into it.

The harsh reality swam around and around in her brain. Married. She was to be married to the Duke of Westmoreland. The cold, distant, haughty master of Compton Hall. The very man who had discovered her innermost secret places and made her ache for his touch at one moment, and who displayed blatant contempt of her the next, was to be her lord and master till death do they part.

The duchess got to her feet. "The announcement will be made this afternoon. I think it best," she remarked, eyeing Lord and Lady Rutledge with scorn, "that you take your leave. Naturally, your"—she hesitated, as if the mere mention of Tina was painful—"daughter shall remain here to receive the necessary instruction on how to conduct herself as future mistress of Compton Hall." Offering Tina a resentful look, she held her elegant gray head high and regally quit the library.

Octavia got to her feet. "A million things to do, come, my dear," she chortled with nauseating cheer. She glanced over her shoulder at her dawdling spouse. "Do come along, Henry," she intoned meaningfully. "His Grace wishes to be *alone* with his bride," she whispered in an exaggerated, coarse manner. Tina's eyes drifted shut. Her humiliation was complete.

Stroking his chin thoughtfully, Roland watched the vulgar duo depart. His gaze drifted back to his intended. Her head was bowed in uncharacteristic submission.

A frown touched his brow. Something was nagging at him. While he was convinced the little witch had a hand in manipulating him last night, he could not reconcile her pale, drawn complexion this morning. Was she regretting her involvement? Was she, too, a fortune hunter who had gotten more than she bargained for in marriage to him?

More to the point, why the devil *had* she refused his offer? That, he had not expected. Her lackluster attitude to their impending nuptials was puzzling, indeed. She had gotten what she was after. Or had she? He was not quite sure. One thing was certain, she appeared genuinely distraught by the prospect. Perhaps she was an innocent pawn in Rutledge's scheme after all.

Something propelled him to find out.

"Allow me to commend you on a most excellent per-

formance. You play your part to perfection, sweeting."
His voice was cold and lashing.

Her head came up. She looked at him as if he were a
candidate for Bedlam. "What part?"

"I think you know," he countered coolly.

"I am not now nor have I ever been pretending."

His momentary pang of sympathy fled as briskly as it
had arrived. "Tell me, I am but curious. Are you accustomed to having men in your bed?" he growled at her.

Her lavender eyes rounded. A twinge of color lit her
pallid cheeks. "Certainly not. Are *you* accustomed to having strange women in your bed?" she tossed back at him.

He offered her a sardonic smirk. "Never strange till
last night," came his biting reply.

She squared her slender shoulders. "Well," she blustered, "I certainly cannot fathom the bizarre circumstance
that precipitated *my* being in *your* bed. That I should ever
. . . that we could possibly . . . that you would . . . want
to . . ." Her voice trailed off as a scandalized blush suffused
her cheeks. Clearing her throat, she bowed her head and
made an unwarranted examination of her lap.

His mouth twisted. "Quite so. It is utterly preposterous," he stated harshly. "But since you saw fit to sneak
into my bed, we shall both pay a rather hefty sum for
your duplicity."

Her spine stiffened. She sent him a resentful look. "I
did *not* sneak into your room," she corrected.

He gave her a dubious look. "Am I to believe you simply materialized out of thin air?"

"I care not what you believe," she flung at him. "I only
know I am entirely innocent of the charges laid at my
feet."

"Perhaps," he allowed at length, his probing gaze lingering on her unhappy face. "Was it your calculating
mother? Did she coerce you into planning my downfall?
Is that how it happened?" he pressed.

She had the nerve to look aghast. "I comprehend your ill feelings toward my family perfectly, but I must take exception to your vile insinuations. What you suggest is not only preposterous, it is impossible. My mother would never compromise my virtue. I am her daughter. She loves me. What you suggest . . . it is . . . is utterly unthinkable."

Sighing, he closed his eyes and stroked the bridge of his nose between his thumb and forefinger. Damned silly chit was either too blindsided or too loyal to see what was right in front of her nose. Clearly, she was unable or unwilling to condemn her mother for what she was—a grasping, callous woman who would stop at nothing to achieve her ends. He almost felt sorry for the small, miserable woman seated before him. Almost.

"Very well." He heaved a frustrated breath. "We will strive to uncover the truth another day when you are feeling less overwrought."

"Time will not alter my feelings. I will never concur with your view. My mother did not lure me to your bed. She could not and would not do such a despicable thing. It is unconscionable. No decent, caring person would sacrifice her own daughter for some misbegotten aim."

He drew an impatient breath. "Regardless of how you happened to be in my bed," he ground out, "the fact remains you were most definitely compromised. And we are going to be living together as man and wife for a very long time. I suggest we make a stab at civility. Honesty would be a good place to start."

Her tongue darted between her parched lips. "I am trying to be honest. I want to remember, truly I do, but everything is so horribly muddled," she complained, rubbing her throbbing temples. "Do you not think I have tried? I simply cannot seem to recall."

"How convenient," he sniped. "Let us hope your amnesia is as fleeting as your morals. We may at last arrive at the truth."

"I am telling you the truth!" she exclaimed with vehemence and winced for the effort.

"Truth?" he uttered with a ruthless snort. "Whose? Yours? Or that conniving witch of a mother? Perchance you think I imagine you had no idea Henry's gaming debts were astronomical?"

She turned a paler shade of green. "I knew he had a tendency to loose a great deal. I overheard them arguing, but I never dreamed, never thought they would garnish my inheritance to pay for his ill-natured habits. I am as distressed by the discovery as you."

He sniggered at that. "I sincerely doubt it."

She drew a deep, fortifying breath. "Upon my honor, I swear to you, I have no recollection of anything prior to the moment of discovery in your bed. Despite your obvious disgust of me, I have not the slightest intentions of trying to trick you. Marriage is the furthest aim from my mind."

His angry gaze blazed her over. *Quite right*, he added silently, *money is her aim*. Her suggestion only confirmed his worst fears. She was a fortune hunter. "Somehow, Miss Rutledge"—his low, gravelly tone belied his anger—"I find that extremely hard to believe."

Irked by his constant insinuation that she deliberately set out to dupe him, her temper flared. "I am certain I have no control over your thoughts," she imparted swiftly, "however unbecoming they may be."

He gave her a crushing glare. "If I am to believe this little gambit of yours was completely unintentional," he snarled in a fierce tone, "then you must allow me a few minor inquiries."

"I myself wish to be exonerated."

He surveyed her keenly. "Last night, whom did you imagine me to be?"

She flushed. Her gaze skittered away. She had imagined him as her fantasy lover. Of course, on this occasion, her reverie had been quite wickedly tempestuous and outdone by any previous dreams she had had. Ever. But she would rather die than admit such childish fancy. Aside from being magnificently tall, wonderfully broad shouldered and breathtakingly handsome, there was precious little to recommend the man. He was completely devoid of charm. Most of the time, he lacked all signs of any real imagination. Verily, she wondered if the man knew what a fantasy was. One thing troubled her. She could not reconcile her feelings toward the tedious duke and her burgeoning passion for her sumptuous lover. How could they be one in the same?

"I think I must have been dreaming," she murmured, ill at ease. She glanced up at him from beneath her lashes. "Whom did you take me for, Your Grace?"

Color flooded his face. Reluctant to relate the sordid details of last night, he tugged at his shirt cuff and cleared his throat. "It hardly signifies at the moment," he countered swiftly. "Let us not forget it was you who cast fate to the wind last night and crawled into my bed."

She squeezed her eyes shut. *"Oh!"* she bristled, stamping her feet in frustration. "For the last time. I did *NOT* crawl into your bed! *You*, Your Grace, are the very last man on earth I should ever wish to bed!" The moment the words escaped her lips, her hand flew to her mouth. Her cheeks flamed bright red.

"You've made your point," he uttered coolly.

Taking a hard swallow, she got to her feet and stood tall in the face of total ignominy. "If your interrogation is intended to be all one sided," she averred calmly, "I shall take my leave." Collecting her skirts, she turned on her heel, fully intending to leave the hateful man right where he stood. But her legs went wobbly. Her world turned topsy-turvy. To her acute dismay, she had to clutch the back of the chair to steady herself. The room felt stifling hot. Her throat tightened. She felt sick, quite horribly ill.

"Are you feeling quite well?" he asked, eyeing her with concern.

Her head was spinning. "I very much fear I am going to be sick," she choked out, covering her mouth.

To her horror, instead of allowing a hasty escape, he came to her aid. Before she could gainsay him, his arm slipped around her waist. Easing her against his lean, muscular chest, he half carried her to the casement window and threw it wide.

"The fresh air will do you good."

Acutely aware of his hard, lean body pressed intimately against her, she leaned her head out the window. Drawing several deep breaths of the cold winter air, she prayed God she would not lose the meager contents of her stomach in front of him. To her relief, the wave of nausea subsided.

When she managed to regain her composure and opened her eyes, he was watching her. His direct gaze focused intently on her face. Lord, she could practically *feel* his dark, piercing stare. It was as though he were trying to see into her soul. The way his hooded gaze traveled the length of her was enough to put any girl to the blush. But she was not just *any* girl. She was the bothersome child he was being forced to wed. She wanted to prove her innocence. But she knew better than to try to elicit his fine opinion. He had decided that she was a wild waif with a penchant for irascible behavior like swimming in the nude in *his* lake and sneaking into *his* bed in the middle of the night.

Flustered, she turned away. "Thank you," she mumbled. "I am better now."

"Not at all," he replied, ever the courteous duke as he eased the window shut. "But I do think you should see a doctor."

Keeping her back to him, she shook her head and walked toward the door.

He watched her cross the room. A shadow of doubt

lurked in the back of his mind. He could not shake the uncomfortable feeling that this recent performance was genuine. What the deuce kind of game *was* she playing?

He scowled. The tug of sympathy he felt for the wily chit irked him no small degree. She was a woman. And he had learned the hard way they were all alike, cunning little witches. Still, she looked positively green.

"If you are truly ill, we might postpone the ceremony," he offered, making a stab at congeniality. "Provided you agree to remain discreet."

Stung, she pulled up sharp. "Your kindness nearly overwhelms me, Your Grace," she imparted with thinly veiled sarcasm. "But I am fine." She hesitated for a moment at the library door. Turning her head, she cast him a fleeting glance. "Who was she?"

His brows snapped together. "Who?"

"The one who gave you such a dreary opinion of all women?"

He fixed her with a withering glare. "A wild nymph with ebony hair and wild eyes to tempt a man to sin," he said unkindly.

She cocked a sultry brow. "Well, in that case, Your Grace, you would be well advised to avoid her at all costs. No woman would like to be responsible for corrupting a soul as pristine as yours."

So saying, she slipped from the library.

His jaw clenched. He hit the estate book with his fist. It toppled onto the floor.

"Little witch," he spat under his breath. Hell and the devil! She drove him to distraction. He could not decide what vexed him more, the passionate beast that unfurled at her slightest touch, or her wanton, unbridled response. Whatever the reason, he was having a confoundedly difficult time controlling his thoughts, let alone his actions.

* * *

Two days later, Roland rubbed his tired eyes and expelled a lusty yawn. Blurry-eyed, he glanced at the library clock. Nearly three o'clock. It was past time he found his bed for the night. Expelling a tired sigh, he closed the leather-bound estate book and sleepily got to his feet. He was tired and irritable. Bloody well furious. Tomorrow he would be wed. And it was not a winsome prospect. He retrieved the taper from the desk, intending to head to his chambers.

Damnable thing of it was he could barely wait to take legal possession of her ripe, eager body. He chaffed at his disgusting lack of self-control. But he could not deny his smoldering need to possess her. She was devilishly bewitching. Damn her. Even now he could recall the soft, slick petals of her feminine core, wet with sweet honey beckoning him into the sensual fray. Why was he damnably attracted to the cursed woman? Perhaps it was his lack of experience with the fairer sex that made him fascinated by her soft, breathless sighs and sweet, delectable lips.

Shaking his head, he made his way through the darkened house to his bedchamber. Given the lateness of the hour, he took pity on his faithful valet. Setting the taper on the table beside his bed, he strode to the window and was about to draw the heavy velvet drapes. It was a blustery cold night. A silvery full moon illuminated the lawn. He thought he caught a fleeting glimpse of a small figure hurrying across the frozen grounds. His brow furrowed. He strained to make out the dark night. His lips thinned. Pure rage pumped through his veins.

"Damnation!" he spat under his breath. Storming from his room, he tore down the hall. His booted feet blazed a path down the front stairs. He did not so much as pause to rouse the servants. No, this ignominy he would suffer alone. To raise the house at this ungodly hour only to suffer further humiliation at a woman's hands once more was unconscionable.

Donning his heavy wool greatcoat, he bolted outside. The swirl of the icy wintry winds kicked up. A storm was brewing. Cupping his hands to his mouth, he shouted to her.

She glanced back. At seeing him, she picked up her skirts and hastened her gait.

"Cursed little fool," he growled under his breath and ran after her.

The wind swirled around him like a whip, lashing his face with ice-cold spines. He chased her over the frozen grounds through the fields, toward the woods. He shouted for her to stop. But she paid him no heed. As his booted feet sped across the frozen, uneven terrain, his temper simmered to a fevered pitch. When he caught her, he would paddle her ungrateful backside for this. He closed in on her just before the thick bracken. He grabbed her from behind. Stubborn to the end, she twisted against him. She lost her balance and toppled with a hard thud to the icy ground. He landed hard on top of her.

"Agh!" she cried out, in protest of his great bulk laying heavily atop her.

The frigid night air howled and swirled around them. She bucked and thrashed beneath him. "Let me go!" Catching her flailing fists, he slammed her arms to the ground, bracing them on either side of her head.

His breathing was rapid pants. "What the bloody hell do you think you're doing?" he asked savagely.

"Running away," she sniped, her bosom heaving against his rock-hard chest.

He snickered. "Obviously. Where the devil did you think you were going?"

"What does that matter?" The wind tugged at her hair, tossing it wildly about her face. "You care nothing for the likes of me."

His dark, furious eyes drilled into her. It struck him then that she was wrong. He did care. More than he wanted to. The harsh expression in his angry eyes softened with smoldering desire. "Little fool," he breathed, "you might have been hurt."

"So what if I were? What concern is that of yours?" Even in the moonlit shadows, he could see the fire in her defiant purple eyes.

His nostrils flared. By God, she was like no other woman he had known. She brought out his worst side, made him lose all sense of control and forget his well-regulated sense of conduct.

"Damn you," he breathed angrily. He did not want a harridan bride. He did not want to be mesmerized by her touch, enslaved by passion. He did not want to be possessed by any female, least of all, this one. But he was helpless to cage the beast within. Hating himself in that moment for wanting her and longing to punish her for being so damned desirable, his mouth covered hers in a fiercely possessive kiss that was meant to dominate and subdue, but had the opposite effect. His open mouth twisted over hers, hard and punishing. His tongue thrust aggressively into her mouth. When at last he uttered a strangled groan and pulled away, he stared down in the moonlight, his breathing harsh and labored. He braced himself for the hard rebuff across his cheek. It never came. A lady would have slapped his face. A lady would have been scandalized, insulted. But she slipped her hands around his neck and tugged him near. And then her lips, were on his and she was kissing him. Wickedly. Deliciously. Incredibly. Her tongue teased and stroked until he thought he would go mad. Uttering a guttural groan of desire, he crushed her to him. His mouth slanted over hers, bruising her lips with his passion. One burning need drove him. He longed to possess her, body and soul. The all-consuming kiss should have tamed her, quelled her spirit. But it hadn't. Her fingers were in his hair, tugging at his nape. Her mouth was hot and wet and open. It was as if they wanted to devour each other whole, meld their bodies into one for all eternity. The insane desire to strip her naked and plunge himself deep inside her in the middle of the freezing cold field brought him back to his senses.

He tore his lips from hers. He gazed down and struggled to draw a calming breath. Her softly parted lips were swollen and wet from the heat of his kisses. Neither one spoke; the reality of their startling passion rendered them both speechless.

Shoving away from her, he got to his feet. "We should return to the house," he said gruffly. She stood as well. His arm slipped beneath her knees, and he swept her into his arms.

"I am capable of walking," she protested.

He grunted. "Yes, I know, capable of running away, too," he muttered, shifting her weight more comfortably in his arms. "I don't fancy another midnight chase through the thorny bracken."

She tried to ignore the heady scent of bay rum that invaded her nostrils. Being carried back home like a wayward child should have humiliated her. But quite the contrary, the feel of his strong arms cradling her against his rock-hard chest had the opposite titillating effect.

He paused for a moment to shift her weight in his arms. "Put your arms around my neck."

Happily complying, she rested her check against his shoulder and breathed a sigh.

He stiffened. "Must you do that?" he snapped irritably.

"Sorry," she murmured and tucked her face inside his shoulder. So, she thought with a satisfied smile, he was not as unaffected as he appeared. When he kissed her, she seemed to forget herself. Perhaps she had been starving for affection for so long that she would accept it wherever she could find it, even with a cold, distant oh-so-proper gentleman.

By the time they reached the house, a torrent of icy rain pelted down on them. His booted foot kicked open the front door. As he tramped across the expansive black-and-white marbled hall toward the library, she realized it was his intention to speak to her.

Good Lord! After that torrid encounter, the very last thing she wanted was to talk. It was bad enough to be carried in the heat of his arms and to have her face pressed against his neck and to feel his hard, sinewy muscles beneath his shirt. She really could not endure anything as civilized as dialogue with the man. Not after she had just kissed him and nearly lost all sense of reason in his arms.

He let her feet slide to the floor.

She shivered.

Glancing at her drenched clothing, he frowned. "You'll catch your death. Sit by the fire," he ordered. "I'll fetch some blankets."

Teeth chattering, she huddled before the smoldering embers in the grate.

A moment later, he returned, blankets in hand.

"Get out of those wet things."

She darted him a surprised look.

"Modesty has never been your forte."

Hot color suffused her cheeks. She snatched the blanket and presented him with her back. Her ice-cold fingers made quick work of her cold, wet garments. When she was warmly wrapped in the cozy blanket, she turned around.

Her heart skipped a beat.

He had removed his wet clothes as well. His skintight britches left very little to any woman's imagination. Her greedy eyes pored over his broad shoulders, hard, muscular chest and narrow, tapered hips.

Sensing her perusal, he looked up. She quickly turned around. He crossed the room to the drinks table and sloshed a large amount of brandy into two glasses. Turning around, he handed her a glass.

"Drink it."

She shook her head. "I never drink spirits."

He laughed deep in his chest. "Tonight, you'll drink it and like it. You need it."

Color streaked across her cheeks. She accepted the brandy. "Thank you."

Slurping a small amount of the amber liquid, she grimaced. "It tastes like bitter tea," she complained and set the glass on the table.

His brows hiked. *"Tea?"* He drained the contents of his glass. "Where the devil did you get that idea?"

She opened her mouth to reply. But he lifted his hand to silence her. "Never mind. I am persuaded your reply would only baffle me to distraction." Crouching down on his haunches, he stoked the fire until a warm, crackling blaze glowed.

She settled into the cozy chair and glanced about her. This was the same room where she had been sentenced to a life of drudgery as his future duchess. A smile stole over her lips. Tonight, somehow it did not feel like drudgery. Oh no, not at all.

Straightening from the fire, he turned toward her. "You thought to run away." It was not a question.

She lowered her gaze to her lap. "Yes," she admitted, "I thought it best."

"Where did you plan to go?"

She shrugged. "I don't know. Away from here."

"Away from me?" he corrected.

She nodded.

"Your Grace," she beseeched him. "You do not love me any more than I harbor the slightest regard for you."

He pulled a face. "Good God. What has that got do

with the price of silver?" He dropped into the wing-back chair across from her.

"We do not even *know* one another."

He arched a sooty brow. "How much better acquainted do you fancy we could be?"

Turning beet red, she averted her gaze and rambled on, "We are clearly as ill-suited as any two people can be."

"You believe, you actually imagine, you've the right to be disappointed?" A hint of derision crept into his voice.

Her jaw clenched. "There is a good deal of difference between the two of us. Or hadn't you noticed?" she asked, her tone sharp.

"Oh, I noticed," he stated far too plainly to be complimentary. He set his glass down on the table beside his chair. "Rather difficult not to." His disparaging gaze weighed heavily on her windswept, damp hair. "It is your penchant to break every rule in the book."

"While you are determined to militantly follow them," she tossed back tartly.

He shrugged. "Most would not find that an objectionable trait in a husband."

"I am not like most young ladies."

He offered her a sardonic grunt. "For once we are in complete accord."

She heaved an irritated groan. "At least you concede that we are mismatched."

He shrugged a careless shoulder. "Like millions of other people. Is that any reason to run off like a headstrong colt in the middle of the night?"

"I had to get away. Before . . ." Her voice trailed off; she averted her gaze.

A mantle of anger swept across his face. "Before we exchanged our vows and you were sworn to me, the ogre duke, for all eternity," he supplied bitterly.

"I have no wish to be your wife."

"Enduring my wealth and position too much for the likes of you?" he taunted with a nasty edge.

She released a miserable sigh. "You are being impossible." Was she not trying for a way to avoid disaster for them both? Must he always regale her with insults?

"And you are being a child. Foolhardy. Insolent. I do hope you see the futility of trying to escape. In future, I should very much like to forgo the midnight romp through the woods."

She glared at him spitefully. "Indeed, Your Grace," she countered, her tone pithy, "I have learned that not all calamities are avoidable. Regardless of how unpleasant."

He fixed her with a murderous look. "A fact I have already come to discover at your hands."

She glanced away from him in anger and noticed the enormous leather-bound books piled on the desk. "I am so very sorry to have detained you from your well-appointed rounds with your enthralling ledger books," she derided with biting sarcasm.

How dare she disparage his strict sense of discipline. He had responsibilities. People relied on him. He must keep abreast of the handling of his estates.

"Despite your seemingly unlimited propensity for impropriety, you would do well to remember as the future Duchess of Westmoreland you may not go forging through the night like a wood spry. One can only wonder if you possess an ounce of sense in that head of yours," he muttered, his tone disparaging, "or, for that matter, decorum."

"Certainly not," she concurred hotly. "Given what a pedantic prig you are, it would be difficult for any mere ordinary mortal to win your admiration!"

"Whereas you would have us both conduct ourselves with a disgraceful lack of dignity and decry any sense of honor!"

Gritting her teeth, she fumed. "Very well, you are determined to think the worst of me at every turn, so be it. I've nothing more to say on the subject."

"That would be a relief to us both, I am sure," he muttered cruelly.

She got to her feet, heedless of the precariously placed blanket that fell to the floor. But he wasn't. His heated gaze pored over her thinly veiled nudity with rabid hunger.

Snatching the blanket off the floor, he shoved it at her. "Go to bed," he ordered sharply, "before that courtesan figure makes me do something we will both regret."

Tossing her long mane over her shoulder, she clutched the blanket to her bosom and marched from the room with as much dignity as she could muster.

Resting his forearm on the mantle, he gazed into the fire. A litany of oaths fell from his lips. Confounded woman acted as though marriage to *him* was hardship for *her!* God's sake, he was a duke. She was a wild, tempestuous imp. She lacked all sense of propriety and, for that matter, common sense. He still could not believe she had taken off on a stormy night on foot across the woods to escape him. A sane man would not take a second look at a virago like her. He must be barking mad. He wanted to do a hell of a lot more than merely look at her.

Four

The marriage ceremony was accomplished in shockingly little time and absolutely no merriment. In fact, the small gathering in the resplendent gold and white salon looked positively grim. The balding vicar and his chubby wife made a stab at gaiety. It fell flat in the face of the duke's antipathy.

But that was not the worst, oh, no. The moment the unceasingly gregarious Octavia appeared with her bedraggled Henry in tow, Tina braced herself for the insupportable events that were sure to follow.

Dressed in an elegant brown velvet canezou and champagne-colored silk gown, her black hair perfectly cut in the Titus style, her mother floated into the room and dropped down on the elegant gold brocade settee beside Tina.

"We long to know how our poor little girl fairs," she demurred, patting Tina's pale, drawn cheek with her ice-cold hand.

Tina paled, inwardly cringing at the impression her mother was making. She was frightfully overdressed for the occasion. It was her gauche habit to wear pearls and diamonds in the morning. No well-born lady would do such a thing.

Tina darted a nervous look at Roland. A look of disdain was indelibly etched on his chiseled features. He could have no good opinion. And in truth, Tina could find no fault with his scorn. Her mother's conduct was deplorable. She noted with a stab of unwanted attraction that he cut an elegant figure. Impeccably attired in a pristine brown claw-hammer jacket, striped percale waistcoat, buff pantaloons, and burgundy silk cravat, he stood tall and proud, looking every inch a duke. While she huddled on the settee, her shoulders slouched, in a plain muslin gown. As if sensing her perusal, he raised his dark brown eyes to hers. Unbidden memories of the night they had shared flooded her mind. She tried to no avail to thrust away the lusciously wicked sensation of his tongue dueling with hers in a fiery game of wills and the incomparable feel of his hot, wet open mouth suckling at her breast. Color streaked across her cheeks. She dropped her lashes. She must be demented to find him so appealing. The telltale signs of attraction nettled her sorely. The man loathed her.

"I can barely contain my excitement," Octavia exclaimed, clasping her hands together with glee. "Today is your wedding day." She wagged her finger at Tina. "I told you something wonderful would happen at the Valentine's Day ball, did I not?"

Tina shot her a quelling look, but the dense woman continued to chortle with delight as if nothing untoward had precipitated this squalid little arrangement.

"You do us proud, my girl," Henry concurred with a knowing wink, his round, chubby face beaming down at Tina.

"How appropriate, too. Saint Valentine is the patron saint of star-crossed lovers, and you have snared a duke!" her vulgar mother crooned.

"Mother, *please*," Tina whispered fiercely, wishing she would cease her obnoxious caterwauling. Was there to be no end to the calamities Tina must suffer this day? How could she behave as though this was a love match? It was beyond the pale. It was all Tina could do not to rail at her.

"What?" her mother decried. "Can I not be proud of my little darling daughter?" She loosed a depreciatory glare in the unfailingly correct duke's direction. "Is that forbidden, Your Grace?" she asked him in a loud voice. "Am I to restrain my delight for such an excellent match?"

The muscle in Roland's cheek pulsed. He looked appalled. His disgusted glance moved away.

Ignoring his haughty disdain, Lady Rutledge turned back to Tina. "Well," she said, clasping her small hand between her long, bony fingers, "I must say you look a frightful mess." Examining Valentina's simple blue muslin dress and wild, tussled ebony curls, she pulled a frown. "That dress simply does not do you justice, my dear. Still," she said on an offhanded sigh, "henceforth you are going to be very well cared for, indeed. Just imagine! You shall have a thousand dresses from which to choose," she remarked with a ribald wink. Tina's eyes drifted shut. She willed herself to disappear into thin air.

Behind her, the salon door opened, signaling the arrival of the duchess. As she made her grand entrance, in a gray silk morning gown with matching lace Bestie, she looked elegant beyond words. Back ramrod straight, head held high, she crossed the room to take her place at her son's side.

Tina's heart sank. She could never hope to fill her shoes, no matter how hard she tried. She realized the enormous social import of the family into which she was about to marry. A renewed sense of apprehension engulfed her.

At seeing her majestic counterpart, Octavia's lips thinned. "At last," she said briskly, ogling the duchess's subtle grandeur with a jealous eye, "we are all here."

The duchess cast a disparaging glance at the gauche woman. "If you are ready?" she asked Roland.

He inclined his perfectly groomed head. "Let us begin." Turning to address the vicar, he said, "Shall we?"

"Indeed." The vicar motioned him toward the fireplace.

Henry lumbered to the front of the room. "May I say, Your Grace, it is well-pleased I am to be giving little Tina away this day?" He rocked on his heels with pride.

Roland fixed the rotund fool with a withering glare. "No, you may not."

The smile slid from Henry's portly countenance. Shifting from one pudgy foot to the other, he mumbled something about it being an honor and fell blessedly quiet.

Octavia practically hauled Tina from the settee and thrust her at the duke. Standing before the hearth, he awaited his sentence to life with the uncouth child bride. The aged vicar stood in preparation, his Bible open and ready, to commence the ceremony. Taking her place at Roland's side, Tina felt as though the events unfolding before her were surreal. The vicar read the opening prayer. She bowed her head. Turning to Roland, the clergyman addressed him. "Do you, Roland Harwicke, Duke of Westmoreland . . ."

With each recital of his seemingly endless names and titles, Tina felt herself shrink inside and wither into diffident oblivion. She glanced at the silk-papered walls lined with gilded portraits depicting the old curmudgeons who had doubtless gone before the current duke. She felt horribly small and insignificant. Her inadequacies loomed very large in the face of marriage to a duke. All her girlish dreams revolved around images of a loving husband who would cherish her for her. Not an angry, forbidding duke standing before a puny gathering of unhappy faces, witness to a swift, prosaic ceremony that would be over in ten minutes and alter her life irrevocably because they had been caught in his bedchamber.

But as the duke's strong, deep, resonant voice declared his intention to love, honor and cherish her all the days of his life permeated her addled brain, she knew her infantile fantasy of love and eternal devotion was over. Now the harsh reality of ruin was all that was left to her. And a proud, austere man who would henceforth be her lord and master.

Her mother's voice hissed in her ear, "Say the words, child. They are waiting for you. Go on, girl!"

Wrenched from her misery, Tina turned to face the vicar.

"Repeat after me, child. Don't be skittish," he urged, smiling down at her. "I, Valentina Marie Rutledge . . ."

She opened her mouth. The words tumbled forth, but their meaning never reached her heart.

"You may kiss the bride," the vicar proclaimed with a happy smile.

His wife wept softly into her lace hankie. The duke shot her a confused look of concern.

"I always cry at weddings," she sniffed by way of explanation.

He frowned and looked away.

Closing the Bible, the vicar waited for Roland to embrace his new bride. And waited and waited.

As if fashioned out of wood, he finally turned to face her. Summoning every once of courage, she met his cold, unwavering stare, saw his taut, pallid features and read the bleak expression in his eyes. The strain of the day weighed on him. At least they shared that, she thought ruefully.

"Pray, dispense with the kiss, Your Grace," her vulgar mother urged. "I am positively famished."

Valentina's eyes drifted shut. This would be her future, snide remarks and disdainful glances. She belonged neither in his world nor her own.

Clasping her by the shoulders, he drew her near. Bending his head, his lips pressed lightly against hers.

"Well, it is over and done with," the duchess murmured, her tone morose.

"Now onto the scrumptious wedding breakfast!" Octavia exclaimed. "I simply cannot wait to indulge in your most excellent ham, eggs and delightful pheasant."

The duchess drew in a horrified breath. She looked appalled at the mere possibility of that woman sitting anywhere near *her* elegant breakfast table.

Roland ushered the vicar and his wife from the room. Closing the door in their wake, he clasped his hands behind his back and addressed his mangy in-laws. "As to the matter of the wedding breakfast, I must ask you to leave this house and never return. Your conduct has been deplorable. You, madam, are quite possibly the most vulgar woman I have ever had the misfortune to meet. And you sir"—his heated gaze skewered Henry where he stood fumbling about—"should be ashamed. Your lack of honor is shocking."

Octavia's mouth fell open. For a full minute she gaped at him. For once, she was deprived speech.

"Well, I never!" she fumed at last. "Such incivility does not become you, Your Grace."

"And such a display only confirms my ill opinion of you, madam."

"What of my Tina?" she blustered angrily, gauchely pointing at her daughter.

"*Your* Tina is now *my* wife." His gaze slid across the room to where Valentina stood. Pale and drawn, she looked devastated by the ugly scene. "And as such," he imparted in a cold, implacable tone, "she will do as she is told." His harsh, exacting gaze brooked no disagreement.

She lowered her gaze to the floor.

Octavia knew when she was bested. Gathering her skirts, she stormed from the room. Tail between his legs, Henry trudged as quickly as his short, stout legs would carry him from the elegant salon. The acute humiliation was more than Tina could bear. Tears pricked her eyes. She blinked them back.

"If you will excuse me," she choked out and hurried toward the door, desperate to escape this ghastly mess. "I passed a terrible night. I am frightfully indisposed at the moment."

"Valentina!" The sharp tenor of her husband's deep, commanding voice gave her pause. She flinched at his harsh display of temper. He had never raised his voice to her.

Unable to look at him, she paused, clutching the doorknob for much-needed support. "I am persuaded you will be content to take your meal without my insignificant presence," she murmured and quickly crossed the threshold.

"Damn and blast," he muttered under his breath and slammed the door in her wake.

"I hope you do realize, Roland," Tina heard the duchess rail at him, "her conduct will never do. She is entirely too headstrong. I warned you. This is a most impolitic union."

"Must you dwell on her every flaw? And constantly berate me?" came his heated rejoinder.

"The little tramp has nothing but flaws!"

Covering her ears, Tina ran up the black-and-white marble staircase in search of her bedchamber. Tears blurred her vision and fell unchecked from her cheeks.

The February sky turned cold. The dusk of evening fell. An amber mantle of darkness signaled the onslaught of night. Ensconced in her bedroom, Tina requested a Spartan dinner be served on a tray. Snuggly warm by the fire, engrossed in her book on antiquities, she was just finishing her meal of cold duck and chutney when a tap sounded at her door. Expecting the servant girl to retrieve her tray, she swallowed the last bite and bid her enter.

Roland stood on the threshold. Wearing a heavy, dark green brocade robe and precious little else from what her pensive gaze could ascertain, he seemed to fill the doorway. His chiseled, handsome features were tense and drawn.

She took in her breath.

He stepped into the room.

He did not actually expect *her* to share the night with *him?*

She swallowed.

Good Lord.

He did.

"You wished to eat alone?" he observed, easing the door shut behind him.

She resumed her reading, murmuring a noncommittal, "Obviously."

"You are reading." His patent attempt to breech the ever-widening abyss tumbled inelegantly from his lips.

"Yes."

"About what, pray?" he pressed stoically, cordial in the face of her aloofness.

"Antiquities."

Dumbfounded, he gawked at her. "I beg your pardon?" he repeated in surprise. "What did you say?"

She heaved an irritated sigh. "I am interested in antiquities. Greece, Rome, that sort of thing."

"I know what they are. The question is why?"

"Why what?"

"Why are you reading about antiquities?"

Slamming the leather-bound book shut, she offered him a heated glare and tossed the book aside. "Oh, I don't know, perhaps it is my horrid bluestocking tendencies rearing their ugly head again. Or maybe I am an incurable eccentric. But whatever the reason, I happen to find ancient Rome of interest."

He took a step closer. "You do," he said, his tone carefully inoffensive.

"Indeed, Your Grace, it might interest you to know that the harbinger of your own ill fate, St. Valentinus, was a martyr not unlike yourself. Only his punishment was death not matrimony. Claudius the Eleventh had him executed on my birthday A.D. 270. Valentinus's story is a legacy of love and friendship. It is a recognized miracle—"

"Good Lord," he gasped out loud. Dragging his hand through his hair, he blew the air out of his cheeks. He had come here for . . . well, for what all men come to their wives bedchambers for on their wedding night. Instead, she was giving him a lesson on antiquities. "You are the most singular woman I have ever—"

One ebony brow arched. "Married?" she supplied, her voice dripping sarcasm.

Not wishing to argue, he offered her a self-deprecating smile. "Forgive me. I do not mean to suggest that your expertise is lacking in any way. It is just that you . . . rather surprise me at times." *All the time.*

"Then, we are well matched, Your Grace," she said in an acerbic tone.

"Tina," he began awkwardly, using her surname to break the icy barrier that was firmly erected between them. "I . . . This morning's display was utterly deplorable. And for that, I am truly sorry. It is my hope that we may put the disagreeable nature of our union behind us."

"That would be a relief to one of us, I am sure," she muttered bitterly.

He took an angry step toward her. "What the devil do you mean by that?"

She drew a weary breath. "As far as I can ascertain, you are a man completely devoid of any normal feeling. You cannot accept anyone who strays from your strict sense of propriety."

He stiffened and fell into a brooding silence. His eyes studied her with a curious intensity. Perhaps she was right. At times, he might appear to be too rigid. And occasionally, he might adhere too strictly to his sense of honor and duty. But she would certainly be a blissful remedy for what ailed him.

While not at all conventionally attractive, she was nonetheless confoundedly appealing, wildly so. She would certainly *not* be considered noteworthy by any of his peers. But he had to allow, there *was* something about her. Perhaps it was her sparkling dark lavender eyes. Or her untamed dark curly hair. Or her flawless ivory skin.

Whatever the reason, he had to admit, she was like a breath of fresh air in his otherwise stagnant life of mundane conventionality. And he wanted her more than he had ever craved anything in his life.

"If you mean my emotions are under admirable control, then in truth, I must disagree with you. I can find no fault with such traits. They are noble and just."

She gawked at him. "Must every emotion be under strict regulation? Is it beyond the realm of possibility that one might err and be human for once? Or are we all meant to be cast in stone and live a life of dreary resignation?"

Appalled, he stared at her. "Is that what you think of me?" he asked in a bare whisper.

"What else can I think," she complained, disconcerted by the weight of his stare, "when you conduct yourself as you do and harbor such obvious disgust of me? My every flaw is accounted for by your probing eye."

"*Disgust?*" he echoed in surprise. "I did not intend," he remarked clumsily, "I never meant to malign you. I will allow the circumstance has vexed me greatly. My mood has been understandably foul, at times."

She heaved a weary sigh. "I suppose your attitude is

warranted. The horrendous condition in which we find ourselves is hardly ideal."

The lines around his mouth tightened. "Being my duchess is a hardship for you, then?" His voice held a bitter, icy edge.

She met his resentful gaze with one of her own. "I realize it is yet another of my lamentable character flaws. But yes, it is. I know you think me entirely unsuitable. Perhaps I am. I won't pretend to know the first thing about being a duchess. Nor can I help the circumstance of my birth. I am who I am. I am such a grave disappointment to you, I know."

He placed his hands on her shoulders. The warmth of his touch spread like wildfire. "You are not a disappointment." His kind reassurance weakened her resolve slightly. "We are man and wife. I shall, of course, endeavor to treat you with respect and admiration." His strong, masterful hands softly kneaded her tense shoulders.

The telltale signs of attraction made it extremely awkward for her to remain resentful for long. His benevolence, however fleeting, gave her hope that they might share a complaisant life together. The knowledge that she longed in her heart for his approval startled her. It was useless to deny it. Pleasing him was important to her, although she could not think why.

She offered him a tremulous smile. "An ounce of civility would do us both good, I expect. I shall try to do better. It is a rather indelicate situation."

He withdrew from her as if she had scalded him. Shoving his hands deep in his pockets, he turned away to pace the room. A fleeting pang of longing stabbed at him. He sighed and scrubbed his hand over his chin. At times, he envied her direct, easy way with words. Lightness of being always seemed to evade him, no matter how hard he tried. She had the ability to speak her mind without the slightest hesitation. Or, for that matter, concern for the etiquette, he thought with a frown.

Pausing at the window, he pulled back the drapes to study the diamond-studded night sky. He had been raised to believe that his emotions should remain under strict control at all times. Discipline over one's thoughts and actions was always in good regulation. And yet he had the most unbecoming desire to take her in his arms and smother those full, enticing lips and worship her body in a very wicked manner that would scandalize the good vicar.

He glanced over his shoulder at her. *His wife.* Good Lord, the thought stunned him still. She looked incredibly soft and deliciously feminine sitting there in her gossamer thin nightgown.

"I do hope the weather holds through the weekend," she said in a vain effort to ease the silence. Profoundly ill at ease, she darted an uncomfortable glance at the large canopied bed. Her fingers fiddled nervously with the satin ribbon at her cleavage. She could not imagine how this evening could be more awkward. The very last person with whom she dreamed of being on a romantic wedding night was Roland Harwicke. Of course, the night of fleeting passion they had shared was another matter entirely. He seemed . . . different somehow. Magnificent, was a better word. Her cheeks burned at the memory. She found herself recalling with vivid clarity the feel of his hard, muscular frame bearing her down against the soft, downy mattress. Clearing her throat, she forced herself to school her thoughts. Why the devil did he not speak? She darted him a shy, sidelong glance. White-hot desire lurked in his smoldering gaze. She swallowed. Her gaze darted away.

It was decidedly odd the way he kept staring at her. No, not odd, completely unnerving. Zounds, he looked more like a rabid dog than a duke!

Flustered, she said bashfully, "May I make a suggestion that might suit us both well?"

Shoving away from the window, he smiled. It was all warm and seductive. "I sincerely doubt there is any way I could stop you."

She flashed him a nervous smile. "I propose a compromise."

Hesitating, he eyed her with trepidation. "Such as?" he prompted.

"Let our marriage be in name only."

Unaccountably angered by her suggestion, a furious glint lit his dark eyes. "Why the devil should you suggest such a thing?" he demanded.

"Well, we . . . I . . . ," she sputtered. She gulped and told him quite plainly, "We clearly do not suit."

No, they did not suit. But if she knew how much she moved him by her very presence. How much he desired to know her very being. She would be quite shocked. Hell, he was bloody well astounded. Bedding the chit was the one thing for which he counted himself fortunate. And now she wished to forestall him.

"No. It will not do. I am heartfully sorry," he told her in no uncertain terms. "But I very much fear I cannot possibly agree."

Nonplussed, she stared at him, her eyes wide and questioning. "Why ever not?" she breathed in astonishment. "You're a duke, who is supposed to embody all that is decent and honorable in a man. You should respect my wishes and not press me to do something for which I am entirely unprepared," she stated, flabbergasted by his refusal.

"You must understand," he explained, closing in on her like a lean, hungry predator, "I require an heir. My intention in seeking a bride was to fulfill my duty to the title. I very much fear you will have to submit to me until such time as I get you with child."

Her cheeks flushed scarlet. She wet her lips nervously. His hooded gaze followed the line of her tongue and settled on her full, soft mouth. She swallowed. He certainly did conduct himself differently in private.

"I understand a child is important to you," she said softly. "I, too, long for children. But I need more time."

"Time?"

He seemed genuinely baffled by her request, as though complete strangers did this sort of thing every day! Her brow furrowed slightly. Perhaps they did. What did she really know of the world?

"Time to get to know you," she qualified nervously, "to have some regard for you as my—my husband."

He eyed her with misgiving. "And you have no regard for me now?" His voice was low and husky.

"I, no," she replied, dropping her gaze to her lap, "how could I?"

A conceited smile touched his lips. He slipped his finger beneath her chin and tilted her face upward. "My name is Roland. And you will forgive me, but that is not entirely correct. I am not unaware of the effect I have on you. Nor will I deny the attraction I myself feel. It is perhaps not noble or decent, but it is nonetheless a fact." Sensual flame lit his dark, penetrating stare. He drew a ragged, urgent breath. "Oh, my darling girl, I desire you more ardently than any other living creature on earth," he professed, his deep voice growing husky with need. "I must possess you or go mad with longing."

His declaration quite took her breath away. "Desire is not the same thing as devotion," she murmured softly, her eyes searching his.

He caressed her cheek with the back of his hand.

She trembled.

The intensity of his dark eyes held her captive. He smiled. "I never said it was."

She took a hard swallow. "What you propose is impossible," she maintained, her tone unyielding.

He flashed a wolfish grin and chuckled deep in his throat. "I think not."

Her eyes rounded slightly. "Do you intend to force your intentions on me?"

He uttered a low rumble of laughter and shook his head at her. "It shall not be rape."

"You cannot imagine that I will submit to you merely out of obligation?"

His brow drifted upward. "Obligation? No, my sweet." He grinned down at her. "Obligation"—he bent his dark head and brushed his lips lightly against hers—"I have discovered, is not a word in your vocabulary."

Lost in his gorgeous dark brown eyes, she whispered against his lips, "Then what, pray?"

"Pleasure," he murmured in a wickedly low voice. The warmth of his hands caressed her shoulders. He eased her to her feet. His arms enfolded her. Her soft hips and thighs melded against his hard, muscular frame. "Sweet, raw, intense pleasure," he murmured, trailing hot, wet kisses along her neck. His lips brushed against her earlobe and kissed the sensitive spot behind. She sighed and angled her neck to better receive his kiss. He buried his face in her neck to breathe in her heady scent. "You smell like honeysuckle. All wild and sweet. I cannot wait to taste you."

Taking a hard gulp, she wrestled with her pulse. It was careening out of control. "What you ask is impossible. I . . . I cannot agree."

She heard his deep, resonant laughter, felt the warm caress of his breath against her jaw. He breathed a kiss there. "Your body betrays you," he sighed, pressing warm featherlight kisses against the edge of her mouth.

"It does not," she countered, mortified by the truth.

His hand lightly caressed the ivory column of her

throat. "We are beautifully matched, you and I," he told her, his voice gruff with hunger. His strong, powerful arms encircled her. Her soft, warm body yielded to his lean, muscular strength. He covered her mouth with his own. His hands ran over her back, her hips, and cupped her buttocks, urging her closer to his powerful thighs. She felt the hard evidence of his desire and quivered. His lips stroked, caressed and worshiped her open, eager mouth with a wild, hungry abandon that stole her breath. Dizzy and breathless with need, she surrendered and leaned into him. Her soft curves molded against his hard, lean hips. Her hands crept around his neck. She clung to him, reveling in the heat of his kiss. With shockingly little effort, his arm swept under her knees. He carried her across the room, their mouths clinging together hungrily. He placed her on the canopied bed and followed her down. He tore at his robe and shrugged it off. Her bold hands ran over his finely attenuate chest and lean torso. She threaded her fingers through his thick, coarse hair and smoothed her palms over his broad, muscular shoulders. Lifting her softly parted mouth to his, she pulled him near. As his mouth covered hers, his fingers fumbled with her night rail, desperate to feel her soft, silken breast beneath his naked, coarse-haired chest. Covering his hand with hers, she made short work of the tiny round pearl buttons. His mouth closed on her breast, sucking and nibbling and squeezing the hard rosy pebble with such delicious intensity, her womb tightened with raw pleasure. She threaded her fingers through his hair and arched her back, welcoming the luscious sensations that washed over her again and again. His hands slid over her hips, kneading her soft, round buttocks. His mouth trailed hot, wet kisses down her rib cage and across her stomach. Her muscles contracted beneath the stroke of his tongue. As if her body knew the path of love that was to be taken and longed for the pinnacle of pleasure, her thighs parted, beckoning his tantalizing touch. Taking her lead, his hand slipped between to stroke and tease her soft, slick folds. Finding the hidden small sensitive nub, he caressed her. She writhed and panted, in the precipice of ecstasy.

"Please . . . oh, *please,*" she moaned, unsure of what she craved but knowing he held the key.

He came over her, resting his weight on his forearms. "My bold wanton," he whispered huskily against her lips, "how you bewitch me."

Clasping her hips, he thrust deep inside her soft channel and cried out in exultation. She was his from now until eternity. She completed him. His wife. His lover. His life.

He heard the sharp intake of breath, felt her entire body tense beneath him. Her hands shoved instinctively against his great bulk to dislodge him.

Burying his face in her dark ebony tresses, he drew a harsh, ragged breath and struggled for some semblance of control. She wriggled beneath him, trying to adjust to his large invasion.

"Don't," he breathed hoarsely. The feel of her tight, wet passage sheathing him like a second skin was nearly his undoing. "God, to be inside you"—he shuddered a sigh of pure ecstasy—"it is such sweet heaven." He strained above her in an effort to resist the almost overwhelming need to love her with hard, fast strokes and spill his seed.

Her hands curved over his taut shoulders and smoothed down his back, holding him once more.

Wrapping his arms around her, he uttered a deep, heartfelt groan and kissed her with savage desperation. Following a primitive driving need, he withdrew slightly and thrust deep once more. She uttered a soft cry; her legs wound around his back. He sank deeper still. She lifted her hips and met his deep, powerful, driving thrusts. He should have been mindful of her virginity, he should have tried to be gentle, but he had long since lost all control. Swept away by a tumult of emotion, the only thing that moved them was a force well beyond his reckoning. Their lovemaking was wildly uninhibited, born of a burning urge to find heaven in each other's arms. Their bodies moved in a passionate frenzy. He was helpless to slow the wild, deep thrusts. Until all at once he felt himself on the edge of release. He sensed that his world was about to explode. He gloried in her cry of blissful rapture and drove deep once more, spilling his seed deep inside her.

When at last the world came into focus, he lay heavily atop her, reluctant to withdraw. She was splendidly small and soft and warm. He could have slept in her arms but roused himself. Pushing up on his elbows, he looked down at her. A smile crept over his lips. It was purely male and completely satisfied.

"We shall deal very well together, you and I," he said softly, kissing her lips.

"I was unaware that the marriage bed could be so— so . . ." Her voice trailed off; she lowered her lashes. "I will try to be more ladylike next time, Your Grace."

A deep, husky laugh rumbled in his chest. He brushed her damp, sable locks back from her forehead and framed her head between his hands. He smiled down at her, his heart in his eyes. "Ladies be damned. My wicked little temptress, you please me very well, indeed. I would not have you to change."

She glanced up at him. She wound her arms around his neck; a sly grin touched her lips. "In that case, Your Grace," she purred, "I must share the most delicious on-dit of the season with you."

He cocked a sultry brow. "Indeed?"

"Your bride is equally gratified with the arrangement herself."

He kissed her deeply then. Savoring her soft, supple lips. With a reluctant groan, he withdrew and gathered her in his arms. His fingers lazily stroked the luscious curve of her back.

"Tell me more about this unusual pastime of yours," he said, drowsily. "I am curious to learn more about St. Valentine."

Folding her arms across his chest, she rested her chin on her hands. "Well, as it happens," she said, warming to her subject, "while imprisoned, he taught his jailer's daughter religion and arithmetic. The girl was blind. And the legend says through her faith she gained her sight. After he was put to death, she planted an almond tree as a symbol of her deep, abiding affection. It is said, the pink blossoms still appear today."

"Ah well, in that case," he murmured in a low, sultry tone, "I shall have to plant an almond tree in Compton gardens for you, my lovely Valentine, shan't I?"

"Oh, I should love it," she whispered breathlessly, covering his mouth with her own.

As the two soared to heaven in each other's arms once more, she thanked God for her misguided cupid.

Five

The next morning, Tina woke to find herself alone. She frowned her disappointment. Throwing back the covers, she hopped out of bed and hurried through her morning ministrations. She raced down the marble staircase and breezed into the breakfast room with a bright smile on her face, expecting to encounter her passionate playmate.

Instead, she was greeted by a dignified, proper smile. Her face fell. Quickly recovering, she schooled her features and took her seat. His withdrawal was like a stab in the heart. His mood was polite and kind; she could find no fault with it. But it saddened her to realize he was capable of revealing himself to her only in their quiet moments together.

A secret smile touched her lips. She had time. The rest of their lives. She could bring him out. And bring him out she would. It would be a formidable task. She was fighting a lifetime of restrictions that had been placed on him. But his growing affection for her would be her ally. If last night was any indication, he was as eager to begin their life together as she was.

"Well, my dear," the dowager duchess remarked, entering the breakfast room. "I assume you passed a pleasant evening? And your husband is pleased with you," she murmured, eyeing Tina with haughty displeasure.

Tina nearly choked on her coffee. She managed a

nebulous, "Yes, thank you," and darted a startled look at Roland. He offered her a wicked grin from behind the corner of the *Times* and winked at her. Clearly, he was pleased with their lovemaking. That warmed her heart.

"Directly after breakfast I shall endeavor to instruct you on a proper wardrobe," her mother-in-law derided, looking down her considerable nose at Tina's simple pink morning muslin.

Sipping her coffee, Tina made a mental note to rid this household of her mother-in-law as soon as possible. If Roland had any hope of emerging from beneath his tiresome yoke, that horrid woman must go. Yes, she thought, a smile blossoming on her lips, London would be lovely this time of year. And a change would do the duchess a world of good.

The butler's arrival interrupted her whimsical fancy. Bearing an ivory parchment note that reeked of lilac water, he extended the silver plate to Roland. "This letter just arrived, Your Grace."

Roland's brow snapped together. Folding the *Times*, he placed it on the table and accepted the missive. "That will be all."

Bowing, the butler took his leave and closed the white-paneled double doors behind him.

Tina watched as her husband open the fragrant letter. His eyes moved across the page. Red-hot color flooded his cheeks. Shoving back from the table, he got to his feet.

"Forgive me," he said awkwardly, "a matter has arisen that I must attend to forthwith. I must away for London immediately." With that nebulous statement, he turned on his heel and quit the breakfast room.

Tina's face fell. She very much suspected the scented letter was from his mistress. Her heart sank. Who else would send such a letter?

"Come now, my dear," the dowager advised, "with your husband called away, we must seize the moment and commence your lessons. I do not want my son married to a gauche country chit any longer than is strictly necessary."

Tina dismissed the old matron's insults by ignoring them. She drew a weary sigh. Well, she thought as she braced herself for a morning of fittings and rank directives, she almost touched a tiny piece of his heart.

The following afternoon, the duke had not yet returned from London. Valentina received several desperate messages from her hysterical mother begging her to pay a visit. Against her better judgment, she took pity on her. It was late afternoon before she returned from Morely House. Her dabble gray, Champion, crossed the sprawling lawn that led to her new home, Compton Hall. Her mood was decidedly grim. Shifting her bottom on the hard sidesaddle, she grimaced at the discomfort of the leather contraption beneath her knee and adjusted the green-velvet and white-satin bonnet on her head for the third time. The enormous coq feathers tickled her nose.

Garbed in the matching satin and velvet gown better suited to a ballroom than a horse's backside, she tugged at the restrictive costume. She heartily resented her mother-in-law's insistence the she wear such lavish clothes. Her one hope as Champion meandered back toward the estate was that the duke was not yet returned. After hearing of her mother's desperation, she needed to sort out her feelings and was not at all prepared to face him.

She neared the long gravel drive and caught sight of a black lacquered carriage. A smartly dressed gentleman in a black greatcoat, beaver hat and immaculate Hessian boots disembarked. Her heart plummeted. She pulled Champion up sharp. Darting a look about her, she decided to make a dash for the stables in the hopes of imploring one of the kitchen maids to let her sneak upstairs. Anything was preferable to suffering an agonizing encounter with her husband fresh from his mistress's bed.

In her haste, she kicked her mount too hard. He reared at the bit and took off. She tried to rein him in but to no avail. Wrestling with the reins, she struggled for control. But he bounded across the hard, icy turf. Unaccustomed to riding sidesaddle, she lost her seat. She hit the ground hard. Champion stood stock-still beside her. Ignoring his dislodged rider, he happily nibbled on the dead grass. Dazed and breathless from the fall, she heard the sound of footfalls beside her. The duke's harsh features etched in concern came into view. Dropping down on one knee, he bent near.

"Are you hurt?"

She opened her mouth to utter a reply, but the wind had been knocked out of her. She could make not a sound, nor could she seem to move.

Reading the fear in her eyes, he slipped his hand under her head. His arms, strong and sure, eased around her waist, drawing her close against him. Before she could object, he hoisted her from the ground and cradled her in his arms. She snuggled closer and felt absurdly safe. Paper-witted fool! The man had just returned from his mistress, and she was cooing in his arms! But she could not seem to help herself.

He smiled down at her.

Her heart melted.

"It is all right; you've lost your breath. Don't be frightened." His voice was deep and caring and wonderfully reassuring. She foolishly allowed herself to bask in his strong embrace.

"I'm quite recovered," she said, when at last she could draw breath. "You may release me."

He set her feet gently down. His gaze swept over her. Taking in her ridiculous attire, a glimmer of mirth lit his gaze. Sweeping across the ground, he handed her the hideous object that had once graced her head.

"These, ah, clothes"—he gestured toward her voluminous gown that threatened to overtake her slim figure—"are they henceforth to be your normal attire?"

"Yes," she bit out, her dark locks tossed in hopeless disarray.

He grimaced slightly. "You'll forgive me, but do you intend to dress in satin and velvet every day?" he pressed.

Still smarting from his hurtful departure the morning after their wedding night, her lips pursed. "On the contrary, your mother suggested my wardrobe. I have no choice in the matter."

"Alas, I am certain with fortitude such as you possess, you will easily foil my mother's attempt to civilize you. But I will speak to her and ask her to be less preoccupied with your attire. Will that suffice?"

Not diverted in the least, she offered him a frosty smirk. "You are kindness itself, Your Grace." She snatched her mangled feathered hat and brushed the grass and dirt from her ornamental riding gown.

He bit back a smile. "Do you intend to provide such winning theatricals daily? Was this engaging display of horsemanship meant for my benefit alone or were you perchance hoping the entire household to be present?" he mocked her gently.

Abandoning her untidiness for the moment, she glared up at him. "I've just come from Morely House. I thought you were away on urgent business in London," she huffed, her deep lavender eyes luminous with hurt. "I never intended to make your address. Nothing grieves me more, I assure you." She had spent a long, lonely night in their tester bed, fretting over her obviously unwarranted feelings for him, while he was entertaining elsewhere. She knew he was free to do as he pleased. She could not help feeling horribly used.

Disregarding her jibe, his brows snapped together. *"Morely House?"* he uttered sharply. A dark, angry cloud swept over his features.

"Yes, Morely House," she echoed with deliberate audacity.

"There must be some mistake." His voice held a note of warning.

"On the contrary, Your Grace, you make no mistake. I went to visit my mother in her hour of need. It seems that Henry's pockets are all but to let. His gambling excesses are more than even you could possibly imagine. She is in a state. Verily, I have never seen her so undone. I suspect she may be on the verge of a total collapse."

He slammed his fisted hands on his hips. "Did I or did I not expressly forbid you to ever entertain their society again?"

"You seemed so fit to take yourself off, I decided—"

"You decided? What a headstrong, infuriating piece of baggage you are!"

Her chin came up, ready for a fight. "You surprise me, Your Grace. I thought no aspect of my lamentable character had escaped your notice. How is it that you have overlooked that rather pertinent detail? I have a mind of my own and fully intend to use it."

He looked away. His lips twisted with displeasure. "Doubtless, it was my aversion to the objectionable trait," he drawled, plowing his hand through his hair.

"I have the right to visit my mother now and again."

He glanced back at her. "Allow me to explain, as you seem unaccountably confused. I do not give a tinker's damn about that bloody woman. I wish you never to make such a visit again."

She opened her mouth to object, but he held up his hand to silence her. "I have not the slightest regard for your feelings in the matter, nor am I inclined to ever entertain their appalling society for your benefit or out of a sense of duty or any generosity of feeling you might wish me to possess. I regret that you have been inconvenienced in this matter, but I have some news that might serve you well—"

"Inconvenienced?" She spat in anger. "While *you* perhaps do not welcome my mother in your home, she is nonetheless *my* mother. I cannot help but feel an obligation to her. Despite her obvious frailties and her many defects, she is my only living relative."

He stared down at her, surprised by her unceasing loyalty to a woman who was utterly undeserving. "Am I to understand that after the calamity they deliberately caused, you sincerely wish to maintain civility?" he asked, amazed at her generosity of heart.

Her face flamed red. She averted her gaze. "You need not fear," she replied stiffly. "I have no intentions of entertaining them at Compton Hall. You may rest easy." She wet her lips nervously. "There is, however, a matter that bears mentioning. I beg of you," she entreated him, clutching at his sleeve, "for my sake, could you not be merciful? She is desperate for funds. Could you not see your way clear to extending some meager portion of your generosity?"

He hesitated for a moment, despising the desperate look in her beautiful violet eyes. Heaving an irritated sigh, he swore under his breath. He knew he could deny her nothing. "I suppose something might be done. For your sake and only because you ask it of me," he strictly enjoined her, "I will be lenient." A frown edged his full, sensual mouth. "I cannot very well have my father-in-law's name in the *Gazette,* no matter how much he may deserve it. Although, letting him rot in debtors' prison is deuced tempting."

"Oh, Roland!" she cried. Throwing her arms around his neck, she hugged him for dear life. "I am forever in your debt."

He gently removed her arms from around his neck and clasped her hands against his chest. "I give you fair warning, if I so much as see your misbegotten relatives again without my consent, I very much fear I will not be responsible for my actions." His tone was playful and quite wickedly suggestive. "I want you all to myself." He nuzzled her ear and kissed her neck. "No gauche relatives filling Compton Hall."

He was not being very proper. In fact, his tongue was doing deliciously wicked things to her ear. He was never improper. "Are you feeling quite the thing, Your Grace?" she asked, a little breathless as he pressed a kiss to her nape.

One end of his mouth curled slightly. "As it happens, never better." Smiling down at her, he threaded her arm through his. His hand covered hers possessively. "Shall we walk a spell? Or have you caught a chill? I have some news which I think may be of interest to you."

Pain stabbed at her heart. Now he would tell her, explain the fashionable situation he arranged with his London mistress, and she would be forced to accept it. Disheartened, she shook her head. "I am not cold. I welcome the fresh air." *But I dread your news.*

He grinned down at her. "Ah, yes, my wild, wayward wife," he mused, brushing a stray lock of hair behind her ear. "I'd quite forgotten your penchant for the outdoors."

She offered him a wane smile and set her mind on tolerating the terms of their arrangement. Despite her budding feelings for him, despite the mindless passion they had shared, she had no real hold on him. She had no choice but to comply. They walked a long while in companionable silence.

"I received a letter yesterday morning," he began.

She braced herself for the worst. "Who was it from?" she dared to ask.

"Lady Newell."

She stared straight ahead, unable to look at him. The winter chill bit at her cheeks, numbing her. Now he would say it. And she would nod her agreement. So much for happily ever after.

"At first, I was not at all pleased"—he slanted her a sidelong glance—"as you were undoubtedly aware. But upon reading its contents and meeting with her in person, I feel I owe you a sincere apology."

She stopped short. "Roland," she said, incapable of enduring another moment, "I have no claim on you. If you wish to entertain painted ladies, I can have no objection."

He burst out laughing. "How direct you are, my sweet!" He pulled a frown. *"Painted ladies?* I have no such inclination. In truth, I have never been attracted to such lewd frivolity." His hands clasped her shoulders, drawing her close. "And after our wedding night," he said, his voice wickedly low and softly sexy, "I sincerely hope that I left you with very little doubt that yours is the only body I have the slightest desire to worship."

She blinked at him. "The letter? From Lady Newell? Was it not an assignation, then?"

He shook his head. "Quite the opposite, she was a witness to your mishap and provided the details you yourself could not recall."

Her eyes were quizzical. "How is this possible?"

"She came upon your mother and stepfather in the hallway outside my bedchamber. Henry was laboring to carry a woman."

"Me?" she breathed in horror.

"At first, Lady Newell believed you to be ill. But on reflection she found their covert whispers puzzling. And in the aftermath of our hasty nuptials, their intent was quite clear."

"You mean to say that this entire mishap was a product of my mother's scheming?"

He nodded. "They must have drugged you and placed you in my bed."

Her brow furrowed. "The tea. It must have been the tea."

"What tea?"

"Mother insisted I share a cup before I retired that night. It was odd, but I thought it better to comply than suffer her badgering. It tasted horribly bitter. I should have guessed it. I should have known something was amiss. The next morning when I felt so wretchedly ill, I should have considered that I had been poisoned somehow. But I never dreamed, never thought . . . I couldn't let myself belief it was true. My own mother. How could she do such a thing? It is unconscionable." It all made sense to her now. Hearing of the duke's firm rejection during the Valentine's Day ball, her mother had been strangely overset. She had railed at Tina mercilessly. Clearly, she was vexed that nature had not taken the course as she had hoped. She and Henry were forced to scramble and devise a new foolproof scheme. Oh, what a blind, dim-witted idiot Tina had been not to see through her grasping mother's wicked ploy.

"Your tea was laced with laudanum, I expect, and perhaps a touch of brandy to mask the taste." He flashed a winsome smile. His palm lovingly cupped her cheek. "You are the only person I know who likens brandy to bitter tea, my love."

"Oh, Roland," she cried, covering her face with her hands, "what you must think of me. I am heartily sickened by the news. This vile machination is too much to be borne. What a hen-witted fool I have been. I should have realized."

He pulled her hands away and peered down at her pale, stricken face. "Do you not see? Lady Newell has vindicated you. If anyone should be filled with regret, it is I for not believing you. I should have taken you at your word and not demanded proof of your innocence."

"Nonetheless, my shame knows no bounds. That my own mother could behave in such a despicable manner." She bowed her head in disgusted humiliation. "It is unthinkable."

He pulled her into his arms and hugged her tight. "Oh, my sweet, wonderful Valentine, their conduct does not reflect badly on you. You were a pawn in their wicked scheme, as much as I."

"No," she said, shaking her head with vehemence. "It must be said. You are too kind." She drew a deep breath. "I have, Your Grace, inadvertently forced you into an unwanted, unsuitable union. Now allow me to set you free." Looking up at him, she gazed into his warm ebony eyes. "You need have no fear of scandal. I shall be as silent as the grave."

He tucked another stray lock of hair behind her ear. "And what of my future?" he whispered, his eyes capturing hers.

She swallowed back her tears. "You can find a bride far more fitting than I will ever be. One of your own choosing."

"But I do not want another."

"Yes, you do. I am not proper. I—"

"I want you, Tina. And only you."

Amazed, she stared at him, her eyes searching his. "Are you in earnest? Do you truly want me as your wife?"

He nodded. "More than anything in this world."

She caught her lower lip between her teeth and expelled a dreary sigh. "Oh, Roland, I very much fear I shall make you the most dreadful duchess."

A smile spread across his handsome features. "Do you, darling?"

"But what of the terrible circumstances that lead to

our nuptials? How can you possibly put all that has gone before aside?"

"Whatever transpired prior to our marriage is of little consequence now. We are man and wife. You are utterly perfect for me in every way. It is my most sincere wish that you might come to love me. I feel such regard . . . I care so deeply. My feelings . . . They are difficult to express. I am horribly awkward," he remonstrated, frustrated with his lack of charm, "not at all proficient with words. You deserve far better."

An impish smile blossomed on her lips. She beamed up at him, her eyes glistening with unshed tears of joy. "Roland! Silly man. I have exactly what I want. And I very much fear I am already half in love with you."

Wrapping his arms around her, he drew her near and whispered against her lips, "Then, you have made my life complete." He kissed her with all the love in his heart, enough to last a lifetime.

The Bachelor and
the Bluestocking

Karen L. King

One

"Cecelia Louise Clemmons, what have you done to Mrs. Parmont?"

Uh-oh. Cecelia recognized her guardian's exasperated tone. That he had shouted her entire name reminded her of the way her mother had scolded her as a child . . . back when her mother had been alive. Although her guardian, Devin Nash, known to all high society as Lord Beauchamp, resembled a mother about as much as a grouchy lion might remind a chick of its mother hen.

The steady tread on the stairs rising ominously toward her made Cecelia scramble out of her stained smock. She capped the glue and ink pots with shaking fingers, grabbed the book resting on the side table, and unbolted the door. She didn't open it any wider than she needed to slip between it and the jamb quickly, and ever so gently she pulled the door shut.

Flipping open her book, she moved to the top of the stairs just as Lord Beauchamp's golden head rose into view. Life just wasn't fair, she thought with a forlorn familiarity. Her guardian had a beautiful thatch of wavy golden hair, sky blue eyes and not an unmanly bone in his Greek-statue body. To make it worse, he had a smile that sent jolts of electricity zinging through the air.

As if to prove it, he stopped, leaned against the rail, shook his head and smiled at her. Cecelia did her best to note the effect and store it in her head. The fluttering in her stomach, the rat-a-tat beat of her heart, the urge to smile back. Instead, she dipped her eyes to her book and tried to make sense of the squiggles and lines that normally formed letters.

These bodily sensations could be due to the fear of getting caught, she reassured herself.

When she thought she could speak without sounding breathless, she said, "Whatever is wrong with Mrs. Parmont?"

"She's leaving."

"Oh." *Another chaperon bites the dust.* Cecelia suppressed the giggle that rose in her throat. "Why?"

"Why, indeed? I presume you could tell me."

No longer trusting her voice at all, Cecelia shook her head.

He stared at her, his head cocked to the side, waiting her out.

Cecelia dipped her head to her book, determined to string at least two words of print together. Reading had a way of making her feel in control.

"Cecelia?" he prompted impatiently. He rose another narrow step.

She bit back the urge to fling her arms in front of the attic door and bar all entrance. Instead, she stepped down as if she intended to descend to the third floor. She would have to scurry back up and lock the door. Not that Devin would exert himself enough to explore her private sanctuary, but he might send one of his servants to do it for him if he grew curious enough.

"Did you ask her why she's leaving?" Cecelia asked.

"She's bored. You're never around for her to talk to. And if you are with her, you have your nose stuck in a book. You never want to go out. She feels useless and unnecessary."

"Well, if you know why she's leaving, why are you asking me?"

"Cecelia," he drew out her name, enunciating each syllable. "You know we both can't live here without a chaperon. You can't attend functions without a chaperon. We won't ever find you a husband if you don't attend at least an occasional at home or soirée."

She drew to a halt on the riser above him. She was rather pleased at being on eye level with him. "Well, I don't want a husband, and I told Mrs. Parmont that she should have friends call on her here, or she could attend any amusement she wished. I didn't mind. I knew you wouldn't mind. I didn't know she was so distressed."

"How could you? Have you spent above fifteen minutes in her company in the last month?"

Cecelia knew that she hadn't done much to make Mrs. Parmont feel welcome, but the woman was always harping on her. *Sit up straight, Miss Clemmons. You shouldn't wear that, Miss Clemmons. Your fashion sense is deplorable, Miss Clemmons. Your hair is a mess, Miss Clemmons. You'll ruin your eyes with all that reading, Miss Clemmons. How will you ever attract a husband if you wear spectacles, Miss Clemmons?* Frankly, Cecelia didn't need any help to feel inadequate in the husband-attracting department.

"Well, heavens, if you would have told me it was my job to entertain my hired companion, I'm sure I would have exerted more effort in that direction. Although, I'm not quite sure that we should have arrived at an equitable level of compensation for the duties."

"Perhaps the amount it costs me to move to a hotel or rent quarters every time a chaperon leaves would be enough," he shot back.

Maybe being on eye level with Devin was not such a good idea. She felt suitably guilty, although she didn't feel *he* needed to know. Too late she remembered he had quite recently given her a generous allowance. She had just been too busy to notice Mrs. Parmont's distress. Or to realize that it was more than her usual griping.

"I'm sorry, I really am. I didn't realize she was about to leave. You know, you could just send me to live on your estate and forget this whole chaperon business."

He pushed away from the wall. "Do you want to live in the country?"

Living buried in the country would definitely make it more difficult to pursue her goals. "No."

He leaned his palm against the opposite wall. "Good, then, because as your guardian, I should think it would be difficult to watch over you there or help you get settled."

Settled. The word made her want to scream. Why must she marry? What man would want her? And what man would she ever want after a year of living with Devin? "Oh, bother, you weren't supposed to be my guardian, anyway."

"Yes, I'm sure *your* father meant for *my* father to be your guardian, but as they have both entered those pearly gates in the sky, and your father named me by title in his will, the responsibility for you and your future has fallen into my lap."

Cecelia wished she dared dart around him on the narrow staircase. She looked to see if she could duck under his arm. "Your responsibility ends when I reach age twenty-five, and I assure you, I do not expect your hospitality to continue forever."

He rolled his eyes. "Cecelia, love, that was if your father had left you a farthing to fly with. But everything is gone. He had debts on his debts. I had to sell his estate; you have nothing to live on, let alone a place to live."

"Yes, I am quite aware of my situation." Which was terribly dependent on Devin at the moment, but she was changing that.

"Well, I have thought on it, and I see only one solution."

Cecelia didn't like the idea of Devin thinking on anything. She went on much more comfortably when he wasn't paying her any mind. She liked even less that the corners of his eyes had just the slightest crinkle around them. "What?"

"Since you have refused to look about for a husband and you really have no other option but to marry . . ." He studied his nails for a moment, wiped them against his jacket and studied them again.

Cecelia was ready to burst. Yes, he had quite lovely hands with long, tapered fingers and neatly trimmed nails. She supposed Devin could look upon them with as much appreciation as the next person, but did he need to do it now? "What?"

He looked up as if reminded she was there. "You'll have to marry me."

Two

Devin watched as Cecelia blinked. Her fawn brown hair hung in a lopsided twist from one side of her head, and she had a smudge of something gray on her cheek. He resisted the urge to rub it off.

She blinked again, looked at one wall, then the other, down at her book and then back at a wall.

He didn't know what he expected her to say.

The silence stretched on, and he could not remember ever rendering her speechless. She wasn't chatty by any means, but she usually said what she thought.

He studied her dark chocolate eyes. Were they brighter than normal? Was she about to cry? He had never seen her cry. Not even at her father's funeral.

She blinked rapidly and lowered her gaze to her book. Blast his kidneys, *she was* going misty on him. He hadn't meant to make her cry.

Perhaps he should have gone down on bended knee. But it hadn't exactly been the formal proposal, more a statement of intent. Good Lord, would she say anything or just run for her life the minute he stood to the side and allowed her to pass?

Bloody hell, he had his ward trapped on the stairs to the attic, and she looked as if he had just told her to drink sour milk. He hadn't thought marriage was such a bad idea. What in heaven's name was she thinking? The wait for her answer, any answer, made his stomach sink. "We get along well enough, don't we?"

"That's just *silly!*" The words practically erupted from her mouth. She looked startled at her own vehemence. Gripping her book with both hands, she dropped her gaze to the pages.

"I'll have you know there are many young ladies who would think marriage to me would be quite a feather in their cap. Beautiful young ladies, the toasts of the season." Devin knew that he was overstating his case, but he had thought this out. He disliked the immense amount of pondering he had done being called silly.

"And I'm sure if you really wanted to marry, you'd ask one of them. No, you just don't want to move out again. You're just being lazy, like you always are."

She raised her face and pushed her spectacles up on her nose, which was actually quite an effective way of blocking him from seeing if tears still filled them, or even reading her expression.

She continued tearing apart his reasoning. "I know it must seem like a simple solution. You need not exert yourself much to marry me, but truly you needn't worry. I will work out the problem of my future. Don't waste any more time thinking on it."

She stepped down so they stood on the same stair and shuddered as she brushed past him.

Now, that was uncalled for, he thought. It wasn't as if he were some repulsive beast.

"Cecelia."

She stopped with her back to him.

Thought after thought collided in his head. Was she saying that he hadn't done this right? Or was she saying she didn't want to marry him at all?

He had been dodging the hankies tossed at him so long, he really hadn't quite thought that any woman might *not want* to marry him.

He put his hands on her shoulders. She stiffened under his touch. "Is there someone else? Some penniless aspiring writer you've bumped into in a bookstore? A starving artist you adore? A half-pay soldier home from the war?"

"Why would you think I would be so foolish as to fall in love with a man of no means?"

Devin could feel her wince as well as see it. "I'm asking if there is any impediment to my suit." Good Lord, when had he begun to sound so pompous? Was there someone else? He held his breath.

"There's no one else," she whispered.

He exhaled. "Good, then."

"I'm not marrying you."

"I'm moving back in my home, in four weeks, chaperon or not," he answered.

"Stay for all I care. I'm not marrying anyone, so it shouldn't matter if my reputation is ruined."

"Your reputation isn't the only one at stake here, Miss Clemmons." He moved his hands to her falling hair and fished out a pin to secure the chignon to the center of her head. Her hair felt incredible against his fingers, as feathery soft as the caress of a summer breeze.

What would it be like to remove all the pins and let it flow across his hands, his pillow, his body?

He stepped back, startled at the image he had conjured. Well, marriage did include that, although a man usually looked to his mistresses for pleasure and his wife for duty. He absolutely couldn't consider staying in his own home while she was here alone. Although it wasn't much better for her to stay here unsupervised.

She stood still as a deer, her head bowed forward . . . over her book. He walked around her. Although it was dark in the upper passageway of his London house, he could see her watching him out of the corner of her eye, before she dropped her gaze back to the pages.

"You're not reading that."

Her head popped up. Was there more than the usual pale pink in her cheeks? She had unusually fine skin, like a porcelain doll's. Was its texture as inviting as her hair's?

"It's upside down." He tapped the page.

She looked at it and smiled. "No wonder I was having such difficulty."

She turned the book over, stuck her nose in it and skirted around him, walking along the passageway. She paused only briefly at the top of the stairs leading down to the main floors.

"You don't read upside down."

"Of course I do. It's just not as easy as reading right side up."

"Do me the favor of not reading on the stairs, so as to not break your neck as you descend. I should much prefer a bride who can walk."

She rolled her eyes. "Perhaps I should try to talk Mrs. Parmont into staying."

"She's already gone." He had made sure of that.

Cecelia escaped the library and returned to her bedroom before Devin found her. Not that he would be searching for her. She stepped up to her looking glass. The same plain reflection with hair that refused to stay pinned, which always greeted her, looked back. "Oh, bother."

If Mrs. Parmont had stayed just a few more weeks, Cecelia wouldn't be in this pickle with Devin. He would have gone about basically ignoring her as he always did. She sat down at her secretary and wrote:

When you asked for my hand
I did fly so high I never thought I should land

Cecelia frowned, then scratched through the line. Dipping her pen in ink, she began again:

When you looked at me with eyes of blue

And declared your love so true
My heart sprouted wings and flew

She growled and wiped her pen dry and closed the ink. Obviously now was not the time to compose love poems. No, she would do better to leave the love poems to those who knew what they meant.

Damn him anyway.

She grabbed her satchel and tiptoed down the hall. She crept up the attic stairs. It was growing late, and she needed to make her daily rounds.

Devin stared at the brandy he had just poured in a glass. It was to calm the jolt to his nerves, he told himself. He swirled it around, allowing his palm to warm the liquid to the proper temperature. Brandy was a patient man's drink.

He was about out of patience.

How could she have refused his offer? Without even giving it any consideration?

He yanked on the bellpull, and when his butler appeared, he said, "Send the carriage for Aunt Marsh."

"Oh, sir," protested Barnes.

"It's either her or drag my mother home from Italy." Aunt Marsh wasn't really his aunt, but a distant cousin once or twice removed.

"I see. Well, Mrs. Marsh it is. She won't like it a bit."

"Tell her it's only for four weeks, maybe less."

Barnes raised an eyebrow.

"This *is* the last time. Do whatever you can to make her comfortable."

Aunt Marsh was eighty if she was a day, a wrinkled and bent old bird. She had been his mother's governess then companion before he blighted her days.

As a chaperon she provided little more than a body. She certainly wouldn't budge from in front of the fire to escort Cecelia about town. Not that Cecelia made any effort to gad about, or that Aunt Marsh would notice one way or another. But as a distant relative of his, not to mention dependent on the pension he supplied her with, she would provide protection for Cecelia's reputation, in appearance if not in practice.

Devin resigned himself to giving up his favorite chair for the duration of the old woman's stay. He needed to tell his valet to pack a bag for him, since he doubted that Aunt Marsh would allow herself to be transported in such a hurry-scurry fashion as to travel above two miles an hour and arrive tonight.

When he entered the front hall, Cecelia nearly plowed into him on her way to the front door. He grasped her shoulders out of a strong instinct for self-preservation.

Her poke bonnet covered her messy hair, and a burgundy pelisse concealed her wrinkled black bombazine dress. She looked almost fetching, he thought with a start. After he had settled her out of danger of crushing his cravat, he asked, "Going out?"

Perhaps she regarded the question as rather chowder-brained, since it was quite obvious she was on her way out the door. Perhaps that was why she blinked her dark velvety eyes at him above her spectacles. Good grief, when had he grown so fond of her eyes?

Without a book to bury her nose in, she was well and truly caught staring back at him. Just as he felt the exchanged gaze was growing rather heated, she pushed her spectacles up her nose and broke the connection.

"Perhaps I should ask, Where are you off to?"

"Hatchards."

Books. He should have figured. "I'll accompany you."

Cecelia backed toward the door. "No need. I have my maid *and* a footman."

"Just the same, I shall tag along, too." He was eager to test this newfound attraction to his ward. When he thought of marriage to her, he knew she was quiet, rarely in his way. She didn't expect him to entertain her, but would engage in a conversation if he wished. She had never been coy or cloying, things he detested in a woman. He thought he could be quite comfortable with a woman who didn't require his constant attention, but her refusal to his immanently reasonable suggestion of marriage had caught him off guard.

"Don't you have another oppressive corn law to pass?"

He retrieved his great coat and hat. "It's Friday. We save our oppression laws for Tuesday." The House of Lords only sat on Friday in an emergency.

"Oh." Her mouth twisted sideways as if she were trying to think of another way to dissuade him from accompanying her.

"Don't twist your mouth up like that."

She rolled her eyes. "Now you sound like Mrs. Parmont."

She had no business comparing him to her departed companion. He couldn't resist antagonizing her. "Puts me in mind of a woman needful of a kiss."

She raised her gloved fingers in front of her lips and glared at him.

"I don't expect that sounded much like Mrs. Parmont." He pulled on his coat.

"I have a lot of shopping to do."

She wouldn't get rid of him that easily. He extended his arm. "Shall we go?"

"I'm walking."

"Then, I shall contrive to keep up to your pace." He jogged his elbow, reminding her he still held it out.

She placed the tips of her fingers on his sleeve. He put his hand over hers supplying the pressure she wouldn't apply.

Outside, the maid and footman stood waiting. After exchanging surprised glances, they fell in step a respectable distance behind Devin and Cecelia as they made their way to Piccadilly.

"I've sent for Mrs. Marsh," he said.

"Oh, you shouldn't have."

"Then, I should apply for a special license?"

"Absolutely not. I shall look at the advertisements in the *Post* tomorrow. I'll find a new companion."

"No."

Her fingers trembled against his arm.

"No more paid chaperons. Mrs. Parmont was the third in six months. It is starting to look like they leave because of improprieties."

Cecelia blushed furiously. "That's just stuff and nonsense. The first grew sick, and"—she scowled—"you're counting Mrs. Marsh, who never wanted to leave her cottage in the first place, and was only temporary until I found Mrs. Parmont."

"I should hate to send for my mother."

Cecelia blinked at him. "I've never met your mother."

"She might not come home anyway."

"Even if you asked her to?"

"She always does as she pleases, especially since my father's passing." Now, how had he started this line of conversation? Best to change the subject immediately. "What sort of book are you looking for?"

Cecelia shrugged.

"Mathematics? A treatise on animal husbandry? An ancient text in Latin? Another novel?"

"If you must know, poetry."

Poetry? He absolutely had to pay more attention to what she was about. He had known her to read about the driest of subjects and then plunge into a popular novel, but poetry?

The bookstore and lending library was surprisingly crowded. Cecelia disappeared into a row of shelves while he chatted with an acquaintance. She had ducked away before he had a chance to reintroduce her. Since the woman who had snared his attention had two daughters of marriageable age, he supposed she was no more interested in exchanging small talk with his future wife than Cecelia was interested in being social.

When he finally located her, she had a book open and was studiously engrossed, not just pretending this time. He looked over her shoulder and read the most syrupy love poem he had ever seen. He felt like gagging as he read *An Ode to a Fine Pair of Blue Eyes*. Was this what Cecelia wanted?

He studied the short hairs just below the edge of her bonnet. The curve of her neck enchanted him. He wanted to lean forward and press a kiss there, or wrap his bare palm around her nape and feel the fragile feminine arch of her neck.

Good Lord, she was a woman, and perhaps in spite of all her practicality, she wanted to be wooed, persuaded of the violence of his affections.

Trouble was, he rarely bothered to feel violently about anything.

The most excess of emotion he had felt lately was when she had called the corn laws, which he had voted to pass last session, "A foolish blunder of overprivileged landowners doomed to cause no end of trouble." That he had come to the conclusion she was right hadn't made him any less angry.

"Find what you wanted?"

With a start, she snapped the book shut and hid it behind her back as she spun around to face him.

He watched her struggle to drop the impervious mask over her face. A welling of tenderness crept under his breastbone. "Love poems, Cecelia?"

She dropped her arms to her sides, one hand clutching the slim collection of poetry. "'Tis the season."

Absurdly a Christmas carol played in his head, but

Boxing Day had passed already. And while they were done with January, it was still a long way from April and May. His confusion must have shown on his face.

"Saint Valentine's Day is coming soon," she said.

He had completely forgotten about the lovers' holiday. He put his arms behind his back and said inanely, "That it is."

She rolled her eyes. "I have several more stops I need to make."

"Shall we move on then? Give me your book; I'll take it to the counter."

"I can buy—"

"Don't be absurd, Cecelia. You're my ward."

"—them."

She picked up her spectacles from the top of the stack of books on the shelf beside her and put them on her nose. Then she handed him the stack. Her expression was a cross between belligerence and embarrassment.

He couldn't help but grin at her. She snorted and moved past him toward the counter.

He read the titles as the charges were added. *Verses of Love. A Collection of Love Sonnets.* He couldn't wait to get out of the shop and put the books into his footman's hands. It was too much to hope that the man couldn't read. What had happened to his sensible, practical, unemotional ward?

They stopped at a perfumer where Cecelia bought scented ink. They stopped at a milliner shop where she picked out several lengths of patent lace and a slew of delicate ribbons. She bought several slips of foolscap and the thinnest pasteboard they carried at another shop. He stewed about how to convince her to marry him.

They stopped in front of another store, an emporium this time, and Cecelia swung around to face him. "Would you wait for me out here?"

The window contained a display of ornate cards. *Let*

your sweetheart know with a Valentine card read the banner draped above the display.

"By all means:" He gave a slight bow. "I'll just look at these silly fripperies"—he gestured toward the window—"while you make your purchases."

Cecelia blanched white and then blushed furiously. She ducked her head down before she entered the store.

Whatever she needed to purchase in there, *she* might consider more embarrassing than all the volumes of love poetry he had paid for at Hatchards. He doubted it. He stared at the cards decorated with lace and love knots, and a plan began to form.

Inside Hartley's emporium Cecelia kept her body between her satchel and the front window as she removed a bound parcel and handed it across the counter to the proprietor.

He unwrapped the parcel she had just handed him and spread the contents across his counter. Cecelia winced, hoping Devin couldn't see the display of her wares.

"These are smashing. Can you bring me more by Tuesday next?"

Cecelia nodded. "Are the big ones selling well, then?"

The man smiled. "Not yet, but they will. There 'ave been a lot of govs looking at 'em. Like the cove out there looking at 'em now."

Cecelia winced, knowing he must be talking about Devin, who hadn't even realized Valentine's Day was approaching and considered her cards silly. "Looking isn't buying."

"They'll be back. The ladies are the one's buying 'em now. I 'ave orders for a dozen more like this." He tapped one of the smaller cards. "Ladies seem to like to give the simple ones, but expect to get the fancy ones."

He reached to the bottom of the stack in the display

case and handed her a card with the lace dangling off the edge. "Could you repair this?"

Her heart sank as she saw the damaged edge where the glue had come away with a chunk of pasteboard. "I don't know." She tucked it in her satchel. "I'll try."

The proprietor knelt down and removed a lockbox from under the case. He opened it and handed her a small bag and a handwritten list. Cecelia's eyes swam as she stared at it.

"Is it all in order, miss?"

She peeked into the heavy bag and gasped at the sparkle of gold guineas and silver crowns winking back at her. "So much?"

"Raised the price when the first lot sold so fast, I did," said the shopkeeper proudly.

"Thank you." She scrambled to get the shock out of her voice. "Quite astute of you to do so. I knew it should be to my advantage to work with you."

He touched his forehead. "To both our gain."

He gathered up her work, handling them like they were made of the most delicate china. She didn't handle them so nicely.

She folded the list and pulled the purse closed and tucked both in her satchel. Who would have thought? Well, she had hoped, but this kind of success she hadn't expected.

Now she needed to go outside and pretend nothing was out of the ordinary with her unsolicited companion.

"Where now?" Devin asked, as she stepped on the sidewalk.

She pulled on her gloves. "I'm done."

"Should you like to go to Gunther's for a shaved ice?"

"It's rather cold for frozen treats."

"They serve tea and cakes, too."

"Do we have to?" She was appalled that those words had slipped out of her mouth.

"No, of course not." A frown marred his forehead.

Perhaps the walking had worn him out and he wanted to rest on their trip home. Anxious to get back to her workroom and count the money in her bag, she had allowed her overset nerves to overrule her civility. "We can stop if you'd like."

He gestured toward the maid and footman, sending them on home with her purchases. He turned toward her, and his blue eyes searched hers.

Heat rose in her face. Perhaps shaved ice was in order. "I'm sure I should enjoy a cup of tea."

That was as long as he didn't ask her what she did upstairs in the attic. She would tell him eventually. After all, when she had raised enough money to strike out on her own, she would have to tell him. But her fledgling business venture needed dry wings before she would risk flapping them about. He would probably think she was all wet anyway.

"Good, because I have something I wish to ask you."

"I quite think you shouldn't."

"I shouldn't?"

"Well, yes, you have asked too much today."

"Really?"

He looked adorably puzzled. Had he forgotten he had asked her to marry him earlier in the day? Or, actually, he hadn't asked. He had suggested that marriage to him was the only reasonable solution. Although, since she knew it wasn't, Cecelia didn't know why she was fretting about it. It had probably slipped his mind, which was a good thing.

She turned toward Gunther's and began walking. He fell into an easy step beside her.

"Isn't it time you left off the mourning? Is that why you were buying the ribbons and lace? To trim new gowns? Do you need money for dresses?"

"Mourning?" She had been quite braced for him to ask about the attic, but that was neither here nor there.

"Yes, the black stuff you wear. All your dresses are black, aren't they? You should have switched to half mourning months ago. Have I been remiss in seeing to your clothing needs?"

"I'm not in mourning; I always wear black."

"Why?"

Cecelia shrugged. "I never thought much about it."

He stopped, and Cecelia debated whether or not to continue walking without him. She was hopelessly unfashionable. It had never occurred to her to vary the order she had given the dressmaker every year since her mother died, black bombazine and crepe.

Last season she had been in full mourning, so a single black ball gown and a couple of black morning dresses were fine at first. Later, her first chaperon had tried to outfit her in the latest fashions and colors. Cecelia had pulled up her heels after the first court dress with yards and yards of lace and a cost that was far too dear for a penniless ward.

It wasn't that Cecelia hated lace. It looked rather pleasing in small bits on her cards, but she didn't like being draped in the stuff. It was itchy, and she felt like a decoration. She was not meant to be a diamond of the first water, or even the second or third water.

She simply didn't have the looks to carry off being an ornament. She felt like a fraud all wrapped up in fine linen. Better to stick to her basic black. Besides that, the court dress was little more than shreds now, the lace all pirated for her card designs, which had been a terrible thing for her to do, she realized with a guilty start. Devin had paid a pretty penny for that dress, and she had sacrificed it on a whim. A lucrative whim to be sure, but a whim nonetheless.

He spun around and started back the way they had come. She stared at him.

He returned to her side and reached for her elbow. "Come on."

"Have you changed your mind? You don't want to stop at Gunther's, after all?" One could of course hope. Perhaps he had realized he didn't want to be seen with such an unfashionable creature as her. In which case he would quite realize he wouldn't want to marry her either. She sighed.

"You need new clothes. Why don't you tell me these things, Cecelia?"

She dug in her heels. "I don't need new clothes."

"Yes, you do. I should have noticed sooner."

"I don't *want* new clothes."

He tugged; she resisted.

"Cecelia, we're here on Bond Street. We could at least buy material to have dresses made up. You have to quit wearing black all the time."

"Why?"

"Because I can't see you in the shadows."

He had spent the last twelve months barely noticing her; why would he want to start seeing her now? "I'll contrive to stay in the light."

Damn, she wished he wouldn't grin at her like that. It made her toes curl and her knees weak. She shoved her spectacles up on her nose. When she forced herself to look through them, everything developed a nice haze. His looks grew blurry, and her heart didn't beat quite so hard when his perfection was a little smeared.

As if to say what was he going to do with her, he gave a tiny shake of his head.

If she had it her way, not a blessed thing. Or everything. She hated not being able to make up her mind.

Three

Cecelia sat down across from Devin and pulled her napkin across her lap. She was enshrouded in black again, and her hair was pulled back in a simple braid. At least that way she seemed to have control of it. He carefully refolded the *Morning Post* and set it down beside his breakfast plate.

One of the servants poured coffee for her and brought her a plate with seared ham and poached eggs. She eyed the newspaper folded beside his plate.

"Good morning, Cecelia."

She looked up, startled. "Good morning, my lord. Was your hotel comfortable?"

Devin rolled his eyes. Trust Cecelia to pull up polite after previously ignoring the niceties of formality. "Not a bit. I miss my own bed."

"You shouldn't have left, then. Oh, look, they pulled a body from the Thames."

Now, there was a conversation stopper, he thought. She wasn't getting off the hook that easily. "Yes, a young woman. Probably did herself in."

Devin was rather glad she wasn't squeamish like most women he knew, but he was quite sure the retrieval of another body from the Thames was inappropriate conversation for the breakfast table.

She took a bite of eggs. She had never even given it a thought.

"She was wearing a lawn nightgown," Cecelia commented.

"Maybe she was walking in her sleep."

"And walked right into the Thames? More likely she was murdered."

Devin glanced at the paper at his elbow. Cecelia was leaning across the table, reading—upside down. She chewed her breakfast while straining to read the article. She looked up halfway through her meal as if feeling the weight of his gaze upon her.

"What?" she asked.

"You've made your point."

She flashed him an innocent look and then lowered her gaze when he met it skeptically.

"Might as well read it the easy way." He turned the paper over for her, so she could actually read the news right side up. He slid it across the table.

She picked it up with her left hand and read while she finished eating.

"She probably exasperated her guardian," said Devin.

"It's too bad she didn't have you as a guardian, then," said Cecelia.

"Meaning . . . I wouldn't exert myself to the point of throwing a willful creature in the Thames?"

"Of course you wouldn't." Cecelia didn't look up from the newsprint. "It's kind of sad. No one even knows who she is."

Devin supposed he should be glad she didn't think he would ever resort to murder, but then, she probably thought he was too lazy to bother.

Barnes entered the room, the silver salver used for correspondence and calling cards in his hand. "Miss Clemmons, this has just come for you."

She blinked and looked up, hesitating for a long moment. She folded the *Morning Post* and set it beside her plate and reached for the frilly confection of lace and ribbons on the tray. "Thank you, Barnes."

His butler bowed and tucked the salver under his arm and left the breakfast room, leaving the two of them alone.

She drew the valentine into her lap, below the edge of the table out of Devin's sight. Not that he needed to see it again. He was more interested in her reaction. The shopkeeper, possibly sensing Devin's unease at buying the card, had assured him that *all* women adored the cards.

Cecelia's eyes widened, and her surprise and shock were easy to read.

"What have you there?" he asked when the silence stretched thin.

"Nothing important." She shoved back from the table and rose from her chair so violently she jarred the table. Coffee slopped into his saucer. With the card pressed against her chest, she flew out of the room.

Well, he couldn't count the card a total loss. It had raised an excess of emotion in her. He sipped his remaining coffee. What emotion, he could only guess.

Once out of the breakfast room, Cecelia made a dash for the staircase. Seeking the sanctuary of her bedroom, she took the steps two at a time.

At first when the card arrived, she had thought there was some problem with it; the lace had come unglued, the love knots loose. She had thought one of the shop owners had sent it back for repairs, but when she had read the signature, *from your Secret Valentine,* she wasn't sure what to think.

All kinds of possibilities ran through her head. The card had been misdirected or misdelivered. Unfortunately, there was no direction on it. It surely couldn't be for her.

She pressed her fingers against her warm cheeks. How could she have a secret admirer? She didn't know many people. It had to be a mistake.

But, zounds, how her heart had pounded when she

thought the valentine might be for her. Was this how the recipients of her cards normally felt? She had to admit it was a frightfully nice feeling for a moment or two before she realized it had to be a mistake.

She could perhaps question Barnes where it had come from. But without a name on it, it was unlikely she could get it to the person it was intended to charm. She propped it on her dressing table near her looking glass.

It could serve as a reminder that people actually bought her cards. She gathered her supplies purchased the day before and headed to her workshop under the eaves. She needed to keep up with the growing demand.

Late in the day a noise out of the ordinary brought her out of her work stupor. She had spent the last hour copying verses from her poetry books onto the cards she had assembled all morning. She shook her cramped hand. The scented ink was starting to make her head ache.

She capped the bottle and scattered sand over the last of the words she had penned.

As she descended the stairs, she heard the front door open and close several times. By the time she reached the ground floor, Devin was leading the even more bent and stooped Mrs. Marsh into the front hall.

"I don't know what business you have sending for me again. I should have stayed home, instead of being rattled all about the country in that bone-setting carriage." Mrs. Marsh punched her cane against the floor as if to punctuate her statement.

Cecelia knew that was a lie. Mrs. Marsh would do about anything Devin asked, but her more gnarled condition startled Cecelia.

"I wouldn't have sent for you at all if Miss Clemmons would quit chasing off her companions." Devin rolled his eyes in Cecelia's direction, while supporting the woman and leading her across the floor in mincing steps.

Cecelia reached for the drawing room door, since the butler and footman were engaged in carrying in bandboxes and valises.

"What's wrong with you, gel?" Mrs. Marsh turned her still bright gaze in Cecelia's direction. "Why aren't you married?"

"She's refusing perfectly sensible offers."

Mrs. Marsh cocked her head ever so slightly. No doubt her curiosity was piqued.

"How many offers have you gotten, child?"

"No sensible ones," Cecelia answered, taking Mrs. Marsh's other arm, before Devin dragged her across the room.

"See now, I'm just going to have to marry her myself."

If she were a dozen years younger, Cecelia would have stuck her tongue out at him. She settled for a scalding look which he met with a carefree smile.

"Yes, you should and leave an old woman to her fire."

"Shall I help you with your bonnet?" asked Cecelia as she helped Mrs. Marsh into Devin's favorite chair. She undid the strings, wondering how Mrs. Marsh had managed to get the bonnet on at all with her arthritic hands.

The old woman nodded. "Don't stand there gawking, boy. Fetch me a lap robe."

Devin stepped to the door to issue the command.

Mrs. Marsh sighed as she settled into the armchair.

Cecelia took the bonnet to hand over to Barnes. She stopped near Devin.

"Was she this bad last time?" whispered Devin.

Cecelia shook her head. "Where have you put her?" She whispered, too.

"She needs to be in the room next to yours."

"That's three flights of stairs, Devin. She can't handle

that. We'll need to make up a room on the ground floor. The library—"

"Not the library." He frowned and glanced at the older woman.

"The breakfast room, then."

He nodded reluctantly. "It'll be warmer there above the kitchen."

"Quit whispering about me and come sit down," said Mrs. Marsh.

"I shall just order tea," said Cecelia. She put her hand on Devin's sleeve. In a low aside, she said, "I'll get the servants started on rearranging the furniture."

The heat of his hand seared through hers, and he nodded. Cecelia snatched her hand out of the sandwich between his arm and hand, surprised that his touch affected her so much. What made it worse was she had initiated the contact.

"Well, hurry, gel. All that traveling in the cold has made me quite stiff."

It wasn't really Mrs. Marsh's urging that had Cecelia hurrying from the room.

When Devin went to find Cecelia an hour later. He was told she was in her attic. He told one of the maids to fetch her while he went to see how the manservants had faired with converting the breakfast room to a bedroom.

He joined two footmen in wrestling the wool under-mattress from upstairs through the door. When he sensed Cecelia behind him, he said, "What is it you do in the attic all day?"

"Boil toads and lizards."

He spun around, yet not really surprised by the answer. "That would explain the black, then. You are practicing witchcraft."

One of the footmen gasped and started to cross himself.

"It's all a hum. She doesn't want to tell me what she does up there."

"Actually, I was rearranging things so the breakfast table might be stored there." She turned toward the two footmen and pointed at the table now leaned on its side against the wall. "If you would be so kind as to take it up there and put it in the attic room I use."

The two men heaved the heavy piece of furniture up and bumped their way out of the room.

"Use the main stairs," called Cecelia after them. "When they don't see any cauldrons, will they be reassured?"

"No, they'll just think you affected their vision with a magic spell."

She sighed. "I suppose I shall have to show them."

"What *do* you do up there?"

Cecelia shrugged. "I haven't come by any toads in weeks, and the lizards are far too dear to waste with boiling."

She would show the footmen, but she wouldn't tell him. "Is it anything I should be worried about?"

She flushed and shook her head. "No."

He stepped closer to her. He wanted to tell her he wouldn't belittle whatever it was she did. She was such a bluestocking, he suspected she might be penning a manuscript. If that was what it was, he would like to see it, when she was ready. "Just harmless white magic?" He brushed a stray hair from her cheek. "Love potions and the like?"

She flushed more, and he wanted to lean closer, sample the heat in her skin with his lips. Aunt Marsh on the ground floor would not be enough protection for his ward.

"Something quite like that." Her voice had grown breathy.

She felt the pull of attraction, too. He knew she did.

She didn't have a book to hide behind, and her spectacles, for once, were nowhere near her face. But he knew better than to overplay his hand with a naive female. That she was under his guardianship made any impropriety on his part that much worse. He dropped his hand to his side.

She turned away and grabbed the last chair to remove from the room. "Is Mrs. Marsh all right?"

"She fell asleep after drinking her tea." He stepped over and took the chair from her. "I'll get that."

"Barnes is breaking down the bed in the mistress's room to bring downstairs."

Devin winced and wished that she hadn't mentioned beds, let alone that his mind leaped ahead to the realization that she would have to share his bed if the other bed in the master suite was removed—if they married, and he had every reason to think they would. It only required his campaign of valentines and gifts to be successful.

"I thought it would be more comfortable, and they wouldn't have to carry it so far."

"That's fine." He croaked out. He set the chair down out in the passageway and turned to find Cecelia's liquid brown eyes trained on him. "You know, I thought witches had to be ugly."

"Plain will do."

"Then, you, most definitely, are not a witch."

He continued on to the stairs to pack several bags. His plan to return home to sleep was not workable. Mrs. Marsh was not an adequate chaperon to circumvent the mad thought that kept spinning in his head, that if he well and truly compromised his stubborn ward, she would be forced to marry him.

Cecelia stared at the retreating back of her guardian. Had he just given her a compliment?

No. Of course not. It was far too offhand to mean anything. Well, other than he didn't think she was plain. Or that as her guardian, he should bolster her confidence.

As the servants trickled back into the room, carrying pieces of the spare bed from the master suite, she directed the positioning and reassembling of the bed.

When the room was arranged satisfactorily and the fire lit and a maid assigned the duties of assisting Mrs. Marsh, Cecelia headed back to the morning room, which would probably function as the drawing room for the duration of Mrs. Marsh's stay.

Devin descended the stairs. His valet behind him carried two valises, which he parked by the door. Then the man disappeared into the back of the house.

"Are you going somewhere?"

"Back to the Grillon's hotel, until my solicitor can find me some other lodging." Devin pulled on calfskin gloves.

"Why?"

He gave her a wry look.

"Just because Mrs. Marsh isn't lodged on the same floor as I am, doesn't mean she isn't adequate supervision."

"Oh, and if I decide to seduce you on the floor of the morning room, will she wake up long enough to dissuade me?"

Cecelia took a step back. Her senses went into double time. Her heart pounded madly. "Don't be silly. It's not as if you would do something like that with me."

He took a step toward her. "Wouldn't I?"

No, he wouldn't. If he had truly wanted to seduce her, he had had plenty of opportunity in the past year. He had never really given a thought to her as a woman before he had come up with the absurd idea to marry her. He wouldn't be acting this way now if there wasn't something else amiss.

"You're mad as hops, aren't you?"

He stared at her. "Quite. Cross as crabs. Not fit company for a lady. Forgive me, Cecelia. I shouldn't have said that."

She wouldn't have minded so much that he said it if

he had only meant that he wanted to seduce her. But he had only meant to shock her into not arguing.

He turned toward the front door and said, "I shall be back in time for supper."

"I'll make sure Barnes knows."

He hesitated with his hand on the doorknob. "When did she get so old?"

So he was upset by the deteriorated condition of Mrs. Marsh. Truth to tell, Cecelia had been a little shocked herself, but not surprised. She had been through the same thing with her father. Mrs. Marsh was quite stricken in years.

She moved across the hall and put her hand on his shoulder. "It's good that she is here now, and we can see to her comfort."

He leaned his head against the door. His voice was flat. "You mean in her last days."

"She isn't on death's doorstep yet, but she won't live forever." Cecelia wished she could give him more comfort, but the truth was Mrs. Marsh was of an age where she might live a dozen more years or meet her maker next week. She squeezed his shoulder. "You should not let her see how very distressed you are. It should only serve to make her feel badly."

He turned and pulled her against him. Her breasts encountered the solid wall of his chest. Crushing her against him, his arms folded around her, solid bars against her back. Her nose squashed against his shoulder, she couldn't help but breathe in the scent of him, warm, musk, linen and leather.

"I know. I'm not the type to wear my heart on my sleeve."

Hearing his voice above her ear and pushed against him so tight she could feel each breath he drew, she felt awkward. His hold on her relaxed and became an embrace she could slip away from any moment. She wanted to escape the odd tingling sensation that invaded her breasts. Yet, she wanted to give Devin the comfort he craved.

Slowly she moved her hand around his shoulder and raised her other hand to join them together behind his neck. She wanted to slip her fingers into his golden curls and pull his head down toward hers. To what purpose—she had no idea.

His hold changed again. He slid his gloved hand across her shoulders down to fit into the small of her back and splayed out his fingers. He dipped his head down, his cheek resting against her hair.

Tension simmered under the surface. She could feel it under her fingertips as she pressed them against the rigid muscles on either side of his spine. Was she doing this wrong? Hugs were meant to soothe, yet her breathing quickened in cadence. His, too.

Emotions swept through her in a windstorm frenzy. She wanted this embrace to be different. That he would see through her to the desperate knowledge that she didn't even know how to offer comfort pounded at her. She shifted against him. He grabbed her shoulders and pushed her away.

He stared at her.

Cecelia could have slunk to the ground in mortification. Her chest heaved, and his gaze dropped. What had she given away in that embrace? Had she confirmed that she was just as smitten as every young miss who had thrown her cap in his direction at his tiniest encouragement? How had this gone so wrong?

He slowly leaned toward her, narrowing the space between their faces.

The door opened behind them, and the rush of cold February air was like a glass of cold water thrown in her face. She stepped back so quickly she rammed against the bottom newel post on the stairs.

The smart of pain nearly brought tears to her eyes.

Devin stared at her as if she suddenly sprouted a healthy witch's wart on her nose.

"The carriage is in front, sir," said Barnes. "Shall I have these bags taken out?"

"Please." He gave a tiny shake of his head.

His eyes were so intensely blue that it hurt Cecelia to look at them. Where were her spectacles when she needed them?

He spun around and stamped out the door.

Cecelia grabbed the balustrade to steady her weak knees. What had she done?

Four

Devin rubbed his gloved hand over his face as he walked down the street. He had told the coachman to transport his valet and luggage to the hotel and he would meet them there in person, leaving his servants shaking their heads.

They weren't the only ones. How had he assumed Cecelia's offer of comfort was anything more than that? Just because holding her in his arms had fired his blood to a slow boil, he had leaned in to kiss her. If not for Barnes's timely interruption, seducing her on the floor of the morning room wasn't so far-fetched.

Bloody hell! What was wrong with him?

Her embrace had been so tentative, yet had driven him wild. What cracked notion had made him find her lukewarm reception stimulating beyond measure? Her look of horror afterward said everything.

He knew why. Because she had initiated the touch after he had warned her his feelings and urges weren't so aboveboard anymore. Or, well, they were marginally above contempt since he intended marriage. But they had nothing to do with respect and regard, with the way he should treat his future wife, let alone any female deserving his protection.

He wanted to possess her body in the worst possible way. And because he knew he would be the first, the last, to reach the hidden depths of passion hidden in Cecelia, to make those velvet brown eyes turn liquid, he had a sense of being a conqueror of old. Which was a pretty odd thing for a man who prided himself on being civilized, urbane, unflappable. Bored.

Devin couldn't recall ever feeling this ferociously, this alive, ever before. Possibly because he had never had to work hard for pleasure. No, most often it was thrown in his lap. But this situation was unique and tricky. Cecelia wasn't the type of woman who would be won over by brute force and the strength of his desire. She was too intellectual for that.

She had passion, but she would have to be totally convinced in her brain box that exploring it would be worth the while. And she was buying books on *poetry*.

He had made it to the shopping district. He stared in a window, his thoughts churning at a furious pace.

The package arrived midmorning. Across the room, Devin looked around his newspaper at her. Cecelia pushed her spectacles up on her nose so he became a hazy blur she could ignore. Now, if she could just ignore the way she seemed to develop a medical condition every time he looked at her. Perhaps she needed a small dose of foxglove to get the wayward tempo of her heart to rights.

Cecelia asked Barnes to have the package sent to her room.

"Don't you want to open it, gel?" asked Mrs. Marsh.

She gave a tight-lipped shake of her head. What could it be, besides some of her valentines being returned to her. Her heart sank. One of the merchants carrying them must have had trouble selling them. She surely didn't want to open it in front of Mrs. Marsh and Devin.

Devin folded his newspaper. Cecelia could tell that by the crinkling sound. He moved across the room, and Cecelia held her breath until he sat down by Mrs. Marsh.

He leaned forward and took her mittened hand in his. "I shall write a letter to my mother this afternoon. Is there any message you wish for me to relay to her?"

Mrs. Marsh looked over at Cecelia where she perched on the edge of her chair. She slowly turned her birdlike head back in Devin's direction. "I should imagine your news is enough. Time she came home."

Cecelia wondered how those two comments fit together. If she weren't in such a stew about the contents of the box that undoubtedly had found its way to her dressing table by now, she would have paid better attention.

"I can hardly read her letters anymore, my eyesight is getting so troublesome."

"If you should like to borrow my spectacles, they might help," offered Cecelia.

"Surprising a gel your age needs them," said Mrs. Marsh.

"I read too much, ruins my eyes," explained Cecelia.

Truth was she had plucked them off her father's desk after his death and put them on trying to feel closer to him. But they weren't going to make something happen that hadn't happened in life.

That was how Devin had found her, and she had discovered it was much easier to view him through the distortion the lenses caused, rather than stare at that perfect face, knowing her plain face hadn't even inspired her father to love her.

She suddenly couldn't stand delaying opening the box any longer and fled the morning room.

Sitting on her bed, she set the box down and untied the ribbon. The box was wrapped fancily for a return of merchandise. She would have expected brown paper and string, not pink tissue and a blue satin bow. She opened the box, and as expected, she saw one of her more elaborate valentines.

An odd queasiness in her stomach kept her from

reaching inside. The lace and satin decoration on the card seemed intact. The words she had penned in tiny letters on the front, *Faithfully yours,* weren't smeared. There wasn't a note explaining the return as she would have expected. As if her hand could stand the suspense no longer, she watched herself reach inside and lift the card and slowly turn it over to the blank back side of the card. In a script not her own were the words:

For the hands that hold my heart

From your Valentine

The box yielded a pair of lavender kid gloves. She gingerly touched the butter-soft leather.

This couldn't be right.

She twisted, looking around until she found the plain white card that had been tucked under the ribbon. She scanned it, hardly believing her eyes. No mistake. She was the only Miss Clemmons at this address. She was the only Miss Clemmons she knew.

Who could be sending her own valentines back to her? Devin? No, he would never go to that much trouble. Besides, he wasn't enamored of her. He was far too good-looking himself to even think of her as a love interest. No, he simply thought she was a problem he needed to solve.

And yesterday—well, he wasn't the kind to turn away a gift thrown in his lap. She knew enough about his life and had seen the way he had been pursued by young women after marriage—those he sidestepped quite adroitly—and young matrons after something entirely different—those he didn't sidestep, but he put out next to no effort in the chase. But then when all one needed to do was flash that smile in the right lady's direction—

Cecelia cut off her thoughts about Devin. One of the shopkeepers who was blown over by her merchandising efforts? Possibly. But which one? One of the young men that she had met last season before she had finally dug in her heels and refused to attend another ball where she clung to the wall in terror someone would ask her to dance?

There had been one spotty boy who had kept her company more often than not. One who had not been put off by her urgent plea that he not ask her to dance as she detested dancing. What she detested was not knowing the steps and looking like a six-footed lummox as she tried to follow the other dancers in the complicated patterns.

A tear trickled down her cheek. Whoever it was, she was incredibly grateful that someone was sweet enough to use her creations to woo her. Even if it proved to be no more than the gratitude of a shopkeeper who had found their association lucrative. It couldn't be anyone who knew her well or he would realize how little she deserved such special treatment.

She pulled the gloves out of the box and drew them on. They fit as though they had been made for her. She leaned back on her bed and put a gloved hand against her cheek. She envisioned a new batch of valentines with the phrase *For the One Who Holds My Heart*. The words would wrap in an oval around a pair of hands.

She sprang off the bed and headed up to her workroom.

Aunt Marsh poked him with her cane. "She know it's from you, boy?"

"Not yet."

"You planning on telling her soon?"

"In a couple of weeks." Devin paced toward the window.

"Turned you down, eh?"

Devin pulled back the brocade curtain and looked outside at the dismal February afternoon. The sky was the blanched gray of winter. Cold seeped off the panes of glass. He didn't answer.

"Good for her."

"I thought you'd be on my side."

"I'm rather fond of the chit."

She was hardly a chit, Devin turned around to argue, but he realized to one as stricken in years as Aunt Marsh, they were all children. And what could he expect; women flocked together.

"You could use new clothes, couldn't you?" He changed tactics. "If I have a dressmaker brought in, you could pretend it was for you. I'd gladly have a couple of dresses made for you."

"What's this about?"

"Cecelia, Miss Clemmons, she's still in her blacks. I believe she's refusing to have new dresses because she doesn't want to feel like she's charity. If you could persuade—"

"Is she charity?"

"There wasn't anything left of her father's estate." In fact, there had been several debts he settled. "But it's not charity. I want her to have clothes fitting her station."

"What station is that?"

Aunt Marsh seemed a little short with him. As a poor relation dependent on the pension he had given her, he supposed she felt an affinity for Cecelia's situation. But Cecelia had a decent marriage proposal.

"As my future wife."

"And if she continues to refuse your offer?"

Why would any woman refuse him? He held a peerage; he was considered handsome, charming; he didn't pick his teeth in public. He told himself to calm down and answer the question at hand. One sometimes had to sidestep passions. He supposed what he would do if he didn't want to marry her. "I could settle an adequate dowry on her."

"But you haven't."

"I never thought about it."

"Didn't you have her out last season? How did that go for a gel without prospects?"

He had put her through last season without any hint that she would be provided for regardless of her father's debts. "Not well, and this year she's refusing to take part in anything. Although the attendance is thin still."

Aunt Marsh shifted in her chair. Her pursed lips spoke volumes of disapproval.

"That's not fair. I was still sorting out her father's affairs last season." Although it hadn't taken him long to realize there wouldn't be anything left for Cecelia. And she had known the lay of the land long before he had sat her down and gone over the grim truth with her. "She doesn't seem to like the balls or Almack's. She didn't put much effort out to interest a suitor."

Truth was he never thought much about what it was like for her not having any money. He had always had more than enough. Until he caught Cecelia selling her father's books in December, books he knew were precious to her, he hadn't even given her any pin money. He had thought telling her to have her bills sent to him would be enough. But, he realized now, it was less than adequate.

"How old was she when her mother died?"

"Thirteen, almost fourteen."

"Bad time for a gel to lose her mother."

Devin studied his nails. Aunt Marsh obviously saw a connection he didn't see. Did losing her mother on the eve of becoming a woman make it harder for Cecelia to behave as one?

Truth was he should have assisted Cecelia more, but he hadn't been prepared to suddenly become responsible for a young woman of marriageable age. He didn't like Almack's much either. He felt like a delectable morsel sacrificed on the altars of ambitious mamas with marriageable daughters. He always felt lucky if he made it out of there without being swallowed whole or shredded to tatters.

He had never taken Cecelia to the literary salons and soirées he enjoyed. Partly because he wanted to escape the way her unassuming, but hopeful, gaze made him feel, and partly because he hadn't seen many young unmarried misses at those types of gatherings. Usually older women, married women, political hostesses attended. Miss Bluestocking Clemmons would probably have adored those types of events. He hadn't known enough about her then to realize. A mother would have known.

"Is there ever a good time to lose a mother?"

Aunt Marsh's reply was a soft snore, which was absolutely of no help at all. For the first time in his life, he could have used some advice, instead of being the one handing it out.

For the second time in a year and this week, Devin climbed the attic stairs. Cecelia had just finished binding up her packets of freshly made cards and was getting ready to start on a new card, when his rap on the door startled her.

"Cecelia, we need to talk."

There were slips of foolscap on her workbench with the ink and pens arranged nearby. Watercolor paints rested near the cut pieces of pasteboard. Her poetry books were propped open to various verses she thought would work well on her cards. Lace and ribbons flowed out of baskets under the table. While it seemed obvious to her, there was really nothing that would give her business away.

She tugged off her bleached muslin smock and stuffed it under the table and opened the door. She returned to her stool and sat down as if it were normal to let him into her private sanctuary.

He hesitated in the doorway. "Do you want to go downstairs?"

She stood up. "If you do."

"No, I just didn't think you wanted me up here." He crossed the threshold.

"I don't when I'm working, but I suppose you must see for yourself there aren't any wax effigies of you."

"I haven't experienced any unusual pains lately."

Devin looked around, his gaze skimming over the workbench. He seemed more interested in the baskets of lace and her sewing supplies underneath. His interest landed on her smock and stayed there an inordinately long time.

"Just a lady's craft room," she said nervously. Just because she had let him into her private sanctuary didn't mean she wanted him to go over every inch with a fine-tooth comb.

His gaze jerked to her face, and Cecelia wished she had thought to put on her spectacles. There was just something so penetrating about his look, as if he was seeing her in her drawers. She looked for her eyeglasses, and he beat her to them. "You don't need these, do you?"

"Did you come up here to talk about my vision?"

"No." He folded the spectacles and held them by the nosepiece.

At least he wasn't smearing the lenses with fingerprints.

"I think you should attend some—"

"No. No more balls, dances, champagne breakfasts."

"How about some soirées, some salons. I think you would enjoy that sort of thing, talking about politics and literature with other people as widely read as you."

Cecelia had felt so outcast by the *ton* that so embraced Devin. She didn't think he could possibly understand how isolated and alone she could feel in the middle of a crowded room. "No."

"Cecelia, I made mistakes last year. I would make it better for you this time."

What was he up to? He must still be concerned with finding her a husband. He would put more effort into it this time. He must be very worried he would have to marry her himself if he didn't rise above his normal complacency and exert more energy in the hunt for a suitable suitor for Cecelia.

"If you don't want to go to Almack's or balls, you don't have to. We could go to the theater, the opera—"

"Perhaps I should just put on mobcaps and be done with it." She didn't know why she didn't just consign herself to the ranks of spinsters. Certainly at twenty-three she could consider herself on the shelf, a veritable ape-leader. A mobcap would just confirm the fact and relieve Devin of the need to worry about finding her a husband or stepping into the role himself.

She opened her mouth to tell him about her business and that he needn't worry about her needing to marry and found she couldn't make her voice come out.

"Don't you want children? Don't you want a husband? Don't you—"

"I want a lot of things I can't have. I want my mother back." Where in the stars had that thought come from? "I'm used to not getting—"

"—want me?"

"—everything I want." Had he said what she thought he said? But she was rolling and couldn't stop. He had no idea what it was like for her. Everyone adored him; everyone doted on him; everyone gave him everything he ever wanted. Even her. "If I ever marry, I'll have it all. I shall have the poems written to my eyes and someone who"—she grabbed her poetry book and searched desperately for the passage—"yearns to—"

He yanked the book out of her hand. "Quit hiding in books, Cecelia. Quit hiding behind your spectacles. I can't give you your mother back, but you can have most everything you want. Just tell me what it is you yearn for."

Didn't he understand that the one thing she wanted was the one thing she never deserved? What woman could expect a man's love when her own parent couldn't love her?

Devin took a step toward her. Time seemed to hang in that odd pre-explosion standstill, until he turned on his heel and stalked out of the room.

Cecelia spent a lot of time in her attic assembling cards as fast as she could. Business was picking up, and she wanted to be sure to keep up with the demand. In less than two weeks her opportunity for this year would be over. Work helped her not think about anything else.

The valentines kept arriving daily. A set of fine lawn handkerchiefs, which she was invited to toss in her secret valentine's direction, was delivered. How she was to manage that when she had no idea who he was, she didn't know.

Next a beautiful Coburg bonnet with a burgundy ribbon around the brim arrived with a message that she should not hide inside so her valentine would have more opportunity to gaze upon her loveliness. Which had the effect of making her smile when she tied it on to go out and make her rounds.

Devin had asked why she was smiling. She had said, "No reason at all."

"New bonnet?"

"Well, yes."

"That's it, then. New bonnets have a way of making women smile."

Which had served to make her frown, and he had traipsed around with her with a perplexed silence. Until he started asking why she had to visit several similar stores. Couldn't she get everything she needed at just one of them?

Then came a set of pearl-studded hairpins, which would tempt her valentine to remove all her pins and run his fingers through her silken tresses. Cecelia wondered if the usual tangles would stop him.

Her secret valentine was a romantic. That was sure. She encountered her spotty friend one day on the street while taking her cards to be delivered. He had been less spotty, but hadn't pressed to delay her. Still, it could be him.

There was one shopkeeper's son who seemed to gaze at her worshipfully from the back when she entered the shop, but was too shy to come out unless another customer required attention. It could be him.

Then there was Devin, who was behaving like a baited bear since their argument. She was tempted to throw a raw fish and honey pot at him and tell him to pick his indulgence and settle his spleen, but it was partly her fault, so she kept her mouth civil.

She thought his refusal to return home and sleep in his own bed was largely the reason for his distemper. But someone in a mood as foul as his wouldn't be capable of composing sweet romantic messages.

She tried to convince him that he should just move back into his home, but he growled at her and then invited her to ride in the park with him. She refused and made an excuse of not fitting into her old habit. Really, she didn't have the time until Saint Valentine's Day passed.

She was so thankful she could count on him leaving the house for Parliament at least three days a week. It gave her a chance to make her deliveries without him hanging on her sleeve. There had been too many times lately when he had insisted on accompanying her and raised his eyebrows at her repeated purchases of colored ribbons and lace.

She had given each of the maids and the footman a

specially made valentine card and sworn them to secrecy, but she didn't feel right enlisting their aid for deliveries when they were in Devin's employ.

She stepped into the emporium that displayed her cards in the window. The store was crowded, and Cecelia hung back, looking at the merchandise. Finally, the harried shopkeeper, Mr. Hartley, pointed her over to the curtained doorway while he had his assistant take over.

She stepped behind the curtain into a storeroom with a jumble of boxes, crates, and bolts of material piled haphazardly everywhere. Or she supposed there was some order, but it was hard to discern from the sheer volume of goods crammed everywhere. The scent of cinnamon and cloves, wool and rosewater, hung over everything. She took another step in among the clutter, and the smells shifted.

In front of her was a half-unpacked crate with small wooden boxes inside. She lifted one up and nearly dropped the exquisitely painted box when it chimed.

The curtain swished behind her, and Cecelia turned to see the shopkeeper.

He looked at the box she held.

Cecelia felt suitably chastised when he took it out of her hands.

"Just in from Vienna." He turned the box over and wound a key on the bottom. He held it out and lifted the hinged top, exposing a small, red satin-lined cavity.

A waltz played with tinkling clear notes.

They stood there as the music box played out the few measures before it wound down.

"That is lovely," said Cecelia, sad the music had stopped, but enchanted by the piece.

The shopkeeper smiled and set it on the table with the others that had been unpacked.

"I'll take all the cards you've got."

He was back to business, while she still felt as if fairies hovered in the air.

Cecelia hesitated a minute. She had deliveries for other stores in smaller packets, but ironically this shopkeeper who had doubled the prices they had set was selling twice as many as anyone else. Her more elaborate cards were selling for as much as ten pounds. She pulled out the other two packets. She would have to deliver something to the other shops tomorrow and send round a note today. She would have to use Devin's footman.

"Do you 'ave more? I 'ave got one cove who buys one or more every day."

"Really, what does he look like?"

"A gentleman," as if that explained all. He handed her the bag of money and the list. "I need more of these. Now that Valentine's Day is getting closer, I need a 'undred or more for this coming week. Plus the order list is getting longer."

She swallowed. Was he bamboozling her? No, his look was sincere. "I'll get you as many as I can. They take time to make."

He handed her cards with tally sheets clipped to them. "These 'ere are the backorders. Can you get these done, too?"

Cecelia swallowed hard. She noticed the heart-in-hands theme seemed especially popular. Her heart started to flutter. "They won't be exactly alike."

"I tell 'em no two are *zactly* alike." The shopkeeper's serious mien broke, and he gave her a wicked smile and a wink. Was he the one sending her valentines back to her?

She hadn't considered him before. He was, well, not old, perhaps in his thirties with dark hair styled like a gentleman's. He was attractive in a slick, dark way. But she could only see him being romantic when it served to gain him something. She blinked.

"You can do it, can't you?"

It was as much a goad as a challenge. She wasn't sure if she could do it, but, oh, she wanted to try. The idea left her breathless with fear and tingling with nervous excitement. "I may have a footman make my deliveries over the next few days, then."

"And the money, miss?"

"I'll be round for it, eventually."

"Good 'nuf, miss." He touched his forehead. "Never thought when you first came round, things could be so good."

"Me either." A shadow passed over her excitement. She had done so well that there wasn't any doubt she had raised enough money to live modestly on her own. Her dependence on Devin would end soon. In spite of his recent bearishness, that thought made her sad.

Five

Cecelia returned home to find a calling card with the corner turned down waiting for her. She checked the name. Her spotty friend from last year. How odd. He had never called on her last season.

Of course, he had been young, younger than her and as green to town as she was. But they had grown friendly. Yet, his calling on her at her guardian's house would signify a serious turn in their friendship. Was he now looking for a wife? Could he possibly be considering her?

Cecelia tapped the card against her lips. Really, he was a nice boy, but he hadn't stirred more than fondness in her. With Devin around, how could any suitable man compare favorably?

Still, if her spotty friend had such a keen romantic streak, perhaps she should at least stop thinking of him as spotty.

"How much of this would one need for a lady's riding habit?" Devin asked the shop girl.

"Would depend on how large the lady is, milord."

"Slender like you. Give me what you think you would need plus a couple of yards in case I'm wrong."

The shop girl gave him an amused smile. Without thinking much, he grinned back. But if she was hoping he would be back come closing time, she was mistaken.

There was only one woman's favors he wanted these days, and she was oblivious to him. Well, not quite oblivious, but so naive she didn't understand his frustration.

The shop girl handed him the brown velvet tied in tissue. Chocolate brown they had called it. He had picked it because it reminded him of Cecelia's eyes. Dark, rich, velvety—damn he wanted her. The valentine cards here weren't as nice as at the other shop, but he was running late. And he still needed to compose a message on the back.

He returned to the quarters his solicitor had found for him just off Bond Street.

"I need a pen and ink, if you would be so kind," he said to his valet, who had to double as a footman in his rented rooms. At least he didn't have to cook, as they both returned to his town house for meals.

Devin shrugged out of his coat and rolled back his sleeves.

His valet set the requested items down on the writing desk. "That's not one of . . ."

Devin looked at his man. "Not what?"

"Not like the others, milord." He picked up Devin's jacket and brushed the sleeves as if the care of his master's clothes were the most engrossing task in the world. Of course, he was well paid to care about Devin's clothing.

"I know it's not as nice, but I didn't have time to go to the other shop." Devin picked up the pen, dipped it in the ink and hesitated. Hell, he had to get it done. Just write something, he told himself. He could only hope the cards and gifts were working, because he wasn't making any progress in person. In fact, his charm seemed to have deserted him at a time when he needed it most.

For the first time, Cecelia received a valentine that wasn't made by her. In fact, she thought the simpler card

much inferior to her creations. *Get off your high horse,* she
told herself.

She had already smoothed her fingers across the rich
dark brown velvet, when she flipped the card over.

*The color reminds me of your beautiful eyes. I could make a
habit of drowning in them.*

Your Valentine

It wasn't poetry, but it was poetic. She leaned across
her bed to see in her looking glass. Her eyes were the
same color as the plush material. That didn't make them
particularly fine. Devin's brilliant blue eyes were much
more coveted. But then hers weren't bad as far as peep-
ers went. They did at times have a sparkle to them.
Although lately they were getting a bit red.

The color of the material pleased her. Dark brown
wasn't such a jarring change from black. She set the
package aside. Perhaps she could have a riding habit
made of the material—after Saint Valentine's Day.

Her life was starting to separate into two pieces. Making cards as quickly as she could now, and everything she
could postpone until after the holiday. She had tried to
streamline the process by having several cards in different stages of completion instead of finishing one at a
time. Next year she would start much sooner. Like
maybe the week after this Saint Valentine's Day.

A knock on her door sent her scrambling off her bed.
She picked odd times to daydream, Cecelia thought. She
should have gone back up to the attic to work a few more
minutes before being summoned downstairs for dinner.
She left her room to descend the stairs.

The delivery had been late today. Perhaps her secret
valentine was growing tired of the game. She stopped
with one foot suspended above the next stair.

The card today hadn't been hers. That meant the
money-making shopkeeper and the son of the other one
couldn't either one be her secret valentine.

Take A Trip Into A Timeless World of Passion and Adventure with Kensington Choice Historical Romances! —Absolutely FREE!

Let your spirits fly away and enjoy the passion and adventure of another time. Kensington Choice Historical Romances are the finest novels of their kind, written by today's best selling romance authors. Each Kensington Choice Historical Romance transports you to distant lands in a bygone age. Experience the adventure and share the delight as proud men and spirited women discover the wonder and passion of true love.

4 BOOKS WORTH UP TO $23.96— Absolutely FREE!

Take **4 FREE** Books!

We created our convenient Home Subscription Service so
you'll be sure to have the hottest new romances delivered
each month right to your doorstep — usually before they
are available in book stores. Just to show you how
convenient Zebra Home Subscription Service is, we would
like to send you 4 Kensington Choice Historical Romances
as a FREE gift. You receive a gift worth up to $23.96 —
absolutely FREE. You only pay for shipping and handling.
There's no obligation to buy anything - ever!

Save Up To 30% On Home Delivery!

Accept your FREE gift and each month we'll deliver 4 brand
new titles as soon as they are published. They'll be yours
to examine FREE for 10 days. Then if you decide to keep
the books, you'll pay the preferred subscriber's price. That's
all 4 books for a savings of up to 30% off the cover price!
Just add the cost of shipping and handling. Remember, you
are under no obligation to buy any of these books at any
time! If you are not delighted with them, simply return them
and owe nothing. But if you enjoy Kensington Choice
Historical Romances as much as we think you will, pay the
special preferred subscriber rate and save over $7.00 off the
bookstore price!

We have 4 FREE BOOKS for you as
your introduction to
KENSINGTON CHOICE!

To get your FREE BOOKS,
worth up to $23.96, mail the card below
or call TOLL-FREE 1-800-770-1963
Visit our website at www.kensingtonbooks.com.

IIl..l..lll...ll.l.l.l.l.l..ll.l.l.l.ll.l..l

KENSINGTON CHOICE
Zebra Home Subscription Service, Inc.
P.O. Box 5214
Clifton NJ 07015-5214

PLACE
STAMP
HERE

Cecelia chewed her lip. That narrowed the field to two.

"Are you coming down, or just going to stand there in the middle of the stairs all night."

"Stand here, of course."

Devin glared at her. He had truly lost his sense of humor.

"Well, I thought I should wait until I grew hungry."

"I'm starving." He muttered something else under his breath, but apparently she wasn't meant to hear it.

"I shan't dally, then."

"Oh, we could dally, if you've a mind to." He stepped up a riser.

Lately there seemed to be a caged energy about him that made Cecelia wary of getting within biting distance. "If sleeping in a strange bed is making you so miserable, you should move back home, Devin. I don't know why you're being so stubborn about this."

"Perhaps obstinacy is in the water here."

"Yes, but—"

"You don't understand what would happen if I moved back in."

He gained her side and held out his arm. She reluctantly took it.

She sighed. "Well, no. I don't understand why you put such a great importance on my reputation, when I don't care a fig for it. It truly shouldn't matter."

"We are well beyond considering damage to your *reputation* . . . or mine."

Which was so cryptic she wanted to stomp her foot and demand to know why he couldn't speak plainly. "What would be so horrible?"

"Well, I should hope it wasn't horrible. Just rather shocking, and I haven't totally eliminated it as a plan of action should my first campaign be exploded."

Since they had reached the bottom of the stairs, she

pulled her hand free from his arm and planted both her hands on her hips. "What war are you waging?"

"I asked you to marry me. I want all the husbandly rights and duties that go along with that."

She blinked. An edginess slid down her spine.

"Shall we go in?" He gestured toward the morning room cum drawing room.

"No."

He caught her elbow which was conveniently akimbo for him to latch on to.

She snatched her arm free, alarmed by the impact the warmth of his hand had on the condition of her heart. "What is it with you? Hasn't anyone ever told you no before?"

"Only you."

"Gracious me, that's it. You can't stand to be told no. Just being told no is enough to make you think you should have something, whether or not you shall wish to keep it or not."

"We're not talking about an it, Cecelia. We're talking about you. Come on, Mrs. Marsh is waiting, and I can't even talk civilly to you anymore. So much for the Nash charm."

"You haven't lost your charm, Devin. It's just . . . It's just *useless* on me."

"Why?"

"Because I know better."

His voice dropped lower. "You do, do you?"

The question and his tone had her doubting the strength of her convictions.

He stepped closer; his chest brushed her shoulder. The odd tingles in her breasts started, as if her skin had been put to sleep and was waking, much the same as if one had sat on their leg and was reminded with the pinpricks of returning circulation, only this sensation was pleasanter. But it couldn't be normal, nor could the frenzied pounding of her heart. As soon as Saint Valentine's Day passed, she would need to visit a doctor and ask what should be done about these palpitations.

He brushed his fingers across her cheek.

Her lips parted in an effort to draw in more air, which suddenly seemed in short supply. Why did his touch affect her so? His gaze became heavy-lidded, and his attention focused on her mouth. He leaned closer. His breath whispered across her lips. Her eyes fluttered closed.

The click of the basement door sounded like a cannon shot.

She sensed Devin turn away, and she opened her eyes. Barnes stood looking as if trapped and wanting for all the world to race back downstairs to the kitchen and restage his entrance with much more noise.

The butler swallowed and said with much less than his usual aplomb, "Dinner."

Devin recovered first. "Thank you, Barnes."

Like a grateful watchman relieved of his overlong duties, Barnes scurried back to the basement door. He hadn't even added the customary "is served."

Of course, he didn't usually announce in the front hall.

Devin straightened his cuffs as if nothing untoward had happened. But then nothing had happened. The almost kiss was averted. Saved by the dinner bell. He showed no interest in continuing his lovemaking. Did it mean so little to him? Was it all just a pathetic attempt to convince her he would bite the bullet and marry her?

If he really wanted to wed her, why was he so miserable? No, he just wanted to dispose of his problem of her future. Last year he had ignored her, perhaps in the hopes she would solve the problem for him. This year he had come up with this jingle-brained scheme to marry, and he grew increasingly testy with her.

Cecelia backed away from Devin. "You really don't want to marry me, Devin. I know you think you do because I said no. But if you just think on it, I know you'll realize that we would never suit."

"Cecelia," he started.

But his tone sounded exasperated, and she didn't want to hear what he had to say. "Trust me, you don't need to worry about my future. I have it well in hand."

Cecelia needed to escape his penetrating blue gaze. She opened the door to the morning room. "Dinner is served, Mrs. Marsh."

During dinner, Devin watched Cecelia. Her face looked pinched and white. She stirred her food around her plate. Why were his attempts to convince her he wanted to marry her going amiss?

The easiness they had once enjoyed in their relationship had turned into edginess. He knew that was his fault, and she didn't understand how thin a thread held his control.

She had never mentioned the valentines he was sending or the gifts. She had worn the bonnet and the gloves, but something was changing about her.

She had a book in hand less often now, and her spectacles weren't always perched on her nose, ready to provide a barrier between them. Were his gifts the cause? Or was something else at work?

When she had come to live with him, he had thought she was a socially inept, totally withdrawn, dependent female. In short, a burden he hadn't wanted. But he had found she was well read, had strong and often insightful political opinions. His staff was suddenly polishing the girandoles and waxing the sofa legs weekly. He had failed to notice that those things weren't being done before. And his staff, instead of resenting the increased workload, adored her.

"Aunt Marsh has requested a mantuamaker come in and make her a couple of new gowns. I've arranged for her to come two days hence. Perhaps you could have a couple of gowns made up at the same time, Cecelia."

Cecelia looked up at him, her eyes full of accusation and questions.

"Yes, I need a new dress for a wedding I'm to attend," said Mrs. Marsh as she stabbed a piece of salmon.

"I could send round a note asking her to bring extra bolts of material. Black if you insist," Devin said.

"I don't need any new gowns." Cecelia looked at her plate.

"Yes, well if you want, she'll be here for a couple of days. If not . . ." He shrugged.

"Who is getting married?" Cecelia asked Mrs. Marsh.

"A distant relative of mine."

"Is it anyone we know?"

Devin choked and reached for his wineglass.

Cecelia gave him a distracted look.

Mrs. Marsh calmly finished chewing her bite of fish. "I'm not at liberty to discuss the parties because the engagement hasn't been announced yet." She turned toward Devin. "Did you receive a letter from your mother, too?"

Devin shook his head. Mrs. Marsh was a wily one.

The old woman looked directly at Cecelia. "You might want to consider having one gown made. It is considered bad form to wear black to a wedding, unless one is forced to by circumstance."

Cecelia looked at Mrs. Marsh and then at Devin.

"So what news of my mother?" he asked. It was far too soon for his letter to have reached her yet.

"As soon as she's able to settle her affairs in Italy, she's coming home. She said she hated to travel in uncertain weather, but thought she could be here by late March."

He wasn't sure how he felt about his mother's return. His father had been considerably older than her, but he hadn't been in his grave above a fortnight when she sailed off to the Continent where she had taken up with an Italian count only a half dozen years older than Devin.

At least, he hoped Mrs. Marsh was just throwing Cecelia off the scent and not warning him that his mother was bringing her young lover back with her.

The two ladies withdrew after dinner, and Devin nursed his brandy alone. The practice was silly when there weren't any other men to enjoy blowing a cloud and conversation with him. He tossed back the drink with only a small wince for the bad form of drinking like a sailor instead of savoring the wine as he should.

Cecelia was tiptoeing out of the morning room as he approached.

"Is she asleep already?"

"Yes."

"Shall we repair to the drawing room, then?"

"The fire isn't lit in there."

"The library, then."

"I was about to retire."

He winced. She wasn't about to retire. She was about to sneak up to her attic sanctuary. He supposed he should just call it a night and slink off to his bachelor's quarters across town. Or he could join some of his cronies at a club.

He didn't want to leave. He wanted to stay and study the hint of roses in her cheeks. He wanted to talk, but he didn't really know what to say. He wanted her to talk. She read the newspapers. Surely, there was some current event she could discourse about at length, and he could listen to the soft flow of her voice.

He could close his eyes and imagine that she were lying beside him in bed and sharing intimate thoughts with him. Her words would circle and encompass him and leave him feeling . . . a part of her world. She was such a private person, when she let him in, he felt as if he had been allowed into the secret garden of her soul.

Instead of scurrying off to the attic, she stood waiting. The pause had grown awkward.

"Then, allow me to escort you to your attic."

"No!"

He swiveled away, stung by her forcefulness. With each attempt he made to get closer to her, she shut him out. "I apologize. I didn't mean to trespass upon your . . ." he didn't even know what to call the room, "your craft room."

"It's just that I don't want you to see what I'm working on there, yet."

Yet? He slowly turned back around. He remembered what he thought she might be working on up there. With the lace and ribbons and heap of white muslin stuffed under her workbench, he had thought she must be sewing undergarments for herself. Drawers and shifts edged in lace and tied with ribbons. Perhaps a nightgown. His imagination was running riot with imagining seeing her in lacy drawers.

"Perhaps you could give me a hint."

She had backed up against the wall, her body half hidden in shadows. The soft gaslight caught the high lines of her cheekbones and the luminousness of her dark eyes. "I shall show you in good time, I promise."

He cut off his runaway thoughts. No, she was absolutely too calm to be talking about showing him her undergarments. Perhaps she was painting. He had seen half-empty watercolor vials and well-used paintbrushes along with several pens and pots of ink. Illustrations? "Are you writing a book?"

She cocked her head sideways as if the idea interested her. "No."

"Are you sewing something?"

"Are we playing twenty questions?"

"If I guess right, will you answer?"

She pressed her lips together and shook her head. "No, I'll just have to stick pins in a little doll of you."

"I told you before, you are far too pretty to be a witch."
All right, he was going to finish what he started earlier.
He would kiss her and leave her with her worthless chaperon. He couldn't count on Barnes to save him from
himself this time.

Her dark eyes widened, and she shrank back against
the wall. Her words came out in a rush. "Do you think
your mother is going to remarry?"

Was Cecelia trying to avoid being kissed? He pulled
back, about to make a remark that would show his nonchalance. "God, I hope not."

"Why? Wouldn't you want her to marry again?"

"I don't know. You women drive me crazy. My mother
wouldn't put on mourning, and you won't take it off."
Devin turned and leaned against the wall beside Cecelia.
"I wouldn't try to stop her."

Cecelia waited in a companionable silence. She
wouldn't continue to pry if he didn't want to talk, but
she understood there was much more to be said.

"Her lover is barely older than me."

"I see."

"What do you see, Cecelia? Because I don't really understand why she had to run off to Europe and go wild."

"Your father, like mine, was so much older. She wouldn't
have had a chance to be young before he died, and there's
not much time before her own youth runs out. It drains
something from you when your spouse is decades older. I
don't think my parents had a very happy marriage. Although, I know my father adored my mother."

Devin turned and watched Cecelia talk.

She paused. "I think my mother loved my father, but
it wasn't the same for her. I think your mother loved
your father, but she needs to be free now."

But she had left so soon after his father had died. He
had begged her to stay, told her that he needed her. She
had patted him on the cheek and told him he didn't

need her; he would be fine. She had been right. He had been fine. Then he had inherited Cecelia.

"Things would have been better for you if she had stayed."

Cecelia smiled softly. "I wouldn't have wanted her to hold back living for my sake. I think your mother must be incredibly brave. She's thrown open her arms and embraced life."

Perhaps she had, but Devin couldn't quite get past that she had needed to turn her back on him and society to do it.

Six

Devin looked at the selection of cards. He noticed several with a pair of hands painted in the center of the card with the words *For the One Who Holds My Heart* circling the hands or underneath. And he had thought he had been original with that phrase.

He picked out two of the frothy confections, one with the hands, and reluctantly, one with a long poem penned inside on slips of foolscap between the outer pasteboard folded in half. It was almost like a miniature novel, with ribbons lacing it together. If Cecelia wanted love poems, he wanted to give them to her. He just wasn't going to be the one writing them. That much was clear.

"You must 'ave many sweethearts," said the shopkeeper.

Devin looked up, startled. "No, just one. I send her a card and gift every day. Can you deliver these?"

"Certainly, sir."

"Along with the gifts?"

The shopkeeper touched his forehead and gave him a smile. "For a small fee, say sixpence for anything under a stone."

Devin handed over the box containing a gold locket. "This is for tomorrow. Sixpence to include some fancy wrapping and a bow."

The shopkeeper nodded. "I'll need an address."

"May I use your pen?"

The shopkeeper passed the pen, ink and a plain white card across the counter. Devin wrote out her name and his address. He turned the first card over, and the shopkeeper watched him. Devin pushed the address card across the counter.

The shopkeeper picked it up and jerked back.

Devin looked up, startled. He couldn't even say what had broken his concentration on thinking what he wanted to write on the back of the valentine.

The shopkeeper set the address card back on the counter and darted to a curtained backroom. "Be right back, gov."

The fellow was a little cheeky, and had a gimlet eye to his profit, but Devin didn't mind. He signed the first valentine and opened the one with the poem. His mind went blank. He needed gifts, too. He had planned to send more material for dresses, but for some reason Cecelia seemed uncomfortable with the idea of having dresses made up for her.

What did she want? What did she need? He closed his eyes and thought about what he had seen in the attic. Lace, ribbons. She had plenty of those, and it might not be entirely appropriate for him to send the makings of undergarments. There also had been the pasteboard ladies liked to use for paintings. There had been paints, and if he remembered right, the vial containing red was nearly empty; the one with white was only about a quarter full.

"Do you have paints, watercolors, perhaps a case for them."

The shopkeeper set a small painted box on the counter in front of him and hurried off in another direction. He came back with a large black leather case and opened it. Inside were removable trays and several bottles and jars and camel-hair brushes. Pens and different-colored inks were on the other side. Well, if she was penning a novel, the pens and inks would go over well, too.

"I'll wager that is just over a stone."

"Just under," shot back the shopkeeper with a steady look.

Devin grinned, knowing he would pay this man one way or another. "Fine for Saturday. Can you deliver something on Sunday?"

"If I have to do it myself, sir." The shopkeeper held up the painted box he had set on the counter. He lifted the lid. "I'd stake my eyeteeth she'd love this."

Devin listened to the waltz play and shook his head. "She hates to dance."

"Don't 'ave to dance to like music. Ladies love these. I'll throw it in for Sunday. You pick out another card." The man pulled out the most extravagant card in the display and put it in front of Devin.

There had been times he had been sure that Cecelia tapped her slippered foot in tempo with the waltzes played at the balls. What the hell, if there was the chance it would bring her pleasure, he wanted to give it to her.

Something had happened last night as he leaned against the wall beside Cecelia. He had wanted to kiss her, but he hadn't wanted to violate the moment. For that space in time, just being with her had been enough to soothe him.

It struck him as ironic that she lived in his home, yet he only had stolen moments with her in the front hall. He was eagerly anticipating Saint Valentine's Day when he would reveal that he was the one giving her the gifts.

Cecelia knew there was another box waiting in her room, but she was getting desperate to finish the orders in the few days before Saint Valentine's Day. One of the shopkeepers had sent a note complaining that he had sold every last one of her cards and needed more.

Yesterday had been a golden locket in the shape of a heart.

So that my heart might be near yours.

Your Valentine

She could feel the weight of it against her skin under her dress. But the locket was empty. She was starting to feel a vague uneasiness about the gifts. The gifts and words that accompanied them were so right, almost uncannily right, as if someone were studying her and knew her almost better than she knew herself. How could anyone know her so well, and without her knowing who he was?

It couldn't be Devin. He was just—well, too self-absorbed to be that aware of her. Not that she faulted him for it. He had simply been raised to believe he was entitled to everything he wanted because he wanted it. He had never been encouraged to think of anyone else's needs.

He could have made it easier for her to be introduced to society. He could have let her get her feet wet before thrusting her into the glittery world of the *ton* where all the other younger marriageable misses were dressed in dazzling white. She in her blacks stood out like a buzzard among swans. He had thought she would know how to go on because she had been born to the right parents. She hadn't known anything.

But it hadn't taken her long to realize that his attitude was the one everyone took as their lead. She was to be tolerated, but not welcomed. He performed introductions, but he didn't go out of his way to do it. She didn't think he meant it to work that way.

He had engaged a suitable chaperon for her and then gone about his merry way. Not that he hadn't tried to pull her into the center of attention. When he had asked her to dance a cotillion, she had refused vehemently. She had known as he walked away shaking his head that it had never occurred to him she didn't know the steps. She had been too mortified to clarify later.

So when he had asked if she would bite the head off of any gentleman he sent to ask her to dance, she confirmed she would. She had told him, when she was ready to dance, she would find her own partners. So it was partly her own fault that she had been left to her own devices.

She knew enough about him now to know that if she had confessed her shortcomings, he would have seen to it she learned to dance. If she had told him her fears, he would have done what he could to allay them. But he never would have thought about her problems if she didn't point them out to him.

"Miss, the dressmaker is here."

Cecelia sighed. She stood up and capped her ink. She didn't have time this week. Couldn't he have scheduled this for next week or the week after? No, she answered herself. How could Devin have known that she needed every second this week for her work?

She stopped in her room and eyed the gift on her bed. Unable to postpone any longer, she untied the ribbon and removed the paper. Inside was a leather case. She opened the case, and bottles of paints, pens and different-colored inks were inside. Now, this was like someone who knew she was creating her cards would send her.

She reached for the card. It was one of her more elaborate ones with a poem inside. Impatiently, she flipped to the back.

Your Valentine

No note?

She put it aside and ran down the stairs and found the butler. "Barnes, I need to know who is sending me these gifts."

Barnes looked uncomfortable. "I can't rightly say, miss. They're always delivered."

"By whom. A footman? Is there livery?"

Barnes shook his head. "Boys."

"Pages? You have to delay the delivery boy next time. I have to know where these gifts are coming from."

"Yes, miss."

"Cecelia, the mantuamaker is waiting for you in the sitting room."

Cecelia swirled around and stared at Devin, who had leaned out of the library. "Are you doing it?"

He folded his arms across his chest. "Doing what?"

Cecelia wanted to sink into the carpet. Of course he wasn't sending the gifts. He was Zeus and Apollo and every god there was rolled into one, society's darling, the catch of the century, and she was a penniless dependent, a mere mortal, a buzzard among swans. She was a problem to be solved. "Sending me gifts," she said in small voice.

"What gifts?" He watched her with those intense blue eyes.

The realization that she wanted him to be the one giving her gifts squeezed her heart. There were still four days left before Saint Valentine's Day. She didn't want to know it wasn't him now. She wanted to stretch out the dream a few more days. And then what?

Her business was successful, lucrative. She would start looking for a house for herself, perhaps in one of the outlying towns. Someplace with enough space to set up a large work space. And the gifts, perhaps she needed to return them when the sender revealed himself to her.

She turned and walked toward the morning room. "Never mind."

"Cecelia, is there something I should know about?"

"No."

"You keep too many secrets."

It had to be the slick shopkeeper. Who else would know to give her what she needed to create her valentines? His intentions were honorable. He had sent the handkerchiefs she could toss in his direction anytime. But she didn't want him.

"I know who it is."

"What?" said Devin.

The shop owner must have sent her the other card to throw her off the scent. Every time she went around to his shop, he had grown more personable. More smiles and winks, an offer to make her tea the last time she had been there.

He was sharp as the razors he sold. He watched his customers and knew exactly what merchandise they looked at. Would it be so far-fetched to believe that he had noticed what caught her eye as she wandered around his store waiting for him to be free? He seemed willing to sell anything that would make a profit for him. And it was his business to notice what people wanted.

Hell's Bells, he would probably be Midas rich some day. She reached for the door handle. "I didn't think he could afford the gifts, but well, of course, he can." After all, he could get them wholesale.

Devin stared at the door of the morning room. He ought to barge in and demand to set the record straight, but there was a dressmaker in there and every chance one of the ladies could be in a state of undress. Not that he wouldn't mind seeing Cecelia in her undergarments, but he did not want to see Aunt Marsh anything other than fully clothed.

Bloody hell, was some other bloke getting credit for his gifts?

He should have just given in to his baser instincts and made her his. He couldn't stand to hang around waiting until they were done with the dressmaker. He had committed to attending a pugilist match weeks ago. Maybe he needed a bit of solid, straightforward, male companionship. It certainly couldn't foul his mood any more. He slammed out of the house.

* * *

Devin watched Cecelia drag into the breakfast room and signal for coffee. He folded the *Morning Post* and studied his ward. Her dress was wrinkled, and her eyes were bloodshot. She looked like a female version of his cronies after a night of hard carousing, as if she had never been to bed at all.

"Cecelia?"

She sat up straight and looked as guilty as he had ever seen her look. "Gracious, they still haven't identified that poor girl." She pulled the newspaper across the table. "Does she look like anyone you know?"

Devin looked at the line drawing on the front page, knowing perfectly well Cecelia was diverting his attention.

"No, no one I know."

"That's so sad. They're going to have to put her in a pauper's grave if no one claims her soon."

"Cecelia, she's probably just another soiled dove who decided she'd be better aloft. It's tragic, but there's nothing you or I could do to undo her death."

Cecelia pressed her lips together and shook her head. "They examined the body. She wasn't a prostitute, not that she would deserve to have an unmarked grave if she were. And she didn't drown. Someone threw her in the Thames after she was already dead."

He looked at the paper again, studying the drawing intently. She looked like a moderately pretty young girl, but not even vaguely familiar. "If I had an inkling of who she was, I would do something."

Cecelia nodded and sipped her coffee. "Yes, I know you would. I just wanted to be certain you looked closely."

"What I want to know is why you look like death warmed over?"

She stared at him with her velvety brown eyes and lied

outright. "I got so engrossed in reading I didn't get any sleep."

"Reading what?"

She stared at him a second too long before she said, *"Childe Harold's Pilgrimage."*

Figured she would throw out a story about a depraved rake written by a dissolute hedonist. "Reading about a pilgrimage or were you on one?"

Her confident expression shattered. "What do you mean?"

"It wasn't reading keeping you awake last night."

She looked away. "I was so reading."

What in blue blazes was she up to? And when had she stopped carrying around a book all the time?

Later, he found both her and Aunt Marsh asleep in the morning room. He tried to shut the door quietly, but Cecelia sprang up from the chaise lounge. A few minutes after that, as he was getting ready to leave the house, he looked outside and saw her hand one of his footmen a packet. Then his footman headed up the street.

She entered the front door as he descended the steps.

"What are you doing?" He folded his arms across his chest. "Reading?"

Her expression looked strained, on top of looking exhausted, but she still managed to be flippant. "Arranging a secret tryst."

"That's not funny, Cecelia." He hated being caught in this strange place between being her guardian and responsible for her well-being, and being a suitor. "You obviously didn't go to bed last night, and your jest about secret trysts does not amuse me."

"If you must know, I sent him to a shop."

"To do what?"

"Pick up some thread. I sent a sample of the material so the color could be matched, and then, of course, he is to get some toads if they are to be had."

Devin wasn't entirely satisfied, but he couldn't pinpoint what made him uneasy. Her explanation, aside from the toads, seemed reasonable. "You trust a footman to match colors?"

"No, I trust a shop girl."

"Cecelia." He tried to think of what he wanted to say. She looked at him expectantly.

"You know you may always rely on me, don't you?"

"I know I have depended on you too much this past year."

He shook his head. He didn't see that she relied on him at all. "If you are ever cast in the briars, I would . . ." This wasn't coming off the way it should.

"You would help pluck them from my backside?"

He smiled. "And I should enjoy it mightily."

She folded her arms, too. "Inflicting pain by removing thorns or that I put myself in pain in the first place?"

"Not the pain part, for I should never want to see you hurt."

She looked away. There she went again closing off to him. He wanted to grab her shoulders and shake her. He wanted to kiss her until she melted at his feet. He wanted to spirit her off to some secluded castle until. . . . But none of those things would make her open up to him, so he did nothing. He had destroyed what closeness they had developed with his suggestion of marriage.

He looked over his shoulder at the stairs he had just descended. "You know I could look about my attic anytime I have a mind to do so."

Her gaze darted back to his, worry lines etched into her forehead.

"But I keep waiting for you to invite me in."

Cecelia dropped her arms and tried to smooth the crinkles from her skirt. He could have told her the effort would be futile.

"I did once," she said in a small voice.

"Not really, not with open arms." He descended the remaining stairs. He drew on gloves. "I trust the session with the dressmaker went well."

Cecelia nodded and shrugged in the same motion.

"You are having her make up a new riding habit, aren't you?"

Cecelia watched him like a wild animal would, tense, unsure if he was friend or predator. Truth was he was probably both, so even though her caution stung, he couldn't quite fault her for it.

"She's coming back Thursday next."

"I have a bay I bought at Tatt's this last Thursday that I think might suit you."

"I don't wish to be so indebted to you."

He moved to the door. "One should not feel an obligation to repay gifts freely given. I would buy you the moon, should it make you happy, Cecelia. But I fear you would regard it as a burden meant to chain you."

He had already sent for his horse. A groom should have brought it round to the front by now. He stepped out the front door. Had buying her gifts been the wrong way to go with her? He felt at a loss as to what he should be doing to persuade her to marry him. And he was quite worried his suggestion that she needed to commit to marriage had forced her down some reckless path. A path she never would have sought if he had not made her feel settling her future was urgent. Was she so opposed to marrying him?

He no longer believed his proposal should go as well as he had thought it would when he first conceived the idea of wooing her with valentines.

He had finally figured out what bothered him about her explanation for sending his footman out on an errand. It was Sunday. No shops were open on Sunday.

* * *

Cecelia stared at the word she had just written. How on earth did one misspell heart? But sure as day *h-a-r-t* looked back at her. In her own poem, too. There was no way she could squeeze in the *e*. Lately, she had taken to composing her own poems on the cards rather than rely on the ones out of the books.

She was exhausted. She had stayed up all night last night working on the back orders.

She was worried that her poetry too often centered on being kissed. But somehow her words written in the soft blue ink from the new kit seemed less tawdry than before.

She needed to make enough cards today to send to the other two shops selling her wares. They would need some to sell in the last two days before Saint Valentine's Day arrived on Wednesday.

She should just tell Devin what she was doing. There really wasn't any reason to delay any longer. There was enough money under her mattress to repay Devin a large part of her expenses from the last year and see her through a year of modest living, as long as she didn't frivolously spend money on fashionable dresses she didn't need.

But when she told him, the possibility of marrying him had to be put completely aside. She would have to begin the process of severing ties with him. After all, society's darling couldn't consort with a woman in trade. She had lowered herself to the level of shopkeepers and tradesmen, or perhaps lower because a woman in business was a more distrusted thing.

He would be able to move back into his own house and resume his carefree life. He wouldn't be troubled by her secrecy and aloofness or the problem of what should be done with her if she no longer resided under his roof. He could once again have his gentlemen friends over for dinner, and he could attend all the balls he wanted. He could spread his kisses to women he wanted to kiss.

If there was one thing she would regret, it was that those few times when he had come near to kissing her, they had been interrupted. But perhaps it had been best that way, because he had meant to do it only to prove that he would fulfill his obligations as a husband and perhaps didn't find the idea of making love to her appalling. But she remembered the one time she had seen him with a young matron in an alcove. His kisses then had been amorous, passionate, and Cecelia had been mortified to stumble across the pair. She had tried to quietly back away, but he had seen her and followed her.

That was the kind of kissing she wanted. Unrestrained. Wild. As though it meant something. As though he wanted it with every fiber of his being. But then she wouldn't get that kind of passion, because he didn't love her and wasn't likely to. She put her head on her workbench and imagined what it would be like for Devin to grace her with that kind of ardor and fell asleep.

She had a crease on her face when she woke up to a knock on her door. She rubbed at it as she answered, "Yes?"

"Miss, your package has arrived."

Barnes himself had come for her? She noted that there was an acceptance, even an expectation, of her daily gifts.

She sprang out of her chair and opened the attic door. He handed her a small package.

"I took the liberty of asking the delivery boy from whence he came."

She undid the bow. "And?"

"He is employed by Hartley's emporium."

She pulled back the paper and saw the music box that she had admired just a few days ago. Cecelia felt her heart plummet. That clenched it, then. It was the shopkeeper all along. What a silly dream to think it might be Devin.

* * *

Devin tossed in his bed. He couldn't sleep. Concerns about Cecelia kept tugging at him. Her obvious lack of sleep from last night and that she had sent one of his footmen off to—well, not to buy thread from a closed shop on Sunday. Had she told the truth the first time? Had she actually sent *his servant* to arrange a tryst?

He didn't believe she was that foolish, but she had been ridiculously naive at times. Finally he tossed back the covers and called for his valet.

He would just go home and make sure she was safe in her bed where she belonged.

Cecelia couldn't believe she had been featherbrained enough to run out of glue. On Sunday night there was nowhere she could go to buy more. She grabbed her lamp and raced down the stairs. She could only hope that Devin might have some in his desk.

The house was entirely dark. The servants had found their beds hours ago. She took a glance at the bracket clock on the mantel of the library: two-thirty-two. Not so very late. Well, if she were at a ball, they would probably just be getting ready to go down to supper.

She had slept too much of the day away and needed to work through the night, although she had tried to maintain a semblance of normality by letting her maid help her into her nightgown and dressing gown before climbing to her workroom.

She set the lamp on the desk and started rummaging in the drawers. *Ink pots, pens, paper, twine, sealing wax. . . . Oh, please let there be glue.* Could she use the sealing wax instead? Could she sew the lace on the cards instead of gluing it? Maybe if she pieced two pieces of pasteboard together to cover the stitches, but that would require glue.

Seven

Devin unlocked the front door and carefully let himself in his dark house. The gas jets in the wall sconces had been turned down, but there was enough light to see his way about. He would just peek in her room. He would stand in the doorway and not cross the threshold. He just needed to know she was safely tucked in her bed.

She wasn't. He could see the flat, tidy expanse of her bed. The covers hadn't even been turned down. He crossed the room to be sure. All right, so now he had broken every rule. He was in her bedroom in the middle of the night, alone. But, one couldn't compromise a maiden who wasn't present.

A giant hand twisted his innards and yanked with savage glee. Bloody hell, where was she?

Fearing and dreading and trying to decide what he should do, he reeled to the door. How could he find her? If she had arranged to meet a yellow-livered cad, Devin would have to find the wayward pair, rescue her, then shoot, strangle and stab anyone who dared ruin his ward.

He told himself to calm down. She could be in the attic. Hope surged through him as he flew to the narrow staircase, but before he had gone up more than a few steps, he could see that the door to her attic hideaway stood wide open. There wasn't even so much as a flicker of illumination from a single candle. She wouldn't be up there in pitch darkness.

Or if she was, he needed a light to see. With fear and anger churning in his gut, he made his way back downstairs. Questions assaulted his brain. What could he do? Where was she? How was he going to find her?

And there was someone thumping around in the library. He did not need an intruder on a night when he had to find Cecelia.

Nearly roaring with impatience, he flung open the library door.

Cecelia jumped back from his desk, flaying her hands forward to catch something he had startled out of her grip.

Glass cracked against his desk; then the remains of the thing thumped on the floor. Fury and relief surged through him in equal measures, making him shake.

"No," wailed Cecelia. She dropped down on her knees.

Devin crossed the floor in one leap and yanked her to her feet. "What are you doing?"

With his hands clamped like manacles around her upper arms, he tried to relax his grip before he bruised her.

She raised her startled eyes to his face. "Are you all right? You're shaking, Devin. Are you ill?" Concern radiated from her brown eyes. "Do you have an ague?"

He wanted to shake her for making him worry; he wanted to lock her up so she could never escape; he wanted to devour her whole. Blood raced through his veins with a scorching fury.

She watched him, concern turning to confusion. She tentatively reached out a hand and placed her cool fingertips against his brow. "Devin?"

Fevered. He was fevered with fear and fury, and a new heat churned underneath and threatened to obliterate all else. He crushed her to him and buried his nose in her hair. His fear that she had run away was unfounded.

His heart still beat madly, unwilling to accept the relief he should feel. Shuddering breaths racked his throat. Her softness against his chest, her breath against his neck, sent a whole new visceral wave of awareness throbbing through his body.

He buried one hand in her hair and tugged her head back. Her lips parted as she watched him with a look crossed between concern and confusion.

"I shouldn't be here."

She began to reply, but he cut it off, pressing his lips against hers and plundering her mouth.

He should go gently, but his blood had boiled his brain, and he was no more capable of restraint than a fire fueled by kerosene.

He pressed her back against the desk, his hips thrust against hers. His heart thundered, and her taste swirled on his tongue and invaded his brain.

A tiny voice kept calling him to stop. She was an innocent. She didn't know how to protect herself. He was advancing far too quickly. He was going to hurt her. Yet, she was so soft and supple, her skin velvety and her scent ethereal and earthy. Her hair was like a caress, and she kissed him back with an enchanting eagerness that made up for any lack of skill on her part.

His hand against her ribs, he slowly pushed upward until he felt the curve of her breast. Her breath spilled into his with a huff.

He bent over the desk, forcing her back as he tore open her dressing gown, so only her nightgown lay between his hands and her body. Brushing his palms over her curves, he wanted more, so much more. He wanted to touch every inch of her satin skin; he wanted to taste her breasts; he wanted all she had to give.

They needed a bed, not the top of his desk.

His bed was upstairs. Better yet, her bedroom had a fire in the grate. He yanked her off the desk and started to sweep Cecelia up to carry her up the stairs, when her gasp cut through his befuddled senses.

She yanked her foot up and grabbed it with both hands.

"Cecelia?"

"I think I stepped on broken glass." Tears filled her eyes, and she averted her head.

He lifted her up and set her on the desk.

Gently he pushed her hands away and pulled back the unadorned material of her nightgown. He took her slender, delicately arched foot in his hand and held it up. The inch-long shard of glass was still embedded in the center, near the ball of her foot. He gingerly gripped it and extracted it.

"The glue is spilling." Blood dripped down her foot.

"Forget the glue." He whipped off the kerchief he had tied around his neck and pressed it against her foot. "Hold that."

He wheeled around and grabbed the brandy decanter. He slopped some on his handkerchief. Holding her foot with one hand, he wiped away the blood, trying to be sure there weren't any remaining splinters of glass. Her stiffened intake of breath cut through to the quick.

Christ, his impatience, his near ravishment of his ward, had caused this.

"The glue—"

"Dammit, Cecelia, you're bleeding. Forget about the glue."

She bit her lip and stared forlornly at the puddle of glue on the floor.

What had he almost done? He tugged so her foot was by the lamp on the far side of the desk and examined the wound, wiping the oozing blood away. "This is why I can't stay here."

"Because I spilled the glue?"

He tied his neckerchief around her foot. "Because if you hadn't stepped on glass, I wouldn't have stopped."

She stared at him with her velvety brown eyes. Didn't she understand?

He impatiently picked her up off the desk and carried her to the library door. He set her down, far away from the danger of more broken glass. "Go to bed. And lock your door."

She looked back at the desk wistfully.

"Go. Now." He pointed toward the stairs.

"Maybe you should carry me."

He fisted his hands in his hair. No, he should marry her, before he got so carried away by passion. He had to anyway; she may still be technically an innocent, but he had gone way too far. The thought of her breasts under his fingers, the heady cadence of her breathing, the earnest participation in the one endless kiss, made his pulse pound.

She took a step back into the room. She looked past him to the desk as if she would return to the scene of his transgression and seduce him into repeating it.

His control was about to snap. Earlier he had been thinking of murdering anyone who seduced her. As her guardian his sin was ten times worse. It would take so little for him to totally lose control. "Get. Out. Of. Here."

Her expression faltered, and she turned and hobbled toward the stairs. He wanted to call out to her and tell her everything was his fault, but he feared if he opened his mouth, what would come out would be a plea for her to stay with him, sleep with him, gift him with her innocence and sate his hunger, and never, ever leave him.

Using the handrail to pull herself up, Cecelia gingerly stepped on the side of her foot. The instep throbbed painfully, but she would have gladly suffered the discomfort to remain in Devin's arms. But he didn't want her there. He didn't want her at all. The venom in his voice when he told her to get out stung much worse than the cut in her foot.

Aunt Marsh poked him with her cane. "What's wrong with you, boy?"

"This isn't going well."

When Cecelia showed up in the morning room, on top of being bleary-eyed, she had been armed with a book and her spectacles. She hadn't met his eyes once. When he had tried to discuss what had happened in the library, she had brushed him off with a, "Don't mention it." She understood it was all a mistake.

"I don't know what I'm doing wrong." Perhaps his only mistake had been in not finishing what he had started.

Cecelia had already disappeared up to her attic before he had made it home late after spending several hours wandering around looking for the perfect gift. He had thought Aunt Marsh was asleep.

"Don't worry about it. She adores you."

"No, she doesn't."

Aunt Marsh harrumphed.

The door opened, and Barnes looked in. "Excuse me, milord, madam." He shut the door.

What the blue blazes? Devin shot out of his chair. He opened the morning room door. "What is happening, Barnes?"

"Miss Clemmons has a visitor. I've sent a maid up to fetch her." Barnes walked away as if it were normal for Cecelia to receive visitors after dark, at—Devin pulled out his watch—nearly seven-thirty at night.

Cecelia came down the stairs and shot him a tired look. She went down the stairs through the servants' quarters and out the kitchen. Devin followed her to the back of the house.

She walked through the garden to the servants' and tradesmen's gate at the back of the yard by his stables.

Barnes moved in front of the kitchen door before Devin made it across the room. "She won't be but a minute, milord. We keep an eye on her."

He stared out the kitchen windows at his ward and a man. Devin could see his dark hair and the despicable flash of the cad's smile in the dim light of the moon and what little light spilled from the surrounding houses.

Cecelia took the heavy purse from the shopkeeper. He had told her there was more money than he liked to keep around in his shop for fear of a robbery.

He reached out and patted her hand. "Only a couple more days. Then we'll 'ave to think on 'ow to keep our partnership going." He smiled his slick smile.

Cecelia wished she felt something, but she didn't. He seemed a nice man, but she didn't believe he really cared deeply about her. She wanted to say something, but she didn't want to force him to acknowledge the gifts before he was ready. The only thing she could think of was, "Thank you."

He touched his forehead. "The pleasure's been all mine." He nodded toward the house. "Who's the toff watching you?"

Cecelia turned and saw Devin clearly through the kitchen window. "My guardian."

"Interesting. Doesn't know who I am, does he?"

"I shouldn't think so."

"Don't tell him. Does he know you make the valentines?"

Cecelia shook her head.

"Well, I'm off before he decides to draw my cork." He leaned forward and brushed a kiss against her cheek. "Good luck."

The peck startled Cecelia. She put her hand against

her face. The shopkeeper disappeared into the darkness almost as if he were deliberately avoiding the light.

She still had her hand against her cheek as she entered the kitchen.

"Who the hell was that?" Devin thundered as she closed the door.

A scullery maid dropped a bowl, and the servants in the kitchen stared.

Cecelia was too tired to think of anything intelligent to say, "The Prince of Darkness."

"As your guardian, I demand to know who that man was."

"Milord," interjected Barnes.

Cecelia held up her hand. "My business partner."

"What?"

Cecelia took advantage of Devin's confusion to cross the room to the stairs leading up to the main part of the house. "My business partner. If you must know. I've started a business, and he sells my merchandise."

The servants stared, but they all knew she made valentines. A couple of the ones she had given the servants were tacked up on the kitchen walls. One would think Devin might notice, but then when had he ever entered his own kitchens before now?

Once she reached the ground floor, Cecelia ran toward the stairs and up to her room.

"Cecelia!" Devin had started after her, but a hand on his sleeve made him stop.

"Milord," said Barnes more urgently.

"What, Barnes?" Devin was impatient to be done with whatever his normally noninterfering butler had to say.

"There wasn't a delivery for Miss Clemmons today."

It took a moment for what Barnes said to soak in to his anguished thoughts. "What?"

Devin suddenly became aware of the stares of his servants. "Come upstairs, Barnes."

In the main hall, Devin was torn between racing after Cecelia and tearing apart the dressmaker who should have delivered the valentine and gift today. Better yet would be pouncing on the man at the back gate and ripping him to shreds. "Who was he?"

"No one important, milord. A shopkeeper, I believe."

"What's going on, Barnes?"

"I'm sure Miss Clemmons will confide in you when she's ready, sir."

"He kissed her."

Barnes gave him a skeptical look. "I'm sure you're mistaken, milord. About that delivery?"

Devin raked his hands through his hair and glanced up the stairs. This was not going well. Not going well at all.

"I'm not sure it makes any difference."

"It absolutely makes a difference, milord."

"My coat, if you would, Barnes."

Half afraid that Devin was summoning her downstairs to discuss this evening's events, Cecelia reluctantly answered the tap on her bedroom door.

Her maid stood on the other side, holding a large, flat box. "This just came, miss."

Had Mr. Hartley dropped it off after he had given her the money? Cecelia didn't even know his first name, and he had just kissed her cheek.

How was she going to get herself out of this pickle?

"Looks like a dress box."

Cecelia took the box and set it on her bed. "You might as well stay and get out my nightclothes."

Staring at the box as if it might contain poisonous snakes, Cecelia chewed her lip. She would have to return all these gifts to Mr. Hartley or at least reimburse him for the price. The gloves and bonnet she had worn; the pens, inks and paints she had used.

"Open it, do," said the maid.

Cecelia reluctantly loosened the bow and lifted the lid. She folded back the tissue paper. Wine-colored satin glistened under the card.

"Oh, how lovely," said the maid.

Cecelia lifted the valentine out and turned it over; all the while she noticed it was not just material, but a bodice with a gathered bosom and a fully made dress.

The signature read:

Like a fine wine, you are worth waiting for.
Your Valentine

But the word *waiting* had an odd smear of ink as if the writer had been anything but willing to wait.

Her maid, obviously impatient with Cecelia's sluggishness, pulled the evening gown from the box and held it out. "Oh, try it on, do. Stand up so I might unfasten your dress."

In a state of near shock, Cecelia stood up. How could Mr. Hartley have had a dress made up in what looked like her size? Could he know the dressmaker Devin had arranged to come to the house? The idea was too preposterous for even her to believe.

Her maid had pulled the new dress over her head before Cecelia realized what the girl was doing. "No, my nightgown."

"You have to try this on. It is so lovely."

Cecelia resigned herself to learning if the gown fit. It explained the dressmaker taking, what Cecelia had thought at the time, too many measurements for the simple walking dress she was having done.

Had Devin ordered this gown made?

As the maid fastened the tapes and pinned the closures, Cecelia realized the dress fit her perfectly.

"We should have a hairdresser come and do your hair, miss. I'm not very good with it myself."

She stared at her looking glass, seeing the elegant

drape of the simply styled gown. There was none of the fuss and furbelows of current marriage-mart-miss fashions, but the dress was beautiful in its simplicity, with only a small demitrain and a gathered bodice that dipped lower than Cecelia was used to wearing.

In a haze, Cecelia reached for the door and flew down the stairs to the morning room.

Only Mrs. Marsh was inside.

"Where's Devin?"

"I believe he's gone home to his quarters," said Mrs. Marsh. "What a lovely gown, Cecelia. Are you going out this evening?"

Cecelia shook her head.

"That color is quite good on you, brings out the blossoms in your cheeks."

Cecelia shook her head again and backed out the door. She pressed her hands against her burning cheeks. It just couldn't be Devin. Could it?

For the second day in a row, Cecelia didn't show up at the breakfast table. Devin pressed his palm against his forehead. Was she avoiding him? Or was she in her attic hideaway?

He finally summoned Barnes to check on her.

"Miss Clemmons's maid informs me that her mistress is still abed," said Barnes upon his return.

Devin pushed back from the table, unable to linger any longer over his cold coffee. "Have her sent a tray when she wakes." He folded the *Morning Post*. "Put this on it."

There was a small piece on the unknown girl found in the Thames. Apparently a few people, including him, had stepped forward with funds to give the girl a decent burial. Cecelia would want to read about it.

He paced the morning room like a caged animal until it was time for him to head for Parliament. He had no choice but to continue with his plan of valentines and gifts. He was almost totally convinced he was doomed to fail.

Except for that kiss in the library. In which case there was always plan two. If a woman could participate in a kiss like that, her affections must be engaged, and he could make short work of any resistance. But he didn't want her forced into a marriage with him. He wanted her to *choose* him.

And he wanted to kill that visitor of the night before last so there was no choice left but him. Which made absolutely no sense.

Cecelia woke late in the day and wondered if she had dreamed about the dress. She was so groggy from three sleepless nights of churning out her valentines and from fretting about the identity of her secret admirer, she didn't feel she could think straight.

A breakfast tray was brought to her, even though she hadn't requested it. She had barely eaten a bite of buttered eggs when her maid began hustling her into a day dress, because there was a visitor downstairs.

She entered the drawing room, and her gentleman friend of last year greeted her. Cecelia felt a wave of panic thread through her. Was it him, after all? Had he somehow learned the dressmaker was to visit and coerced the woman to measure for a dress he wanted to give Cecelia?

No, there was no way he could know her so well.

A few minutes later, she was more confused than ever. Her once spotty friend had come to tell her he was leaving England to take the Grand Tour, and he wished her well. She bid him a safe journey and happiness.

It couldn't be him. He hadn't even asked to write.

Could Devin have really gone to so much trouble to

persuade her to marry him? Could he have stood silently as she received gift after gift without a word to him?

Devin returned home for supper, and Cecelia watched him covertly. Mrs. Marsh chatted up a storm about absolutely nothing at all. By the time Mrs. Marsh and Cecelia had withdrawn to the morning room, Devin had exchanged no more than polite pleasantries with her. Was he waiting for her to acknowledge the gifts?

Was he waiting for Saint Valentine's Day tomorrow?

When Devin didn't join them in the morning room, Barnes informed her that he had left for his rooms across town.

Cecelia sat with Mrs. Marsh long into the evening. She felt almost useless as she had no more valentines to make. Her gift last night had been quite late, but when the clock struck eleven, she stopped waiting. No gift would be delivered this late at night. She trudged up the stairs to her bedroom, knowing nothing had arrived for her.

Disappointment weighed her down as she entered her bedroom . . . until she saw the box on the bed. Her heart galloped, and she tried to slow her frantic breathing.

Unable to contain herself, she ripped open the box. One of her newer cards with a poem she had composed about yearning for a touch of her lover's lips lay inside. Cecelia blushed as she reread it.

She turned it over.

What can I say? I yearn for more than your kisses, so this one is for me.

Yours,

Devin

She peeled back the tissue paper and discovered a quilted dressing gown with petal pink watered silk on the outside, and matching fur-lined, leather-soled house slippers. She folded back the edge of the dressing gown and discovered a filmy, nearly sheer, silk nightgown lay inside.

She shuddered as memories of the encounter in the library spilled out of the locked corner in her mind.

She pulled her feet up and hugged her knees to her chest. The dressing gown and scuffs were pretty and practical, but the nightgown was another story. And if he wanted *that,* why had he returned to his rooms so early? Besides, did his wanting *that* mean anything? She had seen him, well, not actually seen, but known him to do *that* with women he didn't care a fig about. So his wanting to bed her didn't mean he loved her, did it?

Hell, did he even really want to bed her? The other night she had all but offered herself to him, and he had been furious with her. He had sent her away.

Her chest began to hurt. She should have told him sooner he didn't need to marry her.

Cecelia looked wan and pale when she joined him in the drawing room following his summons. She perched on the edge of the sofa and twisted her hands in her lap.

As soon as Barnes shut the door, Devin stepped forward and said, "Happy Saint Valentine's Day, Cecelia."

He took the lack of a book and spectacles as a good sign, except she seemed disinclined to look in his direction. Which might be a good thing, for she might see how very uneasy he was. It wasn't every day that a man asked a woman to become his wife, especially not one as unpredictable as Cecelia.

He moved to stand in front of her and pulled the card from behind his back. He held it in front of her. She stared at it as if it might bite her. He placed it on her knees as he dropped to one of his.

"Cecelia, will you do me the honor of—"

"You don't have to marry me, Devin." Her forehead puckered, and her expression grew pinched.

"I don't think it's good form to interrupt in the middle of the proposal."

She turned the card around. But the message was inside this one, along with the ring tied with the ribbons threaded through the lace. "I made this."

He was surprised, but not surprised. It made perfect sense: the ribbons, the lace, the foolscap, the pasteboard, the inks and the paints. "Yes, and it's quite exquisite."

She pierced him with her dark brown eyes. "Did you know?"

"No, not entirely. May I continue?"

She dropped the card to the sofa. "I've built a successful business. I know that must shock you, but since my father left me penniless, I felt I must support myself somehow." She sprang up and paced across the room. "You see, I have earned well over five hundred pounds."

"A monkey, that much?" he murmured. Feeling rather stupid on bended knee in front of an empty sofa, he settled into the place she had just vacated. Actually, it was quite rude of him to sit while she stood, but under the circumstances, he felt vindicated.

"I know it must not sound like much to you, but it is more than enough for me to repay you for any expenses I may have generated in the last year, and enough for me to live on my own . . . modestly."

"Yes, extremely modestly," he agreed. He crossed one ankle over his knee and spread his arms across the back of the sofa. Cecelia wrung her hands. He had never seen her quite so panicked.

"Well, I have modest tastes."

"I know that."

She stopped pacing. "So you see, you may consider yourself relieved of all responsibility for me. I shall do quite well on my own. I will begin looking for a cottage to rent, and you shall be able to move back home."

"Would there be room for me in your cottage?"

"Devin!" She turned three different shades of red, one right after another, and then turned her back to him.

He moved off the sofa to stand behind her. "I should find it a come down to live in a cottage, but I should like to live with my wife."

"I'm telling you, you don't have to marry me."

"I never did *have* to marry you." He leaned over and brushed his lips against her nape. "The question has always been, would you marry me?"

Cecelia shivered. He put his hands on her shoulders and guided her back to the sofa. She allowed herself to be lead.

This time when he went down on bended knee, he laid his arm across her legs so she wouldn't get up. "I should quite like making it so I *have* to marry you, though."

She bit her lip.

He grinned at her. He didn't quite understand her objections, but he had hope he was getting to the bottom of them. "Was there some problem with the gifts? I wasn't quite sure about the music box, but . . ."

"I treasure that," she blurted out.

"I thought since you didn't like to waltz . . ." His words trailed off as an awful truth came to him. "You don't know how to dance, do you?"

She slowly shook her head.

"Bloody hell, Cecelia, I can't believe how dense I was."

"It's all right. I should have told you."

"I'll teach you."

She looked away at the wall and then the other wall, and then she blinked rapidly. He took her hand in his. "Come, Cecelia, what objection do you have to marrying me?"

A tear dripped down her cheek. "I can't believe you've worked so hard to convince me I should."

He wiped the tear away with his thumb. There was still some barrier he hadn't breached, but he waited patiently.

"You can't possibly love me," she said in a tiny voice.

Was that all she feared? "Have you ever known me to put so much effort into a seduction?"

She shook her head. "You've never had to."

Well, that was certainly true, but he had never wanted to before either. "Perhaps, you should read the card."

Cecelia shook as she picked up the card from the sofa. Her fingers nearly refused to cooperate as she opened the folded pasteboard to the slips of foolscap in between. A gold ring was threaded through one of the ribbons. She turned it over noticing the love knot had been retied in a slipknot.

"Read it."

She turned it back over and flipped to the last inside page.

I love you, Cecelia.

Devin

Her heart threatened to leap out of her chest. She risked meeting his intense blue gaze. His lazy grin was for once absent.

"You've changed me, and I don't think I could live without you, so say you'll be my wi—"

She pressed her lips against his, and he eagerly followed suit. Before she knew what he was about, he had scooped her up and plunked down on the sofa with her in his lap.

"If you don't say yes soon, I shall go mad."

"I don't think you've finished the question."

He clapped his hand over her mouth and laid her down on the sofa, twisting until his body covered hers. "Will you do me the honor of becoming my wife?"

He lifted his hand.

"Devin, not that I have much experience, but isn't this an odd position for a proposal?"

"Let's try this again. I love you. Will you marry me?"

"So in other words—"

He pressed his hand over her mouth again. "You have to say yes or no, Cecelia. Those are the rules."

Her heart pounded madly. Surely he could feel it with their bodies pressed so closely together. She knew she should believe in his love, but did he really love *her*? *Her*, Cecelia, the valentine card-making, bluestocking, dressed unfashionably in black? Or did he plan to change her into some fashionable tonnish creature she wasn't?

He lifted his hand slightly and cocked his head sideways.

She tried to turn away from his penetrating blue eyes, but couldn't bring herself to say no, to say yes, to say anything at all.

He gave her the slightest shake. "What objection? What makes you unsure?"

"I want to keep my business," she said in a timid whisper.

He pressed his forehead against hers. "Absolutely. Fine. Of course you should." He pulled back and looked at her lazily. "It makes you more . . ."

"Exasperating?"

"Well, yes that, but more"—he shrugged as if apologizing for his inability to say it better—"you."

"More me?" Tears threatened to spill out of her eyes. She blinked them back. He couldn't have said it any better.

"Don't you understand, Cecelia? I love you. Whether you're hiding in your attic, or in a book. I just—"

"Yes." For once, she would trust the messages of hope and love she wrote about so freely in her cards. "Yes, I will marry—"

He made it quite clear from that point on why he had chosen to propose lying on the sofa. It was quite some time before either of them was able to say anything more, but she managed to make out his disjointed murmurs, *"this afternoon"* and *"special license."*

Which sounded lovely to her and quite the best Saint Valentine's Day gift of all.

Love Letters

Patricia Waddell

Dear Reader:

The Victorian era was known for its love of the written word. Poets and their sonnets thrived, romantic novels found their place in literature, and valentine cards and letters became extremely popular.

Men and women exchanged these cards, which contained dedications of affection, and on occasion, even proposals of marriage. Young ladies, schooled in perfect penmanship, wrote eloquent verses, hoping to touch the hearts of their gentlemen friends.

The cards were embellished with symbols of birds, flowers and hearts. Lace, beads and ribbons were attached to the outside of the card to accent the personal note or verse to be found inside. The envelopes were often as elaborate as the cards, making it almost impossible to send them by post. Most cards were delivered in person or by courier.

Imagine what might happen if one of these private messages got delivered to the wrong person?

One

Sebastian Delacour Worthington, Viscount Sterling, stepped down from his rain-dampened carriage, oblivious to the heavy mist still clinging to the air. The gaslights, making the windows of the gentlemen's clubs that lined St. James Street glow in the chilly darkness, spilled over onto the wet cobblestones. Sterling had come to his club, as he did each Wednesday evening that Parliament was in session, to partake in an obligatory game of cards with the Duke of Morland and four gentlemanly friends. The weekly commitment had been going on for years, ever since the Viscount Rathbone, the youngest of the group, had lost his father. The old duke had taken it upon himself to oversee the lives of the five younger aristocrats, and none dared to gainsay him.

Sterling was the oldest of the lot. At thirty-six, he was still an upright figure, strong of frame with just enough gray at his temples to add a quality of distinction to his handsome face. He was tall, well over six feet, with impeccable posture, dark chestnut hair and startling green eyes that looked at the world but hid his reaction to what he saw.

Unlike his four friends waiting inside, Sebastian had been married. Shortly after inheriting his title, he had proposed marriage to the stunning Kathryn Belmont, niece to the fourth Duke of Morland. It had been a wonderful marriage, but a disastrously short one. His lovely Kathryn had died doing her best to bring his heir into the world. He had given his heart to his gentle young wife, then willingly allowed it to be taken to the grave. He had mourned his bride for almost three years, living monkishly until he had finally taken a mistress, whom he called upon twice a week. The regularity of his visits paralleled his weekly card game at Brook's. He visited his mistress, discreetly housed near Shatesbury Avenue in the theater district, every Tuesday and Friday. At times, Sterling wasn't sure which obligation stirred more enthusiasm, playing cards with his friends or bedding the dark-eyed Mirabel. Recently, he found himself performing both tasks with a vague sense of ennui.

Sebastian dispatched the carriage, then turned to climb the wet stone steps and enter Brook's. The club wasn't the oldest of London's gentlemanly retreats, that honor being reserved for White's, but it was exclusive and conservative, although its history belied its current reputation. In years past it had been said that the peerage had often wagered its very existence on a game of chance, referring to the gambling exploits of Brook's previous members. The club was still known to have some of the highest staked, respectable games in town.

Handing off his hat and gloves to one of the club's footmen, followed by his Talma cloak with its black quilted collar, Sterling strolled across the tiled floor and into the main salon. As expected, he found four of the night's players waiting. Marshall Hanley Bedford, the Marquess of Waltham, a strikingly intelligent man who had recently inherited his father's title, along with Norton Russell Foxhall, the Earl of Granby, William Fitch Minstead, the Earl of Ackerman, affectionately called Fitch by his closest friends, and Benjamin Edward Exeter, Viscount Rathbone, the most notable rogue among them. While Sterling had attended Eton several years prior to the descent of his four friends upon the esteemed establishment, then gone on to further his education at Oxford, the other four lads had all schooled together. Eton, then Cambridge, had felt the sting of their wild and adventurous ways.

"Good evening, Sterling," Bedford said, coming to his feet and motioning for a steward to bring his friend's customary glass of port. "How are you?"

"As he always is," quipped Exeter, "looking respectfully bored out of his skin."

"The proper amount of boredom is said to be good for the soul," Sterling countered nonchalantly. "You might try the mundane side of life every so often, Exeter. From what I've heard, a little rejuvenation wouldn't hurt you. The widow Downley is known to cast her lovers aside if their daily performance becomes lacking."

Marshall Bedford, the Marquess of Waltham, and the handsomest of the lot, laughed out loud. "That will teach you to tangle with Sterling."

The viscount accepted the reprimand with his customary charismatic smile. "I fear, the widow is the one who's in need of rejuvenation. I left her sleeping like a sated babe not too long ago."

Sterling didn't press the point. If any of the men sitting around the salon table could ride a woman into exhaustion, it was Exeter. The man had an insatiable sexual appetite, one his friends were certain would eventually bring about his untimely demise. One day the viscount would satisfy his hunger with the wrong woman and find himself climbing out a window, bare-ass naked, while the lady's husband took aim and fired.

"The duke should be arriving soon," Fitch said. His remark brought a somber expression to Exeter's face.

Fitch was a second son, the only one among the

group, having inherited his title after serving in the Crimean. He had survived the bloody war, thinking to return and take over the running of several of his father's estates. But like Sterling, fate had dealt him an unexpected hand. The eldest Minstead brother had died from typhoid three months after assuming the designation of earl. Once the liveliest of the group, the current Earl of Ackerman was now serious minded.

"I wonder what old Morland would say if he walked into the club one Wednesday to see none of us about?" The question came from Exeter.

His friends cast him a censuring look. The duke had known each of their fathers. They had inherited the amity, and although each sometimes felt Morland overused the friendship to intervene unnecessarily into their lives, none of them would dare to denounce him. The duke was a cantankerous old man with ironclad principles and biting opinions, but he was, and would continue to be, their staunchest ally.

For Sterling, he was family. It was the duke who had stood next to him the day he had buried his lovely Kathryn, and the duke who had poured the first of many glasses of port the night following his niece's funeral. Sterling wasn't sure he could have survived delegating his wife and unborn child to the Worthington family plot if not for the old man. Morland was as steadfast as he was unreasonable at times, a friend Sterling valued above others he had gained in his lifetime.

"So, Sterling, will you decline another invitation to Lady Goodall's Valentine ball?"

Sebastian set his glass down and leaned back in the tufted leather chair facing the mahogany table. At times, he wished he could share his friends' enthusiasm for the social swirl of London, but there was no enthusiasm in his soul nowadays.

"There are sure to be ladies aplenty." Exeter added his

remark to the question posed by the Earl of Ackerman. "Lots and lots of pattering hearts and fluttering eyelashes. A gentleman's dream come true, if he's careful to avoid the watchful gaze of the predatory mothers who lurk in the shadows, ready to pounce on the first unfortunate soul who passes by."

Sterling smiled, but the expression didn't reach his eyes. His smiles rarely did these days. His firm lips curved upward, but real smiling had been beyond him for a good many years. He was content in his life, mundane as Exeter may view it. Titled, wealthy enough to afford anything he wished and practical enough to realize that life wasn't always joyous, he had come to terms with the loneliness that had overwhelmed him since Kathryn's death.

Now he did his duty, attending the House of Lords, overseeing his estates, playing cards each Wednesday night despite his frequent inclination to remain at home.

"I've no interest in pattering female hearts," Sterling remarked. Raising his glass, he sipped on the rich port he drank as routinely as he played cards with the duke.

"Why the hell not?" Exeter demanded arrogantly. "Mirabel's beautiful, but mistresses can be boring after a while. How long have you been attending the lovely lady? Five years now. I can't imagine shedding my trousers for the same woman for five years. How do married men do it?"

"It's easy enough when you find the right woman," Sterling told him. The somber tone of his voice brought an end to the conversation. It went without saying that he would decline Lady Goodall's invitation, the same way he had declined it for the last several years.

Blessedly, the Duke of Morland chose that moment to enter the club, preventing any further remarks from the young Viscount Rathbone. The men came to their feet, each greeting the elderly duke with a respective nod of his head. Sterling held out his hand. "It's good to see you, Morland."

"Damn weather has my bones aching," the fourth Duke of Morland replied in a gruff, grumbling tone. He was a tall, somewhat handsome man. His late wife had been exuberant where the duke was skeptical, impetuous where he was cautious, yet they had shared a surprisingly happy marriage. One that had denied them children. His title would pass to an obscure nephew in the north, but not too soon. The Duke of Morland was far too stubborn to die before his ninetieth birthday. "The south of Spain, that's where a man of my age belongs this time of year. Ought to take myself there."

None of the men replied. The duke would no more desert his seat in Parliament than he would forsake his family name. It was simply his nature to complain about anything and everything. The day he stopped, they would all be pallbearers.

Once the majordomo of the club had seen to the duke's coat and hat, he opened the doors of the private room that was reserved for the six men. The card table's dark wood top gleamed in the gaslight. A matching sideboard was stocked with brandy, port, the Irish whiskey Exeter preferred when he was winning, a rare occasion, but one nevertheless planned for, and a box of imported Caribbean cigars. Six black leather chairs circled the table. Three decks of cards, still boxed, were stacked neatly beside a silver ashtray. Caldwell, the majordomo, carried one box of cards to the table, placing them within the duke's reach. Morland always dealt the first hand.

It was nearing the stroke of midnight before Sterling gathered in his winnings and bid his friends good night. Pulling up his collar, he stepped into his carriage and

with a tap of his walking stick against the roof signaled
the driver to take him home. Once there, he retired to
the library, his custom after playing cards. He rarely took
to his bed before two in the morning. Dismissing his
valet for the night, he poured himself a drink, then
slumped into a wing-backed armchair, facing the fire.
The embers glowed in the grate, the ashes piling high
and ghostly gray as he stared into the dancing flames.

He felt tired. Bone-weary tired. Tired of life, tired of
the day-to-day routine that brought contentment, but
never satisfaction. Listening to Exeter and Bedford, both
men of pleasure, go on and on about Lady Goodall's ball
had nearly tested his patience. Why? Because he felt a
compulsion, a desperate need to reach beyond his mo-
notonous life, to touch once again the excitement of his
youth. But how?

He couldn't turn back the clock that ticked methodi-
cally in the foyer, its soft chimes echoing throughout the
empty house. He couldn't bring Kathryn and his child
back from the dead. Without an heir, and lacking a male
sibling or cousin to inherit, his title and estate would re-
vert to the crown upon his death, to be held or gifted to
another as the sovereign saw fit. The prospect wasn't one
that brought him joy. The Worthington family name was
old and honored, one he would be proud to pass on to
his children. But gaining a legal heir required a wife,
and Sebastian wasn't inclined to marry a second time.

Across Hyde Park, near the entrance to Kensington
Gardens, Rebecca Elizabeth Lowery lay in her bed, eyes
open, staring at the ceiling. She should be exhausted
after an evening of dancing, but she was too excited to
sleep. Lord Sheppard had asked her to dance, more
than once, an important indication that he was seriously
pursuing her.

Rebecca had come to London with the same hopes and dreams that filled most young ladies' heads. With a resigned sigh that she might have truly met the man of her dreams, she closed her eyes and tried to rest. Newland, it wasn't proper to use his given name in public, but she could think of him in such a private way without breaching the strict code of etiquette forced upon young ladies by society, was rakishly handsome. Tall, with silvery blond hair and deep-set blue eyes, he was eligible and recently titled. What more could her family want?

What Rebecca wanted was for the handsome young man to get on with things. She had spent the last two years in the country, restricted at the family estate, too young to think about marriage according to her doting father. Innocent of anything but her own parents' contented marriage, she longed for one of her own.

Newland Sheppard would make a very respectable husband.

She was almost certain that she loved him. Wasn't his smile dashing and his manner charismatic? Hadn't her heart skipped erratically when he had asked her to dance that evening? And hadn't he boldly whispered that he would be hard pressed to find a more lovely lady in all of London? He must return her affection.

Thoughts of her future wedding gown turned to worry over the dress she would wear to the upcoming annual Valentine ball held by Lord and Lady Goodall. Like her unattached female peers, Rebecca had been fitted with a new wardrobe the moment her family had arrived in London. There was the sapphire satin, trimmed with white feathers and pearl buttons. It was the most daring of her gowns. Perhaps too daring, she decided. She was anxious for Lord Sheppard to kiss her, but it wasn't wise to tempt a man beyond his gentlemanly control, at least not right away. The lavender silk would do nicely, she decided as her hand covered a deep yawn. Yes, the lavender silk. And she would paint periwinkles on her white bone fan. She liked periwinkles, and everyone knew they symbolized an early friendship. Periwinkles wouldn't outrage anyone, and they suited the lavender gown better than almond blossoms or roses.

Rebecca's last conscious thought was that she would enter her expectations into her journal the following morning. She had taken to keeping a diary of Lord Sheppard's unofficial courtship, wanting to retain each and every detail. One day, when she was much older and advising her own daughters in the ways of love, she could read the romantic words she had penned with Lord Sheppard in mind.

Slipping into her dreams, Rebecca smiled. Life would be perfect once Newland proposed. They would have the customary engagement, then a lavish wedding. She would wear pearls woven into her hair and her grandmother's sapphire necklace. Newland would wait proudly at the altar, the perfect gentleman eager to greet his bride.

Two

Restless because the weather, a dreary mixture of rain and snow, prevented her and her mother from shopping, Rebecca looked toward the window. It was the eighth day of February; less than a week would pass before the Valentine ball. Lord Sheppard had happened upon her and Helen St. Clair, riding in the park the previous morning, and tipping his hat had inquired if she would be attending the gala event. A shy, well-rehearsed smile had been her reply.

But six days seemed like forever, closeted in the house as she was. Her discontentment turned physical, and she began to pace the carpeted room, stopping here and there to inspect one of the porcelain figurines her mother had collected over the years. Gently touching the image of a French ballerina, Rebecca wondered what it would be like to dance alone on a stage with every eye in the audience trained upon her limbs. It was a scandalous thought.

Her parents would be aghast at what she had imagined lately. Dreamy images of a man's body entwined with her own, of soft kisses and gently whispered words, of feeling like a woman instead of a pampered child. It was a vague passage, the one she made in her dreams on a nightly basis, filled with unanswered questions and urgent needs that seemed to spring forth from the very core of her body. Last night she had awoken from a dream, but the man had been a shadow, a phantom come to haunt and tease.

"Too many stewed tomatoes at dinner," she mumbled under her breath as she glanced at the clock, willing it to tick faster, to spin until it was time to dress for dinner and perhaps see Newland again.

Rebecca fidgeted with the lace at her cuffs, then sighed out loud. She had to do something. The white lace brought an idea to mind, and she smiled. Leaving the parlor, she hurried toward the sewing home at the back of the house. A valentine card. She would send Newland a card, decorated with periwinkles, like the ones she had painted on her fan, and beads and a dab of lace. She would say something innocent but provocative, the sort of thing that would start him to thinking. Being twenty and one, she couldn't wait forever for the man to get up the courage to propose.

Customarily, only engaged couples exchanged cards, but it was common knowledge that Lord Sheppard had been extremely attentive to her of late, so it wasn't totally improper to write a short verse of friendship. She would pay the cook's son to deliver it. A copper should get the note to Sheppard's door without delay.

It was late afternoon before Rebecca was satisfied with the card. It had taken her almost an hour to think of what to write. She mustn't seem overly eager, but yet she wanted Lord Sheppard to know that he had touched her heart. Unsure if she was being too bold, or not bold enough, Rebecca took a deep breath and wrote what she considered sufficient words to put Lord Sheppard's mind to working.

The envelope used to shield the elegant valentine was H. Dobbs & Company's best stock. Once it was sealed, Rebecca painstakingly sketched a nosegay of white and blue periwinkles on the left corner of the envelope. The chalk was soft and colorful, giving the design an authentic touch. When she was satisfied that Newland would recognize her favorite flower, she penned his name in a bold, ladylike fashion across the front of the cream-colored parchment, then tucked it safely between the folds of an embroidered tablecloth she had been stitching on for weeks and carried it upstairs.

Tomorrow she would take a coin from the small box she kept in her dresser and send Cook's son scampering toward Mayfair.

The morning was a relatively quiet one. Sebastian was at the breakfast table, reading the *Court Journal*: the various speculations as to how the queen was dealing with the death of her beloved Albert, how long she might be expected to remain at Balmoral, and the usual list of current legislation being debated in Parliament.

Carrying his teacup to the window, he looked out at the gray nothingness that had overtaken the city. The weather was still severe. Hours of sleet, falling continuously during the night, had covered the streets with a treacherous layer of ice. There were few carriages about, the horses unable to hold their footing on the slick cobblestones. A cold mist of rain was falling now, too cold to wash away the ice, adding to the misery instead of relieving it.

Sebastian continued to look out the window, feeling a connection with the weather, the coldness, the bleakness of it all. He wasn't due at the House of Lords until late afternoon. There were ledgers to be balanced, correspondence to be written. His steward was seeking his advice about the crops that would be planted once the snow had melted from the fields on his estate near Warwickshire, but Sebastian couldn't focus his thoughts on the upcoming spring. It seemed beyond reach with sleet covering the front steps and icicles hanging from the window ledges.

His thoughts drifted, back and forth, without attaining any real destination, much as his life had drifted the last years. He could, of course, take up the process of finding a new wife, of filling the nursery with a much needed heir, but beyond the hope of leaving a living legacy behind, a son to carry on the Worthington name, there was no joy in the thought.

Having held one loving woman in his arms, Sebastian couldn't imagine sharing his bed with a perfunctory wife. In fact, his groin couldn't find an ounce of energy whenever the thought crossed his mind. The possibility that he might be fortunate to find love a second time was squelched by the marriages he had seen of late. Few held any affection, based upon money and rank and the necessity of joining families to maintain that wealth.

"Pardon me, milord, but there's a messenger at the door. He insists on seeing you."

Sebastian turned to look at Dames. The efficient butler had come to him along with his father's title. A staunch, unwavering gentleman's gentleman, Dames ruled the household with an iron hand.

Hearing the enunciation Dames had used in saying *messenger,* Sebastian left the breakfast room and walked into the foyer. A young boy, no more than ten years of age, stood shivering in the hallway. His pants were streaked with muck and snow, his plaid cap dripping wet. His freckled nose was red from the cold, his lips almost blue.

"You have something for me, lad?" Sebastian inquired, holding out his hand.

The young boy hesitated, then nodded. "You be the lord?"

"I'm Sterling," Sebastian said, sensing the boy's reluctance. He looked as if he had slid all the way from . . . wherever in the world he had come. He watched as the lad twisted his bottom lip under his front teeth, as if he wasn't sure about something. Amber lashes dropped

over pale blue eyes, then lifted with a shrug of his youthful shoulders.

"Then, here it be," the young boy said, holding out an
envelope that had once been immaculate.

Sebastian looked down at the wet parchment. The
name was illegible, the envelope dampened beyond
recognition. When the boy had fallen, which he obviously had on his way to deliver the message, he must
have taken the envelope into the icy puddle with him.

"Dames, give the lad some hot cider and a sixpence
for his trouble."

"Yes, milord."

While Dames saw the soggy lad shuffled off to the
kitchen, Sebastian inspected the message. It was impossible to tell to whom it had been originally addressed.
The name had been obliterated by whatever mishap the
messenger had encountered. He broke the seal, then
stared down at the distinctively feminine penmanship.

The message was a valentine, unmistakably penned by
a whimsical young lady with a fascination for periwinkles.
White lace had been painstakingly attached as a border,
with a cluster of tiny blue beads forming the center of
each periwinkle blossom. Like the envelope, the writing inside the card was blurred, almost illegible, but
Sebastian could make out the word *Goodall*, which meant
the card could be an invitation to seek the young lady
out at the upcoming Valentine's Day ball, or perhaps a
more daring request for the intended gentleman to
meet her for a private kiss in the garden.

He studied the card for several minutes, intrigued by
its female influence and the unexplained reason it had
fallen into his hands. He was sure the card hadn't been
intended for him. Leaving the library, he sought out the
kitchen, but the young boy had gulped down his cider
and hurried out the back door, or so Cook informed

him. "The lad was in a right hurry," she said, her hands wrist deep in dough.

"I don't suppose anyone asked where or to whom he belongs?"

"The Lowerys, milord." Mrs. Hughes was a large-bosomed, robust woman in her late fifties. She was also the only female employed by the household. Dames tolerated her because she could prepare a tasty bread pudding. "'E's the cook's son, milord. Told me his mother might have a recipe or two to share, if I was interested."

"Thank you," Sebastian replied, sticking his finger into a bowl of apricot jam on his way out. Mrs. Hughes was preparing his favorite, a Manchester pudding. "I'll be sure to be home for dinner," he said, adding a smile to the remark before exiting the kitchen.

Returning to the library, he picked up the valentine. He knew of Lord Lowery, of his preference for his country estates and his conservative political views. Views he shared on most points. Did the man have a daughter? A daughter who planned on attending Lady Goodall's ball. Was the note an invitation to her lover? A daring verse, erased by melting snow and rain. And to whom should it have been delivered? There were several eligible young gentlemen in Mayfair. Apparently the cook's young son had either misread the name or had confused the addresses. Either way, Sebastian was now in possession of the card. If the card meant what he suspected, then a certain young lady was boldly soliciting the affection of a gentleman. The situation called for careful handling.

Knowing the romantic message had in all probability originated in the Lowery household, he could return the water-soaked card, using a reliable courier, or he could . . . What?

Attend the ball himself?

He glanced out the window. The mist had increased to a heavy rain. Holding the valentine in his hand, he felt a sense of expectation, as if the rain drenching the icy ground beyond the wrought-iron gate was somehow washing away the dull layer of dust he had allowed to settle upon his life since Kathryn's death.

Strolling to the door, he shouted for Dames.

"Yes, milord?"

"The invitation to Lord and Lady Goodall's ball. Where is it?"

"Your desk, milord," Dames said. Entering the room, he opened the appropriate desk drawer and withdrew the invitation, along with several others. "Will you be sending your regrets?"

"No," Sebastian announced. "I'll be attending the event. Please have Mr. Merrill clear my schedule accordingly."

Dames quirked a gray brow, but wisely declined making any comment about his employer's sudden change of heart. The butler was on his way out of the room, to send a message to the viscount's secretary, when Sebastian stopped him with another question.

"The ball isn't on Wednesday, is it?"

Dames read the invitation. "No, milord. The ball is to be this Friday."

"Good," Sebastian mumbled under his breath, then set about his normal morning's work, feeling unexpectedly revitalized.

Three

"Sterling," the Marquess of Waltham greeted his friend with a curious glance. "I didn't think you attended this sort of affair."

"I usually don't." Sebastian's gaze briefly scanned the crowded room. "I took Exeter's words to heart," he added as he accepted a glass of champagne from one of the many footmen servicing the room. "Thought a little adventure might spice up my life."

The marquess chuckled. "I wish I could say the same." His merriment quickly changed to a frown. "With my stepmother ill, I've been handed the task of seeing to Winnifred's virtue. This is the third ball in less than two weeks. Be grateful you don't have a younger sister attending the season. It's an exhausting duty. Haven't seen so many hungry young wolves since—"

"You were a hungry young wolf yourself," Sterling said.

"I'm not as young as I used to be, but my appetites haven't changed," Waltham replied, giving a young blonde a long, lingering stare. "The room is overflowing with prime females. Pity they're all looking for a husband."

The two friends were quickly joined by the exuberant Viscount Rathbone. "My eyes must be failing." He directed the remark to the marquess. "Is this the reclusive Viscount Sterling standing before me, much dressed, and joining in the festivities?"

"Enough," Sterling warned him good humoredly. "I

decided it would be more than rude to decline Lady Goodall's invitation four years running. Making an appearance, nothing more."

Exeter didn't believe him. Neither did the Marquess of Waltham. They both knew Sterling too well. If his unforeseen appearance meant their friend was finally ready to put his wife's death behind him, they couldn't be happier.

"Enjoy," Exeter said, offering up the ladies in the room with a spread of his hands. "But be careful. You're out of practice. Don't let their charming smiles fool you. Barracudas the lot of them. Beautiful but deadly."

"I'll be on guard," Sebastian assured him as he excused himself to say hello to the Earl of Granby, whom he had just seen stroll toward the billiard room.

He crossed the room, stopping now and then to say a word of greeting. His presence drew stares, explained by his long absence from the social world. His hostess was enthralled to have him, smiling as brightly as the diamonds that circled her puffy neck and fat fingers. It took several minutes to untangle himself from her enthusiastic welcome. Once he reached the billiard room, Sebastian turned to glance over his shoulder. He looked for some resemblance in the crush of young ladies, but saw none. Lord Lowery was a short, pudgy man with a wiry mustache and bushy brows; God forbid his daughter should look like him.

"Sterling," the Earl of Granby greeted him with a note of surprise. "Didn't expect to see you tonight."

"No one did," Sebastian replied. "Didn't think it would be such a shock. I do venture beyond the halls of Parliament on occasion."

"Can't say that I remember the last time," the earl mumbled under his breath as he set down the champagne he had been drinking and studied the billiard sticks inside a glass cabinet. "So why now?" he questioned in a clear voice.

"I'm not sure," Sebastian lied.

"Doesn't sound like you," Foxhall remarked. "You're the most sensible man I know. Always have a reason for doing whatever you do." He selected two billiard sticks, offering them up for selection. Sebastian took one, not really interested in billiards, but unsure how to excuse himself without increasing Foxhall's curiosity. The younger man eyed him suspiciously, then shook his head. "Don't tell me you're in the market."

"I'm not," Sebastian replied resolutely. Curious about Lowery's daughter, he meant to seek the young lady out, satisfy his inquisitiveness and be on his way. A firm warning might discourage her from putting future love notes into the hands of unreliable young lads.

It was more than an hour before Sebastian escaped the billiard room and rejoined the party. He recognized several of the matrons vigilantly watching over their daughters and nieces. Not knowing Lowery's wife, he had no way to identify the young woman who had occupied his thoughts for the last five days. Not until he spied a white fan spread wide to reveal a bouquet of hand-painted periwinkles. Sebastian found himself staring.

If the young lady wielding the ornate fan was Lord Lowery's daughter, then she most definitely had not inherited her father's lack of good looks. She was beautiful. Midnight black hair framed her face; dark brows and long, thick lashes accented eyes that were neither blue nor violet, but a sparkling combination of both hues. Her dress, a deep lavender with pearls adorning the bodice, was cut low enough to encourage a man's imagination. She was sitting on a narrow settee, its matching chairs occupied by two young ladies of similar age. All three were flushed from the heat of the room, generated from the crush of people, and their latest dance, a polka that had sent the dancers into gaily swirling circles about the floor.

Realizing that he was staring, Sebastian silently rebuked himself. It wasn't as if he had never seen a beautiful woman before. Kathryn had been lovely, with soft blond curls and bright blue eyes, and a sparkle in her laugh. Still, the young lady before him was intriguing.

Making sure his glances were brief and surreptitious, Sebastian spent the next hour studying the young lady who had penned the valentine hidden snugly in his jacket pocket. He discreetly learned her name was Lady Rebecca. It was almost midnight before she slipped from the ballroom, sliding through one of the doors that opened onto the gardens. Sebastian sought and found another exit, then stepped outside into the brisk night air.

Rebecca clutched her shawl snuggly around her shoulders. As hot as it was inside, it was near freezing under the pale light of the full moon. She took several long, deep breaths, thinking to return to the party. Newland had arrived a short time ago, unfashionably late, and she hadn't had a chance to gain his attention. Tingling with goose bumps brought on by the coldness and the anticipation of dancing a waltz with the charming Lord Sheppard, she turned back toward the house.

A man stepped out of the darkness, scaring her out of her wits.

"I beg your pardon," came a deep voice. "It wasn't my intention to frighten you."

The voice matched the tall, shadowy form blocking her path. Mysterious and unrecognizable. Rebecca could see the lights of the ballroom, but for all intents and purposes, they were surrounded by a chilly darkness that increased her trepidation.

"Lady Rebecca," he said, sweeping low into a graceful bow.

"Sir," she replied with stiff politeness, wondering how he knew who she was without her having the slightest idea who he might be. Etiquette demanded that he give her his name, yet he didn't seem in any great hurry to do so.

Sebastian stared down at her. He had the advantage of the moon being behind him, putting his face in shadow while hers was revealed in the shimmering light. She was even more beautiful up close. Young and temptingly well formed. His imagination ran rampant as he envisioned her with her hair down, a thick, glorious mane of raven black curls rippling over her naked shoulders and down her back. Her eyes, he would forever think of them as periwinkle blue, studied him, unsure but curious.

"I have something that belongs to you," he said, reaching inside his jacket to withdraw the valentine. He hadn't been entirely sure that she had actually written the card until this very moment, but looking at her in the moonlight, he sensed she was as bold in nature as she was in appearance.

Rebecca stared in disbelief as he held out what looked amazingly like the valentine she had sent to Newland. But it couldn't be.

"A young lad delivered it to my town house in Mayfair," the nameless gentleman told her. "I fear the messenger's encounter with an icy puddle resulted in the words being all but illegible. And the lace is slightly crushed."

Humiliated to the marrow of her bones, Rebecca took the card from his hand. There was not, no matter how she viewed the situation, any way she could escape embarrassment. How had her card ended up in this man's hands?

"I assume it was intended for another gentleman," Sebastian said, keeping his voice low, although he doubted anyone else had the gumption to brave the brisk northern wind. He was growing colder by the minute, which meant the young lady was close to frost bite. "I would have sent it on, had I known the man's name."

"Thank you," Rebecca replied, her teeth chattering as

she said the words. She stepped forward to pass the man, but he stood his ground, blocking her path. She looked up at him, realizing he was much taller than Newland. And older. His voice revealed that much.

"Not yet," Sebastian heard himself say. He shouldn't keep the lady outside, but once she left the garden, there would be no way to approach her unless he wanted to embarrass her further, which he didn't. His breath steamed before his face as he thought about kissing her. He felt his body warming despite the snow that clung to the evergreen branches and the brittle bite of the wind, felt his senses awakened by the sight of the young woman standing within his reach.

If she could think, she might find a way out of this mess, but Rebecca couldn't seem to think. Never in her life had she been more aware of a man's presence. The authority in his voice held her in check. He believed he had reason to block her path, to imply that she owed him something. An apology, of course, but she wasn't sure how one apologized for such a gross error. He had said the note had been all but illegible, so the few words she meant for Newland couldn't have offended him.

"I'm sorry to have caused you an inconvenience," she said, gathering her shawl more closely. "Please accept my apology."

"None is needed. However, I will rest more easily if you promise to forsake valentines and use your eyelashes and fan to lure a man. There's less chance of the wrong one receiving the message."

As a reprimand it worked wonders. "You overstep yourself, sir!"

"A warning is all I'm giving you," Sebastian said, realizing he had meant to deliver it with a fatherly voice. But he wasn't feeling fatherly. For the first time in years, he felt lustful and eager. Too eager.

He had been a fool to follow her into the garden, a

fool at his age to let the wide-eyed gaze of a young girl get to him. But he couldn't deny his reaction. The soft, silken sheen of her hair in the moonlight, the warm tones of her voice, and the promise of sweet innocence in her eyes were responsible for the wild thoughts.

"Perhaps, I should warn you," Rebecca said, drawing back her shoulders and raising her chin. "My father will not look kindly upon me being assaulted in the garden."

He laughed, low and soft. He wasn't fool enough to think she wouldn't scream if he kissed her the way he wanted to. But he couldn't let the challenge in her words go unanswered. "Nor, do I suppose, would he look kindly upon his daughter sending love notes to Mayfair."

Her eyes narrowed, then sparked. "It was *not* a love note."

"Then, what was it? An invitation for a gentleman to come to a ball, an encouragement for him to meet you in the garden . . . in the moonlight?"

Sebastian couldn't explain his sudden anger any more than he could explain the lust that was riding him. The warning he had meant to deliver turned into a lesson as he pulled her into his arms and sealed her mouth before she had a chance to scream.

Vastly more experienced than the innocent young lady in his arms, Sebastian used his expertise and the shock of the kiss to quickly bring her under control. His lips, hard but gentle, moved over hers. Since she had been about to protest, he had caught her with her lips parted. The additional shock of having his tongue gently invade her mouth was enough to make her go limp in his arms. Sebastian pressed on, gathering her more closely, letting the heat from his body seep into her cold skin, warming her as only a man could warm a woman.

Rebecca had never known a man's kiss, and this man's was her undoing. He sipped at her mouth, his tongue dipping and teasing, his lips warm, his hands holding her around the waist, firmly but tenderly, his arms imprisoning hers against his body. She had never imagined it could be like this. It was wonderfully exciting, an adventure into the unknown. She felt as if she was floating, yet firmly anchored to him.

In the back of her mind she knew she should pull away. But even as her mind called out in alarm, her body responded. His mouth was fierce, but gentle. His touch demanding, but painless as his arms locked around her. The man deserved to have his face slapped. No, he deserved worse. Much worse. But she couldn't gather the wits or the strength to inflict any harm, and his total possession of her senses prevented her from saying anything.

Sebastian feasted leisurely, savoring the taste of innocence, the softly curved body pressed tightly against his own. She was much too young, a well-bred lady, ignorant in the ways of men, but logic had little effect on his actions. He kissed her until he was in agony, hard and heavy, hot and ready to introduce her to the next level of passion, then lack of air and what little common sense he could still muster forced him to end the kiss.

Rebecca slumped against him, her cheek resting against the starched front of his shirt just above a silk waistcoat. She took a deep breath and inhaled the scent of him. She had never been this close to a man before, had no idea how strong their arms could embrace a woman, no concept of how marvelous a kiss could be.

She shook her head and wiggled free of his arms. She didn't even know the man's name! Despite the humiliation of a stranger presenting her card, despite the delicious sensations his kiss had created, her hand lifted. He grabbed her wrist before her open palm could connect with his face.

"None of that," he said, his voice deeper than before. Softer.

"How dare you!" she hissed. Her shawl had come away

from her shoulders. She gathered it close, clutching it with a trembling hand. He was still holding her right wrist, his grasp as gentle and firm as his embrace had been. "Who are you?"

"The man who received your valentine." Sebastian wasn't sure why he wasn't ready to divulge his identity. He had nothing to hide. And there was little possibility that the young lady would go rushing to her father. If she did, she would have more than an ill-delivered message to explain.

"Go inside, before you catch a chill," he said, releasing her hand and stepping back. "And stay inside. A moonlit garden is no place for a lady unless she's properly chaperoned."

Oh! He sounded like her father. But he wasn't that old. She let her gaze sweep over him, but all she could see was the tall silhouette of a man framed by the moon's pale light. But she had felt much more. His strength, his gentleness. She knew his scent and his taste, but she still didn't know his name.

"A true gentleman would announce himself. He wouldn't just snatch up a lady and kiss her senseless," Rebecca declared, her own boldness returning.

Sebastian smiled. "A true lady doesn't give a gentleman a chance to *snatch her up.*"

"You dare to insult me." Her chin lifted despite the knot forming in her stomach. She was sure to be missed if she didn't return to the party soon, and it was freezing outside, although she didn't seem to feel the cold as acutely now.

"A man dares much in his life." He could see her eyes glaring in the moonlight. God, she was beautiful. Fire and moonlight, innocence and pride. A girl waiting to become a woman.

This wasn't the time or the place, and he was even more of a fool to want it to be.

"Go back to the party, Lady Rebecca. While you still can." He stepped to the side, clearing her path.

Rebecca was innocent, but she wasn't dim-witted. The warning in his voice was one even she could understand. Saying nothing more, she hurried up the path to the veranda and, without looking back, went inside.

Sebastian watched her go in a flurry of lavender silk and female indignation. A remnant of snow crunched beneath his shoes as he stooped to pick up the card she had dropped. Smiling smugly, he returned it to his pocket, then strolled unhurriedly behind her.

Rebecca took a deep breath before slipping back into the ballroom. She blushed with a sense of guilt and stole a look around her. Had anyone seen her leave? Did they know she had been in the garden with a man? That she had been kissed? It didn't seem so. The faces she encountered on her way across the room showed no sign of censure, no lifting of brows, no matronly scowls to scold.

She rejoined her friends, Helen St. Clair and Elizabeth Bentley.

"Where have you been?" Helen asked. "Lord Sheppard has arrived."

"I needed some fresh air," Rebecca replied, surprised that she could maintain her composure after experiencing such a wicked kiss from an unknown man. "It's dreadfully warm in here."

"Oh, here he comes," Helen whispered, hiding her words behind a lacy blue fan.

Rebecca looked up to find Lord Sheppard approaching. He was smartly dressed in black trousers and a black evening jacket, his blue eyes gleaming as a smile came to his face. *How handsome he is, and how proper,* Rebecca thought, as he bent into a graceful bow before her. So unlike the dreadful man who had just accosted her in the garden.

"Would you honor me with a waltz, Lady Rebecca?" he asked, knowing full well she wouldn't refuse him.

As if his inquiry had spurred the musicians into action, the strains of a waltz began to fill the air. Accepting his outstretched hand, Rebecca allowed herself to be led onto the dance floor.

"You look lovely tonight," Newland whispered as he placed his right hand at the center of her waist. They began to dance, maintaining the proper distance between their bodies as they turned and dipped in time with the music.

Rebecca smiled, but regardless of how Newland's compliment pleased her, she couldn't shake the memory of how another man's arms had felt holding her so much closer to his person. Enjoying the waltz, because she truly enjoyed dancing, she tried to keep her expression light and her gaze centered on the diamond stickpin holding her partner's cravat in place. Her effort was in vain as Newland guided her through the dance. No matter her resolve, Rebecca couldn't forget the blistering heat of her first kiss. It was as if the fire of it was still warming her body. So much so, that when the dance ended, Lord Sheppard suggested a glass of punch to cool her flushed face.

Why wasn't she delighted by Newland's gracious attention? Why were her eyes scanning the room, hoping to find a tall gentleman upon whom she could cast the blame of her distraction? Why did she want to know his name so desperately? There was little recourse she could take, except to hope that the man would be content with his outrageous victory. If her parents learned of the valentine . . . Oh, my God, she had dropped it in the garden!

It had fallen from her hand when he had pulled her

into his arms. She had to retrieve it, to make sure no one else discovered her folly as he had discovered it.

"Is something amiss?" Newland asked, giving her a questioning look.

"No. Nothing," she assured him. She gave the doorway across the room a quick glance. She couldn't excuse herself, then march out the door. Newland would be sure to follow, and this time it was the last thing she wanted. "Parties can be so exhausting," she mused aloud, playing the role of a faint-hearted lady.

"Then, we shall sit out the next dance," he told her. "I'll bring you something cool to drink."

He left her standing in front of a cherrywood-framed settee upholstered in deep burgundy velvet. Rebecca fluttered her fan, suddenly disliking the periwinkles and vowing to paint over them at the first opportunity. As soon as Newland disappeared into the crowd, she took a hurried look around her, then walked down the hall, hoping to find an exit that would take her back into the garden. She had to get that card, illegible or not.

A shaft of light brightened a half-closed door. She peered inside. The room appeared to be empty, the fire prepared earlier by the staff then forgotten. Flickering light danced over the carpet, long, golden fingers reaching into the center of the room, leaving the corners in darkness. The gas fixtures had been turned down. She stepped inside, easing the door closed behind her. A deep breath filled her lungs as she saw the French doors. Beyond the frosted glass she could see the evergreens that lined the garden walk. Her hand was reaching for the brass knob, when a voice stopped her. It came from the dimmest corner of the room, and it sounded very familiar.

"I see my warning was in vain?"

Rebecca whirled around to face her accuser. Again, he was cloaked in shadows, and once again she felt an unmistakable thrill race up and down her spine. But this time it wasn't fear. It was anger.

"Another rendezvous in the moonlight?" Sebastian asked as he stood up from the comfortable armchair he had been sitting in. His brandy glass was empty. His intentions, until the pretty young lady had posed into the room, had been to call for his coat and hat and bid the evening adieu. "I would have thought our earlier encounter would have diminished your romantic notions."

A sixth sense warned her to keep her temper in check, but she was too upset over being discovered a second time to do more than brush the mental warning aside. "The problem with romantic notions, sir, is that there always seems to be a man about to bash them against the rocks."

"A candid reply," he said with a hint of humor to his voice. "And yet, I find you once again seeking the garden."

Rebecca stiffened her shoulders. There was little she could say but the truth. "I dropped the card. I meant to retrieve it."

"This card?" Sebastian said, withdrawing it from his jacket pocket.

Rebecca took a step forward and held out her hand. "If you'd be so kind."

At the moment, Sebastian wasn't feeling the least bit kind. He had spent the last half hour getting himself under control, letting the brandy ease his nerves while he had forcefully commanded his body to return to its normal disinterested state. The brandy hadn't worked. He was stilled aroused. More so now that Lady Rebecca had made a second appearance.

"I think I'll keep it as a memento," he replied casually, returning the card to his pocket.

Rebecca was caught between outrage and flattery. "The card was never intended for you, sir. As you well know," she stated, wishing he would step into the light so she could see him.

"Then, for whom?" he asked. "You never said."

Knowing Newland would come searching for her if she didn't return quickly, she glanced at the door she had foolishly closed behind her. Perhaps, she could bluff her way out of the room. The man might be arrogant, but he couldn't be such a fool as to think brows wouldn't be raised if they were caught alone. "Lord Sheppard is pouring me punch. I have to get back."

"Ahhh, so it's Sheppard." Sebastian recognized the name, but knew nothing of the man.

"My father is Lord Alexander Lowery," she said, hoping to intimidate him.

"I know who your father is," Sebastian said, stepping out of the shadows.

Rebecca swallowed nervously as he made his appearance known. Calm, green eyes appraised her. Thick, wavy hair, chestnut brown or perhaps darker, was flecked with silver at the temples. He was older than she by a good fifteen years, but not so old as to be in his dotage. Tall, with a somber quality about his features, he was still a handsome man. As the solid lines of his body emerged from the dark corner, a body she had become personally acquainted with earlier in the evening, she couldn't help but admire his posture. As straight as an English oak he stood, staring at her with a heavy, predatory gaze that made her heart flutter and her palms grow damp.

She had never had a man look so blatantly at her before. And she couldn't understand the deep, inner knowledge that she was attracted to him. He was much too old, she decided, no matter his handsomeness. Even in the dim light, she could see the gray at his temples. Of course, it was acceptable for a young woman to marry a man who was her senior.

Marry!

She didn't even know his name.

"And you, sir, are . . . ?"

"My name is Sebastian," he said in that deep, soft voice that had raked over her nerves in the garden, leaving them tingling. "Sebastian Delacour Worthington. Viscount Sterling to those of the peerage."

The name and title meant little to her. But then, she had been in the country most of her life. This was her first season, her first encounter with those beyond her father's close circle of friends.

"My lord," she said. Her father was an earl, so she didn't dip into a curtsy. Nor did she show him any other form of respect. Instead, she scowled up at him, counting the seconds, knowing she had tempted fate far too much already and praying that no other guest would seek out the dimly lit room.

"My Lady Rebecca," he replied, stepping closer.

Oh, how he wanted to kiss that scowl from her mouth, to have her clinging to him again, breathless and aroused by his attention, boldly wanting more. But then, it was a bold night. He had stepped across the threshold of the Goodall's home knowing he was inviting that which should be left alone, sensing that whatever the night brought, it wouldn't be the boring evening he would have otherwise spent alone.

Rebecca did her best to ignore the veiled threat in the viscount's voice, but it was there, telling her if she didn't flee the room, she could expect another kiss. Yet she didn't move.

And why had he addressed her as *"My* Lady Rebecca," as if he had some right of authority over her. Thinking it pure arrogance, Rebecca turned to leave, but his hand reached out to stop her, closing over her upper arm, upon her full-length white gloves and just below the sleeve of her dancing gown. The heat was incredible. His fingers were strong, his grasp inescapable, as he turned her to face him.

"Perhaps a kiss would persuade the card from my possession."

She eyed him wildly as her heart started to pump so fast she feared she might faint. "A kiss? You dare to think—"

"As I said before, a man dares much in his life. As do impetuous young ladies upon occasion. Come, Lady Rebecca, kiss me and the card will be yours."

Astonished by his own audacity, Sebastian found himself unable to release her. One more kiss, that was all he wanted. For now.

By rights Rebecca ought to be scared speechless, but she wasn't. Something about the daring Viscount Sterling stirred her blood, tempting the adventurous side of her spirit, one her mother had warned her time and again would get her into trouble.

Well, she had stumbled into it now. Trouble was a tall, handsome viscount who was demanding a kiss in exchange for her valentine. As much as she wanted to jerk away from the man and storm out of the room, Rebecca declined the idea. Perhaps it was the gleam in his eye, clear but somehow blurred with an indefinable sadness she didn't understand. Or perhaps it was her own bold nature. She would never know for sure.

"A kiss in exchange for my card," she said, frowning uncertainly.

"A simple kiss and the card will be yours again," he assured her.

"Very well," she relented, scowling up at him as he stepped close enough for her to see that his necktie was secured with an emerald stickpin. The green jewel twinkled in the firelight. "A kiss, then. And the card will be mine," she reiterated firmly.

Rebecca waited for him to sweep her into his arms again, to cover her mouth with his warm lips, to take her once again to that exciting place she had visited in the garden. But the viscount didn't move, except to release her arm. He stood as still as a statue.

"At your leisure, my lady," he finally said.

"You want me to kiss you!"

"Precisely." He was a disciplined man, a logical man, but he seemed to have lost that restraint. The more he saw of her, the more stunning she became. The impact she was having on him was unnerving. Standing in the dim firelight, she looked more gypsy than lady, more woman than child.

With her eyes wide open and her hands trembling, Rebecca raised up on tiptoes and placed a swift, chaste kiss upon his mouth, then stepped back.

"That wasn't a kiss."

"I'm a lady, my lord, not—"

"I taught you how to kiss in the garden," he reminded her. One brow arched as he pondered his options. "I suppose I could return the card tomorrow. Will your father be in residence?"

"Very well," she relented. "But you're not to touch me."

Hands at his sides, Sebastian patiently waited for her to get on with it.

When she did, he smiled inwardly. Her lips, as warm as the fire burning on the hearth, touched lightly. It wasn't the most memorable kiss he had ever had, but it was enough to make him clench his fists to keep his hands from reaching out and pulling her closer.

Rebecca's boldness took over. Her breath came in a gasp as his tongue flipped out to beckon hers inside. Having only the kiss in the garden to gauge herself by, she let him drink from her mouth, her tongue touching his. Her pulse began to pound, to roar. The sound blocked out everything but the unbelievable wonder of the kiss. When the viscount's arms slowly encircled her, Rebecca barely noticed. It was so warm in his embrace, such a secure, never before felt feeling. She didn't want it to end. When she would have broken the kiss, he allowed her only a slight reprise, a moment to gain her breath before his mouth covered hers once again.

The sexual duel continued, his tongue dipping, hers hesitantly tasting, his lips gentle but demanding, hers soft and curious. The kiss was persistent, persuasive. Hot and inquisitive. Forbidden and dangerous.

Rebecca's senses whirled away in a shuddering sweetness that left her knees as shaky as her heart when he finally pulled away. She slumped against him in acquiescence, her body trembling, her breath coming in soft gasps, her hands resting on his shoulders, although she couldn't remember putting them there.

Sebastian held her close. It was unthinkable to do otherwise. She fit against him as perfectly as any woman had ever fit, her cheek resting against his chest, her dark gypsy curls tickling the bottom of his chin. What was happening to him? As ridiculous as it sounded, he felt as if he had just been resurrected from the cold ground. His blood was pumping with the vigor of a young man, his body hard and tight, his mind unable to catch and hold a logical thought.

It was more than Rebecca's striking good looks, more than the innocence she represented, and much more than a few simple kisses. The exact explanation evaded him as he slowly released her, setting her back from him, widening the gap of temptation but not eliminating it.

"No more valentines," he said. "And no more kisses. Now go."

The man was beyond belief. Intolerable. Incorrigible. Impossible.

Disbelieving that the night had taken such an unexpected course, Rebecca walked to the fireplace and tossed the card onto the flames. She stood with her back to Sterling as the white lace sparked, curling into brown ashes, then into dust. The paper caught, crinkling until there was nothing but dancing orange flames and the heat of the fire. She was breathing rapidly, her heart still pounding, her senses still outraged, as she turned to face the viscount one last time. All she saw was an empty room.

He was gone. Vanished as if he had been a dream, an imaginary phantom.

If only he had been, Rebecca thought as she quit the library.

If only . . .

Four

Over the course of the following few days, Rebecca discreetly gleaned a great deal of information about the Viscount Sterling. He was thirty-six, the only son of an only son, and a widower. Her aunt, a chatty lady in her late sixties, who had known the viscount's mother and who loved to ramble on about how much more elegant the town had been in those days, supplied everything one could possibly want to know concerning the Worthington lineage. It was an old family, an honored family, not one given to scandal or misadventure. The viscount himself was highly respected, as his father had been, well educated and conservative in his politics.

Rebecca sipped her tea and listened attentively, making an occasional remark, asking what she hoped was a judicious question now and again, until her aunt mentioned the viscount's former wife.

"Kathryn was a lovely child," her Aunt Felicity remarked almost mournfully. "Young and lovely, as bright as a new coin, she was. And she adored Sebastian. They had known each other most of their lives. I daresay, it wasn't at all surprising when he offered for her. Everyone suspected the two would marry one day."

"You said he was widowed. Has his wife been dead long?"

Her aunt looked sad. "Far too long for the viscount to be mourning her as he does. The man rarely ventures into society nowadays. Of course, he attends matters of Parliament, but he's never seen beyond his club, or so I understand. Pity that. As I recall, he was a handsome devil."

Rebecca could recall all too well.

"Why do you ask, child?"

Prepared for the question, she merely smiled. "We were introduced at the Goodall's Valentine ball."

"The viscount attended!" Her aunt's hand stopped midair, a fragile teacup posed between the saucer and her mouth. "Well, that's interesting," she went on to say. "Interesting, indeed." She took a sip of tea before expounding on the possibilities. "Perhaps the man has finally decided it's time for an heir. Poor Kathryn died in childbirth. He lost them both that day. Such a terrible waste."

Was that the sadness she had glimpsed in the viscount's eyes? The loss of his wife and child. If he had mourned them as many years as her aunt indicated, then he must have loved his wife very much. Truly loved her.

His appearance at the ball was unexpected, according to her aunt, who Rebecca was sure knew the exact measure of everything that went on in society regardless of the restrictions her health forced upon her. Why had he come? Surely her card had not brought about his attendance. Was he seeking a second wife and the heir that fate had so cruelly taken from him? And why should she give a whit what the man was seeking? She would be far better off if they never met again.

"What of you, my dear? I understand that Lord Sheppard has shown his attention. Don't know the young man, but I knew his uncle. Hiram, if memory serves me. A dreadfully arrogant man. A dangerous sort in his youth. A womanizer of the highest caliber. I'd be careful of that one. If he's anything like his elders, he bears watching."

"Lord Sheppard is charming. The perfect gentleman," Rebecca told her. "He's asked me to ride in the park tomorrow morning."

"What does your father think?" Felicity asked, her tone somewhat censoring. "He'll not be happy if you encourage the wrong sort of gentleman."

"I've not encouraged anyone," Rebecca lied with a smile and an inward flinch of guilt. "Nor has father expressed his opinion one way or the other. At least not yet. I think he simply wants me to enjoy the season."

"As well he should. You're young and beautiful. There's plenty of time to select a husband. Don't let a man charm you into an unhappy marriage."

Her aunt knew of what she spoke. She had admitted to Rebecca, during one of their long chats, that her own marriage hadn't been one of love or affection. She had been charmed, as she put it, into marrying a man whose only interest had been seeing how fast he could gamble her father's money away. Fortunately, for her aunt, the gentleman fell from his horse and died from the injuries, leaving Felicity to the benefits of both the country life and the swirl of London until age and asthma prevented her from enjoying either one to its fullest.

"I should go," Rebecca said. "The hour is growing late."

"Come again," her aunt insisted. "And bring my dear sister with you the next time. It's been ages since Meredith and I have enjoyed an afternoon together."

Ages actually totaled two weeks, but Rebecca didn't contradict her mother's only sister. Instead, she buttoned herself into a short coat, fashioned after the Algerian troop uniform jacket and all the rage with its rounded front and pagoda sleeves. Placing an affectionate kiss on Felicity's cheek, she bid her aunt a leisurely afternoon nap, then stepped outside. Her father's carriage was waiting.

"You may take me home, Stoats," Rebecca said to the man bundled up in a thick coat and muffler. Stoats had been with her family longer than she had. When she had been small, she had pestered him until he had taught her the proper way to handle the reins. By the time her lessons had ended, she could turn a carriage as well as any coachman.

"Yes, miss," he replied.

The day had arrived with sunshine, and although the streets still displayed puddles and the rooftops patches of soot-stained snow, the air was crisp. Rebecca arrived home, pondering not only what her aunt had told her about the viscount, but her inability to forget the man.

She had retrieved her card, had watched it turn to ashes, so the incident was behind her. The viscount had no cause to hold the evening's events over her head, and she had no earthly reason to delegate it to anything but a lesson hard learned. No doubt, the man's intent from the very beginning.

Entering the house, Rebecca forced herself to dismiss the man from her mind. She was attending the theater tonight and had to dress. There would be time enough to worry about the viscount should he rear his handsome head again.

Sterling was of the same mind-set as he stepped down from his carriage later that evening. He entered Brook's, hoping the upcoming card game would provide a diversion from the black mood that had settled over him since the night of Lady Goodall's ball.

What in the blazes had gotten into him, he still wasn't sure. He had no idea why he had kissed Lord Lowery's daughter, and there was no explanation to be had as to why he had insisted upon a second kiss. None but the simple fact that he had found Rebecca beautiful and tempting. Too tempting for her own good. The precise reason why he should have delivered a firm lecture, given her the card, and quit the festivities. Instead, he had all but ravished her.

It wasn't like him to be impulsive, and he certainly wasn't accustomed to giving young ladies more than a passing glimpse or thought.

Sebastian handed off his coat and hat to the waiting footman, refusing to dwell on his less than perfect performance the previous night. He had called upon his mistress, thinking to purge Rebecca Lowery from his mind. It was the first time in years that he had bedded a woman without predictable satisfaction. Mirabel had insisted that it was her fault; she had been under the weather the previous week and less than enthusiastic, but Sebastian knew better. He had barely been able to bring himself to completion, his member had been so uncooperative. As much as he wanted to blame it on complacency and familiarity, he couldn't.

He simply hadn't wanted Mirabel, a sure sign that it was time to bid the woman a polite goodbye. There were widows aplenty in London looking for a gentleman upon which to visit their affection without obligation or responsibility. He could think of at least three who had openly flirted with him since society had begun its annual migration to London. Regrettably, none of them inspired a sexual spark.

The woman he did want, couldn't seem to forget, had gypsy black hair and periwinkle eyes. She was young and slender, but rounded in all the right places, with alabaster skin and a pert little nose that she held too high in the air.

Sebastian cursed under his breath.

"What?" Rathbone asked, coming up behind him. "Did you say something?"

"No."

"Could have sworn I heard the words 'damnable female.'"

Sebastian fixed him with a steely gaze, but his young friend continued smiling. "I received an invitation from Lord and Lady Whetford. As I recall, they throw a splendid party."

"I doubt that I'll attend," Sebastian replied, not ruling out the possibility. Once he had been seen in society, his desk was now overflowing with invitations. It seems he was still considered eligible, even though it had been years since he had thought of himself as such.

"Have a go at it," Rathbone insisted. "I could use the company. Bedford's taking his newest mistress to the country for a quiet weekend in that old hunting lodge he refuses to tear down. Foxhall's made other plans. He refuses to admit what they are, but I'd bet my new Thoroughbred that they have something to do with Clayburn's newly widowed wife."

"What about Ackerman?"

"Fitch is getting too serious of late," Rathbone said with a shrug. "He's almost as black as old Morland, frowning at every turn."

Before Sebastian could reply, the other players joined them.

It was later, as Sebastian was drawing to a royal flush, that the Lowery name caught his ear. He tensed, then looked up.

"Alexander is far too sensible to allow that to happen," the duke was saying.

"Allow what?" Sebastian asked nonchalantly.

"Sheppard," the Earl of Granby supplied. "It seems the new young lord is in the market for a wife and Lowery's daughter is at the top of the list."

"Didn't know Lowery had a daughter," Rathbone mused, frowning at his cards. "Is she pretty?"

"Better than pretty," the earl told him. "She's rich, or

rather her husband will be. That's why Sheppard is sniffing around her skirts. He inherited a title, but little else."

Rathbone grunted. "There's not enough coin in all of London to make me take a wife."

The duke shook his head. "I've known Lowery most of his life. He dotes on that girl. Sheppard won't get her."

"There are *ways,*" Bedford inserted. "Wouldn't put it past Sheppard to use them. From what I hear, he owes every tradesman on Savile Row."

Sebastian clenched his jaw. The most common *way* was to compromise the lady or her reputation. Rebecca might deserve a firm scolding, but she didn't deserve a forced marriage.

The thought of her being compelled into marriage fired Sebastian's blood in a different way than the young lady had heated it. Anger surged through him. Rebecca's lack of experience made her a perfect target for Sheppard's scheme. If Bedford knew of the young man's financial straits, it was more than likely that the hounds were closing in.

On his way home, Sebastian couldn't shake the feeling that in some way he owed Lady Rebecca Lowery his protection. He looked out the carriage window. The gaslights permeated the fog, glowing ghostly through the heavy mist. The creak of carriage wheels and harnessed horses added to the eeriness of the night. The moon, engulfed by dark clouds, offered little light. It was a bleak night.

As bleak as my life of late. His lips thinned with the thought. The contentment he had convinced himself existed in his life was suddenly replaced with a deep desperation, the kind he hadn't felt since his wife's death. The need was too acute, the gap too large, for a mistress or friends to fill. His gaze fixed on the gaslights, their oil burning feverishly to overcome the darkness, yet they failed. The vaporous glow did little but mark the way, giving no details to the passerby other than a reference to the course they must walk to avoid being run over by a fog-blinded carriage. And what of Rebecca? Would she walk blindly into Sheppard's arms, thinking the man loved her?

A faint tremor radiated through Sebastian's body. He knew it was more than the lust he had felt when he had held Rebecca in his arms. The kisses they had shared had made him aware of just how much his life currently lacked. The gaiety of a woman's smile, the warmth of a feminine body tucked closely to his throughout the night, the laughter.

He missed the laughter the most.

Sebastian breathed heavily as he entered his Mayfair town house. A quick glance at the foyer clock told him it was well past midnight, and it would be even later before he would be able to sleep. A restlessness had overtaken him of late, and he frequently found himself staring at the fire in the library grate until the gray hours just before dawn. Sensing this night would be no different than the others, he stripped off his gloves and tossed them on the foyer table next to his hat. Dames appeared in time to take his coat, giving it a firm shake before draping it over a bent arm.

"Did you enjoy the club, milord?"

"I won more than I lost," Sebastian told him. "As to enjoying it, I'm not sure."

Dames cocked a brow, but said nothing. He remained mute as his employer strolled into the library, shutting the door behind him.

Alone and feeling at odds with himself and the course of his thoughts, Sebastian poured himself a drink and sat down in front of the fire. An intense but indefinable dissatisfaction bore down on him. He thought of the years he had spent alone, of the pattern that had crept naturally into his life, of the predictability of it all. But that predictability had suddenly crumbled, leaving a path revealed that he hadn't known existed until a cook's son had mistakenly delivered a valentine to the wrong gentleman.

Now the possibilities seemed endless, the thoughts unstoppable. Plans and dreams returned; hopes of a family and children peaked anew.

Raising his glass, he studied its amber contents, then set it aside. There was no point speculating about a young woman when he didn't have reason to believe that she would do more than slap his face the next time they met. Justifiably so, he thought, then smiled. Lady Rebecca Lowery might be a young lady of virtuous habits, but she had most certainly kissed him back, and in doing so had announced her boldness. A boldness Sebastian found himself eager to encounter again.

Five

Rebecca entered the shop on Bond Street. She was in need of a new fan, having ruined her favorite one when she had tried to disguise the periwinkles she had painted upon it. The shopkeeper greeted her and her mother with a courteous smile. While Lady Lowery inspected a table artfully laden with ribbons and imported French lace, Rebecca tried to think of the task at hand instead of the intriguing gentleman who had enlightened her with his kiss.

It was growing increasingly more difficult to dismiss him from her mind. In fact, she seemed to be thinking more and more about the handsome Viscount Sterling. Even yesterday morning, riding in the park with Newland, her thoughts had drifted across the green to Mayfair, to the town house where the viscount resided.

She had even taken to comparing the two men, though they had little in common. Newland was bright and charming with the most pleasant smile, while the viscount was dark and brooding. Her riding companion had maintained every propriety, never breeching the bounds of polite society. The viscount's kiss had been brazen. The younger lord laughed as he recited the follies of Parliament. Rebecca knew Sterling accepted his role in the House of Lords much more seriously. She sensed a lot of things about him. His dignity was there on the surface for everyone to see, but underneath his staunch expression and authoritative voice, she sensed a vulnerability. He seemed lonely. Of course, there was no reason to suspect that her intuition contained any substance. Other than a few pertinent facts, she knew little of the man.

But no matter the logic, she couldn't deny that she had *sensed* something about him, and she had certainly *felt* something. If she closed her eyes and allowed her thoughts to drift back to that night, she could still feel it. Not just the physical exhilaration of his touch, but the warm sensation that had crept into her limbs, into the very heart of her.

The day was spent shopping. Rebecca purchased a new fan and a spoon bonnet, with a narrow brim close to the ears. The back was cut away to allow a young lady's hair to flow more freely, that being the current style. The hat had a veil of ivory tulle and dark blue ribbons that accented the color of her eyes. Rebecca opened her parasol as she exited the fashionable millinery shop. A note fluttered to the sidewalk. Puzzled as to how a calling card had found such a hiding place, and thankful that her mother was still inside arranging to have their purchases delivered, she read the name and sucked in her breath. It was from the viscount.

> *If an invitation to the Whetfords' dinner*
> *is received, please accept.*

Sterling wanted to see her again!

But why?

It was four days and eight hours later before her question was answered.

Arriving at the Whetfords', Rebecca greeted her hostess, then followed her parents into the large drawing room where a group of about twenty had gathered to wait for the footman's ringing of the bell, the signal that the evening meal was ready to be served. Rebecca scanned the room looking for the viscount, but he was nowhere to be seen. Was he waiting in the library with the host and other gentlemen, or had he yet to arrive, and why was her heart pounding so fiercely? By all rights, she should detest the man.

It was an hour later, as they were walking into the dining room, that Rebecca finally saw Sterling. He looked even more devilishly handsome than she remembered. Dressed all in black except for a charcoal gray cravat with a pearl stickpin, his presence drew her eye. When she glanced at his face, making sure not to linger overly long lest her interest be discovered, her heart nearly stopped. He offered her a quick, almost tender smile. It was her undoing. The knot that had been in her stomach since the moment she had begun to dress for the evening melted and ran hot through her veins.

The table was laid out, decorated with flowers and flickering candles that danced over the gleaming surface of the polished silver. The meal began with a vermicelli soup, followed by poached salmon and lobster rissoles. Entrees of roast lamb, pheasant and curried rabbit were then served, the butler being most attentive in keeping the wineglasses filled until it was time to present dessert. Rebecca picked at her raspberries and cream, wishing that etiquette and social rank hadn't seated the viscount at the far and opposite end of the table. She couldn't so much as catch a glimpse of him without looking around Lord Nesselrod's head. The plump man had been rambling on for the last hour, doing his best to engage her in conversation. She replied politely, being too well schooled to do anything else, but underneath her calm voice was a burning curiosity as to why Sterling had summoned her to the Whetford's dinner party.

After dinner the ladies retired to the drawing room while the men took their cigars and brandy in the library. Rebecca excused herself. Upon exiting the once small bedchamber that had been converted to accommodate the most modern plumbing available, Rebecca glanced up and down the corridor. Sighing with visible disappointment, she was on her way back to the drawing room when a nearby doorway opened and Sterling ushered her inside.

The room was a small reading parlor, furnished with wicker chairs and chintz cushions. The walls were papered in a gold-and-red floral design. Paintings and home-stitched samplers covered the walls. Every available inch of table space was cluttered with bric-a-brac; blown glass figurines neighbored those made of glazed porcelain and china. A sewing basket sat in one corner, its top raised to reveal a variety of threads.

"My lord?" Rebecca questioned as Sterling closed the door behind her.

He raised his finger to his lips, indicating that she keep her voice pitched low.

A tense silence filled the room for several minutes. Finally, Rebecca had to ask. "You wished me to attend the dinner this evening. May I ask why?"

Sebastian shifted his gaze from her face, slowly taking in the cut of her dress. It was peacock blue. The train was long and sweeping, the bodice close fitting and pointed at the waist. Her dark mane of hair was drawn back and secured with an ivory clip. She was breathtakingly beautiful. For a man so recently fed, he suddenly felt ravenous.

"My lord?" She questioned more urgently this time. It wouldn't do to be missing for more than a few minutes. Her mother was sure to become concerned.

"I find myself in need of your attention," Sebastian said, stepping closer, trapping her between himself and the fireless hearth. "A personal matter."

"Personal." Rebecca felt her heart flutter for a wild

moment. She looked at the viscount. His features appeared more striking this evening, probably because the room was better lit than the Goodall's library had been and she could see the deep green of his eyes.

There was something akin to excitement in his gaze, something strong and warm, and just the slightest bit intoxicating. Rebecca licked her lips.

The gesture was enough to make Sebastian tense. It was best to get things said, then return to the library. It was totally unacceptable for the two of them to be behind closed doors, but he felt compelled to warn her against Sheppard.

"Have you accepted a proposal from Lord Sheppard?" he asked, as his gaze returned to her face and those incredible periwinkle eyes.

"A proposal?"

"A marriage proposal," he said impatiently.

"None has been offered," Rebecca replied, too politely for him to think the question hadn't carried a small degree of offense with it. "As yet," she added, just to let him know she expected Newland to propose any day.

"I wouldn't advise you to accept such an invitation should it come your way," he cautioned her.

"Are you always this bold in your address of a lady?"

"Only when the lady is young and stubborn and in need of advise."

She moved to stand beside a Queen Anne chair with long, tapering legs. She gripped the oval back with one hand and said, "You know nothing of me, my lord, neither my disposition nor my age."

"I know enough to warn you away from Sheppard," he said. "The man's looking for a wife with deep pockets. He's nearly bankrupt."

Rebecca sucked in her breath. Newland's defense was on the tip of her tongue as Sterling moved toward her. When he spoke, his voice was the same deep tone he had used in the garden that fateful night. "Whatever romantic notions you have, he'll use to his own advantage. Find another suitor, Lady Rebecca."

She raised her nose into the air. "Lord Sheppard is an honorable man."

"He's a pauper in the making," Sebastian countered. He wasn't speaking from gossip. After Bedford's remarks last Wednesday, he had taken the time to investigate Lord Sheppard himself. The man was living on the mercy of his creditors.

Rebecca glared at him. "Your concern and attention are unwelcome, my lord. As for Lord Sheppard, my relationship with him is none of your business."

"I'll deal firmly with you, Lady Rebecca. Whatever circumstances brought about our acquaintance are forgotten. You have no reason to think my motives are anything beyond those of a gentleman who sees no purpose served by a peer compromising you into marriage."

"Compromising me!" She couldn't believe her ears. "If anyone has compromised me, my lord, it is you. You kissed the wits out of me."

Suddenly the mood changed. She stared at him, as if preparing to explain what she had just said, but the heat of his gaze caught her.

His lips curved even higher, into a full smile as he stepped closer. There was a challenge in her eyes, one he was only too willing to accept. The tip of his index finger lifted her chin. "Did I?"

Rebecca pulled back. What madness had invaded the room with her? The simplest touch from this man and she was stumbling over her words.

"Did I kiss you witless?" Sebastian asked as he lowered his head to cover her mouth.

She tensed for a moment, then surrendered. Her lips parted and softened under his. The kiss was long and leisurely, hot and fluid, warm and as intoxicating as the champagne that had been served with dinner. His tongue teased hers into responding. Her hand fell away from the chair to find his shoulder. An arm encircled her waist, bringing her closer to the magic as his left hand came to rest on her nape.

His thumb pressed lightly, measuring her pulse beat against the pounding of his own heart. Her taste was sweet and heady, light and innocent, bold and exotic. It went straight to his head. The compulsion to keep her safe was replaced by a deeper need, one that had his loins aching within seconds. The tension in the room followed suit, changing into something much more volatile. Desire became a combustive thing. Heat raged through his body like wildfire. A battle began to be waged, his common sense against the burning need she aroused in him. He felt her tremble in his arms, and common sense lost.

An odd restlessness was building inside Rebecca. She knew she shouldn't be allowing the kiss; it was shameful, if not sinful. But it was also unimaginably delightful. Her body seemed to be tingling all over. His hand moved to her face, his palm cradling her cheek. The restless feeling turned into a warm, quivering sensation. He ran his tongue across her bottom lip. She gasped in surprise. His teeth nibbled ever so lightly. She moaned.

Her body felt damp and hot, as if the cold hearth behind them had suddenly come alive with flames. Her heart drummed against her rib cage. His hand moved lower, to caress the exposed skin just above the neckline of her gown. She lifted slightly, not wanting to lose that touch. Not wanting the heat and smoothness of it to end.

Sebastian deepened the kiss. Slowly, artfully, he used his tongue to tease, to tempt, to bring her even closer to the flame as his fingertips traced the softness of her skin from the tip of her ear to the soft skin of her throat. She was a joy to touch, a treasure to be discovered and savored, a prize to be won.

Brazenly, Rebecca returned the wanton kiss, letting him fill her mouth, filling his in return. He tasted like brandy and cigars, bold and exciting, a flavor she couldn't imagine enjoying until tonight. She felt the tension in his body grow as hers weakened, heard the ragged pattern of his breath as he lifted his mouth from her lips and kissed her neck instead, where his thumb had been resting.

This was madness, she knew, but giving it a name was the only thing she had strength to do. There was no pulling back, no regret, no embarrassment as his hand moved from her waist, inching slowly higher until her breast was cradled in his open palm. The heat from his touch was incredible. She felt drawn to it, enticed to discover just how warm two bodies could become pressed together from knee to thigh, waist to shoulder, mouth to mouth. Hot enough to melt reason, it seemed.

"My God," Sebastian groaned as she raised on her tiptoes, bringing her hands from his shoulders and wrapping them around his neck. She lifted high and tight against him.

His arousal was pressed firmly against her. He knew he should push her away, pull himself back before they both caught fire. But he didn't have the strength or the inclination.

Somehow they ended up in the chair. Rebecca was perched on his lap, her bottom pressing down on his aroused flesh, her arms clinging to him, her lips nipping hesitantly at his own. His arm around her lower back tightened; the hand splayed across her rib cage moved higher, seeking her breast again. Then his fingers dipped into her bodice, touching the soft swell of her flesh and the warm valley in between.

"Sebastian." His name was a breath of air against his temple, her mouth moist as she pressed it there.

The single word, the soft, purring sound of his name, was the end of his control. He pushed her gown away from one shoulder as his mouth found and caressed the top of the breast he had all but exposed. The scent of French perfume assaulted his nostrils. He breathed deeply, letting it mix with the scent of woman, alive and warm and in his arms.

The gentleness of his caresses turned rough, more demanding, as Rebecca squirmed on his lap, unaware that she was driving the flames higher and higher, out of control. All she knew was that it felt wonderful, wickedly wonderful, and she didn't want the feeling to end.

She felt her clothing giving way to his exploring hands; then his mouth closed over the taut tip of her breast. She moaned as he began to suck, his tongue flicking across her nipple, his mouth hot and wet. Something deep inside her began to unfold, to melt until she felt as if she had lost the ability to control a single muscle. And all the while he suckled, his hands holding her firmly in place. His tongue circled, then flicked, then circled again, and Rebecca melted more and more until there was nothing left of her but a hot, uncontrollable heat.

Knowing she wanted, needed, the same thing he did, Sebastian ran his hand down the length of her leg, then back up again. On the retreat his caress bunched petticoats and lace, peacock blue satin and flounces, slowly upward. His hand swept the outside of her thigh, then the inside. He caressed the delicate, never before touched skin and felt her shiver in response. A soft moan escaped her, and he kissed it away, his mouth more demanding now.

He touched her then, there in that private place, and her eyes melted closed.

His fingers trailed lightly over and around the nest of

curls between her legs, then probed again, softly, tenderly, going just a bit deeper this time. She stiffened.

"Easy, love," he whispered as his mouth came to rest over hers. "God, you're so tight, so wonderfully warm and wet."

His kiss brought another blaze of heat. A fire that burned deep inside her. Rebecca let it engulf her just as his touch was engulfing her, overwhelming her senses, making her body hot and molten. His hands were doing such wonderful things. Magical things. Things she had never thought possible. He was touching the very center of her.

Sebastian kissed her again. He knew she was shimmering on the edge, trembling with the first wave of ecstasy. He felt it at the same time she did, felt the gentle rippling of her muscles, the liquidized heat of her body, the instant of tautness before she surrendered to the power of passion. He lifted his mouth away from hers and watched the pleasure wash over her face. Her lashes fluttered. Her cheeks flushed with color; then the softest of sighs escaped her.

"Lovely," he whispered.

The sound of a door being opened, then abruptly closed, brought Sebastian's head up. The Duke of Morland stared back at him.

Six

"Sterling."'

His name, pronounced like a death sentence, brought reality crashing down.

Rebecca reacted as quickly as her befuddled senses would allow. Recognizing the duke's voice, she buried her face against Sebastian's chest and prayed for the floor to open up and swallow them whole.

Sebastian withdrew his hand from beneath layers of white lace and blue satin, then wrapped two protective arms around her. From the duke's vantage point all the older man had seen was a shapely length of stocking-covered calf, but it was more than enough to confirm that what he had interrupted hadn't been innocent.

Keeping Rebecca snug against him, Sebastian addressed the duke. "If you'll excuse us for a moment, Your Grace, I'll see that the young lady is returned to her mother."

"Very well," the duke agreed. Giving Sebastian a look that said the worst was yet to come, he turned away, shutting the door more quietly this time.

Sebastian took a deep breath. Rebecca still had her face buried against his chest. He could feel her trembling in his arms, but it wasn't desire this time. She was shaking with fear and humiliation. He had come to warn her of Sheppard's seduction and had ended up seducing her himself. It was a good thing he wasn't playing cards tonight. His luck was running in the wrong direction.

"Rebecca."

It was the first time he had called her by her given name, and the sound of it was surprisingly soothing. There were half a dozen things she should do, beginning with untangling herself from his embrace, but she didn't want to move. Regardless of all she was feeling, of all that had happened between them, his arms still seemed like the safest place on earth. She lifted her chin as proudly as possible and met his gaze.

His smile was tender and sympathetic. "Are you all right?"

"How can I be all right?" she said, feeling heartsick at what the duke must have seen, of what he must be thinking at this moment, the situation as confusing as her thoughts and the things he had done to her. There was no piecing the puzzle together as long as she was in his arms. "What have we done?"

Gently lifting her from his lap, Sebastian stood up from the chair. He held her around the waist, looking down at the breasts he had bared and kissed.

Rebecca followed the path of his gaze, then hurriedly righted her bodice. "I . . . I have to go," she stammered. Never in her life had she felt so humiliated, so unsure of herself.

"It would probably be best if you excused yourself for the evening," Sebastian suggested, hating himself because he couldn't offer her more than words at the moment. But that would change very quickly. Rebecca was still dealing with the shock of what had transpired between them. While he, on the other hand, knew all too well what the future held.

"I can't just rush out the door," she said, regaining some of her composure, but not nearly enough to think straight. "What will the Whetfords think?"

Knowing that gentility was everything to most young ladies, and knowing that Rebecca was no exception, Sebastian searched for a plausible but acceptable excuse. "Return to the drawing room and inform your mother that the poached salmon isn't settling well on your stomach," he said. "Ask to be taken home."

Her cheeks flushed with color, then went pale. "The duke will tell—"

"No," Sebastian said, stopping her before she could verbalize her fear. "Morland is an honorable man. Being one, he will offer me the opportunity to set things right."

"How can things be set right when everything is so wrong?"

The ramifications of what had happened were finally sinking in. Her reputation was ruined, any possibility of a future with Newland destroyed. She was ruined. Totally ruined. Her head fell as the realization overtook her, slumping downward with shame.

Sebastian caught her chin and lifted it, forcing her to look at him. He captured her hands, trembling and cold, and brought them to his mouth. After kissing each of them, he held them against his chest.

"Return to the drawing room. You look pale enough for Lady Lowery to accept that you aren't feeling well." He kissed her forehead, then smiled reassuringly. "Say nothing. I'll call on you within the week."

"But—"

"Permit me to take charge of the matter." He didn't want to dwell upon what had taken place between them. His first consideration was for Rebecca and her present state of mind. She looked ready to burst into tears. "Calm yourself, my love."

Rebecca looked at him with dismay.

"Calm myself," she said with a dash of anger in her voice. Her wits were back in full force, and she was excruciatingly aware of what had happened, what she had been foolish to allow. She was at the mercy of society and its stringent rules, or at least she would be if Sebastian couldn't convince the duke that her reputation wasn't beyond repair.

He responded with another reassuring smile. "Trust me."

"If my father finds out, he'll demand a wedding," Rebecca said, feeling light-headed at the thought. "I don't want to marry you."

The words were lacerating, cutting Sebastian to the quick, even though he knew they were reactionary. She was upset, rightfully so, and she blamed him. Passion and her own response to it had shocked her. Being discovered by the Duke of Morland had her terrified of the consequences. The emotions he had brought to the surface were foreign to her. They couldn't be controlled the way she had been taught to contain her other feelings.

"Need I remind you that our acquaintance is no longer casual. Do you think me so callous, so selfish, as to not offer you marriage?"

"No." Rebecca shut her eyes, but the image of what the duke must have seen formed all too clearly in her mind's eye. She felt herself blush.

He pulled her back into his arms, stroking her back like a child's. "Does marriage to me seem so horrendous?"

Rebecca didn't want to answer him because she didn't want him to know that her thoughts had taken that direction more than once in the last week. Instead, she untangled herself from his embrace. "Very well," she relented. "I'll leave you to speak with the duke, but nothing more."

Sebastian wasn't going to let her get away that easily. "I fear the circumstances demand more than conversation."

"I disagree," Rebecca told him. "Although my innocence may be tarnished, it is still intact. There is no reason, no demand, that we should wed. If you cannot convince the duke of that, then I shall."

Sebastian started to protest, but the chime of a small

clock alerted him to the possibility of being discovered again, this time by one of Rebecca's parents. Truthfully, he wasn't all that upset over being discovered the first time. It made the situation easier to handle, at least from his point of view. Convincing Rebecca of that would take time they didn't have at the moment.

"I'll speak with the duke," he said noncommittally. "Time demands that you return to the ladies."

For an instant, Rebecca wanted to throw herself back into Sebastian's arms. It was a silly notion, considering the circumstances. She chewed on her bottom lip, determined not to cry, knowing she didn't dare let a single tear escape or she would be at the mercy of the situation. Unable to fight the nervousness that was close to making her stomach sour for real, Rebecca nodded, then turned and left the room. Once she was in the corridor, she hesitated. She was cold and trembling inside and out. At least her mother wouldn't question her request to be taken home, not if she looked anything like she felt.

Sebastian waited inside the small parlor, wanting to give Rebecca time to clear the corridor before he stepped beyond the door. He glanced at the clock, then paced restlessly across the carpet. He knew the duke was doing the same thing, giving Rebecca and her parents time to politely excuse themselves from the party. There could be no connection between the Lowerys' exit and a short, private conversation between him and the Duke of Morland. All must seem as it should be or the gossip mill would churn mercilessly.

Stopping midway between the closed door and the cold hearth, Sebastian regarded his innermost thoughts. The sense of impending doom that should be burdening his shoulders didn't exist. In its place was . . . relief. Relief that his life would no longer be a solitary one.

A few minutes later, Sebastian strolled into Lord Whetford's library and helped himself to a brandy.

The duke was seated near the fireplace. The glance he gave Sebastian was too brief to be interpreted by the other gentlemen in the room as anything more than cursory.

It wasn't until an hour later that the two men could effortlessly make their way to another small seating room, this one furnished with matching bergere seats and a long settee. Sebastian closed the door and faced the duke.

"My apologies, Your Grace, my behavior this evening has been inexcusable."

"I fear it would have been even more indiscreet if I hadn't intruded."

Sebastian didn't argue the point, nor did he defend himself. There was no gentlemanly defense for what he had done, just as there was no recourse but one.

"I must say I'm surprised," the duke remarked as he stopped in front of the fire. "I would have thought Rebecca too young for you."

"She's old enough to marry," Sebastian said, sealing his fate with the words.

"Lowery kept her in the country for as long as he could," the duke said. "She's his only child. Pampered and impulsive from what he's told me, but not unkind."

"The very reason we made each other's acquaintance," Sebastian said, remembering the valentine. "I fear she thinks herself more suited to Lord Sheppard."

The duke's expression turned sour. "Young ladies and their romantic notions," he snorted. "Rest assured their fathers aren't burdened by similar thoughts. Nor any kindness for the men who get trapped by them."

"I will call upon Lord Lowery before week's end," Sebastian assured him, just as he had assured Rebecca. "May I assume that the earl will agree to the union?"

"He'd be a fool not to," Morland responded candidly. "You're ten times the man Sheppard is."

Relieved that the only person he would have to convince was the bride, Sebastian assured the duke that Lady Rebecca would be his viscountess by summer's end.

By the time Lady Lowery had dutifully tucked her daughter into bed with a cup of herbal tea to settle her stomach, Rebecca couldn't breathe a sigh of relief. There was no relief to be found in the circumstances that suddenly surrounded her. She was cloaked in scandal, even if no one knew of it but herself, Viscount Sterling, and the Duke of Morland.

Knowing sleep was out of the question, Rebecca set her tea aside and climbed out of bed. Her blue satin dinner dress had been replaced with a nightgown and bed jacket. There was nothing under the gown to restrict her movements, nothing to cover the places the viscount had touched with his bare hands. Her skin had cooled, but the evocative caresses still burned in her memory.

Her nerves were unsteady as she approached the window and stood staring out into the starless night. She seemed trapped inside a paradox. Her mind knew that everything bright and wonderful about her life had just been tarnished; no longer was she the innocent young lady she had been before meeting the viscount. But her body felt as though it had been set free. Now she knew that intimacy between a man and woman could be powerful, exciting and pleasing.

Beyond the window, the trees were bare. A hansom cab clopped by at the end of the street, the horses' hooves heavy on the cold cobblestones. Distressingly aware of just how close she had come to being completely ruined by the viscount, Rebecca took a shaky breath. If it had been her father, not the duke, who had broken in on them, she would be engaged right now. Hopefully, Sterling was right. Hopefully, the duke would listen to him and agree to keep the indiscretion to himself. If not . . . She refused to think of what that set of circumstances would bring about. Marriage to a man like Sterling wasn't something she wanted to think about. Not tonight. Not ever. He was older and would therefore assume himself wiser. He was established in his ways, she was sure, with no give or take about him. A union between them was out of the question.

And there was, of course, no affection. The attraction she felt for the man could easily be explained away with curiosity. As for him, he was a grown man who had once been married, and who probably kept a mistress. Men such as the viscount were accustomed to having women. Whatever she had aroused in him was simply a man's natural reaction. Nothing more.

Rebecca told herself that as she returned to bed, knowing sleep would come reluctantly. Still, she forced herself to draw the coverlet up to her waist, to fold her hands over her stomach and to close her eyes. She tried to think beyond the night, to the morning and perhaps a day of sunshine and a brisk ride in the park, but thoughts of Sterling, of his kisses, of how he had made her feel, of the shocking way in which he had touched her, wouldn't be dissuaded. They filled her mind, then her body, bringing on a restlessness that made sleep impossible.

When she focused on what had happened, the feelings returned full force, making her body tingle in a mysterious way. There was no being reasonable about them, either. What she had felt that night in the garden, when an unnamed man had kissed her, she felt just as strongly now that the man had a name. More vigorously than she should, since she had convinced herself that she was in love with Newland. Funny that the younger man hadn't so much as crossed her mind since she had stepped into the parlor and come face-to-face with the viscount.

Lord Sheppard's attention was becoming more an inconvenience than a compliment, and Rebecca realized that she had been naive about a lot of things. If he was the fortune hunter Sterling professed him to be, then she was better off knowing now rather than later. It stung her pride to think that she had been that gullible, that indifferent to Newland's true motives. She had wanted to defend him to Sterling, but she hadn't been given the chance. Now his defense seemed unimportant. Regardless of her best laid plans for the future, fate had intervened and, in doing so, had changed everything. Even if Sterling succeeded and gained a vow of silence from the duke, she would never be able to forget what had happened between them.

Realizing that her thoughts were jumping about, going from not wanting to ever set eyes upon Sterling again, to longing to return to his embrace, Rebecca clapped her eyes tightly shut, then began reciting poetry. She struggled to pronounce each word in a fervent whisper, to concentrate on each measure, each rhyme, with such precision as to prevent the smallest flicker of a thought to be led astray by the sensual memories of the evening. It was a trial, a tribulation that took a good hour, but finally, blessedly, she drifted off to sleep.

Seven

Sebastian entered his library the next morning with a purpose in mind. After leaving the Whetfords', he had gone directly to his club to have a drink and a few minutes of public solitude before returning to Mayfair and his bed. Surprisingly, he had slept most soundly. A good thing considering he was going to need his wits about him. Assuring the duke that he would offer marriage to the young and beautiful Lady Rebecca Lowery, he now had to find a way to present that offer. Being older, and supposedly unacquainted with the lady, he couldn't just up and propose.

Society, especially English society, lived by a long list of unwritten but extremely stringent rules. One of those rules was that he and Rebecca must be *formally* introduced. Once that was accomplished, he could ask her to waltz, invite her and a chaperon to walk or ride in the park and begin what would then be viewed as an acceptable courtship. Since he and Lord Lowery were political acquaintances but not close friends, Sebastian had to find an acceptable and inconspicuous way to accomplish a formal introduction.

The season wasn't yet in full swing, nor would it be until after the Easter adjournment of Parliament. There were still families in the country, lords and ladies who would not be returning to the city until late March. Despite this, there were soirées and parties galore, all of which presented matchmaking opportunities. All Sebastian had to do was find the right one and the right person to do the formal introduction.

The morning newspaper presented the perfect answer.

Lady Felicity Forbes-Hammond had donated a hefty sum to one of London's many charities, earning the listing of her name in the *Illustrated London News*.

Lady Forbes-Hammond was Rebecca's aunt, the oldest of the sisters, the youngest having wed Lord Lowery some twenty-three years ago. Sebastian remembered the lady extremely well. She had been a friend of his mother's, a candid woman with an amusing wit. As he recalled, the normal compliance hadn't been bred into her. Lady Forbes-Hammond was strong enough to question what other women accepted without hesitation. A trait he was beginning to suspect her niece had inherited.

He called for Dames, penning a note while the butler waited.

"Have this delivered to Lady Felicity Forbes-Hammond, Park Lane, opposite Lord Crombie's town house," Sebastian instructed. "Tell the footman to await an answer."

"Yes, milord," Dames replied, wondering what had his employer looking and acting so chipper this morning. "Will there be anything else?"

"Have my carriage ready," Sebastian instructed. "Once the footman returns, I'll be paying a call upon the lady."

Dames nodded as he turned to leave the library. Whatever the viscount was about, it wasn't matters of Parliament. The butler called for the footman, hoping the spark he had seen in the viscount's eyes was there to stay. It was past time the man got on with his life.

A sallow-faced maid showed Sebastian into the morning room. Lady Felicity Forbes-Hammond was expecting him. Dressed in dark burgundy with a heavy strand of jet beads around her neck, the silver-haired woman accepted his greeting with a skeptical smile. Once he was seated, she raised her lorgnette to her youthful eyes and gave him a thorough looking over.

"Well, I must say I was more than surprised to receive your note this morning. May I ask what prompted a request to call upon me? Your mother was one of my dearest friends, but I haven't seen you for years," Felicity remarked bluntly. She had never been known to mince her words. Having exceeded sixty, she saw no reason to mince them now. Before Sebastian could reply, she dropped the lorgnette suspended from a neck strap of corded velvet. It came to rest upon her substantial bosom. "Age hasn't harmed your good looks," she said pointedly. "I understand you've been seen about town. I'm glad to hear that you've taken the plunge back into society. We have missed you, my lord."

Sebastian's recollection of Felicity Forbes-Hammond was an accurate one. The lady was as spicy as ever. "I find myself in need of a favor," he announced.

"And what might that be?" She studied him as he poured two cups of steaming tea. Sixty-plus years of peerage life had taught her to trust her instincts. The man was up to something. "Ahhh, could it be what I suspect?"

"What do you suspect?" Sebastian passed her cup across the table. She accepted it, the jewels on her hands blazing with brilliant color.

"I don't believe in coincidences," she replied flatly. "Only last week my niece was sitting in that very chair mentioning that you'd been seen at Lady Goodall's Valentine ball. Dare I conclude that your visit and the favor you're requesting might concern that very young lady?"

"Would it distress you if I answered yes?"

"Good gracious, no! I'd be thrilled beyond words. Rebecca is a lovely girl. Absolutely lovely. And she has spirit," Felicity announced rather proudly. "Of course, most men don't care for spirit in a lady. They prefer mundane attitudes and well-drilled manners."

Sebastian sipped his tea. He couldn't afford to commit his feelings to words as yet. If Felicity was willing to provide the formal introduction he needed, the rest would take care of itself. If Rebecca's aunt encouraged the relationship, all the better.

"What I prefer is to be formally introduced to your niece," Sebastian said, balancing his teacup on a delicate china saucer. "I saw her at the Valentine ball and admit to having my attention captured. Of course, my first concern is that her father will welcome the suit."

"Alexander's no fool," Felicity replied, unaware that she was seconding the duke's opinion. "Rebecca is his only child. He's pampered the girl beyond reason, but he loves her dearly. I'm quite certain my brother-in-law will not be distressed by your attention. He wants to make a good match for Rebecca and, like me, fears that she will allow her emotions to cloud the issue. Marriage is a serious matter."

Sebastian took another sip of tea.

"The opera," Felicity announced after a few moments of careful thought. "Rebecca will be accompanying me tomorrow evening. I keep a box at the Royal Opera House. I would be pleased to make the introduction during intermission."

"Thank you," Sebastian said. "Let's hope your niece finds me as pleasing as I find her."

Lady Felicity Forbes-Hammond appeared to be on the verge of clapping her hands together like a child. "I can't tell you how excited I am about the whole thing," she said candidly. "Rebecca is like a daughter, which indicates how very fond I am of her. And it's equally wonderful to realize that you've decided to marry again." It went without saying that the kind of request Sebastian was making had serious consequences. A gentleman did not ask such a favor unless he was willing to follow his words with suitable actions. "Your mother, God rest her soul, would be pleased to know that you're finally getting on with things. Your title demands an heir. Rebecca will make you a wonderful wife."

"My thoughts exactly," Sebastian said, letting the plot play itself out. Everyone would assume, as did Felicity, that he had finally decided to marry and produce an heir. Given that, and his age, a short engagement would be totally acceptable. No one need ever know that he had come close to compromising his future wife in the Whetfords' sitting room.

Having concluded their official business, Sebastian allowed Lady Forbes-Hammond to reminisce about the earlier years, the parties she had attended and the scandals that had rocked society in those days. When the conversation turned to current politics, she frowned most fiercely. "I daresay things will change once our sovereign comes out of mourning, though God only knows when that shall be. Rumor has it that she's content in the Highlands."

"Parliament is endeavoring to conduct the country's business in her absence," Sebastian replied.

"Endeavoring to do as they've always done, arguing and fussing like a batch of children," Felicity corrected him. "And that ghastly war those Yanks are fighting. I can't imagine such goings-on."

"America is having its share of growing pains," Sebastian remarked dryly. He sympathized with the men fighting in the civil war. England had had its interior conflicts, but none of them had reached the magnitude that was currently being witnessed across the Atlantic.

"Growing pains, indeed," Felicity scoffed. "It's insanity, pure and simple."

Sebastian didn't argue. He tactfully steered the conversation to a less volatile topic, then gradually brought it to an end, thanking Lady Forbes-Hammond for her assistance and assuring her that he would attend the opera.

He stepped outside the stylish Park Lane residence with a brisk step. Once he had directed his driver, Sebastian sat back and wondered how Rebecca was faring this morning. She was probably struggling with equal parts embarrassment and anxiety. He wished he could call upon her, but he couldn't show up on her doorstep without arousing suspicion, and that was the last thing he wanted at this stage. There was also the possibility that he wouldn't be welcomed by the lady herself. No, it was much better to plan their next meeting, to control it by making sure they were seen together in a public place, one where she couldn't unleash her temper.

Rebecca sat, listening to the opera, but not hearing a note of it. She was still trying to assimilate what had happened over the course of the last few days, trying to understand why she was feeling the way she felt, lonely and vulnerable and angry all at the same time. Being sensible and well-educated she should be able to put the matter into perspective. The viscount had taken advantage of her, used her lack of experience against her, and in doing so had compromised her. But while putting the blame upon his broad shoulders offered some excuse, it didn't alleviate her from an equal portion of responsibility. She had penned the fateful valentine, allowed herself to be trapped in a moonlit garden, and she had willingly walked into the Whetfords' sitting room, tempting fate once again. Even if Sterling's intentions had been honorable, she should have avoided him.

What was it about him that drew her like a moth to the flame? There was no point in denying her attraction to him. He was a handsome man. But then so was Newland, albeit a different type of handsomeness. What had taken place between her and the viscount had been the most shattering physical experience of her life. Rebecca closed her eyes and pictured what had happened once again. She had been sitting on Sterling's lap; even after all that had taken place, she couldn't bring herself to think of him as Sebastian. He had been kissing her, touching her in the most intimate of ways, and she had enjoyed every moment.

Her face flushed red in the darkness of the opera box. It was shameful to be thinking what she was thinking, and yet she couldn't banish the thoughts. They had been filling her head for the last forty-eight hours, becoming a part of her. She couldn't shake the image of how tenderly he had gazed down at her or the memory of how gently he had touched her bare breasts. The mere thought of it made them tingle anew, growing hard and painfully taut under the beaded bodice of her gown. But he had touched far more than her breasts. His hands, his fingers, had done shockingly delicious things to her body.

Rebecca flinched as applause filled the opera house. The curtain came down, signaling a break between acts and the intermission. The noise softened as the lights were raised, and people began to make their way to the salon for refreshments.

"Are you enjoying yourself?" her Aunt Felicity asked.

Rebecca managed a smile. She didn't want to tell her aunt that she would much rather be at home, behind closed doors, left to brood over what seemed an impossible situation. Instead, she lied with the practiced ease of one taught to always be charming and affable. She was reaching for her fan, when the heavy curtains at the back of the box parted and Sterling appeared.

Her heart stopped in her chest, unprepared for the sight of him again. He seemed more handsome than ever. Wearing a black frock coat, brocaded waistcoat, and a white shirt and cravat, he stood as tall as an English oak while her aunt smiled up at him.

"Lady Forbes-Hammond," he said, bending gracefully at the waist to plant a kiss on the hand her aunt offered to him. "It's a pleasure to see you again."

Rebecca released a breath she wasn't aware she had been holding when her aunt, smiling all the while, formally introduced her to the Viscount Sterling.

Sebastain saw the surprise register on Rebecca's face. Being a lady of high breeding, she masked it almost immediately, but not quickly enough for him to think his appearance was a total disappointment to her.

"Lady Rebecca," he said, bowing over her hand. He straightened and looked her directly in the eye. "Are you enjoying the opera?"

"Yes," she lied automatically, her mind unable to think of anything else at the moment. The last two days, filled with agonizing hours of wondering and worrying, melted away. Sterling was here, standing before her, smiling down at her as if it was the most natural thing on earth for them to be conversing.

"Please join us," Felicity said, waving her folded fan at one of the empty chairs. The box normally seated four, but could accommodate six when necessary. "Tell me what you've been about lately. It's been ages since I've seen you at the opera."

Rebecca sat, her hands loosely folded in her lap, listening while Sterling and her aunt became reacquainted. The sound of his voice, lowered in respect to their surroundings, reminded her of how he had whispered her name only two nights before. She glanced at him and found him smiling at her. The expression sent a disturbing sensation deep into her body, as though he had reached out and touched her again.

Rebecca blinked, willing away the blush of embarrassment she could feel forming on her cheeks.

"Would you care for some refreshment, Lady Rebecca?" Rebecca hesitated.

"Go ahead, my dear," Felicity insisted good-naturedly. "I'm too faint of breath to climb the stairs a second time. I'm sure the viscount won't mind escorting you."

"I'd be delighted," Sebastian admitted.

Knowing there was no polite way to say no, and not really wanting to, Rebecca allowed Sterling to take her gloved hand and place it upon his arm. With a sense of anticipation and unexplainable excitement, she followed him into the carpeted corridor.

"You look lovely," he whispered as they approached the staircase that led to the lobby.

He wasn't just flattering her. She did look lovely. The dress of apple green silk had a beaded bodice that accented her youthful figure. Sebastian couldn't look at her without remembering how beautiful she had looked lying in his arms, her breasts bared and damp from his kisses, her lips moist and parted with passion, her body soft and melting at his touch. If the duke hadn't intruded, he would have buried himself in that warmth and willingly lost himself to passion.

Rebecca stopped, glancing around her to make sure no one overheard her as she asked, "Why are you here tonight? You never go to the theater or the opera. You avoid society whenever you can."

"No longer," Sebastian told her. "And the reason I'm here should be obvious."

It all suddenly became too obvious: his assurance to her that he would take care of everything, that he would gain the duke's silence, that she should trust him. Having her aunt, an old friend of his mother's family, introduce them in a public forum was the finishing touch. Sterling intended to offer for her hand. As usual in the affairs of ladies and gentlemen, the outcome of their kisses would have nothing to do with love and everything to do with honor and duty. The viscount had compromised her, tarnished her reputation, and now he would offer marriage. It was the way their civilized portion of the world conducted itself.

She looked around again, seeking an escape. What she saw was Lord Sheppard walking toward them. She hadn't known he was attending the opera this evening. She wished he hadn't. What was she going to do when Sheppard and Sterling came face-to-face, and it was only a matter of moments before they did. Newland was walking her way with a determined stride.

"Lady Rebecca," he said, smiling. The expression faded when he caught sight of her hand resting on Sterling's arm. His hand had come to rest lightly upon hers, a sure sign that they weren't just exchanging words as they passed each other in the corridor.

"Sterling," he said, nodding briskly.

"Sheppard," Sebastian replied cordially.

"As always, your presence brightens the room," Sheppard said, turning away from the viscount as if he didn't exist, or wished he didn't. "Are you enjoying yourself?"

It was a double-edged question, and both she and Sterling knew it. Being a lady, she had no choice but to smile and reply as expected. "Yes. I'm here with my Aunt Felicity. She's always been fond of the opera."

Sheppard seemed somewhat relieved, but not totally satisfied. Her remark didn't explain the viscount or why he was anchoring her hand to his arm. Without a direct explanation, he was left to assume what anyone else would assume—Sterling had an interest in her and was displaying that interest publicly.

It was impossible not to compare the two men now that they were standing side by side. Rebecca cast a quick glance at Sebastian. His handsome face reflected confidence and the assurance that he knew exactly what he was doing. Sheppard looked flushed with anger, as if he were straining to keep his temper under control. Rebecca wanted to interpret his reaction as jealousy, but Sterling's accusation that Sheppard was nothing but a fortune hunter came to mind. Putting the allegation aside, she collected herself. "Viscount Sterling's mother and my aunt were friends," Rebecca said casually. "He stopped by my aunt's box to speak to her and offered to escort me downstairs."

"I'd be glad to make sure the lady reaches the refreshment table safely," Sheppard said. "After she's quenched her thirst, I'll see that she's returned to her aunt."

"I'm sure you would," Sebastian replied. "However, I admit to being a selfish man. Now that I have the young lady, I intend to keep her."

Sheppard stepped back, clearly surprised by the cutting response.

Rebecca held her breath. Even if Sterling's words hadn't been crystal clear, his tone was unmistakable. The viscount considered her his personal property. Sheppard was trespassing.

"I beg your pardon." Sheppard stiffened.

Sebastian offered him an apologetic smile. "Sorry, my lord. But you'll have to find another lady to escort about town. This one is taken."

If Rebecca had been prone to faint, she would have swooned dead away.

To her amazement, Sheppard didn't reply. He stared at her for a brief moment, his gaze intense. Then without a word, he turned on his heel and strode away. She drew in a deep breath, then looked pointedly at the man who had remained by her side.

"You were intentionally rude," she said stiffly.

"On the contrary," Sebastian replied. "I was intentionally honest. I don't plan on stumbling over Sheppard every time I want to get near you. If he's the gentleman you proclaim him to be, he'll understand and keep his distance."

"There is nothing to understand," she countered. She tried to remove her hand from his arm, but his grip tightened, holding her at his side. "And there is nothing between us but unpleasant circumstances. If you'll excuse me, I wish to return to my aunt."

"We haven't had our refreshments yet," Sebastian reminded her politely, belying the look on his face that said it would take an act of Parliament to gain her freedom. "Would you prefer lemonade or champagne punch?"

"I'd prefer to never set eyes on you again," she whispered as fervently as she dared. A group of people was strolling toward them, and she didn't dare stir up another scandal. A lady did not lose her temper in public.

"I'd prefer just the opposite," Sebastian said. "Actually, the more my eyes can see of you, the better."

The blatant reference to just how much of her he had seen only two nights past was enough to test Rebecca's temper to the fullest. She jerked her hand again, but Sebastian wouldn't allow it. There was no way she could escape without making a scene. He shot her a warning glance as Lady Torrington sauntered toward them. The woman had more tongues than cats had lives. Rebecca groaned on the inside.

As expected the old woman's eyes didn't miss a thing. They darted from Rebecca's face to that of the viscount's, then quickly down to where Sterling's hand rested upon hers, which was still holding on to his arm. Not by choice, but Lady Torrington didn't know that. Her smile, more prunish than friendly, was a forewarning of the gossip to come.

"My dear," she said, gauging the distance between Rebecca's body and the viscount's with a discerning eye. "How good to see you again. I saw your aunt earlier this week. She mentioned that you were to accompany her to the theater."

That being said, Lady Torrington turned her sharp eyes toward Sterling. "My lord. I'm pleased to see that the gossip wasn't in error. You are, indeed, out and about again."

"Indeed, I am," Sebastian replied, his voice and tone reflecting nothing but satisfaction. "Lady Torrington," he said with a polite nod. "If you'll excuse us, I promised Rebecca some punch."

The use of her given name wasn't a mistake. Rebecca wanted to gasp in unison with Lady Torrington, but she caught herself in time. She glared at Sterling as he led her toward the staircase. "You might as well put an announcement in the *Times*," she charged. "Lady Torrington is—"

"One of London's biggest gossips. If not the biggest, then the fastest," Sebastian supplied.

"You did that on purpose," she accused him, slowing to a halt so he was forced to look at her. "How dare you assume that—"

"How dare I assume what, my dear?" He was smiling again. "How dare I assume that I have certain rights where you are concerned. I assure you, I do. You gave them to me when you melted in my arms."

Rebecca felt herself blushing. The man was impossible. Totally impossible.

She stood in the corridor staring at him, unable to think of anything but the colorful curses she had heard old Stoats grumble under his breath when the horses weren't being cooperative.

A possessive need was flowing through Sebastian, the need to claim Rebecca as he had claimed her that night in the garden, to label her his woman. And she would be his.

"I'm going to marry you, Lady Rebecca Lowery."

She shook her head, and the pearls adorning her ears

and throat gleamed in the light. "We can't marry. We don't even like one another."

Sebastian smiled with cool arrogance. "I think we *like* each other more than enough. Or have you forgotten what happened only two nights ago?"

"Of course I haven't forgotten," Rebecca hissed softly. "It's just that—"

"I had you in my arms, and it wasn't the first time," Sebastian said, stopping her words with his own. "Whatever differences we have weren't an obstacle then. And I won't allow them to become an obstacle now. This evening is a belated beginning, but a beginning nevertheless." His gaze became more pointed, more serious. "It would do you well to recall the nuance of our last encounter," he told her, "and to realize that the results are inevitable. Whatever romantic dreams you have entertained about Lord Sheppard can be put to rest. You'll be *my* viscountess."

The possessive quality of his words brought a new crush of emotions down on Rebecca. She looked away from his face, to the now empty corridor and the paintings that adorned its walls. She had thought of the ramifications, had done nothing else for the last two days, but hearing Sterling announce his intentions so boldly, so irreversibly, made her head spin. Marriage. It was something she had thought of with Newland, but she had never allowed herself to think of it as a possibility with any other man, especially this man. He was too confident, too arrogant, too controlled. And he didn't love her.

Sebastian watched her face, knew she was battling with the realization of what their encounter truly meant, of a future she had unintentionally placed in his hands. Damn. He needed to talk to her, not whispered words in a public hallway. He needed to explain that a marriage between them wouldn't be a disaster, that he would do his best to make her happy.

"Damnation," his frustration came out in a rush of breath. "This isn't the time or place."

"A problem we've encountered before," Rebecca said pointedly.

Releasing her arm, Sebastian looked frantically for someplace they could be alone. He walked to the last door, unattended by a footman, and hopefully void of any opera patrons. Luck was with him; the box was empty, the curtains drawn. Marching back to Rebecca, he took her arm and pulled her along behind him.

"Where are you taking me?" she asked in a panic.

"We have to talk," he said firmly, then closed the door behind them. With the curtains drawn, separating them from those in the audience who had chosen to remain in their seats, the alcove provided a dark privacy they were unlikely to find anywhere else in the building.

Rebecca had imagined another moment like this, alone with Sterling, but she hadn't imagined how powerfully it would affect her. The supple darkness, the roaring of her heartbeat in her ears, the scent of him so close. It was devouring her senses.

When he turned to her, putting his hands on her upper arms, she felt the contact so strongly she flinched.

"Shhh," he said as if she was about to speak. "We only have a few minutes."

"We can't marry," she said wanly, knowing full well that he felt duty bound to court her, to establish the façade of a relationship that would protect her reputation. "You're . . ." She wasn't sure how to protest his attention. He was older than she, but he was titled and respectable and wealthy. Socially there were no barriers between them that would prevent a marriage.

"I know I'm not the man of your dreams," Sebastian replied stiffly. "But what has passed between us is beyond either of our controls now. Surely you understand that."

Rebecca wasn't sure she understood anything. Not

now. Not since she had seen him again, heard that deep, husky voice again. She couldn't think of him as just another gentleman, just another face in the fashionable crowd. There was no ignoring what they had done, no denying that she would much rather him kiss her than waste time talking.

A silent moment passed between them; then as if fate had accompanied them into the empty opera box just as it had joined them that night in the Goodalls' garden, Sebastian drew her into his arms. Rebecca took a quick breath, then relented. Closing her eyes, she allowed herself to be held against his chest.

Sebastian sighed lowly and savored the moment, the feel of her in his arms again. They stood in the darkness, his arms offering comfort, his body growing tight with desire, warming to hers. The curls on the top of her head tickled his chin, and he smiled. She was delicately built, but all woman. Bending his head, he kissed her temple. "Will you do me the honor of becoming my wife?"

Warily, she looked up at him. It was so dark she could barely make out his features, but she quivered inwardly with the knowledge that those forest green eyes were looking at her, as well. She was excruciatingly aware of him, of how strong his arms felt, of the lean, hard power of his body, of the manly scent of him, a mixture of soap and brandy and cigars.

"Marry me," he breathed against her mouth before his lips sealed off any possible reply.

Rebecca answered the kiss, unable to do anything else. She was lost again, a willing prisoner of the warmth of his embrace, the sensual security he always seemed to provide. She knew it shouldn't be happening again, this insanity, this unexplainable surrender, but he assaulted her sensibility, her very sanity.

Closing his arms more tightly around her, Sebastian made a halfhearted attempt to suppress the desire racing through his blood. One hand wrapped around her nape to hold her in place while his tongue dipped and tasted in a sensual rhythm that foreshadowed what he really wanted to do to her. His fingers played with the wisps of hair that covered her neck. He felt her shiver in response, a delicate shuddering that any experienced man could recognize.

She wanted him. Of that much, he was certain.

Helplessly, Rebecca felt the last of her reason deserting her as Sebastian's hands held her tightly. It was the first time she had said his name in her mind. *Sebastian.* It suited him just as his kisses suited her. She moaned against his mouth, needing to breathe, but not wanting to break the kiss, not wanting to give up the wonder of it all.

Several moments later she rested against him, her breath coming in short, soft gasps while he ran his hands up and down her back, silently counting the endless buttons he would have to undo to feel more than apple green silk beneath his hands. Her hands lay passively against his chest, her cheek pressed tightly against his perfectly tied cravat. She hadn't answered his question, hadn't said yea or nay to his proposal, but they both knew she would be his wife.

"We have to get back to your aunt," Sebastian whispered softly. His voice was huskier than before, soft and seductive, like the darkness that concealed them.

Rebecca nodded, then pulled away from him with a grace that had been learned over the years. "It's all so complicated."

"Not if you don't allow it to be," he replied. "There is something between us. You can feel it as surely as I do. Let's start with that, shall we?"

She didn't seem to have any choice in the matter. Sebastian had taken control of the situation, just as he seemed to take control of her with the slightest touch. "Very well, my lord. I'll consider your proposal."

Frustrated that he didn't have time to kiss her again, but content that she had at least cooperated, Sebastian released her. He opened the door, giving the corridor a quick glance in both directions to make sure the coast was clear, then motioned for her. She went, allowing him to escort her downstairs where everyone attending the opera could see them.

As expected, a ripple of whispers raced through the lobby of the opera house. Those of society who had heard that Sterling was back in circulation had their suspicions confirmed by the attentive way he led Rebecca toward the table of refreshments. The Viscount Sterling and Lady Rebecca Lowery presented themselves as a striking couple, his respectability accenting her beauty, his age her innocence. By morning, the gossip mill would be churning full force, the speculation of a marriage predestined and approved by the wagging tongues that thrived on speculation and suspicion.

Sebastian knew exactly what was going on behind the surreptitious glances and polite smiles. For the first time in his life, he welcomed it. A quiet dinner, following the opera, with Lady Felicity Forbes-Hammond and her lovely niece would put the official stamp on the matter. He would escort the ladies home, then call for Rebecca the next morning. A chaperoned ride in the park would be the crowning touch. The last domino to fall would be their first waltz. Lord and Lady Thurman's ball would do nicely enough. It was scheduled a few weeks hence. He had already made a discreet inquiry and discovered that the Lowerys' had accepted an invitation. Lord Thurman was a blunt old codger, a political bulldog of sorts who fervently fought for the current conservative viewpoint. His wife thrived on parties in and out of season. When Sebastian led Rebecca in the first waltz of the evening, they would be looked upon as privately engaged. The official announcement would come later. Then the wedding. Late summer would be best.

As Sebastian accepted a cup of champagne punch from an opera house servant, he smiled to himself. Thoughts of a wedding brought visions of a wedding night to mind. He looked at Rebecca, standing gracefully at his side. She met his gaze and smiled, unaware that his thoughts had her stripped naked and lying in his bed, her arms lifted in greeting.

"People are staring," she said under her breath.

"Let them stare," Sebastian said, handing her a cup of punch. "You're beautiful."

Rebecca maintained the cordial expression she had donned just before entering the lobby. As much as she was enjoying being on Sebastian's arm, she would much rather be in his heart. If they married, and it seemed more a possibility than an impossibility, then she wanted him to care for her. No, not care. Affection wouldn't be enough to last a lifetime. She wanted love. He had loved his first wife. Could he love her as well? Could she resurrect his heart, a heart he had once given freely to another woman?

Eight

The question of the viscount's true feelings plagued Rebecca for the next few weeks. Just as Sebastian had stepped out of the shadows that night in the Goodall's garden, surprising her, he had now stepped into her life. But this time it was daylight, in full view of London society. They rode in the park, attended the opera under the watchful eye of her aunt and mother, and dined at the best restaurants after leaving the theater. He was attentive, suddenly the perfect gentleman, always courteous, always careful of his speech and manners. There had been no more kisses, no more stolen embraces. It was the most frustrating of times for Rebecca, yet she found herself being drawn into the web Sebastian was weaving so carefully around her.

Knowing she was trapped didn't keep her from enjoying his company. As the days progressed, she found herself actually liking the man. He was sharp-witted, charming and even humorous at times, making her laugh at the little things in life. Just the other day, while riding in Hyde Park, accompanied by two of her father's grooms and Helen St. Clair, who thought Sebastian devastatingly handsome, he had amused her with tales of Parliament and the stately gentlemen who ruled its halls.

They never discussed the intimacy they had shared the night of the Whetfords' dinner party, or the heated tension that existed between them no matter how casual the occasion. But it was there, always shimmering between them, always reminding Rebecca how wonderful it had felt to be in his arms, to have his mouth devouring her, his hands touching her.

Nor did they speak of marriage. Or of love. Or of the past marriage that had left Sebastian mourning his beloved wife for more than eight years.

Dressing for a ball to be held by Lord and Lady Thurman, Rebecca resolved to bring an end to the indifferent conversation. She needed to know how Sebastian truly felt. Feeling herself falling slowly, surely in love with him, she had to know if his heart would always belong to his darling Kathryn. Sterling's proximity over the last several weeks had erased all thought of Lord Sheppard from her mind, just as it had dampened the young man's attention. Newland deliberately avoided her these days, having turned his interest to another young lady, one Rebecca had heard was quite wealthy. Now all her thoughts and expectations centered around Sebastian Delacour Worthington, Viscount Sterling. If she became his wife, if she gave him a child, would they forever be substitutes for the original ones, cared for but never truly cherished?

Sebastian helped himself to a drink in Lord Lowery's library. He had arrived before the family's departure for the ball, unbeknownst to Rebecca. A short note had arranged the meeting between the two gentlemen, one anxious over the outcome, the other paternally curious.

Turning away from the dark cherrywood liquor cabinet to find his host patiently waiting behind his desk, Sebastian smiled. "I suppose you're wondering what I'm about," he said.

Rebecca's father smiled knowingly. "I would say from your behavior the last few weeks that it's obvious." Lord

Lowery relaxed in his chair. "Can't say that I'm surprised. Not completely anyway."

"Then, you have no objection to a marriage between your daughter and myself?"

Lowery shook his head. He was dressed in formal attire, just as Sebastian was, but his stout size paid no compliment to his expensive clothing. "No objections that come to mind." His smile faded somewhat. "Rebecca's my only child. Proud and precocious and pampered, I admit, but she has a good heart. I want her happy." He paused to finish his drink, then added, "I was afraid that young fool Sheppard was going to turn her head. He would have had hell's own time getting me to agree to the marriage, but thankfully, it never came to that."

"I'll do my best to see that Rebecca is happy," Sebastian said. He sat down in a lush ruby red armchair. It was time to get down to details. "I'll arrange to have my solicitors call upon you at your convenience. With your permission, I hope for a summer wedding."

"My wife will be happy to oblige you," Alexander replied. "She's noted your attention of late, as has everyone in London." A gray brow arched, then lowered. "Not that anyone's surprised. You're old enough to know responsibility. Your title and estates have to be considered. And a man needs a family. Mine has brought me years of happiness."

Sebastian smiled for the first time that evening. "As I hope my new family will bring you. I want children."

"Good," Lord Lowery said. He came to his feet, offering Sebastian his hand across the desk. "A grandson would be a welcomed addition to the family. Always wanted to have a young lad to take fishing."

The two men exited the library to find Rebecca and her mother descending the staircase. Lady Lowery was of average height with dark brown hair and soft brown eyes. Even in her youth, she wouldn't have been called lovely, but her features were pleasing and her manner gentle. Beside her, Rebecca shone like a dark-haired angel in a lavish gown of yellow taffeta. The sleeves were garnished with white rosettes, the full skirt boasting the same design at the hem. Her hair was worn up, away from her face, calling attention to the vivid color of her eyes. The cut of the gown was modest compared to most, but it suited her perfectly, the color bold and bright. Long white gloves covered her hands and arms; a bracelet of amethysts and pearls decorated one wrist.

Sebastian heard the whisper of taffeta over starched petticoats as she moved toward him. It seemed that no matter how prepared he was to see Rebecca again, when the time came, she always stirred his senses. He would kiss her tonight, ending the long weeks of forced abstinence. A kiss, several kisses, to confirm the engagement Lord Lowery had agreed to announce. Then, if he was lucky, the months between a chilly March and a warm July would pass quickly. He wanted her desperately, but he was determined to wait until their wedding night, until she could walk into his arms without shame or regret.

Rebecca swallowed hard at her first sight of Sebastian. He cut a daring figure in his black coat, a black-and-gray-striped single-breasted waistcoat and black trousers. His tall, lean body was accented by his impeccable posture and handsome features. Reminding herself that she couldn't let the physical attraction between them mask what had yet to be said, she accepted the hand he offered to aid her in stepping off the bottom stair onto the polished tile floor.

He greeted her mother, then her. Rebecca's mother looked pleased to see him, as did her father, and she suspected that Sebastian had been up to no good again. Her suspicions were confirmed as her father led her mother to the far side of the foyer, then spoke in a low voice.

Before Rebecca could ask what they were whispering about, the butler appeared with both her and her mother's wrap draped over his arm. Sebastian helped her with the white fox stole, then leaned down to whisper. "Your father will announce our engagement tonight."

She glared up at him. "I haven't agreed to marry you yet."

"You will before the night is over," he promised, sounding much too confident for her peace of mind.

He joined them in the carriage, sitting across from her while her mother and father welcomed him into the family as if her wishes didn't mean a thing. Rebecca knew she was being callous. She hadn't cut the viscount or his intentions, nor had she spoken anything but kind words about him whenever asked, but it still galled her that neither of her parents seemed to think she might have doubts about the man. Of course, they were thinking of her future, of the comfortable life the viscount's wealth would offer, of the honored family name he would bestow upon her during the ceremony, of the contentment of believing they had met their obligation as parents, raising a well-bred young lady who had gained a favorable proposal. All that was well and good, but Rebecca wanted to be loved above all else.

It was a good two hours later when the musicians struck the strands of the evening's first waltz before she could voice her doubts to Sebastian himself. His hand, resting on her waist, was distraction enough as he led her into the graceful twists and turns of the dance. Rebecca tried to keep her gaze focused on the black pearl stickpin securing his cravat as she spoke, looking at him in any way was disorienting.

"I would have preferred to know your intentions this evening," she said very pointedly. "You spoke to my father without my consent."

Sebastian didn't falter as he swung Rebecca around

the floor, the skirts of her yellow gown billowing out as she matched his moves as though they had been dancing together for years. "You gave me permission the night of Whetfords' party," he replied. "And every day since then. Deny it, if you can."

"What happened one evening weeks ago isn't the same as mapping out my entire life as though it's yours to do with as you please," she retorted. "I know little more about you now than I knew then. And you don't know me at all."

His smile was smooth and seductive. "I know all I need to know," he told her. "As for knowing me, I'm not in costume. I have nothing to hide, no ghastly secrets that will jump out of the closet to frighten you." His hand tightened ever so slightly around her waist. "What of your secrets, Lady Rebecca? Is there a fantasy I should know about? A secret longing that will transform my opinion? If so, then I confess curiosity."

"Don't torment me," she said, wishing they could be alone. They hadn't been since that night at the opera. "I'm just not sure . . ." She hesitated, wanting to make her words palatable rather than insulting. "I'm not certain we are as well suited as you believe."

Sebastian knew what she wanted. Words of love, spoken softly, but he wasn't about to offer them in the middle of a crush, on a dance floor crowded with people. As for loving Rebecca, he wasn't sure of his feelings. What he felt for her was vastly different than what he had felt for Kathryn. But then, he had been younger when he had married the first time, more open to the confusing emotion. He wanted Rebecca, more each time he saw her, but love . . . if only things could be explained so easily. There was a remnant of his heart that would always belong to Kathryn, a part of him that would always remember the past with love and longing. Could he love again? He suspected he could, but his feelings for Rebecca had come upon him so suddenly, so unexpectedly, he couldn't define them that way. He had grown up with Kathryn. Living on a neighboring estate, he had watched her bloom into a young woman. Rebecca had come out of nowhere. He had read a water-smeared note, then waited for its author in the moonlight. It was the kind of story one expected from a fairy tale. This was real life.

As the music came to an end, Rebecca finally met Sebastian's gaze. Something was happening between them, something that could be wonderful and exciting with the possibility of lasting a lifetime, but it lacked the commitment only love could offer her.

"Perhaps it's time for another forbidden rendezvous," he suggested in a whisper. "The night isn't overly cold."

The thought of meeting Sebastian beyond the walls of the ballroom, of being held in his arms while no one was watching, made Rebecca's pulse quicken. If they could be alone, then she would have the opportunity, the time, to ask him outright how he felt about her. She had to take the risk, dare to ask, for she would never be content until she knew the answer.

"I'll be close by. When you find the opportunity slip into the garden."

Before she could agree or disagree, they were being congratulated on their engagement. Rebecca's mother hadn't been able to contain herself for more than a few minutes and had told their hostess. Lady Thurman was known for giving grand parties and for being an enthusiastic gossip. With Lady Torrington in attendance, the news had swept the room like a tidal wave.

Sebastian stood by her side as the well wishers approached them. When the Earl of Granby stopped in front of them, she smiled, knowing he was one of Sebastian's closest friends.

"Lady Rebecca," he said, lifting her gloved hand to his mouth for the customary kiss. Handsome in his own right, the earl was known to be one of the best catches in London, if only he could be caught. "Seeing you brings about a full understanding," he remarked. "No wonder Sterling's kept you so close." He turned to face his friend. "She's lovely, Sebastian. And you're a lucky man. Be happy."

"I plan on it," Sebastian replied, speaking honestly.

Within the span of an hour, Rebecca found herself being introduced to more of Sebastian's friends. She wondered if he had intentionally gathered them together, to present her on the night their engagement was announced. There was the Marquess of Waltham and the Earl of Ackerman, both equally handsome and equally wealthy. When Viscount Rathbone, the handsomest of the lot and the most brash, invited her to dance, Sebastian turned her over, but not without a word of warning for his young friend.

"He doesn't trust me," Benjamin Exeter said teasingly as he escorted Rebecca onto the dance floor. "I adore lovely ladies, and you're the loveliest one here. Are you sure you wouldn't rather have me?"

The viscount's reputation was known all over London. He was the one man her father had warned her about. "I'm afraid not," Rebecca replied candidly. "I'm hopelessly in love with Sebastian."

Saying it, she realized it was the truth. She wasn't just falling in love; she had fallen. Had her heart stumbled that first night in the garden or had the viscount trapped it somewhere between their first kiss and this very evening?

The music began, and Viscount Rathbone led her effortlessly into the dance. "I'm glad," he told her. "Sterling's a good man. Love him well, my lady, as I'm sure he loves you."

The advise was unexpected, coming from a man with his reputation, but Rebecca sensed its sincerity and smiled. It was another hour and three dances later before she could make her way to a small parlor off the ballroom. From there, she watched and waited, wanting to make sure no one saw her open the glass-paned doors and slip outside.

She was just about to reach for the doorknob when Sheppard appeared. His smile was as dazzling as ever.

"I was hoping to have a moment alone with you," he said. "Sterling always seems to be on your skirt tails of late. Tell me it isn't true. Surely, you're not going to marry the man. He's old enough to be your father."

A rebuke was on the tip of Rebecca's tongue, but before she could defend Sebastian, he did it for himself.

"Hardly that," he said, coming up behind them. The gaze he set upon Sheppard was cold enough to freeze the English Channel solid. "As for marrying me, the lady has agreed. We've received her father's blessing. The announcement will be in the papers by week's end."

Sheppard bristled. "I had meant to present my intentions for Rebecca. You knew that, as did she." He glared at her then, his smile completely gone now. "I'm loath to think that you dallied with my affections, Lady Rebecca."

Sebastian stepped between them. He didn't have to say a word; his actions spoke loud and clear. It was like watching two terriers outside the den of a solitary fox. Sooner or later one was going to go for the other's throat.

Sheppard's hands clenched into fists, but thankfully remained at his sides.

"You will apologize to the lady," Sebastian said. "Then you will take yourself back to the party and whatever heiress you're currently trying to seduce."

"You insult me, sir!"

"I'll do more than insult you. I'll pay off your creditors and call the note the very next day." There was no threat in Sebastian's voice, only a promise that he would do exactly what he said.

Sheppard stared openmouthed for a moment, then looked away. The expression on his face confirmed what

Rebecca hadn't wanted to believe. If he married, money would be the motive, not love. Her heart sank a little, more in pity for him than in regret for herself.

When Sheppard looked at her again, his face was void of any emotion. "My apologies, Lady Rebecca," he said. "And congratulations."

"Thank you," she replied. He turned to walk away, but she stopped him by saying his name. Sebastian stood by her side now. She reached down and took hold of his hand. "I wish you well, Lord Sheppard."

His combativeness faded for a moment. A sad smile came to his face, a silent call for forgiveness as if he knew that she would have married him if Sterling hadn't intervened; then he turned and walked away.

Feeling increasingly sorry for him, Rebecca watched until Sheppard disappeared into the crowded ballroom. It was several minutes before she looked up at Sebastian. He was studying her, and she knew he was looking for signs that the young lord's retreat had broken her heart. She almost wished she could give him one. Why should the man be any more certain of her than she was of him?

"I'll meet you in the garden, just beyond the fountain," he said.

"Only to talk," Rebecca cautioned him. "There are things that need to be said between us."

Sebastian didn't agree or disagree. He merely smiled a smug smile, then left her to make her way into the garden while he found another exit.

The night air was cold, but refreshing. Rebecca took a deep breath as she glanced around. She had waited a good ten minutes before coming out, needing the time to compose her thoughts. Standing on the flat stone pathway, listening to the music of another waltz, she hoped she had the strength to resist Sebastian's warm arms long enough to confront him on the subject of the marriage. Recalling the way he always swept her off her

feet, she made her way into the garden with its manicured evergreens and shrubs. The glow of a cheroot
gave her pause.

"What have we here?" Sebastian's unmistakable voice
came out of the night. "A night nymph sent to tease me."
He tossed the cheroot aside.

The next thing Rebecca knew, she was being pulled
into his arms and kissed until she didn't have any breath
left. When he finally released her, she slumped against
his chest. So much for good intentions, she thought as
he held her, providing warmth along with what she
prayed was love. Fog filled the far corners of the garden,
illuminated by a cloud-covered moon and the glow of
the gas-fueled chandeliers suspended from the ballroom
ceiling.

"I want to kiss you again," Sebastian said, nudging her
chin up so he could look into her eyes. "I'm a starving
man," he whispered. "Starving for the taste of you."

Before he could accomplish his goal, Rebecca raised
her hand and place two gloved fingertips to his mouth.
"Not yet," she said, still breathless from the debilitating
kiss he had given her. "I need to talk to you first."

Reluctantly, Sebastian loosened his hold on her without releasing her completely. "About what?"

"Your first wife."

He had expected the question before now. Kathryn
and his previous marriage weren't a secret. Everyone
knew of them. It wasn't surprising that Rebecca would
approach the subject eventually, although Sebastian
wished she had chosen a different time and a warmer
place. They couldn't stay in the garden for long; the
wind was too brisk, the night air too cold.

"Her name was Kathryn," he said.

"You loved her very much, didn't you." It was more declaration than question.

Keeping his arms around Rebecca, he took a deep

breath and answered. "Yes. I loved her. She was bright and young and beautiful, and she made me very happy."

The emotional upheaval that had been tormenting Rebecca for days suddenly became a sinking feeling. She felt her hopes fading, her dreams evaporating. "I'm sorry," she whispered. "I know there would have been a child."

"Yes, if she had lived," Sebastian replied. He tipped her chin up again. He could see the doubt and fear in her eyes, the hesitation written all over her face. "That's in the past," he said. "I can't undo it, even if I wanted to, which I don't. I'll always treasure the time I had with Kathryn."

"I know," Rebecca said. Honesty was better than deception, even if the words were hard to hear. But another question still demanded asking. "Is that why you want to marry me? Because I'm young and healthy and I can give you an heir?"

"A son would please me," Sebastian said. "As do you."

He stared down at her, his expression both passionate and tender. Then he kissed her again, his mouth warm and demanding. His hands cupped her face, sheltering her from the wind, making her feel momentarily treasured. One kiss led to another and another, and suddenly the cold night vanished completely. In the warm cocoon of Sebastian's embrace, all Rebecca could do was respond. Her body melted bone by bone, muscle by muscle, until she could barely stand.

"We have to go back inside," she found the breath to say, although she didn't have the slightest notion how she was going to accomplish it. She was too weak to walk.

"One more kiss," Sebastian said. He was testing the very limits of his tolerance as he captured her mouth one last time. He had never been this aroused, this hungry for a woman. Forcing himself to keep the kiss from becoming the fiery demand his body wanted it to be, Sebastian kissed her long and leisurely, as though they had all the time in the world. "If I don't let you go now, you'll be truly compromised," he said, taking a deep breath of cold air. It didn't serve the intended purpose. He couldn't resist placing a quick kiss on her upturned nose. "Now that we're officially engaged, I'll be lucky to steal a moment alone with you."

His prophecy came true.

There were congratulatory balls and soirées, luncheons and afternoon teas that consumed the remainder of the season. The wedding was planned for the twentieth of July. They would marry in the family chapel in Warwickshire. Every Worthington bride had assumed the role of viscountess in the chapel. Rebecca would be the tenth one to do so.

As the Lowery private coach approached the Sterling estate, Rebecca couldn't help but wish she had pressed her case more forcefully. Sebastian had remained attentive and protective even after the announcement of their engagement, but he had yet to say that he loved her.

Everyone assumed he did—his friends, her parents, even Felicity insisted that she had never seen a more besotted gentleman—but Rebecca still had her doubts. Doubts that were growing by the day. She hadn't seen Sebastian for almost two months. Both he and her family had departed London shortly after Parliament's adjournment as had most of genteel society. Sebastian had gone on to his country estate, to supervise the spring planting and to make preparations for their wedding.

Rebecca's time had been consumed with fittings for her gown and trousseau. Aunt Felicity had offered her expertise in helping to decide who would be honored with an invitation. The ceremony would be small, since the Sterling Hall chapel could comfortably seat only a hundred people. Her aunt had come ahead, insisting that the viscount would need a woman in the house to make sure all the last minute arrangements were seen to properly. Marshall Bedford, Marquess of Waltham, would stand with Sebastian. Helen St. Clair would be Rebecca's only bridesmaid. Her father would escort her to the altar while the Duke of Morland and Sebastian's closest friends watched from the pews.

The closer she came to Sebastian's home, the more Rebecca realized that she had a lot of soul searching to do before she walked down the aisle. She knew that she loved Sebastian. His recent absence from London had been a confirmation of how much she enjoyed his company. Her heart leaped at the very thought of him. But there was more to consider than her heart or her body. Once she became Sebastian's wife, the frills and pampering of her childhood would be left behind. She would be expected to be a wife and eventually a mother, to manage a household and supervise servants. Surprisingly, none of those things frightened her. As the carriage rolled down the tree-lined roadway, Rebecca realized that she wasn't simply substituting a husband for a father, as so many young ladies found themselves doing. Sebastian wasn't anything like her father, although he would care for her as thoroughly. He was a man, and she was a woman, two people who would share more than a bed. They would share days and nights, sickness and health, all the things attested to by the vows they would soon speak.

The revelation came with a normal amount of apprehension, but no real dread.

A short time later, Rebecca stepped down from the carriage to find Sebastian waiting. He smiled and kissed her on the cheek, permissible since they were to marry the following day. But it was the words he whispered in her ear that brought a blush that colored her cheeks.

"I've missed you," he said. "I want to kiss you all over. Everywhere."

With her parents standing behind her, Rebecca kept her composure, but being with Sebastian again was taking its toll. She was growing more nervous by the minute. Once they were inside the old Tudor house, she looked around. This was going to be her home. As expected from a full staff of servants, the chandeliers gleamed and the wood glowed.

Dames took charge of her parents, escorting them to their room while she was swished off to the parlor. "Your aunt is waiting," Sebastian told her. "She's an adorable old tyrant who insists that she see you right away. I'm to make myself scarce until the wedding."

Rebecca frowned. She had hoped for one last opportunity to speak with him. Sebastian had convinced family and friends of his affection, but he had yet to convince her. "I had hoped . . ." She paused as he looked down at her. His gaze was intense, and she knew he wanted more than words. "I wanted to talk to you."

Sebastian gave the foyer a quick glance, then pulled her toward the stairway. He opened the door to the customary closet that could be found under the staircase of almost any English manor house and pulled her inside. Stuffed with mops and cleaning cloths, the small closet smelled of beeswax and lemon oil. The door clicked shut, leaving little room and no light.

"We've got the rest of our lives to engage in conversation," he said, then kissed her.

There was no time to protest. Rebecca's parted lips, on the verge of saying something, were penetrated by his daring tongue. He lifted her against him, silently cursing the layers of clothing that made up her traveling suit: a jacket, skirt, blouse, corset, chemise, petticoats. He didn't have enough time to do battle with each and every button and lace. But that didn't stop him from kissing her witless.

"Tomorrow," he promised, releasing her reluctantly.

Rebecca caught her breath while he opened the door, scanned the foyer a second time, then tugged her along behind him until they reached the parlor doors. "Your aunt is waiting."

Before she could call him back, Sebastian was gone, leaving her alone and flustered. She took several long breaths, then putting a smile on her face, opened the parlor doors and walked into the room. Her aunt was sitting near the window, reading.

"Rebecca, my dear," she said, lifting her face for a kiss on the cheek. "You look lovely."

"I look tired and nervous," Rebecca corrected her. "Does getting married always do that to a woman?"

"It should," Felicity replied candidly. "Show me a mundane bride and I'll show you an unhappy woman."

"Then, why do I feel so unhappy," Rebecca sighed, sinking onto the settee as if the weight of the world had put her there. The burden she had been carrying grew heavier as she looked across the room. The portrait of an angelic young lady was hanging over the mantel. Rebecca knew it was Kathryn, Sebastian's first wife.

Felicity followed her gaze. "I hope you're not thinking what I think you're thinking, child."

"She was lovely."

"Yes, she was," Felicity agreed, looking rather put out over the direction the conversation had taken. "But then, so are you. Extremely lovely. And intelligent enough to know that Sebastian cares deeply for you. He isn't the kind of man who takes a wife as casually as a new hunting hound."

"How do you know if a man truly loves you?"

"One thing you don't do is sit around looking like a melancholy puppy," Felicity said impatiently. "My goodness, girl, what has gotten into you? Sebastian is a fine man. You're lucky to have caught his eye."

"So everyone tells me," she said wanly.

Felicity snorted; there was no other way to describe the sound. "I remember the last time I was in this house. It was the morning of Kathryn's funeral. The light went out of Sebastian that day. I didn't see it shining again until he visited me before we attended the opera. That man loves you, child. If you can't see it, it's because you aren't looking closely enough. Now, stop pouting and get yourself upstairs for a good nap. You'll feel better after you've had a nice rest."

Rebecca did her best to smile. "I'm sorry," she said, walking to where her aunt was sitting and taking hold of her hand. "I do love Sebastian. But he's never spoken those words to me. A bride should hear them, don't you think?"

Felicity's impatient expression softened. She patted Rebecca's hand, then smiled. "My dear, I'm sure that Sebastian is just as nervous as you are. I daresay, he never expected to marry again. Be patient with him. All will be as it should be."

Rebecca nodded solicitously. There was little more she could do or say without revealing that the real motivation behind her and Sebastian's wedding was honorable obligation not love. But that had been months ago. Now, feeling as she did, Rebecca wanted it to be love. Perhaps Felicity was right. If she was patient, if she tried to be a good wife, then perhaps one day Sebastian would come to love her. It was a bittersweet thought, but Rebecca took what comfort she could from it as she left the parlor and went upstairs.

Nine

Rebecca's wedding day arrived with brilliant skies and a bright sunrise. Everyone was up and about early; servants scurried about like liveried mice seeing to the comfort of the guests and family members. Rebecca sat perfectly still as her maid brushed and styled her hair. Then it was time to put on her wedding gown, a white satin creation with a mantle of pearls and lace. The sleeves ballooned at the shoulders, growing slimmer as they approached her elbows, then slimmer still as they reached her wrists. The skirt was full, blossoming out into a ten-foot train at the back. Her veil was sheer, the cap studded with pearls and lace rosettes.

Looking at herself in the cheval glass, Rebecca couldn't help but wonder what a woman did when she wasn't entirely sure if she should walk down the aisle or bolt like a frightened rabbit. When there was no evidence that the man she was about to marry held more than a casual affection for her, no heartfelt reason for their lives to be entwined, did she pray for the best and maintain her dignity or did she demand that the ceremony be delayed until he announced his true feelings?

"It's time," Lady Lowery announced with tears in her eyes. She walked to where Rebecca was standing and hugged her, being careful not to crush the fragile lace of her wedding veil. "You're so beautiful," she whispered.

"Your father and I love you so much. Always remember that."

Blinking back her own tears, Rebecca smiled. "I love you, too."

Lord Lowery was waiting in a small room off the chapel vestibule. "By jove, you're lovely," her father announced proudly.

"I'm nervous," Rebecca admitted, clutching a bouquet of white roses and blue periwinkles as if they could guarantee her happiness.

"Don't be," her father said in the reassuring voice she recognized from her childhood. "Sterling's a good man. He'll take good care of you."

The church bells began to ring, calling all who would witness the ceremony to their seats. Sebastian exited the small antechamber where he and the Marquess of Waltham had been waiting. He was as nervous as the bride, although no one could see the signs. All they saw was a tall, impeccably dressed groom standing before the altar.

Finally the pair of closed doors at the front of the chapel opened, and music flowed through the church. Two chapel attendants rolled out a runner of dark blue velvet, and Rebecca took the first step down the aisle. Everyone stood and turned to watch the bride. Sebastian felt the nervousness fade from his body. A deep contentment took its place. Love had seemed unobtainable a second time, beyond his reach, forbidden happiness that couldn't possibly occur twice in one man's life. And yet, now, watching Rebecca move toward him, he knew he was the most fortunate of men. For he had found love, or rather, it had found him.

Rebecca felt every nerve in her body begin to shake as her father stepped back and handed her over to Sebastian. His hand felt warm as it grasped hers ever so gently, his smile warm and welcoming as they stepped to the chancel before the altar. The ceremony began, then ended with a kiss as the church bells began anew, proclaiming the union of husband and wife.

The reception was filled with music and congratulations from all the guests. Her aunt, Lady Felicity Forbes-Hammond, gifted her niece with some advice as she made her goodbye. "Be happy, my dear. And don't be nervous about tonight. Sebastian's been married before, he understands your fears."

Fears.

There were too many to list as Rebecca changed from her wedding gown into a sheer white nightgown with long sleeves and pearl buttons at the neck and cuffs. She dismissed the maid once her hair had been taken down, choosing to brush it herself. It fell to her hips, long and thick and as black as jet. She brushed it until it gleamed, reflecting the light from the candles the maid had lit before leaving the room. The minutes ticked by as she tried not to be nervous, fought not to think of the future, only the night before her.

Hearing a noise, she turned to find Sebastian standing in the doorway. He was wearing a dark blue smoking jacket with black velvet lapels and black trousers. His feet were bare. It was the first time she had ever seen a man without a cravat or shirt. Although the jacket was sashed snugly around his waist, she could see the sprinkling of dark chest hair where the jacket formed a deep vee.

His gaze moved over her, and Rebecca felt herself tremble.

Sebastian couldn't keep himself from staring. He had seen Rebecca in lavish ball gowns and stylish riding habits, in expensive day dresses and only this afternoon clad in pristine white satin, but he had never seen her look more beautiful than she looked at this very moment. Her hair cascaded down her back like a rich, dark waterfall. Her eyes, bright with apprehension, were wide and unwavering as he stepped into the room, shutting the door behind him.

Instead of speaking, he walked to the table and poured two glasses of champagne, then silently passed one to her. Rebecca accepted it with a trembling hand she was unable to stop from shaking. This was her wedding night. She and Sebastian were finally alone. There were things she wanted to say, questions she longed to ask, but all she could do was lift the glass to her lips and drink.

"You're beautiful," he said quietly, then took the glass from her hand.

Unsure what she should do, Rebecca did nothing.

Sebastian held out his hand. "I'd like to kiss the bride again."

The gentle tone of his voice was Rebecca's undoing. She moved into his arms, wanting to be there more than any place on earth.

His lips came to rest over hers, their touch light and delicate, undemanding as his arms moved around her. She had come home, home to the warmth and security that this man had offered since their first fate-filled meeting. His touch, his scent, the strength of his body pressing gently against her, was what she had longed for all these months. Knowing she loved him, knowing her heart was truly his for the taking, Rebecca surrendered to the kiss.

For an eternal instant there was only the meeting of their mouths, a kiss so sweet, it stole Sebastian's breath and his bride's. *His wife.* His to cherish and protect and love. He had thought about this time; little else had occupied his thoughts these last few months. He had held himself in check, controlled his desire, wanting their wedding night to be perfect for her, as perfect as he could make it. He would use his experience: the memories of a previous wedding night when Kathryn had shied at the thought of removing her clothing, of the nights spent in his mistress's bed, of the things he had learned about women, what brought them to completion, what allowed them to soar with the passion, what they enjoyed and what brought satisfaction to both woman and man.

He wanted Rebecca to feel all those things, the shyness that would evaporate once he had joined his body to hers, the excitement of passion, the contentment of pleasure. All that and more. So much more. He wanted her to moan his name, to cling to him, her body flushed and damp, her womb open to his seed. But most of all he wanted her to tell him that she loved him. The words hadn't been said by either of them, a rare thing between two people who did love each other. Sebastian could see the love in her eyes, feel it in the soft surrender of her body as he pulled her more snugly into his embrace. But like her, he needed the words.

It took a moment for Rebecca to realize that she was being lifted, carried to the bed, and laid gently upon the cool sheets. The night was warm. An open window allowed the summer breeze into the room, but it did little to cool the need she felt. Sebastian's hands were as hot as fire as they moved over her, molding the sheer fabric of her gown to her body, reacquainting himself with the feel of her.

His kisses were intoxicating as they moved from her mouth to her throat. Then his hands were moving too, undoing the tiny buttons at the neckline of her gown, pushing it gently off her shoulders until she was bared to his eyes. He looked his fill, his eyes gleaming in the dim light, his words soft as he smiled and told her not to be afraid.

"You liked what I did before, didn't you?"

"Yes." The confession was a breath and a moan combined. His touch was burning her, his fingers gentle but skilled as they moved over her breasts, making them harden almost instantly.

Then his mouth was there, covering her, sucking gently at first, then more demandingly, bringing back the fire she hadn't felt since that night in the Whetfords' parlor. It was wonderful, this heat, this yearning he created within her, this need that made every muscle in her body go taut, every nerve ending sing with anticipation.

When she thought she would nearly go mad, Sebastian eased away from her. He shed his jacket hastily, then returned to the bed. Rebecca's breath caught as he moved to lay beside her, his chest pressed against her bared upper body. She had never imagined the pleasure of naked skin to naked skin, and it was wonderful. So wonderful she wanted to touch him, to learn him the way he was learning her.

Sebastian saw the need in her eyes and smiled. He found her hand and placed it on his shoulder. "Go ahead," he encouraged her. "Touch me."

She did, hesitantly as first, then more boldly, letting her hands glide from his shoulders down his arms to the tips of his fingers. It was incredible how different he felt, how strong and warm and solid. She smiled in spite of herself.

"We're married," Sebastian whispered as he lowered his hand to find the hem of her nightgown. "Don't be shy or afraid. Don't worry about pleasing anyone but yourself and me."

More advice, but Rebecca listened this time. She did want to please Sebastian, to make him think only of her, to somehow push the memories back into the past, where they belonged.

Patiently, Sebastian moved his hand slowly up her leg, inching her nightgown with it. He stroked the outside of her calf, then her knee, then the delicate skin of her inner thigh. She tensed. He relaxed. "You're warm and soft," he said before kissing her again.

Rebecca sucked in her breath, ending the kiss as his fingers found the nest of black curls between her legs. If she could feel the heat there, then so could Sebastian.

"Trust me," he said. "No, sweetheart. Don't tighten your legs. Let them relax. Let me pleasure you. God, I've wanted to touch you for so long. It's been an eternity."

The eternity turned into long, mindless minutes as Rebecca let her head fall back against the pillows. Sebastian did more than touch her; he turned her body into a willing puppet that followed his every lead. His fingers caressed then probed, gently invading her, stretching her, making her shiver with need. Her hips arched, wanting more of his touch, more of the searing fire that was melting her insides. Somewhere in the sensual fog that enveloped her, Rebecca knew where he was taking her. She had been there once before. It was an exciting place, a place of sensations and intimacy, an uncontrollable place, a place she had thought about visiting again.

Sebastian watched, smiling down at her, as his fingers continued to glide in and out of her snug passage. She was hot and wet, growing wetter, growing hotter as he gritted his teeth and vowed to endure the torment until she was pleasured, until she called out his name, begging him to take her the rest of the way.

His muscles tightened under the strain of holding back. While one hand stroked and teased, his other hand found the buttons of his trousers. He should have shed them with his jacket, but it had been too soon. He hadn't wanted to shock her. He wanted her twisting and squirming, panting with need, wanting him so much she wouldn't be frightened at the sight of his aroused member. He had never been this hard, this ready.

When his fingers left her, Rebecca's eyes opened. He was leaning over her, his forehead damp with perspiration, his green eyes blazing like a forest afire. "I need to touch all of you," he said, tugging at the hemline of her gown that was bunched up around her waist. "Sit up, sweetheart."

Her senses were so inflamed by now that Rebecca didn't think of being shy. She raised up, allowing Sebastian to pull her gown up and away. He tossed it aside, then rolled off the bed, coming to his feet. His trousers were already unbuttoned, revealing a flat, hard stomach and more crisp dark hair. They came away from his hips with a quick tug, then fell. He stepped out of them, kicking them aside to join her gown on the floor.

Rebecca looked at the taut muscles, the long legs, and the thick bush of hair surrounding his swollen manhood. She closed her eyes and took a deep breath. She was exhaling when Sebastian joined her on the bed, his hands reaching for her, bringing her up against his body. They touched, skin to skin, and she shuddered with the wonder of it all. Then he was building the fire again, fueling it with each stroke of his hands, each kiss, each intimate caress, until she was burning alive.

When he finally moved over her, she was too lost in the storm to understand why he was widening the space between her legs, spreading them apart to make a place for himself. She was exactly where Sebastian wanted her, lost in the moment, lost to the urgent glide of his fingers as they continued to tease and torment and teach her how high a woman could fly. Her maidenhead was fragile, but definitely there. He could feel it, hot and slick against the tip of his fingers, ready to be breached. He sucked in a deep breath, harnessing his control, praying he could keep it long enough to enter her properly, one clean thrust that would put him deep inside her.

When it came, Rebecca flinched, arching her hips to try and dislodge him, but it was too late. He was buried to the hilt, and it was pure heaven.

She wiggled, and he groaned. "Lie still, sweetheart. Relax and let your body do what it was made to do."

With her eyes closed and her body on fire despite the initial discomfort, Rebecca tried to do what he asked. She caught her breath, then released it as he withdrew, then moved forward again, stretching her easily this time. She was amazed that her body accommodated him, yet it did. He continued to moved slowly, filling her, then retreating only to fill her again. The sensual pattern turned into a rhythm, pulling back, pushing forward, a simple dance of bodies that Rebecca learned quickly. To her husband's delight, she arched her hips, matching his lead. He groaned again.

"My God," he breathed against her mouth. "You feel so good. So damn good. I could love you forever."

She smiled, then kissed him. The kiss built and built, matching the tempo of their joined bodies, heightening the tension until it snapped. Sebastian felt her muscles tighten around him, felt the tiny shivers that began in her womb, then moved outward, tiny explosions that forced his body to respond. He joined her then, pushing deep and holding himself there, letting the hot, wet warmth of her wash over him, through him, until it reached his very soul.

Rebecca rolled over, blinking, coming awake slowly from the most delicious dream. The curtains were drawn, allowing only a thin finger of light into the room. It was well after dawn, the light a warm summer yellow as it streaked across the carpeted floor onto the bed. She stretched lazily, a smile brightening her sleepy face as she looked around her. Sebastian was gone, but the sheets were still warm from his body. The soft splash of water told her he was in the dressing room.

She sat up, letting the sheet fall away. The thought of what had happened between them sent a blush of color to her cheeks. She was truly Sebastian's wife now, his viscountess. It was amazing what could change in the course of one night. Yesterday she had been frightened, full of apprehension and uncertainty. This morning some of the anxiety remained, but with it was a determination to make the most of her marriage, to win Sebastian's heart by loving him the way she knew he deserved to be loved.

Suddenly, she was impatient to see him, to hear his deep, resonant voice. She pushed her hair away from her face. The tangled black web of curls had fascinated her husband when he had taken her a second time. He had played with her hair, then, combing his fingers through it, commenting on its color, how it should rightfully belong to a gypsy.

Finding her nightgown folded neatly over the back of a chair, Rebecca quickly slipped it over her head, forsaking the buttons for the time being. She reached for the ivory-handled brush on the vanity, pulling it through her hair.

"Let me do that."

She turned around to find Sebastian leaning against the doorframe of the dressing room. He was wearing his trousers, but no jacket or shirt. His feet were bare, his hand holding a teacup from which he took a leisurely sip. "Good morning, my lady."

The words sent a rush of heat from Rebecca's face all the way down to her toes. She licked her lips, feeling strangely unsure of herself despite the intimacy they had shared during the night. "Good morning, my lord."

"Are you hungry?"

She shook her head, setting her wild black curls to dancing.

"Then, perhaps a cup of tea," Sebastian suggested. "Dames oversees the blending of the household teas. A task normally left to the housekeeper, but one he seems to enjoy."

"Your butler was here this morning?" The thought of the stern-faced servant venturing into the room while she slept contentedly in Sebastian's bed kept the blush on Rebecca's cheeks.

"A discreet knock and a tray left outside the door. Nothing more," he assured her with a smile that made her knees go weak.

She watched as he moved across the room to pour her a cup of tea. Drawing an unsteady breath, she returned the brush to the vanity table and walked to the bed. Slipping between the sheets, she sat back against the pillows. When Sebastian turned, finding her precisely where he wanted her, he smiled.

He carried the teacup to the bed, giving it over to her delicate hands, then went to fetch the brush. "Sit up a little straighter and turn around," he instructed her. "I'll brush the tangles from your hair. Then, I assume, you'll want a bath."

"Yes," Rebecca said shyly.

Instead of brushing her hair, Sebastian gathered it in his hands and draped it over her right shoulder; then he kissed her neck. "You taste as good as you look," he mumbled into her ear.

His hot breath brushed over her skin, bringing goose bumps in its wake. The sensation was so strong that Rebecca had to hold on to her teacup with both hands. She shivered, and then his hands were there, in front of her, taking the cup and setting it aside. She looked over her shoulder at him, saw the need in his eyes. Then he kissed her hungrily, lowering her to the bed. This time their mating was powerful and elemental. Rebecca knew the pleasure that was waiting and welcomed the fire. It burned as bright in the morning light as it had during the warm darkness. Sebastian tried to be gentle, but there was no control left in him this morning. He wanted Rebecca, his wife, with a voracious need that had him ready to explode the moment he entered her. He lifted her gown out of the way, then cursing, pulled it over her shoulder, throwing it toward a far corner of the room.

"I want you naked," he said, bringing his body up and over hers. "I want to watch you when I come inside you." His hands followed the contours of her body, starting at her knees, then moving slowly upward. He kissed the hollow of her stomach, just above her navel.

She lay there, naked, looking up at him, her eyes bright and wild, her lips parted, her breathing rapid. He cursed again at the stubborn buttons on his trousers, at his own impatience to mount her, to find her warmth and plunge into it, deep inside where she was the hottest thing he had ever felt. When it happened, they both caught their breath. Their gazes locked for a long moment; then Rebecca's eyes drifted closed. Sebastian smiled, then groaned as her muscles clinched around him, demanding that he move. He did. Deep and strong. His hips lifted then returned, thrusting hard, filling her, answering the need they both felt but were too breathless to express.

Rebecca gripped his shoulders as he pushed harder and deeper, wanting to touch the very center of her, wanting to make her feel what he was feeling, that tingling excitement of pleasure building minute by minute, thrust by thrust, until it exploded, until he exploded, filling her with his very essence.

"I didn't get to finish my tea," Rebecca said sleepily. She was curled up close to Sebastian, her hand resting on his chest. They were both naked, the sheet covering them as their bodies began to relax.

"If you're fishing for an apology, you won't get one," Sebastian mumbled, feeling weak but unbelievably happy. He kissed her on the forehead, then said something about needing all the rest he could get.

Smiling, Rebecca closed her eyes and slept. When she awoke a second time, she found the room empty. The maid knocked on the door a few minutes later. By the time Rebecca finished her bath, the maid had freshened the bed linens and left a breakfast tray. Surprisingly hungry, she walked to where the tray was sitting atop an oval table in front of the window. A smile brightened her face when she saw the present.

It was a small book of poetry. Rebecca picked it up. Her fingers moved lovingly over the soft leather. The poet was Pierre Teihard De Chardin, one of her favorites. A white rose, taken from her bridal bouquet, marked a passage. She opened the book and read it aloud. The poignancy of the verse brought tears to her eyes.

"Love alone is capable of uniting beings in such a way
as to complete and fulfill them
for it alone takes them and joins them
by what is deepest in themselves."

Sebastian had signed the bottom of the page.

"I love you, Valentine."

Tears slid down Rebecca's cheeks and onto the page. She clutched the small book to her chest, her heart bursting with joy. She turned, intending to go in search of her husband, only to find him standing in the doorway once again. He was dressed, his hair still damp from a morning bath.

"Felicity told me you liked poetry," he said. "It took me weeks to find the right verse."

"Weeks," she said, her voice soft and shaky. Sebastian was staring at her and smiling. Dare she believe the words he had written, the verse he had chosen? Her heart flared with hope.

"Weeks," he said, stepping fully into the room. He laughed softly. "You can't imagine how many verses I read, wanting to say just the right thing to you. They all seemed lacking, until I read the one I marked." He stopped a few feet away from her. "I do love you," he said. "I think I have from the very first moment I saw you standing in the garden looking like a dark-haired angel."

"Oh, Sebastian," she sobbed, overjoyed by the gift and the knowledge that she had finally reached his heart. She rushed across the room and into his open arms. The book of poetry ended up being pressed between them. "I love you," she said. "I was so afraid."

"Of what?" he asked, tilting her chin up so he could kiss her properly.

It was a long time before Rebecca could answer him. He held her close as she tried to explain. "I was afraid that you were marrying me because of some misplaced sense of duty. That you didn't love me. That I wouldn't be able to take Kathryn's place."

"My duty has never been misplaced," he said. "And you don't have to take anyone's place. *Your* place is in my heart. In my home." He picked her up. "And in my bed."

"Again!" Rebecca laughed with joy.

"Forever," he whispered against her mouth.

As he kissed her, Rebecca didn't think forever would be long enough.

Historical Romance from
Jo Ann Ferguson

DO YOU HAVE THE
HOHL COLLECTION?